James Bartlett Wiggin

The Wild Artist in Boston

A Story of Love and Art

James Bartlett Wiggin

The Wild Artist in Boston
A Story of Love and Art

ISBN/EAN: 9783743388925

Manufactured in Europe, USA, Canada, Australia, Japa

Cover: Foto ©Andreas Hilbeck / pixelio.de

Manufactured and distributed by brebook publishing software (www.brebook.com)

James Bartlett Wiggin

The Wild Artist in Boston

THE

WILD ARTIST IN BOSTON.

A Story of Love and Art in the Actual.

BY

J. B. WIGGIN.

BOSTON:
PUBLISHED BY J. B. WIGGIN.
17 BROMFIELD STREET.
1888.

BOSTON
S. J. PARKHILL & CO. PRINTERS

CONTENTS.

3

4 CONTENTS.

THE WILD ARTIST IN BOSTON.

CHAPTER I.

THE TRIBE OF BARTLETT.

IT was the last week in June, and New Hampshire never looked handsomer. In old Strafford County, not far from the river and the head of tide water, among all the alternations of hill and valley, field and orchard, meadow and woodland, are scattered many farms, which prove the truth of the old Saxon definition, that a farm is a place for provision. And few among them all, that day, for beauty and productiveness, for all sweet home qualities, were more worthy of the name than the Bartlett homestead. The house stood a little in from the road. It had a well-to-do, opulent look. It was ample in size; white, with green blinds; with piazza in front, and each column hidden with a trellis bearing queen-of-the-prairie roses, sweet honeysuckle, Virginia trumpet flower, and woodbine, — the latter going beyond all bounds, away on the roof of the ell, at its own sweet will.

A few steps from the front door began the flower garden, and slightly sloping away from the house, it insensibly resolved itself into herbs, vegetables, summer squash, sweet corn, and early potatoes, in the most profuse manner, until the house and its grounds stood revealed to you as a perfect realization of the wedding of Use and Beauty.

5

The ample barn, farther back, on the right of the picture, was plainly seen against the dark green of the large orchard beyond; and afar off, over field, pasture, and woodland, might be seen — many miles away — the great blue hill in Strafford, and Blue Job in Farmington. In the distance on the left, was a pretty, rolling country, scattered apple-trees, and a few airy and graceful elms. Nearer still, a broad field of grass, which the breeze was moving in waves, which promised well for haying; and in the foreground, on the left, about five acres of corn, in long rows, well set, hoed clean, and lastly, on the last two rows, the side nearest the house, two men — Mr. Guy Bartlett, forty-five years of age, healthy and hearty, the owner of the hundred and fifty acres; and by his side, hoeing the advance row, his son and only child, Royal Bartlett, in his twenty-first year.

Mr. Bartlett was an honest, Christian man. It is the highest praise I can give a human being. Some novels are only a receptacle for the memoirs of villains. This is not that kind of a book. I have known, and do now know some splendid people; I seek such, and cultivate them; and without undue publicity, I will, with their knowledge and consent, put them in this book.

Whether the young man, Roy Bartlett, was worthy of as high praise as his father, you can find out by reading this book; for I am going to tell you more about him; and he had some queer experiences. Certain it is that they both believed in the good things of this world, and they both believed in each other. Roy Bartlett was healthy, hearty, good sized, and — I hesitate to say — good looking. Handsome blue eyes, brown hair, a light golden-brown mustache, red lips, pleasant, winning ways made him a fine ideal of the Bartlett tribe, as I have known them.

"Well, father; this finishes the second hoeing of our corn, and it looks well. Not a hill is missing. Of course the crows got a few hills, but I transplanted enough to fill their places, and I think you will be satisfied with the harvest."

"It looks like it now," said Mr. Bartlett.

"Now, father, I have something to say to you. Our farm work is well up to the season. Nothing is suffering. A little more work in the garden, and we are all ready for haying. You know I am nearly twenty-one years old. And you know that I have always liked drawing and pictures of all kinds. From the time that I have expended, and the interest that I have taken in art, perhaps you have thought that I might make some use of it, at some time."

"Yes, Roy, I have," said Mr. Bartlett.

"Now here is my proposition. I never shall go far away from you and mother."

"I hope not," said his father.

"But I wish to go to Boston to-morrow, perhaps back at night, or may be the next day, to ask advice and get evidence as to whether it is safe and wise for me to try to get a living out of art, especially oil painting. Perhaps I cannot decide it at once, and perhaps I shall try for a while and relinquish it; but at all events I can return to the farm and make a good living from that. If New Hampshire habits and gumption won't win, then I shall consider the fault in me. Are you willing I should try, father?"

"Yes, Roy, I am. Of course I had rather have you

with me every day; but that is not quite reasonable. So do what you think is best."

"Thank you, father. But do not think for a moment that I can consult my own interest, to the neglect of my father and mother. We have improved the farm every way. It is in good order and producing finely. You own it free and clear, and have a good amount at interest. And you have given me a good chance too. I have made some money on the patches of ground I have cultivated for myself, on apples, and on the colts I have raised and sold. So my experiment will be no expense to you."

"Oh, well," said Mr. Bartlett. "You can have help if you need it. Whom have we but you, Roy?"

"I know that, father. But I do not believe, with my health and strength, in wasting much time or money that brings no return. I will go to-morrow and look over the chances. Next week I will tune up the mowing machine, to mow around the buildings, and after the Fourth of July we will cut the grass as fast as it gets ripe and ready."

"We finish our work just in season for dinner," said Mr. Bartlett. "The sun just begins to light the west side of the house, so it is about a quarter to twelve. There! didn't I guess right! There is your mother on the front steps. And she is blowing the horn."

Roy swung his hat in answer, and, following the path that wound through the thick clover, they went to the welcome dinner.

Royal Bartlett inherited his first name as well as his last. His mother's maiden name was Marian Royal. Of good size, cheerful, healthy, and efficient, she was all the

wife, mother, and queen needful for one family, and the
sufficient ruler of heart and home. The table was spread
for four persons.

"Come, folks," said Mrs. Bartlett, "the dinner is all
ready."

"But where is Sam?" asked Mr. Bartlett. "He ought
to be here. He must have heard the horn, and he's not
the boy to neglect his dinner."

"No," said the housekeeper. "Sam Ellet is doing
what he thinks ought to be done; but here he comes
now." And, after an interview with the pump, and pol-
ishing his red cheeks on a crash roller towel, he appeared smiling at the table.

Sam Ellet was an orphan, now eighteen years old. He
had been fed, clothed, sent to school in winter, and
made happy as a member of the family for several years,
for what he could do. Lately he had received large
pieces of silver, and good-sized bank notes, new and
crisp, of the Strafford Bank, which he had judiciously
deposited in the Dover Savings Bank. He had proved
that he could keep money, and was to be trusted. Furthermore, he had learned to despise a man that could not
keep a cent, and he had made up his mind that he could
not "stomach" anything that was not "bone honest"
and truthful. So Sam was trusted and loved. He was
one of the family, and he made friends. He was proud
to be in the Bartlett family. The Bartletts were good
livers. The name is old, and I doubt if her majesty's is
older. At the Norman conquest a Bartlett settled on
the Arun River, near the Earl of Arundel's castle. The
present M. P., who represents the name, can ride fourteen
miles on his own land, and the name now, and for a thou-

sand years, is a part of England's history, coming down
to us through soldiers and statesmen, scholars and gentlemen, through Josiah Bartlett, the first signer of our
Magna Charta, the great declaration, and later he was
chosen the first governor of New Hampshire, — for this,
and all family and personal reasons, these Bartletts rejoiced
in the bluest blood, and a healthy family pride, that,
because they came of good stock, therefore it was their
duty and their pleasure to transmit it quite as good or a
little better than they received it.*

So Guy Bartlett and his family felt that if they behaved
as well, they were as good as anybody. And they lived
wisely and well. So Sam Ellet called them "Uncle
Bartlett" and "Aunt Bartlett," and felt himself bound
to uphold the honor of the family.

"Did you hear the horn, Sammy?" asked Mr. Bartlett.

"Yes, sir; I did. But I was almost done with the
last pile of rocks, and I thought I had better finish the
job. So it is all done, and I think you will like it."

"I am glad of it, Sammy. We will look it over carefully once more, and now, or when the grass is grown,
we can use a mowing machine over the whole back field.
It will make easy work of haying."

* Those who are interested in the Bartlett name can see "Genea-
logical and Biographical sketches of the Bartlett family in England
and America," by Levi Bartlett of Warner, N. H., 1875. Since this
was written, and before printing, an event has happened that I
gladly record here. On July 4, 1888, a magnificent bronze statue of
Hon. Josiah Bartlett was inaugurated in Amesbury, Mass., where he
was born. It cost many thousand dollars, and was the generous gift
of Mr. Jacob R. Huntington, a wealthy citizen of Amesbury. It was a
splendid deed to do, and it was splendidly done that day. And no
man stands higher or purer as patriot, statesman, or beloved physician than my ancestor, Doctor Josiah Bartlett.

"Now, mother," said Mr. Bartlett, "where do you suppose Roy is going to-morrow?"

"I don't know," she answered. "Perhaps up to see Aunt Sarah."

"No. Farther than that."

"Where?" she asked, anxiously.

"He is going to Boston to see about learning to paint pictures."

"Is he going to leave us to be a wild artist?" she asked, in dismay.

"Oh, that is too bad!" said Sam Ellet.

"Not as bad as you think, mother," said Roy. "I shall never leave you and father for long at a time. I shall go to the city in the morning, and perhaps return at night, or next day at farthest; and as for being wild, I do not think I shall go to the bad at all."

"Well, I hope not," she added; "but from some specimens that I have seen, it seems as if art was inseparably wedded to poverty, beer, and tobacco. I do not think it need to be so, but perhaps I may find it better."

"You surely will," said Roy, "for there are as pure and noble men and women in art as in anything. Indeed, it is said Saint Luke was an artist. And some of the old masters painted, as Michael Angelo builded on Saint Peters, for their soul's salvation. See Fra Angelico's pictures, painted on gold leaf. He prayed as he painted. No, mother. Art is not degrading. And it ought to be ennobling. But it is all in the man. He it is that ennobles the work. Now, mother, don't worry. I shall be none the worse for art, and I hope art will be all the better for me."

There was a pause.

"Yes," said Sam. "But what will the farm be without you, Roy?"

"Thank you, Sammy. But the farm will not lose me at all for the present, and not for long at a time in the future. Wouldn't it be nice to visit me for a few days in Boston?"

"Oh, it would be splendid," said Sam. "I had not thought of that. But it would be lonesome here."

"Now," said Mr. Bartlett, "we will stop borrowing trouble, and not try to cross a bridge until we get to it. And, to make it all the prettier, we will put the garden in order this afternoon, for I think there are some green squirrels in it."

"Green squirrels?" said Sam, in wonder. "What are they?"

"Weeds," said the farmer. "Daniel Webster wrote home to his man John, at Marshfield, 'Take good care of my mother's garden.' It is good advice."

Right well the Bartlett family followed it that afternoon. Later, when the weeding was finished, the supper put where it would do the most good, the stock cared for, and the chores all done, the lord of that home walked in that garden in the cool of the day with his helpers, and he saw as much beauty and found as much peace and comfort as is ever found in this bunchy and peculiar planet that is all the world to us, at least, for the present.

Disdaining horse and carriage, Roy, after a very early breakfast, and, as much as anything to put an end to too much vigorous thinking, he waved his hand in farewell to the family, who came to the piazza to see him off, and he took "shank's mare" for a walk to the station.

It is a New Hampshire superstition not to watch a

friend out of sight else they may never return. Of course, no one believes it, but they observe it all the same, and when, a quarter of a mile away, Roy looked back, he saw no one looking, but gazing earnestly for a moment at the landscape, which was so much to him, he exclaimed, "It is a beauty, indeed it is a beauty. I hope I shall one day do it justice in a picture." Then he turned and continued his journey in a run.

Mrs. Bartlett wore a sober face that day.

"Sammy," said Mr. Bartlett, "our work is well up to the season. Have you anything you wish to do to-day? You can have a part or all of to-day, if you wish, only be back at milking time."

"Yes, sir," said Sam, "I should like to hoe my water-melons, and that patch of land you gave me, and, as it is just cloudy enough, I will go up to the brook this after-noon and see if I can get a string of trout, so if Roy comes home to-night, and I think he will, we can have something he likes for supper."

"Good," said Mr. Bartlett, "and mother will like it too." So Sam had his day to himself. With lines enough and to spare, with hooks enough to lose a few, and a tin mustard-box, that used to be, but now containing a good supply of angle-worms, Sam came home with a string of trout that would have delighted a city chap. I know what I am talking about, for many a good fry I have taken out of the same brook, and this novel is a good deal more of a history than you think it is. Heretofore it had been considered that Roy could take the finest string of fish, but Sam had got his thinking cap on, and had fished, like Simon Peter, to some purpose. And Roy went to Boston to seek his fortune.

CHAPTER II.

WHEN a young man leaves the old home, whether it be high or low, and drops into a city where he is nearly or quite a stranger, there is a feeling of all-over-ishness, that comes over him which almost amounts to desolation. But the poet says, "This world's mine oyster, that I with sword will open," and that was Mr. Royal Bartlett's feeling as he stepped into Haymarket Square and walked up town. "J. Sardou, Artist, Room 39," he saw, a modest sign, on the upper end of a line beside a door. He went up four flights and knocked.

"Come in," said a man's voice.

"Can I look at your pictures, sir?"

"Yes, sir. But I have not many in."

Roy did look. There were not many finished, and he could hardly tell what was finished and what was not. Landscapes, cattle and figure pieces, and the usual variety —points of merit in all, some quite good. But nearly all had the feeling that a little more was needed to make it good and complete the art of the picture. Roy praised the noble quality of this group of oaks, the form of this waterfall, the sky effects, and what he could without violence to truth; said he was much obliged for the kindness, and was about to go.

"Do you paint, sir?" asked the artist.

"No, sir; I have drawn some, I love art and am always

14

interested in pictures. Perhaps I may paint some a little later."

"Don't do it, sir; however much you may like art or get the itch of paint, don't do it. You'll be sorry if you do."

"Why, sir?"

"Poverty, self-denial, hope deferred, and perhaps starvation. I do not mean that I am starving now," added the artist, "but I have been very hungry. Oh no! art is not in much demand. You had better let it alone."

"Well, sir," said Roy, "I am obliged for your kind word, and will consider it. It is a great pleasure to see your pictures. What price should you get for that bright moonlight, sir?"

"Fifty dollars."

"And that cluster of oaks?"

"One hundred."

"Does not that pay?"

"Oh, but they don't sell."

"Would they not at a less price?"

"No they wouldn't (fiercely). If a man wants a picture he will have it. But the minute you put your price down you are gone. You can never get it up again. And pupils are no better. At the first of the season I put out ten dollars in advertising for pupils. And they came, sometimes a dozen in a day, looked in, looked over the pictures, praised some of them, said they would see, and that is the last of it. No, sir, take a friend's advice and let art alone."

Roy thanked him and passed out, but as he did so he heard the artist remark in a stage whisper, "I'll bet the fool won't let it alone."

And the young man laughed for the first time to-day. He had seen enough in this one interview, to prove that a different course would bring a different result, and he approved of the' judgment of the average art pupil, that sought an atmosphere not quite so heavy with grumbling and tobacco.

He next called at a picture store. There were many attractive pictures in the window, and among others, two New England home scenes, one summer, the other winter. They were much like his own home, with cattle and all the evidences of life around the house and barn. Over the door the name, long and well known in Boston, " C. Drew, Pictures and Frames." He went in. Several people were looking at the pictures around the store.

" Are you Mr. Drew?" asked Roy.

" Yes, sir."

" Will you please tell me who painted those landscapes in the window?"

" Certainly; Mr. Titcombe painted them, and see the crowd around them. Why! a little while ago a man said he saw one of those cows go down to the water and drink."

" They do look almost natural enough to. What is the price of them?"

" Twenty-five dollars each. They are eighteen by twenty-six inches."

" Does Mr. Titcombe have pupils?"

" Yes, indeed. He paints all sorts of pictures, colors photographs, and I don't know what he don't do in art."

" Does he make money?" asked Roy.

" Of course he does. I sell a great many of his pic-ures, and I send him pupils and custom. Oh·yes, Mr.

Titcombe can get rich if he will take care of his money. He gets enough. Here is his card. Look in and he will show you around."

"I thank you for your kindness, Mr. Drew, I have often heard of you, and I am glad to meet you. Now let me ask you a question. I have studied drawing as an amateur for years. Sometimes artists have seen my work and praised it. Now I wish to try my luck in color. I can take a poor, worn-out farm and make it shine. This is what I wish to know: Can I, with not much genius and only a fair amount of ability, but a strong love for art, — can I, with faithful industry, strict temperance, good management, and hard study, become a fair artist and get an honorable living?"

"Yes, sir, I have no doubt of it," said Mr. Drew. "No doubt at all, for the qualities you mention almost always succeed and compel success."

"Then I will try," said Roy, "and very faithfully too, before I give it up. And now I will use that card and call on Mr. Titcombe."

Roy did so, and to his surprise he found the art school in four large, high, connected rooms, and a dozen pupils at work. Any amount of pictures, mostly in oil, a few in india ink, sepia, crayon, and pastel. He was soon at ease with the artist.

"Of course," said Mr. Titcombe, "almost any one who loves art, with fair ability and hard work, can soon begin to produce something that will sell, if you do not ask too big a price. 'But art is long and time is fleeting,' and to be a good artist is a life work. Your drawing will help you. Before I went to painting I studied drawing. I spent one whole winter," said Mr. T., "all my evenings

and spare time, in trying my best to copy J. D. Harding's
lithograph work on trees."

"Now, just look here, Mr. Bartlett," as he opened
a large folio near him. "Please examine these sheets,
title-page and all. One is my work, and the other is the
press which I copied. Tell me which is which." Roy
looked first at one and then at the other, then from one
to the other, again and again. Then, as Mr. Titcomb
regarded him with a half smile, Roy answered, "I think
the sheets in my right hand are the hand work."

"You are right," said Mr. Titcomb.

"But," said Roy, "it is the finest imitation of a lithograph title-page, and of tree drawing, that I ever saw. I
would not have believed it possible."

Roy engaged lessons. A dollar each for three hours.
Pay cash every time. Stop when he preferred to. So
Roy made a good friend and kept his independence.

"Have you looked into the art stores much?" asked
Mr. T.

"Not much."

"Suppose you look into Child's and into Williams
& Everett's; they always have fine pictures."

Roy thanked him, and continued his calls. He made
the pleasant acquaintance of Mr. A. A. Childs, and he
kept it long afterwards. He called at Williams &
Everett's. It was a treat. There happened to be a
large and fine collection on exhibition, and it was a revelation. Specimens of the best American art. Bierstadt, T. Hill, T. Moran, De Haas, Bellows, Sontag,
Gerry, Geo. L. Brown, Champney, Shapleigh, Ordway,
and I don't know how many more. A kind word of en-
couragement from Mr. Williams completed his happiness

and his day's work. He had covered the ground faithfully, and found an affirmative answer. The five o'clock train bore him home. He was still busy at thinking of the day and what should come of it, when he approached his home. The whole family met him on the piazza.

"I thought you would come, Roy," said Sam Ellet.

"We are all ready for you. Supper is on the table," said Mrs. Bartlett. "I guess you are hungry. What did you have for dinner?"

"I have not had any," said Roy. "I was so busy that I did not think of it until it was time to take the train."

A large dish of fried trout, with warm biscuit made from New Hampshire wheat, and many other farm products, flanked by a pitcher of cider, amount to good eating and drinking, and Roy paid his hearty respects to it, for he needed it.

"You are awful good, Sammy," said Roy.

"Yes, I thought you would like some greased pins for supper," said Sam.

"Yes, Sammy. But these brook trout are too good to be called greased pins. The large ones we dissect, but the little ones are brown and tender, and we eat them bones and all. Mother can beat the world at cooking fish and wild game."

"Yes. And everything else," said Sam.

"Stuffing," said Mrs. Bartlett.

"You are right," said Mr. Bartlett, "and of the finest kind. The fact is we ought to count up our mercies and our reasons for thankfulness, and be thankful accordingly. Now, just think, there is no clearer, cooler,

whiter, purer water than our old well. And there is a
living spring not far off. The farm yields more fuel
than we can use. Our apples and pears are in abundance, and New Hampshire fruit far excels Western
fruit in flavor and eating quality. And see what biscuits
mother has made. No Western wheat ever had so good
a flavor. See these potatoes! Fine, mealy, and of best
quality. Can anybody beat mother's butter and cheese?
How about our pork and beef? How about our lambs
and fatted calves? How about our milk, eggs, and yel-
low-leg chickens? I tell you, boys, there is no better
place to live in than in New England. There is plenty
here."

"The winters are pretty tough," said Roy.

"Yes, I acknowledge that," said Mr. Bartlett. "But
take the evidence on the other side. Last year the
deaths in British India were twenty-three thousand by
poisonous snakes alone, to say nothing of wild animals.
Our winter saves all that. Nothing is safe from the
ravages of white ants. Our winter saves all that. Take,
for instance, the island of Singapore. Thirty miles long,
ten miles wide, and ten miles out at sea. Yet the loss
by its one city of a hundred thousand people is one life a
day, through the year, by tigers alone. But our winter
saves all that. We have no cholera, no Yellow Jack,
very little malaria, in fact I know of none. I think New
Hampshire folks have as much to be thankful for as any
people on earth; you know the Psalmist thought of His
loving kindness and tender mercy. Indeed, I think so
well of my native State that I wrote my opinion in a
poem not long ago. Perhaps you will be pleased to hear
it. Now we have a little time after supper, and I will

read it to you, It won't take long, and need not hinder mother very much. Here it is." And by the light of the evening lamp, Mr. Bartlett read his tribute of love to

"NEW HAMPSHIRE HILLS.

" Dedicated to all who are proud that they were born in the Granite State.

"New Hampshire Hills, fond memory comes to me,
And bids me twine a loyal song for thee;
Where sunshine falls and evening dew distils,
Where summer glory crowns New Hampshire Hills.

"New Hampshire Hills, that catch the morn's first beams,
And linger, bright with evening's latest gleams;
Sweet be his verse, and pure his thoughts who wills
To sing thy praises, O New Hampshire Hills.

"New Hampshire Hills, I turn to thee with pride.
Have not thy children for thee lived and died?
That, while the earth its destiny fulfils,
Freedom may reign upon New Hampshire Hills?

"New Hampshire Hills, thy children proud and free
In every clime, on every land and sea, —
While love and gratitude each true heart fills,
Unite to praise thee, O New Hampshire Hills.

"New Hampshire Hills, forever grand and true,
Forever towering to the heavenly blue;
His patriot heart with new devotion thrills,
Who builds his altar on New Hampshire Hills.

"New Hampshire Hills, what summer pilgrims throng
Where health and beauty verify my song;
Land of sweet waters, and of laughing rills,
O home of beauty — bright New Hampshire Hills.

"New Hampshire Hills, thy fields and forests wide
No tigers keep, no lurking dangers hide;
No serpent stings; there no malaria chills,
But health and safety crown New Hampshire Hills.

"New Hampshire Hills, thy children far and wide
Look back tŏ thee with high New Hampshire pride;
No land so fair thine own place ever fills,
To win their love from thee, New Hampshire Hills.

"New Hampshire Hills, where'er thy children roam,
What good-cheer memories call them back to home;
What loyal work a mother's heart instils,
What mother's love lights up New Hampshire Hills.

"New Hampshire Hills, where'er my feet shall stray,
Among thy pleasant scenes, or far away,
I turn to praise thee, and my spirit wills
My grateful song to thee, New Hampshire Hills.

"New Hampshire Hills, with love and Sabbath bell
Guard thou the dust of those I love so well,
Forevermore. Though death my own heart stills,
God bless my home, my dear New Hampshire Hills." *

When it was finished, Roy asked, " Can I have a copy,
father?"

" I want one, too," said Sam.

" And I will take the original," said Mrs. Bartlett.

" You have got him," he answered, " and I guess you
will all get copies later; but," he added, "it is nine
o'clock, and I think we had better read."

The light-stand with the Bible and hymn book was
set forward. Mother Bartlett read the old hymn, —

* This poem was read before the N. H. Club of Cambridge, Mass.,
June, 1885.

"Thus far the Lord has led me on;
Thus far his power prolongs my days:
And every evening shall make known
Some fresh memorial of his grace."

Then Mr. Bartlett read the one hundred and third psalm. "Bless the Lord, O my soul, and all that is within me bless his holy name." Then two of the four knelt, while one poured out his soul to God, in the rich offering of a thankful heart. How many times I have heard it! And blessing, peace, and health comes of it.

Then half an hour later, "tired Nature's sweet restorer, balmy sleep" had conquered them all. Father and mother in the great bedroom; the boys upstairs; Grimalkin, the great Malta cat, in the arm-chair; the pelican, Roy's fancy name for his mother's very knowing canary bird, on his perch; and Canis Major, the brown and white Newfoundland dog, asleep with one eye open, on a thick mat on the piazza.

When the moon at its full looked down upon it all, it seemed to repeat the eternal promise. "Peace I give you. My peace I leave with you; not as the world giveth, give I unto you."

CHAPTER III.

THE next morning was a June morning in all its glory. About five o'clock there was a noise of opening doors, and Canis Major came pitching upstairs to the boy's room, tickled almost to death to see them. It was his usual morning call, and a most effectual way of waking the boys; for he would be recognized; he would not be suppressed; he would love them and kiss them, and the shortest and sweetest way out of it was to let him; as a woman marries a man whom she wishes was a safer and better fellow, just to get rid of him. But Canis Major was safe and true, and he was welcome. And besides it was milking time, and while Mother Bartlett fought a duel with the cooking stove, and won it, too, the three menfolks, each at the side of his chosen cow, began a solo, ting, ting, with the streams of milk as they hit at the bottom of each tin pail. It was a splendid success, this June morning, "in the height of feed," and the blessing of heaven, and the breath of the clover was in it.

The long procession of cows filed peacefully down the lane, headed by "Speck," a beautiful Ayrshire, with sharp horns, the leader and dominant power, in short, the one that *licked* all the others. The procession ended with Jerusha, a monster cow, the largest I ever saw, who gave a tub full of milk, and was in abject fear of all

24

the others, but on the most confiding terms with all mankind, and with no more fight in her than there is in the
"Sermon on the Mount." These cows are portraits in
both physique and character. I have pictures of some of
them. The men strained the milk into the creamery, and
the horn tooted for breakfast.

"I declare," said Roy, "more trout and larger ones."
Sam grinned.

"Look out, Roy," said Mr. Bartlett, "Sam is getting
ahead of you."

"Sam is a daisy," said Roy. "He is a credit to the
family."

Sam was pleased, and what would he not have done
for Roy, or Uncle Bartlett, or Aunt Bartlett? Why!
We are taught even God himself loves the praise of his
saints, and why should not Sam go toward the kindly
light that was home, love, and blessing to him?

As the meal was concluded, Canis Major let out a
single bark, not as one who gives warning of danger, but
as a notice that some one is coming. And so it was.

Mr. Aaron Hoskins, a farmer, well to do, with an only
child, a daughter eighteen years old, and she was a
schoolmate of Roy's. It was Mr. Hoskins. He had a
kind neighborly welcome.

"I guess I came in a good time," said he.

"Rather late," said Mr. Bartlett, "but there are a few
trout left. Now set up and have some!"

"That is the blessing of having some boys," said
farmer Hoskins. "Now my boys are all girls, and only
one at that, so I get no trout."

"Mother get a plate. There's a good lot left, and I
want Mr. Hoskins to taste these."

He did try them, and to his satisfaction; talking farm-talk the while.

"Now a taste of this cider," said Mr. Bartlett. "You know a fish swims three times. Once in water, once in fat, once in cider. Then they won't hurt you."

It was a neighborly call and a picnic.

"I must go," said Mr. Hoskins. "I thank you all for your kindness. Now, Roy," said he, "do you want to go out and show me your cows, on my way home?"

"I shall be pleased to," Roy answered. And they went out.

Mr. Bartlett added, "Much obliged for this call. Come again, neighbor, and come oftener."

No one said it, but all knew well enough that Neighbor Hoskins wanted to talk to Roy about something besides cows, and he did. They walked out toward the cattle.

"Oh, Roy, how your farm does improve. Mow it most all with a machine, don't you?"

"Yes sir, all of it. We made it possible last week."

"You are splendid farmers, you make the farm shine. But it takes elbow grease to do it."

"Yes, sir," said Roy. "But it is better, cheaper, and easier to improve a field, than to always mow it by hand."

"Yes, Roy, I know it. But I have not the heart to do anything. Now I will tell you my trouble, Roy. You know Mary, and are always good and kind to us all: — Will Glance is always coming to see my Mary; and she is all the child I have. Will Glance steals and lies, he gets drunk and chews and smokes and abuses his mother. He denies it all to Mary, and she believes it all, like a fool. And I know it is true, for good, honest people that I can trust have seen it, and seen my Mary with him, and have come and warned me of it. One day I went, when he was at my house, and saw his mother, and she denied nothing, but wept as if she would die. Still Mary will not give him up. She says if she cannot get what she wants, she must take what she can get. He is rather good-looking, or would be if he looked good, and he is rather dressy. Mary says he will be steady enough as soon as he is married, and that 'a reformed rake always makes the best husband.' Oh, what a mean proverb, and a terrible lie! And it almost kills mother and I. Now, Roy, you know what she is. You have been to school with her, and are older than she is. Can't you go and see her to-night, and tell her what you know about Glance — for you must know him?"

"I do know him," said Roy, "and no good of him. He is a boot-maker; makes good pay when he works, fools away his money, and, as he is related to his employer, he does not get discharged. I am very sorry, Mr. Hoskins, and I do not think she will listen to me, but I will warn her of her danger, although such service commonly comes to no good. If you and Mrs. Hoskins will be over here at eight o'clock, I will call at your house and say a word to Mary."

Mr. Hoskins turned to his home with tears in his eyes, and Roy turned to the house with a job on hand that he did not relish. But he was determined that he would do it to help his friend and neighbor. He was ill at ease all day. His father regarded him quietly, but said nothing about the call, while Sam Ellet gave him a few hard looks that were bristling with interrogation points.

About eight o'clock Mr. and Mrs. Hoskins came over

in the light wagon. Roy had seen them coming, and had gone on his errand by a short cut across lots.

Mary Hoskins was at home, and answered his knock.

"Come in, Mr. Bartlett. You are quite a stranger."

"Busy times," said Roy. "Hoeing and getting ready for haying."

"Oh, you have not been here since the snow flew."

"I acknowledge that; I have not visited much anywhere, but to-night I called to say a word that you ought to hear."

"What is it?"

"Will Glance is not good enough for you, Mary."

"Oh, that is it, is it? Now it is all out. Now I am enlightened. A woman has to do as she can. And if Will Glance is not good enough for me, why didn't you come yourself? You need not tell me you did not want me. That is implied. Then it leaves a chance for Will Glance. Do you know any hurt of him?"

"Yes, Mary, I do. I have seen him drunk, yelling and lashing a stable horse, which he drove almost to death. And I know he has struck and kicked his mother. Now, Mary, as a friend, I do hope you will not grieve your parents and reap sorrow for yourself — lifelong sorrow — by marrying William Glance."

"Well, Mr. Bartlett, I am obliged to you for the interest you take in me all at once. Perhaps it will not be as bad as you think. But a woman has to do as she can in this world, and so, for want of a better man, I am engaged to William Glance. Of course, it will make no difference to you personally, Mr. Bartlett."

"Of course not," said Roy. "But I did want to help you as a schoolmate and friend."

" Very well, then," said she. " I have no favors to ask of you. And as you have not been in this house for six months past, I shall not cry if you do not come into it for six months more."

Roy said he was sorry that his call would result in no good, for he should always wish her well.

Then he kindly said, " Good night, Mary."

She gazed upon the floor.

Again, " Good-night, Mary."

No movement and no answer. Then Roy slowly and sadly closed the door after him, and his footfalls faded out in the silence of the evening. She said she should not cry, but she did. She had gone to her room when her parents returned, and in her own bed she wept until the fountains were dry. I do not say why she wept. You can think what you please. The next day she was very pale and quiet, and a little later in the afternoon she said to her mother, " I think I will walk out, and see if it will cure my headache. I will try to be back to get supper."

She did not get back so soon, and she saw Will Glance and told him the whole story. He ground his teeth with rage. He despised meddlers. He would get even. She forbade it.

Roy had talked but little during the day, nor could he see how he could be of any service to the Hoskins family. His mother had nearly solved the problem. So at supper she said to Roy, " It is a pity that Mary Hoskins goes with that Will Glance."

" So it is," he answered.

" What does Mr. Hoskins say about it ? "

" Oh, he regrets it."

"What does her mother say?"

"Of course she does, too."

"Well, Roy, what can you do about it?"

Roy looked square in his mother's face.

"Oh, you need not look strange. You have been stewing and mulling about it ever since yesterday morning, when you and Mr. Hoskins went out to see our cows. Our cows, indeed. A two-legged heifer, I guess, was the subject."

Roy laughed heartily. He could not help it. And they all did. Mr. Bartlett said nothing. Sam ditto. On the principle that when a mother takes a child in hand it is safest and best for the father to sit on the fence and avoid responsibility.

"Mother, I think we all have the right idea of Will Glance, and that we are not likely to help the case any."

"You are right, Roy. Then will you please to let it alone, or trouble will come of it."

And trouble did come of it.

CHAPTER IV.

ROY WALKS OUT.

Roy dismissed the subject from his mind, and after the chores were done went out back of the house to look around. He was in his slippers, and entertaining a quill toothpick, both for use and to assist him in his meditations. He was thinking that, whatever troubles others had, he had none: for his life was as sweet and peaceful as a pan of milk, when a tall, dark-complexioned man sprang out from among the lilac bushes with a club, and knocked him down. Roy was stunned. The stranger jumped, and sat upon him, and with a curse he growled, "There, I'll teach you to meddle with me. Now, when you come to I'll pound you again."

With the weight upon him, Roy did not revive. Then there came a queer, rushing sound, like the flight of birds, but growing louder, and in a moment more a crashing blow, and Will Glance went down under the fist of Sam Ellet. Glance was confused, but soon rallied. Sam laid him out again, and, catching his club, hit him on both hands and across his nose with that. Then Sam straddled him, and yelled, "Murder! murder! Help! help! Murder! murder!" The old folks were in the garden in front of the house, and were not long in getting there. They were just in season to see Canis Major make a big grab into the seat of the villain's trousers, and hang to him. It must have hurt his feelings, by the way he yelled.

31

Mr. and Mrs. Bartlett choked him off, and tied him up; but it was a job. His eyes were like balls of fire.

The parents carried Roy into the house, sponged his head, wiped away the blood, and found, to their joy, that his skull was not broken. But it was a cruel wound on his forehead. Their help revived him. Then Mr. Bartlett brought out a flat, greenish-glass bottle, with General Harrison stamped on one side, poured out a few spoonfuls of nobody knows what, and made Roy drink it. Then he said, " Now, mother, he will not faint; and you can take care of him." Then he went out. Sam stood a-straddle of the scamp, with the club, ready to strike. Mr. Bartlett took him by the collar, and helped him up, although he still held him fast. Glance cursed, and swore he would kill Roy Bartlett.

" If you do," said Sam Ellett, " I will kill you. I will, and I always keep my promises."

Glance was hurt some in several places, and his head was addled and bruised. Roy came out of the house, leaning on his mother's arm.

" Let him go," said Roy; "he has not made anything out of it, and I am alive."

Mr. Bartlett spoke. " William Glance, you are a wicked man. But it is best that I should leave your punishment to a higher power than I am. If you will promise me solemnly that you will never molest my son, or one of my family, or my property again, I will set you free, and you may go. Otherwise I will unchain the dog, and, when I can get him off of you, I will bind you, and deliver you to the sheriff, at Dover jail." .

Glance thought a moment. He was a fool, but he was not an idiot; so he gave the required promise, and they set him free. Canis Major roared, and tugged at his chain, but did not get loose. If he had, Will Glance would have been translated. They led the scamp out at the front gate, and he limped slowly and painfully down the road towards Dover, with his hands on the widest part of his trousers. He had evidently been drinking, and whether he remembered Lot's wife or not, he remembered Sam Ellet and Canis Major. He did not look back, and they all watched him out of sight, regardless of consequences. His parents supported Roy to the sitting-room. He uttered a mild protest, and soon he lay at his length on the sofa.

"Now," said Mr. Bartlett, "tell me briefly how this came to pass. Mr. Hoskins came to see you?" he began.

"Yes, father, and he wanted me to speak to Mary about Will Glance. I did not wish to, and I told him I thought it would do no good. But I went. The visit failed. She must have told Glance all about it; and you know what he is. The first thing I knew I was struck. Sam knows the rest."

"Sam," said Mr. Bartlett, "tell what you know."

"And tell it exactly as it is," added Mrs. Bartlett, sternly.

Sam turned and looked at her.

"Aunt Bartlett," said he, "could I, or would I, tell anything else? I knocked over Will Glance, and saved Roy, and I would give my life for him."

"I beg your pardon, my son," said she. "Sammy, I was only too earnest. You are faithful and splendid."

Sam was mollified. "You see the work was done, and I have often, when it was pleasant weather, gone up into

the cupola of the barn, and was looking at everything in
sight, — for you can see a long way from the cupola, —
when I saw a man coming across the pasture, keeping
close to the wall, and under the trees, and looking suspiciously around. Soon I knew it was Will Glance.
Then you may be sure I kept my eye on him ; and before
I knew it, he had a club, and, after watching awhile, he
saw Roy, and sprang upon him. I was in the cupola, and
barefoot, so he did not hear me coming. I made awful
flying leaps down, and I came upon him unawares and
gave him my fist, like the kick of a mule."

"You are a treasure, Sammy," said Mr. Bartlett.

"True-hearted and faithful," said Mrs. Bartlett.

"You are as good as a brother," said Roy.

Sam was proud; and when, a little later, Mr. Bartlett
came up to Sam and gave him a small pasteboard box, he
wondered. Sam opened it, and saw, lying on a lock of
pink cotton, a new, bright, gold twenty-dollar piece.
Then Sam's heart overflowed.

Will Glance did not appear in public for a week.

On the third day of July, Farmer Hoskins rose early
in the morning, and as he was going to the barn he saw a
ladder at his daughter's window, and the window was
open. He guessed the truth. Mary was married to
Will Glance. A brief note told the story. The old
folks bore it as well as they could. On the afternoon of
the Fourth of July they came home. Glance said he
would use them right; sorry he was poor. If Mr. Hoskins was willing, he would work for him, as his hired man,
for twenty dollars a month, he and his wife to board with
the family.

Mr. Hoskins could pay it well enough, and, rather than

lose sight of Mary, the bargain was made. Mr. and Mrs. William Glance lived at the Hoskins farm. All the neighbors were sorry for it. All wished them well, but no one had the hardihood to offer any congratulations. New Hampshire farmers are plain folks, and not inclined to be hypocritical.

Roy Bartlett lay on the sofa, and his mother petted him and made much of him, and his father and Sam were most devoted. But Roy was nobody's baby. On the morning of the third of July he sat on the mowing machine, and mowed the dooryard and all that needed an early clip, from the road all around the buildings. And the place looked as smart as a boy that had had his hair cut. Roy rested in the afternoon, but, on the morning of the fourth, he tuned up the mowing machine for active service the next day.

The next day the campaign began in good earnest. Roy was better, and spoiling to get the hay when it was at its best. Bright and early the rattle song of the mowing machine was heard, and it sounded long and well. Every foot of land had been examined with careful eyes; the hollows had been raised, the knolls graded, and now it was the poetry of motion, safe and efficient. Not once did he get pitched a rod away, ahead of the cutter, in spread-eagle style, into horrid danger. No. But he rode a conqueror, through the vast army of spears, until acres of grass lay around him, drying into tons of sweet hay. And never in his life will he look nobler or handsomer, than he did that day. His father and Sam cut the corners of the field, and, great as was the work accomplished, it was easily done. The day was hot, and the hay made well. After dinner,

the horse-rake appeared, with old Tom, a horse who was
the perfection of all honest equines, and the hay was
raked. What a transformation! At six o'clock the field
was covered with the tumbles of hay, all in order for the
night. Beautiful landscape! How different from the
morning. Then, beautiful nature, and now still gloriously beautiful, but almost the despair of art is a haying
scene. As Emerson says: "Nature is various; Nature is
intricate."

CHAPTER V.

ROY PROVES HIMSELF A HERO.

DAY after day the fragrant hay came gayly to the barn, — excuse me, I did not intend to write poetry, but the subject is so full of it that it came involuntarily. At any rate, poetry or not, it is a fact. With ten days perfect hay weather, the best hay was nearly all in. It was Friday evening, and the morrow promised to be not much of a hay day, for clouds were rolling in, as if a break in the hay weather might come soon.

" Roy," said Mr. Bartlett, " our English hay is almost all in. I think we may take it a little easier, and not mow to-morrow. That case that was left out to me as referee, had better be attended to. I want you to take the light wagon and go to Dover in the morning. Sam may go with you. Go to the lawyer's office and get the papers, with all the case and the evidence done up in one snug bundle, and sealed. You sign it with date, day, and hour, and let Sam sign it as a witness. Then go up the Tollend road by the heath house, past Ezra Hayes's and to Elisha Locke's, turn there, cross the bridge, go to the Gonic, and from there to Rochester. Call on the lawyer for the other side, get his case, evidence, and all his statements, have it sealed, sign it the same as the other, and let Sam witness that, too. Then bring the papers safely to me. Perhaps a long, hateful, and expensive lawsuit can be avoided ; and, although I have no personal inter-

37

est in it, yet as it has been referred to me as an honest
man, I must do them all the good I can."

The next morning, Roy and Sam went on their errand.
It was cloudy in the morning, but soon " burnt off," and
was a fair, hot day.   The boys knew nearly every farmer,
by name, at least, from Dover to Strafford Ridge.   Roy
took his sketchbook with him, so that he might take an
outline of rock or tree, house or hill, if he chose to.   It
was a pleasant summer ride.   Past the old Betsey Coffin
place, Peter Cushing's, Nat Eaton's, Joseph Winkley's,
Ham, Hodgdon, Horne, Fernald, Watson, the old Heath
House, with a convivial reputation, Ezra Hayes's, Cater,
Elisha Locke's, and so on to the Gonic.   This is the short
for Squanamagonic, the barbarous old Indian name.
They accomplished their errand at Rochester, and started
on their return.   When they got back to Locke's Mills,
Roy said, " Now, Sam, let us hitch the horse here, for I
want to sketch the falls, the old saw-mill, and the pout-
hole."

" It is a beauty subject for a picture," said Sam.   " I
hope you will get it."

The young men went a few rods down on the east side
of the river, then down the steep bank among the rocks
and trees, holding on carefully, for a slip might be dangerous.   So they climbed down to the water, then by
jumping from one rock to another, they at last stood on
the large flat rock about ten feet long and four feet wide,
which was a little above the water.   Then they stood at
the deep foaming water of the pout-hole.   There were
two young men already on the rock, both younger than
Roy, and one younger than Sam.   The mist of the falls
fell in coolness around them, and, although the boiling

current looked dangerous, yet the older one was un-
dressed for a dive into the dark water.

"Not going into the pout-hole, McDuffie, are you?"

"Yes, I am. I can swim like a duck, and you can't
drown me."

"Don't do it. I wouldn't risk it." said Roy.

"Oh, it is safe enough, I guess. I want a rock from
the bottom. About ten feet down, ain't it?"

"Near that," said Roy. "But it is not safe. More
than one have been drowned in this rough water." Roy
took off his coat with the papers in it, and laid it on a
rock, safe and dry. Then he glanced at Sam. Sam was
wide awake, and appeared to understand.

"Sam," said Roy, "grab that fishing-pole."

He did.

"Good-by," said McDuffie. And he dove, head first,
into the dark water. They watched anxiously, but he
did not appear.

"Sam," said Roy, "go down on that rock and help me
out. Quick, or he is lost."

McDuffie had struck a sharp rock in the bottom, and
was stunned. He was drowning. An instant later, the
white of his body shone for a moment in a place where
the sun shone, and that instant Roy plunged into the
water after him. Roy caught him by his head, and struck
as strongly as he could, with the heavy body, and was
being rapidly drawn down the river when Sam's fishing-
pole reached him. A strong grasp with one hand, while
he had McDuffie's head under his arm, holding on with the
other a moment, while two lives were almost lost, and
then Sam grasped Roy's hand, and the other young man
had McDuffie, first by the hair, then by the arm; then

all three lifted him, scratched and bleeding, upon the hot rock, and Roy climbed and was helped, painfully, after him.

"Thank God," said Roy.

"Amen," said Sam.

They worked quickly, found a plank and laid it from rock to rock, and got the senseless body quickly on a piece of soft grass, which, of course was hot on such a day. They held him head downward for an instant, and they rolled him. They slapped his feet and hands, and his back. They pressed his breast and made respiratory movements, and soon were rewarded with a groan. Then, after the best treatment that the boys could give, they wiped him dry with their handkerchiefs and dressed him. He was conscious, although bleeding from bruises and scratches from the rocks. Then they supported him to Roy's wagon, and with one on each side of him, to hold him up, and Roy to drive, they got him home to his father's house, sensible, but suffering. Sam told them what Roy had done, and young McDuffie heard it and beckoned to Roy. He came and put his hand upon the sufferer's cheek; then McDuffie took the hand and kissed it. It was a full acknowledgment of everything.

"But, Mr. Bartlett," said Mr. McDuffie, "you are all wet through. Come in and get a dry suit, and stay with us."

"No, I thank you," said Roy. "Sam and I will go home. And the horse will do it in double-quick time."

"You have saved my son," said Mr. McDuffie. "We can never repay you. I will see you soon."

"You are all welcome," said Roy. "Good-by, I am glad to be of some service to you. I guess he won't dive into the old pout-hole again, when the water is pouring over the dam."

Mr. McDuffie sent to the Gonic for a doctor who patched the outside, and dosed the inside of young Mc-Duffie, and prophesied that he would do well if he kept away from the pout-hole.

"Do you think you will know enough to?" asked his mother. A decided nod was the answer.

Then Roy and Sam took a fast drive home. He was wet and sodden, and the water quashed in his boots. It was a wonder and astonishment to Mr. and Mrs. Bartlett, but it did not stop them until dry towels, dry clothing, and warm drinks had been administered, until Roy was as hot as a baked apple, and as red as a rooster. He laughed heartily at the way his mother coddled him, and his father looked at him as if he thought unutterable things. That night, when Mr. Bartlett gave thanks to God for being delivered from dangers, seen and unseen, he did it with an unction. And the young hero slept the sleep of the true-hearted, and came out as bright as a button in the morning.

CHAPTER VI.

THE next day was Sunday. The Bartletts had no hay out, and nothing to worry about. There was a quiet hush about the day. Everything seemed to be different from the other six days. It was quieter. Grimalkin walked around as if she knew what day it was, and the pelican sang with a Sunday kind of mildness. Even the flies buzzed differently. I an not writing fiction. I know that in such households there is a Sunday restraint and rest upon everything. I have often felt it, and wondered if the day was not made of sacred material. The house was locked up. Four people rode to Dover in the family carryall, to the brick Orthodox church with the large golden rooster on it. They sat in the Bartlett pew. They came to worship. When the parson gave out the morning hymn, —

> " Safely through another week
> God has brought us on our way,
> Let us now a blessing seek,
> Waiting in his courts to-day.
> Day of all the week the best,
> Emblem of eternal rest," —

then the Bartlett family seemed to find the voice of thanksgiving and praise. Mr. Bartlett sung a strong

42

bass, Roy was a good tenor, and Sam was learning well
on the bass also. Mrs. Bartlett was a good soprano and
an inspiration in church music. To-day there seemed
especial cause for thankful songs. All the large congre-
gation felt it too, and joined with the choir in the well-
known hymn. But, after the loyal prayer and giving of
thanks for all the mercies of life, the parson gave the
subject of his sermon. " By this we know what love is,
He gave Himself for us." Then it did seem as if the
parson knew all about it, and was bound to make this
service the perfection of all Sabbath completeness. And
the day was a rich one.

On the way home Sam remarked : " There is some
stability in a good evangelical church."

" Yes, indeed," said Mr. Bartlett, " I knew a man, Mr.
James Davis, who attended that church for twenty-four
years, and during that time he missed but one half day
from its Sunday service. After that his health failed,
and he was not able to attend so constantly. That is a
record for constancy. I have an old account-book containing Mr. Davis's agreements with his men whom he
employed for the Dover Factory Company, dated 1825,
in which they agree to work for the D. M. Co., and find
the necessary carpenter's tools for so much a month, free
from expense of board or spirit to the company. Other
employers furnished liquor ; he would not. Good men
and good churches are never far apart. Thus Sam was
shown the right, and was made and treated as their
equal. Monday morning came fair and bright. The
grass was wet for it had rained during the night. Bright
and early, Canis Major came tumbling upstairs to call
the boys. They had the start of him, and the three

.friends came down together. The chores on a large farm are no small job to do, but with four strong people, and extra help when they wanted it, they got along nicely. And breakfast is always welcome. When the morning meal was finished, Mrs. Bartlett said earnestly, "Roy, I have two requests to make of you."

"Say on, mother."

"One is, keep out of other folk's love affairs, and the other is, keep out of the Isinglass river or somebody will lose a good man."

Roy laughed and said he would remember it, but would try to do his duty. After breakfast the rattle of the mowing machine began again. Once it sounded new and incongruous, but now it is the most agricultural and bucolic of sounds; now it is quite as much an addition to the music of nature as the staccato song of the yellow-hammer. This time the great clover field yielded up its sweetness. Not the oleanders of Palestine, not the oranges of Florida, not the escholtzias of California, not the rhododendrons of Pennsylvania, or the roses of Old or New England, are any handsomer to me than a splendid field of red clover in the beauty of its bloom. And the prince of the house of Bartlett rode a conqueror over it all. It was eleven o'clock when the horn sounded; too early for dinner. First a single long wind of the horn, then three short staccato toots. It was company come. More short toots would have meant danger, and would have brought them all in on the run. Roy came first, and soon his father and Sam. It was Mr. McDuffie. He greeted them very heartily, and said that Jean was better. "Guess he has learned a lesson. But he will lie on the sofa for a week and get some of the scratches and bruises off him. And my boy knows that Roy almost lost his life in saving him, and he wants to do something for Roy. Jean said that his funeral would have been to-day if it had not been for Roy, and he did not want to die yet. Now he is going to do this. About two years ago his uncle gave him a hundred dollars for his name, and it has been in the Dover Savings Bank and gained something since. Jean says Roy must take it, every cent. Give the interest over the hundred to Sam." Mr. McDuffie laid the roll of bills and odd change in Roy's lap.

Roy's color came in a moment. "No sir," said he vehemently. "Not one cent will I take now or ever, and no present of any kind. Do you want any, Sam?"

"No, indeed," said Sam, "it would spoil all the good of it."

"Now, Mr. McDuffie," continued Roy, "I only did my duty. I am grateful to Jean and his father and mother for their appreciation. And I know Sam is too. You do this. Stay here to dinner; then go to Dover before the bank closes, return this money to the savings bank again, every cent, and perhaps the interest will not be broken. Then tell Jean if he wants to love me I shall be glad to have him. Then he and all of you come and visit us and we will visit you and be friends with you all. Tell Jean when he does a kind, generous act to some one else, to let me know it. When he adds to his bank account, to let me know it. Tell him when any great good comes to him, to let me know it; and I hope often to hear some good of him."

Mr. McDuffie mopped up his face, and some others did. The dinner was eaten with thanksgiving and thankfulness, and the money went back to Jean McDuffie's account in the Dover Savings Bank. Jean soon recovered. He was less headstrong and more faithful. The boy that was with him said, that Jean got a pile of good out of the Isinglass river. But he had a close shave for his life. And that night the fragrant clover lay in several hundred tumbles on its way, with extra help, to its winter quarters in the barn.

Two days afterward the Bartlett family smiled when they heard that Jean McDuffie's parents " had up a note." That is to say, at the next Sunday morning service, the Orthodox minister read a notice, saying, " Brother Elisha McDuffie and his wife desire the church to join them in returning thanks to Almighty God for delivering their son and only child from a sudden and dreadful death." And the parson did give thanks, and the church did join, and meant it, too. It was a common practise for thrifty families to ask the church to pray that they might have special favors granted them at special times. Whereat a quiet and suppressed smile would steal over the faces of the world's people as some graceless one would whisper " that makes the tenth." And often, very often, from sadness and sorrow, I have heard their requests come, " that the death of their beloved one might be sanctified to their spiritual and everlasting good." They learned and loved to bear each other's burdens, coming and going, and, although the devil's children think they have all the fun, there are many, many, both earthly and heavenly blessings that they never know. Indeed, I think they work the hardest, fare the hardest, suffer most, and take the poorest pay all the time.

The haying went on. Every day the big loads went tumbling into the deep bays or on the high scaffolds. All the upland was in, and now they were cutting the runs and meadows. But a little of it got wet. At noon the clouds were rising, and the thunder growled in the distance. Big thunder-heads piled up in the west, and with almost human expression, seemed to war and battle with each other. They got the hay up as fast as they could, and some of it was housed. They put it in larger bunches, and made it to shed water as much as possible. Sam opened the gate that led from the pasture into the lane, and the cows hurried up to the barn. Then, with claps of thunder and blazes of lightning, they ran to the house, not quite soon enough to escape all the shower. An hour later the milking was done and the supper out of the way. It seemed as if all the water in Bow pond, three miles long, had got loose, and was pelting Strafford County, and the crashing of the thunder and the blaze of the lightning increased.

Mr. Bartlett spoke. "Now, mother, you sit on the sofa. It is stuffed with feathers. Sam, you move your chair out of the corner, but not in the centre. Roy, move farther from Sam, so we may be scattered more if the house gets struck."

Mr. Bartlett pumped two pails of water, and sat down apart from the others.

"Are you well insured, father?" asked Roy.

"Yes, very well. Then what more can we do? Nothing. We have cared for all the stock, scattered apart, so as not to be all killed at once if the lightning should strike us. Now we may look on and enjoy what we can of the fearful power of the storm."

It was hours before there was any abatement, and then one part seemed to follow the Cocheco River, and the other the Bellamy, off toward the ocean. And whoever had it was welcome to it. They had had enough of it.

CHAPTER VII

DULL WEATHER IN HAY TIME.

THE next day was no hay day. It was cloudy. Mr. Bartlett did not feel like doing anything but haying, and that could not be done. So they sat in the big kitchen talking.

"Father," said Roy, "have you made your decision on that referee case?"

"Yes, I have."

"What do you get out of it?"

"I suppose I could charge a reasonable fee, but I shall ask nothing. I have put my answer on the basis of truth and justice, and they will value my decision more if I do it for peace and right than if I do it for money. Here comes Captain John Q. Hayes now after the papers."

He rode into the yard, and was soon in the sitting-room. The papers were delivered, and the compensation declined. Then Captain Hayes sat down, saying he would sit and chat awhile. He had not made a call in a long time, and he was welcomed. Roy went down and drew a pitcher of rare old cider, which seemed, like Dimmesdale's love, to have a consecration of its own. It was not neglected.

"Did you ever see such a rain?"

"Not often," said Mr. Bartlett.

"Why," said Captain Hayes, "I should think the old

49

Orthodox parson that lived near the Sudbury River, had
prayed for it. Did you ever hear the story?"

"Please tell it," said Roy.

"You see, the old parson was a matter-of-fact man, and
believed in prayer. So when he prayed for a thing he
just meant it literally. One time there was an awful
drouth. Oh, ever so dry, and the country all drying up.
One Sunday morning he could stand it no longer. So he
prayed, 'Oh, Lord, thou hast taught us to bring all our
wants to thee. We need rain. The crops are all drying
up, and everything is afire. Oh, send us rain, now. Not
a big thunder shower that will rip things and wash all the
taters out of the hills, but a regular drizzle-drozzle,
drizzle-drozzle, that will soak in and do us some good.'
Of course it rained. And it kept it up all the week. It
was enough; but the parson did not feel at liberty to
interfere with the weather unless he had a grievance.
And the grievance came. Ha! ha! ha!" laughed the
old captain. "It rained all the next week, and the old
parson got enough of it. So he prayed again, 'Oh, Lord,
stop this rain. We have got enough of it, without you
intend to drown us. Some of the country is under
water, half our hay has gone down into the Concord
River, and the rest of it is as black as your hat.' Then,
they said, the rain stopped."

They were all amused at the captain's story, for he was
good at stories. Of course, nobody could vouch for the
truth of such good stories.

"Now I will tell you a true story," said Mr. Bartlett.
"Some years ago I happened to be in Cambridgeport,
Massachusetts. At that time, Rev. Joseph W. Parker
was pastor there, a man of dignity and scholarship, I

think as near my ideal of perfection as a minister, as I ever saw. One Wednesday evening when the bell sounded, I went into the weekly prayer-meeting. It had been terribly dry for a long time, and the air was heavy with the smoke of forest fires. The pastor read a short lesson, and, after a hymn he prayed, and this is his prayer, nearly word for word; I remember it distinctly. O Lord! Thou hast taught us to bring all our wants to thee. O Lord! send the rain, the needed, welcome rain. For the heavens are as brass, and the earth is parched with fervent heat, and men and beasts are suffering. O Lord, send the rain! O Lord, send the rain. Then the breeze blew fresher into the windows, the thunder was heard, and in the last half of the one hour long meeting, it rained splendidly, gloriously. Then Mr. Parker, since Dr. Parker, in the fulness of his heart, gave thanks. O Lord, we thank thee for the rain. Thou hast heard our prayer. We thank thee for the glorious, welcome rain. When the meeting was over I stayed and shook hands with him, and thanked him for praying for rain. And I got my jacket wet going home. This is exactly as it occurred."

Said Roy, "Captain, must we consider these things sent in answer to our asking?"

"What does the book say?" he answered. "'All good and perfect gifts come down from the Father of lights,' and it also says, 'In everything give thanks.' Now whenever we get a good thing we know who to thank for it, don't we? It seems Elisha McDuffie did."

Roy was answered. Sam showed his ivories. Mr. and Mrs. Bartlett enjoyed it. They always relished a good truth, well put.

"I heard a good story," said Sam, "a little while ago, and it is strictly true. There was a farmer named Sherman who lived in Wayland, Mass. He had a piece of corn near a piece of woods and the squirrels dug it up to eat, so he carried out a large box trap, baited with corn. He set it on the fence and fastened it, so it could not get away. It remained a long time but caught no game. One day he saw it sprung, but there was nothing in it, so he left it. He saw it once in a while, but it was an old trap and he let it stay out all summer, until the corn was gathered. One day in the fall he thought he would carry it home, and lo! it was too heavy. Soon bees came buzzing around his head, and he found his trap had a swarm of bees in it and was full of honey. The bees went in at the spindle-hole and filled the trap."

"A good story," said the old captain. "I have two swarms at home now, that I found in the woods. I located them in warm weather and felled the tree and sawed them off in snapping cold weather, and set them upon my bee stand. I know where there are two swarms now in Greenhill woods, and I mean to get them as soon as the weather is cold enough. I get a swarm or two, almost every year. The fact is, that the man who lives in the country can be a very sharp, wise man and get a great deal out of his wisdom if he will, as there is always something new in the country."

The boys always enjoyed a call from Captain Hayes. He was always entertaining.

Roy tried again for another story. "Captain, did you ever know a witch?"

"Yes, indeed, and been bewitched by them, time and again, when I was of your age."

Sam shouted.

"And I have not got beyond their influence yet," he added, laughing.

"Tell us a witch story, captain."

"Do you want it, Sam?"

"Yes, sir, please tell one."

Well, then; up in Barrington, take the road that leads through Fly Market, then up around by Jerry Kingman's and Eliphalet Foss, over Muchdo hill, past Robert Stacy's to Hardscrabble, and there on till you take the road that leads over to the Leatherses, and when you are pretty well on your way, you will pass an old cellar-hole. There was where the old witch lived, and her name was Moll Ellsworth. She lived alone, except a black cat without a white hair on it. She planted her own garden, and raised enough for her. She went out carding and weaving. Sometimes she laid out the dead and watched all night with them alone. She would take no money but silver, and she always bit it when she took it, else it would have worked harm to her, as a witch. Even witches have their limits like other people, Everybody was afraid of her, and so but few ever went into her house. There used to be lights in her house at all times of night, and some people said that Henry Tufts (see *Harper's Magazine*, March, 1888, Vol. 76, page 605), used to make it one of his hiding-places, and pay her well for it, for no one would dare to look there for him, and the sheriffs and constables always wanted him. Now Nick Scruton used to live a little ways beyond her, and he used to sauce her when he went by, and she scowled and bit her thumb at him. And Scruton's horses were lame, and his cows were gargety, and the milk was bloody, his wife was sick, his pigs died, and Scruton was just sure that old Moll was at the bottom of it all. Then, as he was coming home from Dover one day with too much rum in him, he saw the old witch walking along the road. He tried to scare her, by seeing how near he could come to her, and not hit her. He rode too near and knocked the old woman head over heels into the Canada thistles. She got up awful mad, cursed him, and vowed revenge. Then Scruton's chickens disappeared. His dog died. His cat was found in the well, with bones and old boots, and one night when the cows came home, he found a long brass pin sticking through the teat of one of them. He had as much as he could do to pull it out the cow kicked so. He got it out, but it took all his strength to hold it. He told his wife to bring a teakettle of boiling water, and to put a piece of silver and a leaf out of the New Testament into it, and she did. Then Nick Scruton, by main force, put the pin in it. Such a blood-curdling screech as came out of that teakettle you never heard, no, nor never will. The next morning the old woman was found at her own door, badly scalded. Soon she disappeared, cat and all. Doctor Fernald said she went over to Lee to live with her brother. But some folks said the devil flew away with her, some such night as last night was, and if you don't believe the story, I can take you up to Barrington and show you the cellar-hole.

"Do you believe the story, Captain?" asked Roy.

"Me? Yes. I believe it is about the biggest lie I ever told, but that is all the kind you can have, if you want a witch story. It must be fictitious. Ha! ha! ha! But I have stayed too long. I shall not get home to dinner. Good-by. Come up and see us."

Now, if you have never been present at a farmer's call, or, it may be, that it was prolonged to a visit, you have, at least, read one. Many a time, on a rainy or snowy day, or of an evening, have I drawn the cider, got the apples, cracked the nuts, and heard the stories of the Revolution, the War of 1812, of ghosts, witches, fairies, enchantments, hunting, fishing, Indians, cooking, bee hunts, farming, woodcraft, and, goodness knows what, of the folk lore of old Strafford County.

CHAPTER VIII.

THE haying was done, and well done. Of course, a good farmer is always on the lookout to increase the amount of food for house and barn alike, in order to increase the income of his farm. But Mr. Guy Bartlett liked a good variety of home comforts, and made it a point to secure asparagus, tomatoes, and many others of the vegetable kind, and the wild berries as well. So, early in August, after breakfast, he said : "Now, boys, your mother and I think it will be best to take a drive to the heath, and pick some blueberries and huckleberries, to dry for next winter. We can take a lunch with us, and it will be a picnic to-day, and puddings and pies next winter."

This suited Roy and Sam, and speedily brought old Tom and the express wagon, with two seats in it, to the door; while luncheon, with pails and dippers galore, speedily hid themselves under the seats, ready for use. About four miles from the City Hall, in Dover, is the Tibbett's farm, now called the Heath House, and for half a mile beyond it, to Ezra Hayes's, is the birches. It is a huckleberry swamp that, if you will reckon far enough back, and charge enough for your fruit, has raised berries enough to pay off the national debt. I like to keep right down to hard-pan fact. Not every year are they a bonanza, but this year they were. Roy drove off the road in a winter path, for security against visitors. Old Tom was made comfortable to leave, and then the picking began. It was a sight to behold.

"There," said Mr. Bartlet, "I have seen most of the fruits of the earth, growing in their native soil. But I never, in my life, saw a finer natural fruit than these half-high and high-bush blueberries, when the bushes are blue with them, as these are."

They picked with a will, four of them. Sometimes they were low and required stooping. Then, again, they were from six to ten feet high, and often blue with berries. Then came a bush of black ones. Then, again, a bush of purple choke berries, that were handsome to look at, but useless to eat. Nature likes to show us what she might have done, in order to show us how good she is. And busy hands and plenty of berries gave a rich reward. Often, Roy or Sam collected the berries, and bore them to the wagon, and, with a kind word for Tom, returned to picking. Mrs. Bartlett moved quietly to the next bush, when, whirr! went a large bird away from her feet with a loud noise that startled her. She looked, and there at her feet was a little home, a partridge's nest, with ten beautiful dark speckled eggs in it. They were all pleased to see it, and to look at it attentively.

"Come," said Mr. Bartlett, "let us all move away, and pick elsewhere. The old lady will want to cover her eggs again, and she has her rights in the world as well as we."

It was done. A few minutes later, Sam stood beside a large clump of bushes, picking industriously. In the middle of the clump was a birch tree, whose roots parted like an old-fashioned light-stand, and it left a hollow un-

derneath, and there, behold! in peace and safety was
another home, and in it sat a wild rabbit. Sam smiled,
and, motioning silence, he called the others just in time
to see puss scud out and away from the strangers. It
was a sensible wild home. It was up above the water,
sheltered from the rain, with several avenues of escape,
for those whom God has given no means of defence. It
is a pitiful story here, but they look at it differently, after
seeing how rabbits multiply in Australia. There they
are a calamity.

"Come," said Mr. Bartlett, "it is luncheon time."

It was spread on a nice shady spot of grass, near the
wagon, and old Tom quietly took his oats and watched
the proceedings. The boys were a little curious to know
what kind of a surprise Aunt Bartlett had prepared for
them. It was a good one. A stuffed fowl, bread and
butter, doughnuts and cheese, an apple turnover each,
and a bottle of cold coffee.

"This, with plenty of berries, is enough," said
Roy.

"Then enough is as good as a feast," said Mr.
Bartlett.

"It strikes me that this is a feast," said Sam.

"I am glad you like it," said Mrs. Bartlett.

So they sat or reclined, at their own sweet wills. They
made remarks, relevant and irrelevant. and they voted it
a harvest, a picnic, and a red-letter day generally. They
told stories. They rested and listened to the voices of
the woods, as Thoreau listened.

"It is a revelation," said Mr. Bartlett; "what wisdom
it is to make the best of everything, and to have a happy,
thankful time. Not to wrong or rip anybody, and to

keep sweet yourself. I remember Gail Hamilton puts it most beautifully, in one of her essays. She says: 'Life is a burden, but God has laid it upon us. Whatever you make of it, that it will be to you. You may make it a millstone around your neck, or a diadem upon your brow. Take it up bravely, bear it on cheerfully. Lay it down triumphantly.' It is a splendid sentiment. Ha! what is this, boys? I have found a prize; I think some one has camped here before. It is a fine pocket-knife. It is almost new, and evidently lost but a few days. I guess I am about seventy-five cents or a dollar in, by finding this nice knife."

"Good luck," said Sam. "Here, Aunt Bartlett has found a partridge's nest, I have found a rabbit's form, Uncle Bartlett has found a knife, and now, Roy, it is your turn."

"Very well," said Roy, "I think I will find some more berries."

They resumed picking, but did not need to work much more. The pails were filled again, and Roy began to look about him. As he stepped away to a heavily laden bush, he saw something on the ground. He touched it with his foot, and a merry smile spread over his face, as he called to his mother: "Mother, come. I have found my prize!"

She came. They all did. And Roy, with a mischievous laugh, held up a woman's stockings, and — er — garters. "Evil to him who thinks evil of this," said he.

Said Mrs. Bartlett, "She was of good size, and tall; for these are long. And her feet were small. These are hand-knit, and she was a splendid knitter. They are fine, and first-class, and the elastics are tasty and costly. They have lain here only two or three days, — only since day before yesterday, when it was so hot. She took them off for coolness, and lost them by going a few steps from them. But, oh, it was risky to go to Dover without them."

Sam looked at Roy in the queerest way, and chuckled and laughed, to the amusement of them all.

Said Roy, " I guess I had better get out of this swamp, for my luck is so peculiar for two months past that heaven only knows what I shall run into next. Now, mother, you please take charge of these articles. If Carlyle had found them, he might have written another ' Sartor Resartus ' about them. Father is right in saying, that one is always finding something new in the country."

" This last beats them all," said Sam. " I have been reading a Swedenborgian book lately. It tells of correspondences. I think there is something in it. Aunt Bartlett has found a nest full of eggs. It means home and plenty for her. I found a rabbit's form, which means that I shall have a home and be a farmer. This suits me. Uncle Bartlett has found a knife, which means that he shall cut his own bread easy, and in abundance. But this last find beats them all. It means that Roy shall have a queen of his own, who is a woman to be proud of; and I expect it."

" Thank you, Sammy ; and the same to you," said Roy.

Often the remembrance of Roy's find brought a smile.

" Come, boys," said Mr. Bartlett, " if Roy has a super-stition about this place, I think we will go home. We have a fine lot of berries to-day ; enough to black our mouths up good several times." The team was hitched up again, and, as the shadows lengthened, they rode home just in time for Aunt Bartlett to get supper, and just in time to find the cows lowing in the lane for admission to the barn.

CHAPTER IX.

CANIS MAJOR had been left at home on guard, and told to "look out for it." He had done his duty. No one had been allowed to enter the dooryard. But on the square top of the gate post lay a stone for a paper-weight, and just in sight of every one who lifted the latch was an envelope of a letter, and above it was written, so that it was made to do duty as paper and signature, —

"I called, and found Canis Major on guard. I leave kind regards, and will call again soon.

"JOHN Q. HAYES."

"I think it is about that referee case," said Mr. Bartlett; "so we will be at home for a few days, to meet our caller."

It was their habit to look over their farm, and see what permanent improvement was most needed to make work easy and profitable, and to make the handsomest home and pay the most of use and beauty. So when a very dry time came, after haying, some low place, that had at last gone dry, had the black loam removed, then the bed was raised with stones and soil, with suitable drainage, and then the dark loam was replaced over it all, and it was fertilized and sown to grass again; and, oh, you ought to see the herds-grass grow! They wanted no eyesores on their farm.

Said Mr. Bartlett, as he paused on the next improvement, " Boys, life moves in circles. There is an old hymn' which says, ' Thy days are one eternal round ; ' and it is true. Work and harvest are at once cause and effect forever. I was once travelling on a Mississippi steamer, and a Southerner scraped acquaintance with me. He asked as many questions as ever any Yankee did in the same time, and he told me he was going down to New Orleans to sell his cotton, to buy more niggers, to raise more cotton to buy more niggers. So life is the same treadmill."

" Yes," said Roy. " But we have more than the usual amount planted; we have made more than the usual amount of improvements; we can keep more stock, and enrich the farm more. We are gaining every way. I happen to know that Captain Hayes will be at an Orthodox installation to-morrow; so I move that we go on an excursion to the summit of Blue Job."

" All right, Roy, we will go."

It was a beautiful September day. The chores were done early. Then the light wagon, with Mr. and Mrs. Bartlett, was soon followed by Roy and Sam, in another light hitch. Whoever rides for pleasure, in a pleasant time and in a pleasant place, will always find it, if they are pilgrims of beauty, in the way they ought to be. Even the desert is a succession of surprises, and often teeming with life. These people had a good time, for they took it with them. Up the road, passing Green Hill, with its one tree near the summit, past Elisha Locke's house and mills, through the Gonic and Rochester to Merrill's Corner, in Farmington, and farther by a crooked, well-known road, until their horses were left with friends; then, with baskets in hand, the party was slowly ascending the steep sides of Blue Job. Take it easy. There is much to see. How the view extends as you climb up. Not dangerous at all, but still it is a good journey, and it pays well to take it. The summit was reached, and then the view!

Said Mr. Bartlett, "Now look! To the north is the next range of hills, of which the Gunstock Mountain is the prominent one, and just beyond it is Lake Winnepe-saukee. Away to the northwest is the Western Kear-sarge, whose summit is in Wilmot. Near it is Warner, where lives Levi Bartlett, the compiler of the Bartlett genealogy. West of us is the great Blue Hill, larger and higher than Blue Job. South of us is all this beautiful rolling country, with Strafford Ridge and the towns below, extending away to the ocean. There, the three pine-trees that locate Great Falls. Farther to the right is Mount Agamenticus, — and a beauty it is. The fact is, I never feel the majesty of God, and the nobility of man, as when I can see his wonderful works from some mighty mountain top.

> " ' Who loves not Nature suffers every need,
> Who most enjoys it, he is blest indeed.' "

"Then you think," said Roy, "that our best loves are cultivated."

"Yes, I do; and our meaner loves as well. Such as the loves of vice and dissipation."

"Then I suppose," added Roy, "that it becomes us to choose the noblest loves and to reject all others."

"Certainly."

"Well," said Roy, "I feel now a strong love, not a particularly noble one, but it gains on me. Will you please explain it, father?"

"What is it, Roy?"

"The love of my dinner."

"You always had it. Born so," said his mother.

"And you remember, mother, that it is your favorite theory that a boy 'takes after' his mother and a girl after her father. So I came honestly by it."

Sam was much amused when Roy and his mother sparred, and Roy usually came off best.

"Come, mother; you will have no peace until you feed your chickens."

It was done; and while they feasted the inner man, the eyes could wander nearly around the horizon, bounded only by the hills of New Hampshire, from twenty to fifty miles away.

"Aunt Bartlett is a commissary-general worth having," said Sam Ellet. "She always keeps her army well supplied and happy. This makes loyal and good soldiers."

"There is a theory," said Mr. Bartlett, "that it is not good to use a soldier too well. He expects too much, and it makes a molly-coddle of him."

"I think," said Roy, "that saying has very little truth in it. Almost all evidence goes to show that men do better if well used. A 'lean and hungry Cassius' does think too much, and his thoughts are not of the kind they would be if he was better fed. But we have a feast of body and mind both to-day. I do love the hills, and especially the hills of my native State. To be able to picture them in all their might and beauty is a joy indeed. I had rather be S. F. Smith, who wrote, —

'I love thy rocks and rills,
Thy woods and templed hills;
My heart with rapture thrills,
Like that above,'

in his beautiful hymn, and be, like him, the voice of
loyalty, praise, and patriotism through countless genera-
tions, than to be any president since Washington. The
poets outlive the historians, although frequently the poets
are the historians. Bayard Taylor has written in his
fine novel, 'Hannah Thurston,' of one of his characters,
'Nature had not given him her highest gift, that of
expression.' When in the capitol, the forum, the pulpit,
as musician, author, actor, painter, or poet, it is one great
gift, partly given, partly acquired, and it makes a man a
king among men. In these times, a man who ministers
to the sense of beauty, ranks much higher than one who
ministers to the blessings of use."

"Jess so," said Sam. "And Roy has given his opinion
a splendid expression. But, for all that, I suppose that a
hundred people must work for use where one is demanded
as a minister of art, literature, or any form of beauty, and
so, although I will learn to appreciate nature and art,
books and beauty, I shall be content with the beauty that
lies in the greatest use, while I do what I can to feed the
world and keep from being hungry."

"Then it seems," said Mrs. Bartlett, "that we have a
prophet of use and one of beauty, besides an old man and
woman not yet classified."

This made them laugh.

"That is not a good way of telling it," said Roy.
"What we really have is Lord and Lady Bartlett, both
alike prophets of use and beauty, and two young sprouts

who are trying to follow the example of their illustrious predecessors."

"Roy," said his mother, "I should think you had been to Blarney. If you ever do get in love with a woman, she will have to surrender like Davy Crockett's coons. They knew he was a sure shot, so they said, 'Don't shoot, we will come down.'"

This turned the laugh on Roy. They walked around the summit, and drank in the inspiration of the hills.

Said Mr. Bartlett, "I think if we were here in the evening, when a full moon was rising, we should plainly see a long white strip of silver light, which is the ocean. I have seen it plainly from West Northwood, not far from here, where the land is not as high as we are. It is a beautiful sight. You would not think it possible to see farther by moonlight than by day, but sometimes it is so. Now, Roy, if you have that sketch done, we had better bid good-by to the summit and return."

They did return, and by a road more direct, passing through Barrington, at the eastern end of Ayer's pond, and coming down by George McDaniel's and the old Methodist meeting-house, on the road towards Dover. It had been a good day. It had filled their minds with bright, healthy pictures for time to come. A man's mind wants to be furnished and ornamented as much as his body. It had been a lesson in nature and art to Roy.

CHAPTER X.

THE next two days were bright September days.

"Roy," asked Mr. Bartlett, "what ought we to do to-day?"

"There is one job I should like to do before I go away. There are two or three stones in the great field that I should like to sink out of the way of plough or mowing machine forever."

"It is a dangerous work," said his father.

"Then I will conduct it so it will be safe," said Roy.

And he did. On the evening of the second day, the stones that had projected above ground, and had always been in the way, had quietly sunk beneath the surface, away from the plough forever. It was a permanent good. In the evening Sam read the papers; Mrs. Bartlett did her part to make the evenings pleasant; Roy worked on his sketches, played the cabinet organ, or read, and the evenings were pleasant at home.

The day following, it rained. They were in the ample sitting-room. Soon Neighbor Hoskins called in, and he was welcomed. Yes, his family were well; Mary was well and Will Glance was living with them; at present he was steady, and working moderately. All hoped he would do well. So they left it. Nobody rejoiced. A carriage drove up. It was Captain John Q. Hayes. Shake hands and hearty greetings all around.

"Now," said he, "business first, and then I shall not forget it. Mr. Bartlett, your opinion of how that property should be divided and settled, is accepted by both parties, as the fairest and best that can be done, with one exception. You have left out the interest of the best man in it. That is yourself; they all say so. They have signed an agreement, accordingly, provided that you accept fifty dollars for your services; otherwise they won't settle at all, and will act just as bad as they can. Each party contributes half, so you see they look out for your interest as well as you for theirs. Here is the money. I am instructed not to take 'no' for an answer. Here, please sign this receipt."

They all were pleased.

Said Mrs. Bartlett, "Now we can see which the contrary one is."

"All right, Captain. I will take it, but if they have any trouble in settling, they must call on me again, and if they do not settle kindly and peaceably, I must return the money." And the receipt was signed.

"Did you catch many foxes last winter, Captain?" asked Roy.

"Yes, several."

"How did you manage?"

"Ah! you young folks want a story, do you? Yes, I catch foxes when I can, because they eat my poultry, and occasionally steal a lamb. Besides when I do catch one, in the right season, his pelt brings me a dollar and a half, or more. So you see catching foxes helps farming both ways. About forty rods in the rear of my barn is an old oak stump. It is in about the middle of a small, open pasture. I fed the sheep around that stump so as to have a lot of orts scattered around, to make it look kind o' natural. Then when we killed a fowl, or had fresh meat, I put the odds and ends near the old stump. The foxes found it soon enough, so I set a smart, well-oiled fox-trap at the stump, covered it up with hayseed, and next morning I had a large he-fox. His skin sold for two dollars. The next morning I had his mate. Then I had nothing for a week. Then I put my trap down with extra care, — put the bait in a crevice of the stump beyond the trap, and for three mornings in succession I found the bait gone, the trap sprung and turned bottom upward. Then I knew I had an awful long-headed old fox to measure wits with. And here was the problem. An Orthodox deacon playing a game of deceit with an old fox, for his skin. So I set the trap bottom upwards, put a few drops of anise around it, and left it. The next morning I had him by his fore paw. The fool had turned the trap, and then, supposing it safe, had trod on the trencher and got caught. He was a splendid specimen, of a rare kind. He was a silver-gray fox. I got fifteen dollars for his skin. It was a beauty!"

"Gracious!" said Sam.

"Then I caught three young foxes, but well grown. I got one dollar apiece for their skins. After that for a month I got nothing. I put the bait around the stump, but the foxes got the benefit of it. When I came to examine the tracks in a light snow, I found it was one large fox, and some few hairs that he had scratched off told that he was a black one. I wanted his pelt very much, and I studied on it. One night I caught a mouse. He was standing up straight and frozen stiff. I then set the trap in a little hollow, ten feet away from the stump;

I fastened the chain to a spike driven into the frozen ground. Then I covered the trap with a thin dark brown paper, scattered the hayseed over it, and left the frozen mouse fastened to the trencher. It looked alive; you would have been sure the mouse was just ready to run. I found the next morning that the fox had looked at it the same way, for he had run and put both paws on the mouse to catch him, and so I had the fox firm and fast by both fore paws. He was a fine black fox, the only one I ever caught."

"It is a good thing," said Mr. Hoskins, "to have such a Nimrod as you are, to clear out our foxes. It makes poultry possible."

"Did you ever get young foxes?" asked Sam.

"Yes, indeed. We burned over a piece of land on Scruton's plains, last summer, and we got four young foxes, one litter about a quarter grown. They lived and did well. We did not wish to keep them all, so we gave away two of them. They were as affectionate as puppies except when you gave them fresh meat; especially chicken. Then their eyes were like balls of fire until the meat was eaten; but in a moment after, they were on their good behavior again, and, O, so glad to see you. One night the shed door blew open, and the dog got in and killed them both. That finished my foxes."

Said Roy, "Captain, I always like to hear older people talk, for they have had a good experience, and know something. I always learn something new and refreshing. Now please tell me, Captain, did you ever see or know of anything in your own personal experience, that was clearly supernatural?"

"Well, Roy, I doubt if there is or can be anything

supernatural. All life, in the body or out, is natural. I think you mean to ask me if I ever saw any work or movement of living beings with no visible body. Yes, I have known some things that I could not account for. I had a boy once, who worked for me. He was steady, tough, and well as any boy I ever saw. One day he was hoeing in the corn with me, and a little brown bird came and lit on him again and again. The boy could not drive him away. The bird would keep close to him, and did all day. It was his last day's work. He told his mother of it, and she said sorrowfully that it was a sure sign of trouble. He was buried in two weeks, of typhoid fever. I do not know as there was any connection between the bird and the fever, but I think of them to-gether, always."

"Then," said Roy, "although we may regard the story as true, yet the inference is doubtful."

"Certainly. You can infer what you like."

"Now, please tell me, Captain, did you ever hear any-thing of the same kind from reliable people whom you could believe?"

"I will tell you a story, Roy, and you can judge for yourself. If I give you all the evidence and you make up the verdict you cannot blame me. You have all heard of old Aunt Debby Watkins, that lived over be-yond Hick's Hill, on the road to the Gunket. Well, she was an honest, God-fearing woman, and told the truth in all else and why not in this? And here is her story: 'Lige Glen lived a mile beyond her. His right name was Elijah, and no man was less like the prophet Elijah than 'Lige Glen. He was drunken, ugly, profane, dishonest, and dirty, outside and in. His children were neglected

and abused. They all died young. People said, and
some were bad enough to know, that he had sold himself
to the devil for so much money, for, strange to say, 'Lige
Glen did nothing to make any money, but he always had
it. He did not toil or spin. If there was a black, gusty
night, 'Lige was always out wandering round. In a hard
gale or thunderstorm he was always gone, and his wife
left alone. People said he finished her, and I guess he
did. It is always said, if a man is sold unto sin, long
life is not for him, certainly not beyond the common age
of man. So, one foggy afternoon, late, a dark-complexioned man called and asked Aunt Debby if she would go
down and watch with Glen. He was very sick, and she
took her Bible in her pocket, for safety and to read in,
and went to watch with the sick man. There was no one
in the house but 'Lige. There was a little fire in the old
fireplace, and plenty of wood handy. She put on a log,
and asked if she could do anything for the sufferer. He
asked not much, tasted little water, dozed a little, and
waked again about midnight. Aunt Debby was reading her Bible by the light of one tallow candle, when she
was startled by seeing a monstrous big black dog push
open the door, go up to the bed, and begin to whisper in
'Lige Glen's ear. They talked in an unknown language,
for the old windows rattled, and the candle flared in the
wind. She could see the two horrible black heads together, and the dog seemed to be giving orders, while
Glen's eyes opened wider. But he seemed to have no
power to dispute a word, and the horrid dog or devil, or
whatever it was, put his nose into 'Lige's face, and stayed
as long as he liked. Aunt Debby had not power to lift a
finger. After a long time, he moved slowly away from

the bed, out into the kitchen, and, by the noise, he seemed to go down, down into the earth. After sitting a long time, and seeing a light strip of sky in the east, she rose and looked at the old long clock in the corner, then lighted another candle and looked at 'Lige Glen. He was dead and cold. I think this story is a fact," said Captain Hayes. "Now what do you make of it, Roy?"

"I know nothing of it," said Roy.

"What do you, Sam?"

"It sticks me," said Sam.

"Mr. Hoskins, what do you say?"

"Looks fishy," said he.

Captain Hayes laughed. "Mr. Bartlett, you are good as referee. What say you?"

"I should need more evidence before I put in my verdict."

"Mrs. Bartlett, what do you say?"

"Say? Why, I should put in an interrogation point as long as from here to Durham, after such a story as that."

"Well," said the Captain, "I have told the story as she did, as she was a simple, truthful woman. Now, I will tell my part of the story. Later, I was called, on behalf of the town, to look over the farm and personal property, and to appraise them, for 'Lige Glen left no heirs. We found, to our astonishment, that in an underground cellar which connected with the sheds was a lot of counterfeiters' dies and moulds, with some unfinished halves and Mexican dollars. In one corner was a lot of old duds, well felted in with black hair, which told the story of the nest of a large, short-haired black mastiff. This accounted for the milk in the cocoanut. Soon after this the house and its contents were burned. Nevertheless, I think 'Lige Glen sold himself to the devil. Bad men always do. Come, Mr. Hoskins, it is your turn."

"All right then. Did you ever hear old Jake Hodgman tell stories?"

Captain Hayes said he had, for Jake had the reputation of being the biggest liar in Dover.

"Once," said Mr. Hoskins, "I asked him why he told such wild stories. Says he, I will tell you. You know my father had a small farm, and when apples were plenty he had apples enough and to sell, and he made two or three barrels of cider. The old man liked to tell large stories of what his farm would do, but one year he had only one barrel of cider. Along came old Doctor Woodbury, one day, and my father was bragging to him about what his farm would raise, and how much cider it would make, when the doctor said he should like to taste his cider. Father called to me, Jake, Jake, go down cellar and get a pitcher of cider out of the cask that is tapped in the third row. Said I, What do you mean by that, father? You know there is but one barrel in the cellar, and that ain't full. Then draw it out of that, he roared, and I drew the cider. But the old man licked me like the devil for telling the truth, and it broke me of it, so I have never told it since. Whether this was truth or not, you can judge," said Mr. Hoskins. "He always stuck to it that he never told it; but some of these wild romancers are very entertaining people."

Said Captain Hayes, rising, "It is time to go. We have had a sociable time. 'Peace be unto you.'"

"Please wait a moment," said Roy. "Sam, will you please get some cider out of the third row? but if there is only one in the cellar, then get it out of that."

Sam did it with a wide smile. Each one moistened his clay without for a moment suspecting that he was not a temperance man. Guy Bartlett was fifty dollars richer for honor and honesty, good reading and good judgment, and the heirs of a large estate had found a peaceful settlement in place of a long and expensive wrangle. "Blessed are the peacemakers."

CHAPTER XI.

SEPTEMBER was passing away, and it was coming to be well known among the many friends of the Bartlett family that Roy was going to Boston in October. As the evenings grew longer, they had more neighborly calls from many who wanted to give him a kind word before he went. So, almost every evening, the parlor and sitting-room were both lighted, and callers came from Garrison Hill, Dover, Knox Marsh, Littleworth, Tolland, Madbury, or Barrington. It was almost an ovation. Sometimes the evening ended with a " sing," and the old family names of Hall, Wheeler, Flagg, Perkins, Young, Kitteredge, Woodman, Twombly, Hayes, Wentworth, and Waldron were well represented. Smart young fellows and wide-awake girls, with plenty of fun and music. One evening they had debated whether to sing or read selections. They had decided on selections, and as it was well known that Roy sometimes wrote very entertainingly, it was voted that he must read some of his own work. He complied by going to his room and returning with a manuscript entitled, —

The Adventures of Jim Camel in Amazonia.

About fifty years ago, there came to Green Hill a full-sized, roughish-looking man, whom everybody knew as Jim Camel. He stayed at the farms where he first came,

77

working for low wages, if any, and getting food, shelter, and home. There he lived until he was beginning to be an old man and there he died and was buried. But he was a remarkable man. I have heard people say he was an awful liar, but that is not a fair statement for these days. It would be better to say that Jim Camel was possessed of an ornamental and prolific imagination. He recounted the most elaborate fictions, as if he solemnly believed every word he said. He had been a sailor. Many of the tales he told of foreign lands were regular, and did no violence to geography. Some were a little mixed. When he had a large damp of cider or New England rum, his stories were richer, but did not jibe quite as well as usual. For instance; once when in that condition he told of being in a country, and seeing blackberries very, very plenty. Each one was a mouthful, and, he added, you know my mouth is not a small one. He said he had a large, thick club, that he used as a cane to walk with. This he tucked under his arm and for a long time picked blackberries with both hands. Very busy he was indeed not to notice a great black bear as big as a horse, that was picking berries as fast as he was. The bear let out a growl and Jim Camel was awake. He hit the bear on his snout and the bear retreated. Jim followed up and kept that club turning and whizzing in the air so fast that you could not see the club at all, only a big blur before the bear. Camel followed up and kept the bear in full retreat until in about a quarter of an hour he drove him into a big snowdrift and killed him. He saw no inconsistency in such a story, but when he had a good listener he often told new and wildly original yarns, for their benefit alone.

We were talking of chopping cordwood, one day. Pshaw! said he, people around Green Hill don't know what chopping is. You ought to have seen the chopping I did on that voyage when I was cast away among the Amazons, in South America. Holy Moses! trees twelve to fifteen feet through, women twelve to fifteen feet high. Ah! that was a country! Tell us the story of the whole voyage, Jim. But wait; I'll get a mug of old cider out of the heart of a barrel. There now, Jim, how's that. Well, well, that's good. That'll thaw out a man's in'ards so there won't be no icicles on his liver. How that old fireplace does heat up. Guess the weather is moderating, ain't it? The hearers laughed. Now I was just sayin' it was a wonderful voyage. You see, the ship was a large one and an old one, an' she carried a crew of forty men; you see it didn't need so many to work the vessel, but the captain was half owner and he wanted men enough to defend her if she got into a dangerous place. I said the ship was an old one, and some of the men said she was haunted, for she had been more than one voyage catching blackbirds on the coast of Africa. That is enough to haunt any ship and spile her luck. The captain's name was Keniston. I never heard his first name, but I s'pose he had one. Some of the crew said the night before the *Mary Jane* sailed, that the rats went ashore all night long on the gangway plank, an' if I had knowed it I would have gone ashore too. But I sailed in the *Mary Jane* of Boston, with thirty-nine other good men, all told. We went along all right for a few days, an' it was watch an' watch. We had our tin dipper of black coffee, an' our sea-bread an' beef. Now an' then we had a lobscouse, or a duff, or a dundy funk puddin'.

But the captain was surly an' the mate was a hog an' always ready to hit a man. The crew are allers apt to follow a bad example. When we got into the horse latitudes the gales came on, an' then it was, call all hands, an' the ship rollin' bad. The foresail was an old one, an' a puff of wind came, and away she went, split an' blown away. Well, we fought it out but we lost the captain an' two men overboard, so we got along without them. We kept on our voyage for two weeks longer, over a month in all, an' the old ship leaked so we had to keep men at the pumps. An' she creaked an' groaned, so no one could sleep aboard until finally she began to settle in the water an' then we headed her for land that just hove in sight to the west'ard, which proved to be some part of South America. Still the ship kept settlin' lower until we found she was goin' down. We made a raft as well as we could of spars, and, with the long boat, which we loaded with water and provisions, we got away jest in time to see her go down. There wa'n't nobody aboard of her, but we heard some awful yells just as the ship went down to see Davy Jones. Then we began to try to get ashore. We would row a little by day and seem to be just as far off from land the next morning. How hot it was. Soon the provisions an' water failed. Then it began to look serious. The sun rose up out of the ocean like a great red ball of fire as it is. It grew smaller and hotter as it came to its noonday, then it grew larger and larger again, until it went under the ocean again, a great red ball of fire at night. Food and water all gone. The men sat on the raft in the hot sun an' glowered at each other. Pretty soon it began to be whispered that some-body had got to die to save the rest. Then they drew

lots and our number was one less. It seems kind o' bad
I know, but those that have tasted man say he is not so
bad eatin'. I didn't touch a dum mite of it. Things
kept growin' wuss an' wuss, until we had but five men
left. All went the same way, an' they were so weak they
could hardly walk. Then a breeze sprang up from the
east'ard an' the next mornin' there we were right in sight
of hills an' woods an' palm trees an' rich vines, an'
pretty soon we were drifted into a beautiful cove, where
we heard voices an' shouts of laughter. Oh, such a sight
as bust on us. They were in a-swimmin, an' all women,
too. An' the beatermost thing was the size of 'em.
Why! there were women there fifteen foot high, an' lots
of 'em twelve. Well, there was a few little gals, from
five to eight feet high. They frolicked an' laughed, an'
spattered one another. Their hair was long an' black an'
straight an' glossy, an' oh, the purtiest hair. Their complexions was just a little golden bronze color, a good deal
harnsomer than white. Their teeth was white an' even
and when they smiled it was enough to set a sailor crazy.
You know that anything in petticoats is harnsome to a
sailor, but you have no idea what a difference it makes
without the petticoats. An' their forms. Oh, ah, I can't
describe 'em, it wouldn't be proper.

How they played and sported on the white sand that
looked like silver. But as soon as they saw us they
shrieked like any women and ran for their togs. A great
big drum was beat, and it wa'n't five minutes before they
came marchin' in real military ranks down to the water.
The captin, who was one of the tallest women, ordered
us to be brought ashore, when a corporal's guard at once
waded out to us, for the water wa'n't over ten feet deep

and each one of the five took a man in her arms and
brought us all ashore. We was almost dead and they
knew it. We had not seen a man at all as yet. As we
were so weak we could not help ourselves. They had
their sweet wills with us. Their language was a mixture
of Spanish and bobolink. The captain asked a sharp
question of the next officer. I could not understand the
question, but I heard a good square no for an answer.
Then I saw the captain laugh, an' in a minute she called
to a magnificent woman soldier who had a spear eight
feet long, an' a battle axe. The captain gave her an
order. She laughed in a minute, and so did the whole
company. She took a big blanket ten feet square, like an
India rug, and took me right up in it. She walked off
about a dozen steps, each six feet long, I'll bet ye, into
an open door in the side of the cliff near. She closed the
door after her, for it was pitch dark. Dark as a black
cat. She held me kind o' easy, an' in a minute something
slid into my mouth as big as the end o' the pepper box,
an' it beat the world what a rush of rich victuals I got.
Yum, Yum! you see I was hungry, holler clear down to
my heels. I must ha' got about two quarts I guess, an' the
supply runnin' a little lower, when I was shifted ends off,
quicker 'n a wink and then I had it right an' left. It
had a flavor of cocoanut, and I never had nothin' fit me
ekal to it. I just 'tended to my privileges right up to
the handle, whatever they were, when all at once they
got away from me an' my blanket was adjusted. She
opened the door and walked out with me with her pretty
mouth puckered up as if she was about to say pepper-
mint. Then the captain looked me over, punched me in
the stumjack an' grinned, an' says, he's fuller than a tick.

Then the whole crowd laughed an' shouted an' giggled, so that I began to laugh myself. Well, sir, that woman just took to me. She wanted to take me in where the entertainment was every little while. If she had kept on she would have had me into the shape of a bell pear. Very soon I was on my legs again, an' able to eat with the best of them O them amazons were all good to me, an' always giving me titbits when the others war'n't lookin' The other four that were saved were oldish men, old sea dogs, an' these amazons did not distress themselves about them. In about a month I began to pick up their language real fast, an' just then the orders came to leave the beautiful cove. They made a litter like a palankeen, and it was covered with the gayest cloth, an' these women warriors just carried me as easy as open and shet. They were about half naked, with sandals an' fancy-colored skirts like highland kilts, an' short at both ends. Every woman was as nice an' perticular about her toilet, forty times as nice as a man. The trees were often twelve an' fifteen foot through, an' oh, such beauty vines, an' such grapes, an' fig trees, an' oranges, an' lemons, an' mangoes, an' mangosteen. Oh, such flowers! They marched kind o' single file, and often they would cut a flower three feet in diameter and use it for a sunshade until it wilted. These flowers were all colors, an' it made the most gorjus procession I ever seen. Away off you could see any number of palm trees, an' often beyond an' across water, this beautiful country, the immense valley, the coffee-bearing foothills, now and then a feathery waterfall, and beyond it all, came up against the blue sky, the awful Andes, with a big volcano right in the middle among them. It was the biggest, harnsomest sight I ever saw.

The soldier that fed me had just lost her husband, an' that was why she was in the army. She stuck to me close and was dead gone smashed on me. I've often had 'em that way. She told me I must go to the Capital to see the queen. She had her pick of all the men in the queendom, for she was going to marry the smartest one. Now, ye see, that kind o' interested me. I knew the other four could not take the place of a younger man. But all this time I had not seen a man, an' I knew there must be some somewhere, but where? We were passing lots o' houses, only one story high with a door eighteen feet high, clear up to the eaves. Ye see, the women needed such doors, they were so tall. Well, I looked into some o' them houses and I'll be hanged if there wasn't the men, smaller than I was, tendin' babies and washin' dishes. It give me quite a turn. Then I began to laff an' I laffed till I like to a died. But I got used to it. The idea of matin' a woman fifteen feet high to a little runt of a man five feet high. It hurt my feelin's. It is like matin' a drone bee half an inch long, to a queen an inch an' a half. But it kills the drone in a minute. Then the buildin's grew richer an' higher, an' the Capital was the smashinest city, ever so much bigger than Boston. Great domes all covered with gold, an' fancy-colored minarets, an' palm trees among 'em all, an' bands o' music with drums an' cymbals and reed instruments, all blown by women. The fact is, the men were at home keepin' house, and the women run the country. The queen sent for me. She said she wanted the best man for her husband, and, as she had tried the chopping test she had found a man that beat all the others. Now if I could outchop him I should be the happy man. Then

I thought of the girl that had been so good to me at first. Her name was Rumalia. I was afraid she would take it hard. The queen's name was Amazette. Just twelve feet high, an' the handsomest woman I ever set eyes on, an' oh, how she smiled on me.

Wal, the trial came. I don't allow a man to beat me choppin'. The other feller was a smart one. There were a plenty of axes. He took one that weighed about three pounds, an' I took one that weighed six. Then I made 'em bring a bucket of water, an' I laid five more axes in that. We began on a tree fifteen feet in diameter. Oh, holy Moses, how the chips flew, chips two feet long. Soon as my axe began to smoke, I knew I was starting the temper of it an' I took another, an' laid this in the water. If it didn't sizzle, I'm a liar. Well, sir, you can believe it or not, I cut that tree in a little over an hour, three quarters off before it fell my way, an' won the queen. As soon as Rumalia saw the tree fall, she tied a big stone around her neck, an' drowned herself in the lake. Excuse me (Jim Camel brushed his hand over his eyes), I ain't got over it yet.

Well, the queen sot the day for our weddin' and I lived in a palace an' had the richest an' best of everything. Talk about palaces and pearls an' parrots an' peacocks an' palms. What do folks around Barrington know about 'em. Miss Amazette kept an eye on me to see that I wasn't too sweet on any of her officers. But I hadn't the heart to do it, I was thinkin' of poor Rumalia, that cut me up the worst. Just then an insurrection broke out in a distant part of the queen's dominions. I told the queen if she would postpone her wedding two weeks, and give me an escort with my four men to the

place where the trouble was, I could make peace as well
as chop big trees. So she did it. We journeyed several
days with great speed, until we came to the country. I
made a treaty of peace with them and they agreed to
serve the queen. Then I found a large steamer that ran
down a branch of the Amazon until it came to the main
river, and took passage with my four men on board of
her. I sent a messenger to the queen, telling her that I
had pacified her subjects, bidding her good-by, and telling her not to wait for me. In three weeks we were in
Para, in five more in New York, five men of us, the
survivors of forty of the crew of the Boston ship, *Mary
Jane.*

This is Jim Camel's story, more or less faithfully told.
I should like to see it dramatized and put worthily upon
the stage. Joseph Cook says, — When we come to Bos-
ton we expect a little rhetoric. When I go to the theatre
I want a little scenery. I should not end the play of Jim
Camel in Amazonia, with a stolen voyage to New York,
or Jim's lowly grave on the sunset slope of Green Hill.
I would start him off with the embarkation of the captain
and crew, and the ill-omened disembarkation of the rats.
Then the chimes of the North church playing, view of Boston slightly glorified, Boston light and sunset over Boston,
Minot's light and moonlight at sea, big storm, captain overboard, haunted ship, pantomime tricks, ghosts, dismasted
vessel, sunrise and sunset at sea, ship slowly sinking, raft
and long boat, — the sun a ball of fire, despair, and death,
the glorious country of the Amazons, bathing scene judiciously managed, recuperation, interesting soldiers,
flowery land, triumphal journey, men doing housework,
lady grenadiers, mighty distances, feathery palms, golden

domes, tall minarets, bright birds, leaping water-falls, luxurious court, mighty Andes, irrepressible volcano, barbaric music, richest of color, wealthiest of palaces, scenery *ad. lib.*, gracious, condescending queen, poor Rumalia, chopping match, victory, Amazette won, grandeur and gorgeousness, queen's entertainment, woman's kingdom come, woman triumphant, men find their true vocation and stay there, high old revel, triumphant suppression of revolt, queen's gratitude to Jim Camel, saved the queendom, glorious wedding, honeymoon never ends, Jim grows old gracefully, golden wedding, palace full of Amazons, his own daughters of course, splendid manly women, also sons, sweet, affectionate, womanly men. Too sweet for anything. Oh, have the whole thing go off like anniversary week in Boston. Little need of matter of fact, but the widest latitude for the gorgeousness of his own lush imagination.

Roy ceased reading. Jean McDuffie sat close before him with a ripe smile all over his face.

Said Roy. "What do you think of Jim Camel, Jean?"

"Think? why I think it is splendid to the last degree, but it is a little of Jim Camel and a great deal of somebody else."

This reply brought down the house, for it was just what they all thought. With many a kind word and especially from Jean McDuffie, the company went home. As the last team drove away from the house, Roy tarried at the gate, and looked a moment at the house glorified in the moonlight. His heart was full as he asked himself, "What kind of a man ought I to be, with such appreciative friends, with such a welcome home, and with such a father and mother!" It takes a lifetime to answer such questions, and Roy went slowly into the house to rest, but what was most unusual for him, his last hours at home were pulling upon his heart so much as to make a pain that almost banished sleep.

CHAPTER XII.

SORROW TURNED TO JOY.

THE weather was fair and pleasant the day that Roy went to Boston. But it was rather a blue day at the farm. Hereafter the home life was to be like the play of Hamlet, with the young prince left out. With renewed assurances of countless letters and often visits, Roy shook hands with his father and kissed his mother, and Sam drove with him to the station.

He landed at the Quincy House in Boston, fully resolved to take it easy, to be well employed, to make the most of it and not to fret. Sam came back to the farm as solemn as an owl. Mr. Bartlett did not talk much and seemed to be musing and thinking considerably. Roy's mother had her mouth firmly drawn up, as if she had a large amount of suppressed feeling, which, by great effort, she was fully determined to control if it killed her. Long and dreary was the afternoon, and milking time was more of a burden, because Roy was gone. Supper too. There was enough and that which was good enough, but somehow the questions were few and the answers were short and not interesting. Noise was out of place. It seemed as if Sunday had got loose again.

After supper Mr. Bartlett looked at the *Dover Enquirer*, and Sam looked into the fire which shed a pleasant glow from the open fireplace. Aunt Bartlett cleared away the tea-things. When the work was done, she sat

89

down on the wide sofa, and the full weight of her desolation came over her so strongly that she burst into tears.
She wept hard for a few minutes, with her face buried in
the great sofa pillow. Then, when her grief had found a
little vent, Mr. Bartlett arose and took down a large
roller towel, laying it across his easy chair. Mrs. Bartlett looked with one eye uncovered to see what he was
doing. Sam was interested too. Then Mr. Bartlett
went into the kitchen and brought down the big dish-pan
that dishes were washed in, and set it down on the floor
before his chair. Mrs. Bartlett now watched him with
both eyes. She forgot to weep. Sam wondered. Had
Mr. Bartlett lost his mind? Then he went into the
kitchen again, was gone a moment, pumped a little water
and came in, and after seeing the doors all shut sat
down with the roller towel on his knees, and the big
dish-pan between his feet. His two spectators looked on
in wonder and astonishment. Then, with a funny old
snort he made believe burst into tears. "Ah, Boo, Hoo,
Hoo. He is gone, mi bi es gone. Oh, Boo, Hoo, Hoo.
Roy has gone to Boston and we'll never see him again, at
all, at all. Ah wurra, wurra. Ah, Boo, Hoo, Hoo." And
he squeezed a large sponge which he held concealed in
his hand, into the big dish-pan. Mrs. Bartlett and Sam
screamed with laughter. Mr. Bartlett wiped his eyes on
the roller towel and cried again like a big bull calf. "Ah,
Boo, Hoo, Hoo. He's gone to Boston among cannibals.
He'll be bottled up for cologne water. He'll be hung an
drowned an' robbed an' murdered an' sold for a slave.
Ah, Boo, Hoo, Hoo, Hoo." Sam roared. Mrs. Bartlett
laughed until the tears came. Not the briny. Then she
got up, kicked the dish-pan away, threw the big towel

after it, and the sponge after that, and in spite of his pretended resistance, she put her arm around her husband's neck, sat down in his lap and kissed him, saying: "At any rate I have got you left, you old coon, and I am going to keep you." It was nuts for Sam, and as good as a play.

"Now," said Mr. Bartlett, "let us settle this thing right here. I gave my consent for Roy to go. He is a safe, manly young man. Do you wish him tied to a woman's apron string all his life? I travelled far and wide before I was of his age. He will do well. Now, if you will promise not to be sorry or grieve any more until you have cause to grieve, then we will be pleasant and happy just as he wishes us to be. But if you propose to shed any more tears I will have the big dish-pan again."

There were no more tears shed and the remainder of the evening was pleasant, as were the evenings after it.

"But," said he, "it is best that we make a rule to have company one or two nights in a week. Then we will go out some, we will read aloud some, play checkers or something a little, if we wish to, and in general act as if it was our duty and pleasure to keep sweet and thankful just as much as it is to be fed and clothed, and especially as we have so much to be thankful for. We must make life a joy and a thing of beauty, and we must keep Sam as sweet as the heart of a June rose.

Sam showed his white ivories and laughed with both mouth and eyes.

I do like to see old married people act as though marriage was the birth, instead of the death, of love. Guy Bartlett often pretended to court his wife over again, and he called her, Miss Royal, her maiden name. Some-

times she would play off for awhile, and give him no en-
couragement. Then it took more persuasion to bring her
to terms. This time after the dish-pan was put away, Sam
was looking to see what was coming next. Mr. Bartlett,
said, "And now, Miss Royal, if you remember, I was in
Cambridgeport some time ago and attended a silver wedding there. I was invited to entertain the company, and
I did so by reading this poem to them. Shall I read it
to you and Sam?" It was so ordered and read, —

"THE SILVER WEDDING.

"Dear beloved: when we find
A pair to wedded life inclined,
'Tis right that they, of their own wills,
Should treat their friends, and pay their bills.
Now this young man, I'm glad to tell
Has known this maiden quite a spell;
Has boarded with her, and I'll mention
Has paid her very marked attention.

"And more than that, 'tis even said
They thought at one time they were wed;
But lately, come to think about it,
We find them some inclined to doubt it.
The thing is now so long forgot,
They know not if it is, or not;
And so, for fear such fact should grieve them,
We'll have them hitched before we leave them.

"Young man, I charge you solemnly,
If you know why this should not be,
Keep your mouth shut, and hold your yop;
This wedding is not going to stop.
Hold up your head and make no noise;
Set an example to your boys.

" Beloved young lady, can you stand
  To wed this innocent young man —
  Take him with houses, lands, and purse
  For better or perhaps for worse ?
  Change both your single lives to double,
  And bring him one end of his trouble?
  Then his you shall be all your life,
  You I pronounce husband and wife.
    Oh, happy couple, all goes well,
    As merry as a married spell ;
  Your home is warm ; your chamber light ;
  You need no warming pan to-night.
  There's silver music in the air ;
  'Tis silver, silver everywhere ;
  For hearts are warm, and home is bright,
  And silver wishes come to-night.
  The clouds that float along the blue,
  Shall show their silver sides to you ;
  Posterity shall bring its joys,
  I promise you two glorious boys ;
  Also two girls, sometime you'll mind them —
  Don't hurry, for the boys will find them.
  Then pleasant years of life and care
  Shall streak their silver in your hair.
  The moon that glorifies the night,
  Shall shed for you her silver light ;
  When trouble comes, you each can share it ;
  You only have to grin and bear it ;
  While friends, on this your wedding-day,
  Bring silver gifts to light the way.
  Now may this pleasant day in June
  Presage life's golden afternoon.
  Long may you live, and prosper, too,
  With loving hearts and friends all true.
  And so may Heaven's best blessings fall,
  So says each one.   So say we all."

This seemed to please Mrs. Bartlett, for she immediately captured the manuscript, so that it should be put

with the large pile of others that Mr. Bartlett had written for various occasions or publication. Grimalkin was stretched comfortably in Mrs. Bartlett's lap, and Canis Major lay on a rug on the floor in the firelight. It was a beauty picture, and Roy would have said so.

"Now, Sam," said Mr. Bartlett, "it is your turn to edify the company."

"You know that I have often investigated the attic in search of something to read; for there are few farmhouses as well supplied as this, in reading matter, — take the books in the secretary and great book-case, all the newspapers and magazines in the attic, — and among it all, I have had a good chance to read back numbers of the *Morning Star, Dover Enquirer, New Hampshire Statesman, Manchester Mirror, Boston Cultivator, Belknap Gazette*, and I do not know how many more, besides old books and papers away back for a hundred years. Now a story comes to my mind that I liked very much. I cannot tell where I got it. It is so old and so characteristic of the Boston Yankee, that I remember it very pleasantly.

Story of the Boy that was Born in Boston.

Many years ago, when Salem was a power in the land, and the Bertrams did a large trade with Madagascar, and brought Mocha coffee, and Java pepper, and spices, and India and China goods, to Salem; then Boston boys went to Salem, sometimes to go to sea in Bertram's ships. Often it was a long time before they were heard from, even supposing they ever were heard from.

So after the war of 1812, when United States consuls came to be settled in Asiatic ports, away up the Mediterranean, under some of the Democratic Presidents, these consuls had some odd experiences. One thing they often did, was to assist distressed Americans to get home.

One day when a consul was taking his after-dinner nap, he heard a knock and rattle at his gate. The man spoke to him in bad English, and said he wanted to see the consul. I am the consul. Said the man, I am an American. Oh, go away, you are no American! I am, sir, I was born in Boston. The consul opened the gate and let him in, but expected to prove easily that he was from anywhere but Boston. Yes, said the man, I was born in Boston, and the last I knew of her, my mother lived there. That was most thirty years ago. The consul looked him over. A little short-legged chap, dirty and sick looking. He would have looked pale if he could. Where did you sail from? Salem; in one of Bertram's ships, he answered. I have lived at cape of Good Hope, Mauritius, and Tamatave. I have been to Antananarivo, and seen the Queen of Madagascar. I have been in Zanzibar, Mocha, Mecca, Medina, and Muscat. Of course I speak Arabic, like an Arab, else I could not have come out of Arabia alive. I have been in India and China. I could not get into Japan, but I have been in and around Africa and Asia all the time, and never been home. Now I want to see Boston once more, although there ain't a soul alive that would know me. It began to look as if the man had told the truth. The consul thought he would try him. What streets do you remember in Boston? Washington Street, Hanover Street, and Ann Street. Yes, and what public buildings? The State House. Yes, any public hall? He thought hard, but in a moment said, Faneuil Hall, I remember that, plain.   Can you remember what the weathervane was, on Faneuil Hall?'   He looked down and seemed to be thinking just as tight as he could.   He fairly put out all his strength to remember.   Then all at once he shouted, Grasshopper, by thunder, I have not thought of it for years and years.   He was sent back to Boston, and better still, he found his old mother alive to welcome him.

"That is just such a story as I like," said Mrs. Bartlett. "That is, I do not like to have a boy go away in silence, for half a lifetime; that is cruel and mean to his mother; but I am glad he got sent home in the way he did."

"Yes," said Sam, " and every Boston boy ought to remember that the State House is crowned by a pineapple, and Faneuil Hall by a grasshopper."

CHAPTER XIII.

I do not believe there is a city in the world that contains within a radius of half a mile in each direction, reckoning from Park Street Church as a centre, more education, literature, art, beauty, music and song, or more to amuse, entertain, and enjoy, than Boston. Not in the same space, and very few in their whole space. Many theatres of the best, the noblest churches, the strongest missionary societies, State House, City Hall, Athenæum, Public Library, and many lesser libraries, circulating libraries and bookstores; the best of them all, book and art auctions, studios, and art-galleries, missionary, historical, geological, and anatomical museums: and every specialty that the wonder-seeking brain can call for, is almost sure to find its representative, from the plainest cooking to the most elaborate designing that can be wanted.

But first, Roy found what colors and brushes he needed, and with little delay he was at work on his first picture, in oil color. He did not hurry, but took the day to cover his first canvas. He did not feel elated over it: he felt small. He had a great respect for a palette of color. Others said not so bad. Had seen worse. A lie needs some foundation. Roy's picture had no foundation for praise of any kind. He leaned it face to the wall to dry, and walked out. He banished art from his mind,

97

with exercise. He made up his mind to improve that picture to-morrow, and he did it. When not painting, he planned what to paint. It is a New Hampshire proverb that when a job is well planned and begun, it is half done. When Roy went to work, he knew what he intended to do, and what to do while the first painting was drying, until he wanted to take it up again. He did not drizzle away his time, and he did not content himself with having one little canvas only, and then wait for days, for a slow color to dry. He had a stock of a few canvases and panels, and in three or four days, one landscape picture of river, bridge, trees, and mountains, twelve by eighteen, was done. It cut him a little to sell pictures that he did not admire, but he was bound to do it. He wanted them out of his sight. He did not tell who painted them, they were by pupils; and without much difficulty, he took three dollars for the first one. The second was better, and a dealer asked him to bring in some occasionally. He began to visit studios, and to get a little acquainted with the artists; to hear art methods, and art criticisms. He read books of standard value. One day he was in the Studio Building at an artist's exhibition, with a friend. There were a few persons present. His friend asked, " Where are you staying, Mr. Bartlett?"

" I am at the Quincy House yet, but I want to find a quiet family with few or no other boarders, that will be as much like my own home as possible. I should like two meals there and I should be gone at noon. I do not want it with common miscellaneous people, I had rather wait longer."

A gentleman turned and looked a moment at Roy.

The artist said he did not know of such a chance, but

thought there were plenty who would be glad of him for company. That evening, at the Quincy House a messenger brought him a letter, thus, —

"MR. ROY BARTLETT, — I hear that you wish a room in a suitable, quiet family. If you will call on me at No —— street, perhaps I can put you in the way of getting it.

"Truly yours,

"MRS. PARNA WARREN."

The next morning he called on the artist to thank him for so soon finding a chance for him, but to his surprise the artist knew nothing about it. Then who did send the letter or cause it to be sent. The letter looked honest. Perhaps the writer would inform him. So he would call and investigate. He did so. It was a good four-story house, not new, high up on Beacon hill, and not far from the State House. It was situated so as to give a good outlook down a street, and the chambers looked over a large extent of the cities and country around Boston. He was ushered into the parlor. It was a very large one. But in a moment more, a girl-servant opened a wide folding door, and showed the back parlor, sunshiny and pleasant, and a lady sewing on some brilliant silks. She was perhaps fifty years old, slightly gray hair in curls, but with a clear fair complexion, red cheeks, and genuine air of the most undoubted dignity and respectability.

Roy at once knew her to be a real lady. He said, "I am Mr. Bartlett, I received a note from Mrs. Parna Warren."

"Yes, sir. That is my name. Take a seat, sir. I sent the note. A gentleman whom you do not know, and who does not know you, having seen you but once, said he accidentally heard you say, that you wished to get a room in a quiet family, like your own home."

"I do," said Roy.

"This gentleman was impressed with the candor of your remarks, and with your looks, and told me of it. So as he does not know you, to recommend you, if you will answer my questions, perhaps I can be of service. What is your name?"

"Royal Bartlett."

"Where have you lived?"

"At home in Strafford County in southern New Hampshire, near Dover."

"How old?"

"Twenty-one."

"Well situated? and did you leave at peace when you came away?"

"I did; in peace and love with the best father and mother that ever a boy had. I am their only child. They are good farmers and I was very pleasantly situated. But I wanted to study art awhile, and see if it was best to continue in it. It was hard leaving home, but I am not far away and shall see them often."

"Are you a temperance man?"

"I think you will never object to my habits in that respect; undoubtedly alcohol has its uses as medicine, yet a young man as healthy as I am — never sick a day — has little need of medicine."

"How about tobacco?"

"I never use it. I think a man is better, cleaner, handsomer and sweeter, every way, without it than with it. Of course many nice people use it, but they would be nicer if they did not."

"Mr. Bartlett, I have two daughters. One is a teacher in a public school, and the other teaches music. Would breakfast and supper hours such as would be suitable to them, be convenient to you?"

"Just the thing."

"Now, Mr. Bartlett; I and my daughters were all born in Boston. My husband died when they were young. We are comfortably situated, with an assured income, that suffices for us. This house is mine. My daughters need not work, but they prefer to earn something for themselves. If we are all pleased after trial, as we have no man in the house, we should like to have you with us for company. The price will be low, as we do not need to do it for money alone." She named the price. It was satisfactory.

"Now, one thing more. My girls like the society of suitable men, as well as women. But they do not wish gallantry, and they will not flirt."

Said Roy. "I am heartily glad of it. For I will not flirt myself, neither will I give any woman cause to hate me. I like ladies' society, when it is true and sensible."

"Now, Mr. Bartlett, let us see if the room will suit you."

It was in the fourth story, large, light, well-heated, and with a splendid view. Nothing could be better.

"One thing more. My older daughter is Miss Emily and my younger is Miss Sarah Warren. Perhaps you had better call them Miss Emily and Miss Sarah, and to them you will be Mr. Bartlett. You can come as soon as you please."

Said Roy. "I think it will be this afternoon, and, Mrs. Warren, please to speak of anything I can do to serve you."

Roy's call was a beauty. Although he had much that he liked at the homelike Quincy House, and was constantly meeting New Hampshire people there, which made it social for him, yet that afternoon saw him and his trunks domiciled at the Warren homestead, on Beacon hill.

Roy was well dressed, looking well, and feeling well. At six o'clock the supper bell rang. Reader, you can call it dinner if you like. This is a free country. I believe Adam and Eve took dinner at noon, and Roy's ancestors did; furthermore, I do not believe there is a valid reason for changing it now. He descended to the parlor and was presented to the Misses Warren. They were fine specimens of Boston girls. That is the superlative, for this planet. Then Mrs. Warren led the way to the dining-room, and took her place at the ladies' head of the table.

"Now," said she, "I have a problem. Here is a table, and four persons to sit around it. Please tell me, Mr. Bartlett, shall I let Miss Emily sit opposite to me and help us? or would you like to?"

Said Roy, "Mrs. Warren, put me right where you and the ladies want me; where I can do the most service."

"Do you mean it?"

"Indeed, I do."

"Then, please, take the master's place, opposite me; and my daughters will sit each side." He did.

"Thank you, sir," said Miss Emily.

"I am heartily glad of it," said Miss Sarah.

That dinner — er — supper, I mean — was a success. Enough, and the best of everything. Roy fitted into his new place at the man's head of the table, as if it was always so. After supper a little time passed in getting acquainted with the Warrens, in the parlors. Each was glad to find that they all enjoyed pictures and books. Then came suggestions of reading certain authors, and good times together, and Roy ascended to his sanctum.

A little later he stretched himself in his little bed, and found ample length and width for five feet eleven, and his mind ran over what he had accomplished, all in one day. Then with heart and voice he answered, "Thank God for it all." Then, in an instant, his thought jumped seventy miles, to his home in New Hampshire, and he added, "And God bless father, and God bless mother, and God bless Sam, and all the horses, and cattle, and pigs, and hens, and Canis Major, and Grimalkin, and the pelican." Why! the whole thing had been done as easy as rolling off a log.

And I might say of Roy, as the doctor was at last obliged to, in Bayard Taylor's glorious novel, "The Story of Kennet," when the doctor's daughter would not marry Alf Barton, and would marry Gilbert Potter, "Thee was led. Thee was led."

CHAPTER XIV.

LIFE WITH SOME FLAVOR IN IT.

During the rebellion, when all the men were gone to the war, in some families, life was stale, flat, and flavorless. In one family, of a mother and three daughters, it was very monotonous. One day the youngest girl was missed. They hunted for her. Her mother found her in a summer house, in the garden, getting a little flavor out of a stub of a cigar.

"Why! my daughter, what does this mean?"

"Oh, I am only trying to make it smell as though there was a man somewhere round."

Before Roy came it must have been quiet at Mrs. Warren's. Three men living together are a menagerie. There is a Spanish proverb, that a kiss without a moustache, is like a spring chicken without salt. Women only, living together, are a great loss of negative electricity, without the positive to make it enjoyable.

The quartette met at the breakfast table. Mrs. Warren was pleasant, motherly, and a queen of housekeepers. The daughters were pleasant and helpful, while Roy seemed to fit into the vacant chair like the benediction after a long sermon. He helped quietly, quickly, and easily.

After partaking of something, and time to pause and consider had come, Roy said, "There are several ways of doing things, especially eating, — in a hurry, or at reasonable leisure; in silence, or, after hunger is appeased, now and then some pleasant words. Which is the wisest way?"

Said Mrs. Warren, "There is a proverb, 'Let your victuals stop your mouth;' but I do not think it is a good one. I like a good meal well attended to, and it is often much improved by the pleasant things spoken of. To eat and not to speak is prison-like and barbarous."

"I suppose," said Roy, "with the increase of printing, the art of conversation has somewhat declined. But perhaps not."

Miss Emily thought there was more discussion, on all subjects, especially in Boston, than ever before. Even women had taken the platform in great numbers. Miss Sarah had seen it, had heard it, and had not been especially pleased with it. None of the ladies had.

Said Roy, "There is a lady lecturer who, on one occasion, criticised the men severely. Some one asked her, 'Do you hate a man?' 'That depends entirely upon the man,' said she. It is one reason why I am here, that I do not wish too much society of men. I get enough of it in my business. It is another reason why I am here, that you are willing to admit a suitable man here. But it depends entirely upon the man. If a man goes to a new home and gets all of light, comfort, and pleasure that he can, and gives as little as he can for it to those he is with, his selfishness and baseness will soon be apparent, and spoil his welcome. On the other hand, if he is helping, loving, and giving, and is willing to sacrifice a little for others, he will be an acquisition. Therefore, if you ladies need a brother's help, please call on me, and see if I do not give it. I have always worked on the farm, — I like it, — and I am strong, and able to do it. I may have to ask, as a privilege, some real work to do. If a piece of furniture needs moving, or a nail to be driven, a picture hung, or any trouble comes, by day or night, when you need a man's help, you are welcome to call on me. If your help all leave you, and you all get sick at once, then, perhaps, I can show you whether my mother taught me to keep house or not. I have studied medicine and surgery enough to be of good use to myself and others. A New Hampshire Yankee wants to learn all he can of useful things, for he never can tell what he will have to do before he dies."

The ladies laughed at the quaint wisdom, and said that such habits ought to bring success through life.

"Mr. Bartlett," said Miss Emily, " we usually stay at home on Thursday evening, as much as we can, and often plan to have company. It is this evening. Our parlors are very large; indeed, they are one great drawing-room. To-night, perhaps, three or four of the teachers in the school with me may come in. No set entertainment at all, but social chat and, perhaps, some literary talk or select reading. Will you join us?"

The invitation was accepted at once, and Roy was well read enough to like it thoroughly. When the young man took hold of his painting that day it seemed to go as if it had a special impetus, and there began to be a little satisfaction in the improved quality of his pictures. It was a favorite quotation of Mr. Titcombe's, " Art is long, and time is fleeting," and he believed that to be a good artist is a life work. Roy found it true; to be a good judge of sculpture, statuary, oil paintings of all kinds, engravings of all kinds, and books of enough kinds, requires a vast amount of reading and conversation with others who knew more than he did. So each day was full of pictures to study, books to consult or read, or work to do. The evening brought company. Mr. Stacy, who is a teacher, and his wife, who had been a teacher, and three lady teachers, five in all; these, with the quartette, counted nine in the parlor. Mrs. Warren was with her daughters in their enjoyments, and she was well educated, and the best of company. Roy was presented to the new comers, and, after listening awhile, he gradually joined in the conversation.

They spoke of Robert Burns, read selections from him, "Auld Lang Syne" and "Highland Mary."

Roy asked, "If Burns was living now, could he achieve the fame that he won in his time?"

Some thought yes, some thought doubtful.

Said Mr. Stacy, "Mr. Bartlett, please tell us what you like best in Burns, which are his best poems, what you like or dislike in the man, and what you think in general about him." It was a nice way Mr. Stacy had of drawing people out. Mr. Stacy was a fine talker, a good listener, and a very agreeable, profitable companion. Some teachers get these qualities. They still teach, unconsciously, and do it most charmingly.

Roy answered, "What you ask in a sentence could hardly be answered in a sermon. Robert Burns was a wonderful man. Where was it ever done before, that a ploughman could take the crabbed provincial dialect of his own country and compel the world to sing and think in it, as Burns did in 'Auld Lang Syne?' And to write and spell it too. It is the anomaly of the world. But it is the love and humanity, the honest heart that he mingled with the singing 'lilt' of his songs. No finer, truer, nobler words were ever written than 'Highland Mary.' I have heard Professor Blish recite 'A Man's a Man for a' that' most tellingly. Fergusson's Epitaph is a tribute indeed. I am sorry for Burns's faults, — for his drunkenness and his animal coarseness. I am sorry that, among all the songs of this life, that more of them did not contain some promise of the life to come. I know that he wrote 'To Mary in Heaven.' But there is one of his poems that should have had another stanza; it is 'John Anderson, My Jo.' Miss Emily, if you will read it, I will add a stanza of my own." She did so, and Roy added, —

> " An' when we've slept together, John,
>   The sleep that all maun sleep,
> And waked in that bright world, John,
>   Where all maun cease to weep;
> There, in that better world, John,
>   No sorrow may we know,
> Or fear we e'er shall part again,
>   John Anderson, my Jo."

The listeners asked for a copy, which Roy repeated to them as they wrote it.

Mrs. Warren asked: "Mr. Bartlett, have you been in Boston much before?"

"Not very much; only short visits."

"Now, please tell us what has made the most impression on you since you came to live here? What has recurred to you oftenest, and made the most impression."

He answered: "One thing is apparent, the immense interest that Boston takes in art, music, and amusements. But that is not answering your questions. To do so I must tell you a story. A few days ago, just at dark, as it began to show the lights plainly, I was in a West End car, on Charles Street, going from Cambridge to Boylston Streets. A lady and little girl got in. The lady was tall, handsome, and very well dressed ; everything in the most perfect taste, as if she had the best common sense, and also ample means. The little girl was dressed with more ornament, and was evidently the only child. And a most beautiful one she was. They sat in the rear end of the car, opposite to me. Next to them was a dear, motherly looking old lady. Next, a tall woman, in deep mourning. Then a well-dressed man, with gold jewelry, heavy and solid. He looked like an Englishman, one used to command ; an old pirate, dogmatic, and perhaps insufferable. Six of us in all. As soon as the mother and child were seated, the child began to have a frolic, which brought the sunniest smiles to the mother's face. The child would laugh, catch its mother's hand, and kiss it ; then insist upon the other hand, and kiss that ; then take the mother easily by her nose and one ear, holding her off at arm's length to look at her ; then, clasping her arms around the happy mother's neck, would kiss her lips, her nose, her forehead, her ear, in a perfect gale of childish love, laughter, and frolic. Every passenger smiled in joy and sympathy. It continued until the mother arose to leave the car at Boylston Street. There, as the child was in her mother's arms, she turned to us all, and, looking like the radiant angel that she was, she spread her little arms, and said, in the sweetest voice, 'By! by!' The motherly looking woman said, 'God bless you, dear!' The woman in mourning burst out sobbing. The old pirate, in the corner, said, 'God bless her dear little heart. Of such is the kingdom of heaven,' and my own heart smote me in the ribs, and tried to choke me; while my eyes clouded up for rain, until everything looked misty. I have told the story exactly as it was, — time, place, characters, everything. It needed no embellishment. If any one mentioned in it ever sees it, I wish to give kindest, dearest regards to the motherly old lady, my tender sympathy to the woman in mourning, who had lost her loved one. I give my acknowledgments to the old pirate in the corner, for I believe he was a mellow-hearted old Christian. I hereby say, that the thing that impressed me most, and recurred to me oftenest, is the blessing that God gave to that happy mother, that holy love-feast, and the parting benediction of that sweet little child."

Mrs. Warren silently gave her heartiest approval to the story, and wiped it away with her handkerchief.

CHAPTER XV.

ONE evening, after the company were gone, Roy took a trip to the land of Nod, and it lasted until the time when, if he had been at home, Canis Major would have come pitching upstairs to greet him. It was near six o'clock. As soon as he opened his chamber door a succession of shrieks came from the room beneath his, which was occupied by Miss Sarah Warren. They continued, — dreadful shrieks. The door was locked. It was the work of but a moment, to throw his whole weight against it, and, after a hard trial, to burst it in. Miss Sarah was hanging by her hand to a high hook in her closet. She had arisen, and, in her long night-dress, had attempted by standing on a chair, to take down a dress from her wardrobe. It was hitched. In trying to get it loose, a pointed hook had gone inside of a loose gold ring, the chair had tipped over and left her hanging by one finger. It was awful torture. Roy seized her and lifted her up, but could not get it free. Then he held her up, and by reaching up, although it cut and bruised his own fingers, he tore the hook out of the wall, and lay Miss Sarah on the bed in a dead faint. Then with much care, but strong force, he took the treacherous hook out of her ring, and went with flying leaps down the stairs for help. "Come upstairs. Come quick. Sarah is hurt. Bring camphor or ammonia."

111

They came, and after chafing her hands and feet and applying restoratives, she became conscious of her suffering.

"Now," said Roy, "I will go to my room and get a small pair of cutting nippers that I have, and I will cut off the ring, for her finger is too badly injured to take it off any other way. Please get a dish of warmish water and bandages, that.I may close the wound and care for it until a doctor can be called."

The ring was cut off, the finger examined, and the bone found not broken, although the flesh was badly torn and bleeding, and the hand strained and bruised. Roy placed the injured part in the right position, softened and restored the bruises as well as he could, and then he did up the finger and hand with a wet compress. When Roy had given all needed help he went below, leaving Mrs. Warren and Emily to complete her toilet. In a little while they all came down to breakfast. Miss Sarah, although she had a severe strain and a bad wound, was still a young lady of fine courage. Oh, don't sniff at that, reader. A woman will always have a tooth extracted with better grit than a man, and any dentist will tell you so. But if you had seen the thankfulness of Miss Sarah, especially, and also of her mother and sister, you would have thought that Roy had made a good beginning with one of Boston's splendid daughters. Miss Sarah drank her cup of coffee, and lay at ease, as much as the pain would allow her to, upon the sofa, until the doctor came. He uncovered the wound. "Who did up this wound?" he asked.

"Mr. Bartlett, a gentleman who is here with us."

"This is all right. I don't see what you want of a

doctor while he is here." He gave directions. He thought Miss Sarah would let her piano have a vacation for a few weeks. She did. The doctor called once more, and Mrs. Warren said, if any change came for the worse, she would send for him. But morning and night, Mrs. Warren said to Roy, "Now, doctor, will you examine the wound of your patient." Roy did. He dressed it, softening and healing it with castile soap and easy rubbing, and twice a day, half jokingly, consenting to be called doctor, while he was doing a doctor's work. If Mr. Guy Bartlett could have been invisible, and have seen how much good Roy could do with his amateur studying of medicine and surgery, he would have been pleased, and he might have thought he was seeing the dawn of love. If he had known what a woman Sarah Warren was, he would have said, "I will risk my boy, if Mrs. Warren will risk her girl." And he would have been safe.

These young people were splendid, perfect animals. And more than that, the intellectual was equally fine. They were well-read, had seen plays, and I shall not pretend that they did not know the history of the Grand Old Passion. And Roy did a dangerous thing. But he did it safely. One kiss which might have been granted, one show of devotion, one earnest expression of desire for full and lifelong ownership, might have brought a splendid result. But he kept within the limits of help only, and ceased that when it was no longer needed. And so it came to pass, that these young people lost neither their heads or their hearts. I like a man that can hold his horses. The business part of his obligation was paid promptly and fully. After Miss Sarah had recovered and was able to play again, it was a joy to hear her. Her piano was one

of the best Henry F. Miller pianos, and was cared for by
Mr. Miller, from the warerooms. Consequently, it was
always at its best, and Miss Sarah's playing was a surprise
and a revelation to Roy. A little later, he found a package in his room, upon his dressing-case, addressed on the
wrapper only, "Dr. Royal Bartlett," on opening it he
found two large volumes, richly bound in full Turkey
morocco. They were "Rogers' Poems" and "Rogers'
Italy," in the richest style, and with Turner's illustrations.
Henry Ward Beecher once said, "I received a letter this
morning, written as elegantly as if it came from Boston."
On the inside leaf of each book was also written, and
quite as elegantly, "Mr. Royal Bartlett, a present from
Mrs. Parna Warren, Miss Emily Warren, Miss Sarah
Warren." It was a rich, tasteful, artistic, valuable, magnificent present. Roy went downstairs to interview the
ladies.

He said, " Mrs. Warren, of course I am very grateful
for your magnificent present. It is just my taste, with
all those exquisite illustrations. But you give me too
expensive a present, by far. Those books cost no small
sum of money."

"Can you keep a secret?" asked Mrs. Warren.

"I can."

"Then I will give you one, and mind you keep it. I
am glad to give you these books, and you need not worry
about what they cost, for I have not spent half of my income any year, for these last ten years. Now are you
satisfied?"

"I am," said Roy, "but I earnestly hope you will keep
it in safe places, fly no kites with it, and not put too
much of it in one place, like the farmer that put too

many eggs in one basket. In general, I hope you will keep it, so it will be a blessing to you all, as long as you live. Your secret pleases me."

All this time, which was not long, Roy had not been unmindful of his home. He wrote satisfactory letters to his home, but thought he would stay away until Thanksgiving day. He had a kind invitation to go to church with Mrs. Warren and her daughters. "What church do you attend?" "Oh, we go to the West church and hear dear old Dr. Bartol." It is a sign of a good church and a good minister, where they talk so kindly as many Boston families do about Rev. Dr. Bartol. I meet it constantly. Roy said he would be glad to go soon, but had promised his mother that he would go to Park Street church, with friends who had already appropriated him for two Sundays. And so Roy went to church and heard Dr. Withrow, Dr. Bartol, Phillips Brooks, the Tremont Temple pastor, and others. He did his level best to paint better, in purer color, that would not fade or turn green or black. He took his opera glass, which was a good magnifier, to places where many oil paintings were to be seen, and studied them from an easy seat in the middle of the room. A very comfortable, enjoyable way, that does not tire you to death. He used the public library, and it helped him. He went to Harvard College library and saw such books as the elephant folio, illustrated "Piranisi" that shows Roman antiquities, the illustrated "Lepsius" on the Nile valley, the illustrated "Dante," and magnificent folios where only a few copies were printed, some by the first Napoleon, some by the second Napoleon, called Napoleon III., and by the rich and titled men of the world. Such books can only be seen in the great libraries of the world. He attended strictly to his art education. He did not adopt a theory, set up for a critic, pick up an ism, mount a hobby, become a reformer, or a man with a mission. So he was not remarkable in any way. And for this cause he was a very remarkable man. I am afraid this statement is a little mixed, but I do not see how I can improve it.

CHAPTER XVI.

SOME years ago a governor of Mississippi wrote his proclamation like this, — "It is a custom to appoint a day of thanksgiving. All things must have an author, and it is usual to call that author God. Some think it is wise to give thanks to him for the blessings we receive, and ask for a continuance of them. Such a practice can do no harm, and may do much good. I therefore appoint a day of thanksgiving." Such things do not grow in Massachusetts or New Hampshire.

All of the tribe of Bartlett that I ever met had got beyond their alphabet in revelation. When the train rolled into the station at Dover, N. H., on Wednesday evening, before the Thanksgiving that comes on Thursday, Roy Bartlett was there, and was not long in getting a hearty grip from Sam Ellet. If they had been brothers they could not have been better friends. Old Tom was not long in taking them home.

"The prodigal son has come home," said Sam.

"How is the wild artist?" said his father, laughing, as he shook him by the hand.

"The wild artist is all right, and glad to get home to his father and mother."

Mother Bartlett greeted him with a smiling face, which in a moment overflowed with grateful tears. It was a happy home coming. Canis Major was wild with joy.

Nothing would content him until Roy sat down and took his big brown and white head and shoulders in his lap, and let the dog kiss him to his heart's content. Grimalkin came purring around, and was soon in Roy's lap, and while Roy laughed to see it all, the pelican tuned up and sang its very best. Roy's welcome was complete. Then the supper. Chicken pie and sweet-apple pudding, baked in the brick oven, with warm biscuit from wheat grown on the farm.

I once heard a city missionary ask a sailor what he believed in. "I believe in good eating and drinking," was the answer. It is the prevailing faith of the world ; but in practice, only a few people ever know what good living is. I have eaten the food as prepared by many nationalities, and been in high or low places, but never had better food than I have had in the Bartlett Homestead. Roy and Sam Ellet thought so to-night. The thanks were given and every heart was uplifted. The supper was enjoyed, and then and after, Roy was told of all they could think of, that was news to him, from Garrison Hill to Durham, and from Sawyer's mills to Rochester.

Roy asked, " How is Will Glance doing ? "

" Working some, but it is evident that he does not like it, and I believe he is a dangerous man." said Mr. Bartlett.

" I have no confidence in him," said Sam.

" How is Jean Mc Duffie doing ? "

" Well as a man can. His father tells me he is making some money by hauling lumber, and as he has his father's team and all he can make, of course he can do well."

Roy was glad of it.

" Now, father, I expect to be here at home until next

Monday morning. This will give me Thanksgiving, two
others, and Sunday to go to church with you. You know
that children like stories, so Sam and I want one. Tell
us a New Hampshire Thanksgiving story."

"Yes, sir," said Sam.

"Tell them about Frank Garland," said Mrs. Bartlett.
"That is a good story, and it comes straight enough to
be true. It is a good picture of the old times and the
old families."

Mr. Bartlett thought a moment, and then began —

A Thanksgiving Story of the Olden Time.

MOST people like a real story. So do I, and what I
tell you, I know to be true myself, or have heard it from
good people. It can do no harm, for the family are all
gone, years ago. If you were in Dover and take the Tollend road, up by Peter Cushing's, and the Heath House,
and through the birches where the huckleberries grow,
then instead of going to the right by Ezra Hayes's around
Green Hill, you keep to the left, on the old road that
goes over Green Hill, passing Jonathan Young's and the
George Wiggin farm, then half a mile beyond that, on
the right, you come to an old cellar hole, that was the
Garland Farm. A few rods beyond the cellar, just as you
begin to descend the hill, over the wall on the right, is
the family burial-ground. The house was a large one,
two stories high, with as many as twelve or fifteen rooms
in it. The fireplaces were large, and I think there were
as many as six in the house. The one in the kitchen was
nearly large enough to burn wood of sled length. The
house was well built, well clapboarded, but never painted.
The barn was a very long one, and I have seen it well

filled with hay and cattle and large stacks of hay beside. It was six and a half miles from Dover, which is a good market. They raised a great deal of corn, hay, potatoes, an immense quantity of apples, cider, and hogs, and no end of produce. I have seen large flocks of geese, ducks, guinea hens, calling go back, go back, turkeys, hens, and chickens, and several peacocks. There always was a cloud of doves around the buildings, and often I have seen them feed the poultry. It was a sight to behold. A large basket of shelled corn, and when they were called, oh, what a scamper. The doves were not content to catch the corn, that was scattered far and wide, but they flew at once upon the basket and the man that held it, and he was covered with doves. There were several hundreds in that Babel of poultry. He soon scattered the grain and fed the multitude. The farm had wild straw-berries, raspberries, blackberries, and blueberries; beside, in the garden, currants, gooseberries, English cherries, and plums in abundance. Then a plenty of grapes, and, last but not least, the old button pear tree, more than two feet through, very large and high, and altogether the largest pear tree that I ever saw. One neighbor said he had eaten its fruit for over seventy years, and he could not remember the time when it looked much younger than it did then. It bore alternate years, and although it would be hard to find pears over an inch in diameter, yet they were very sweet, and I think its crop would be a large cartful. The ground was well fertilized, so it grew large and lived long. At last it grew hollow. Then the ants moved into it and alas! it blew down. A better servant, farmer never had. The children could not eat much in pear time, they were so full of button pears.

Oh, you need not pity our ancestors much, after the Indians kept quiet, for I can hardly remember to tell of all the good things they had. The Garland farm had horses, three or four yoke of oxen, cows, and young cattle, and plenty of sheep and lambs. The spinning wheel was often whirring, and the linen wheel as well, and in the big, unfinished garret were reels, swifts, warping bars, and a big loom to make woollen cloth. Mr. Garland had about four boys and two girls. As this is a Thanksgiving story, I will say that they had all had an abundant supply of Thanksgiving comforts. Those were stern times. Spare the rod and spoil the child, was often heard, and children had to suffer. Said Mr. Garland to the youngest boy, a little past fourteen years old, Now, Frank, Thanksgiving day is gone and it is almost bedtime. It is time to rake up the fire, to keep all night. Go out and get a back-log that will keep. It was nearly nine o'clock. The back-log ought to have been in before dark, and it ought not to have been left for the youngest to get. It is not best to be too hard on the baby. It was bad management. Too bad. Frank went to the door without his hat. It was dark and cold, with some snow on the ground. He tumbled around on the woodpile, but the big logs were frozen down, and he could only get loose a little one, as big as his leg. This he picked up and carried in. The old man looked at it. He was mad. He jumped up, took down a horsewhip which hung in a corner and hit Frank a dozen cuts with it. Frank bit his lips and took it. When the old man was done, Frank put on his coat and mittens and heard his father's order. Now get a back-log, not a toothpick. Frank went out. He stayed out just seven years, until he was his own man and twenty-one

years old.   Then after dark on Thanksgiving evening he
came and looked in at the window of the Garland home.
The old man was there and the mother and most of the
children.   Frank was a strapping big fellow, with strength
in his back and money in his pocket.   He went to the
woodpile.   He took the biggest log he could find, carried
it in and laid it down before his father, saying, Here, father,
here's your back-log.   So it is, said the old man.   But I
have almost a mind to lick you again, for being gone so
long after it.   You are not big enough, said Frank.   No,
said his father, perhaps not.   At any rate I do not wish
to try, for I have done it once too much already.   Frank's
mother and sisters wept over him, his brothers greeted
him with welcome.   His father showed that he was a
sinner, and as Frank had made money and saved a handsome sum, so the righteous son forgave the prodigal
father, and they lived happy ever after.   The back-log
lasted several days.

    The next morning Canis Major came upstairs in
double-quick time, and there was Roy, sure enough.
The hearty, loving dog almost turned himself wrong
side out with joy.   Then the cattle had to be interviewed
and talked to and petted, the sheep fed, and all the stock
seen and spoken kindly to, even to the hogs, hens, turkeys, geese, and ducks.   When all had been cared for,
and the breakfast enjoyed, they all sat in the large sitting-
room, with Canis Major keeping close watch of Roy to
see that he did not disappear again.   Then there was a
good time for Roy to tell of all that he had been doing
in Boston.   He told them how Miss Sarah had got hung
up in her closet, how he had helped her down, how he
had played doctor, and also of his rich present.

"Ah!" said Sam, "I guess it is coming."

"What?" asked Roy.

"Some splendid woman to occupy those stockings."

Roy said, "He had not found her as yet, and had seen no signs of her except the stockings."

Then Jean McDuffie rode into the yard. Roy and Sam walked out with Jean.

"I wanted to see you," said Jean. "You wished to hear of any good that might come to me. I have been teaming this fall, and have laid up money. I have about three hundred dollars in the Dover Savings Bank. I have met a woman who is awful good to me, and I am to her. Don't you speak of it, because I do not care to have the world know my business before I know it myself. You know I can sing some. She is a fine singer too, and we shall be married as soon as we can fix things to our minds. Father wants me to bring her home to live. She has saved considerably more than I have. So, instead of being dead and buried, I am alive, happy, and very thankful."

The young men congratulated him, and they were all in a mood to appreciate the day. So the golden hours passed on, with kind words from friends, a sermon in the brick church with the golden rooster on it, and all of the blessing of home and friends, and on Monday morning Roy's visit was ended. Canis Major looked discouraged enough. He watched Roy and Sam out of sight, and was not comforted when Sam returned without Roy.

CHAPTER XVII.

THE Warrens were glad to have their young man with them again. And why should they not? He was not a reformer, ready to attack every one whose opinions differed a shade from his. He was not a growler at all. He was not as full of dislikes as a herring is of bones. His young life tasted good to him, and it was his, as it may be almost every one's privilege, to make it so. Some people can never see a brilliant butterfly without spoiling to clutch it. And when they do, what have they? A ruined butterfly and a dirty hand. He fitted into his place, in the home life of the Warrens, better than if he had been born into it, on the same principle that the average young sprig is so devoted to another man's sister, and so careless of his own. But Roy would have been devoted to his own.

The breakfasts were very pleasant, the suppers were a reunion, and a joy to the corporeal, social, and intellectual man. Mrs. Warren enjoyed life well. Miss Emily often met, in her associations as teacher, many enjoyable things; Miss Sarah was an enchantress with her piano. The Thursday evening coterie often came together, and then there was something entertaining.

Sam came to Boston for a week. Then Roy was kept busy. Sometimes one or both of the young ladies went out with Sam. They rather liked the rosy young man with the quiet manners. In one way or another, they managed to keep him busy. They went to church, to the public library, to the Art Club, to the studios, to see Edwin Booth, and to see Denman Thompson, in the New Hampshire play. When the week was over, Sam was thankful and satisfied. He was glad to go home and go to work. There is some sense in such a visit. Have your enjoyment, make it taste good, always be glad of it, and stop when you get enough.

Then Roy bent all his energies to painting better pictures. His expenses were light, and he sold enough to pay his way, and more. One day he went into Leonard's auction room. There were several pictures to be sold, although it was not a regular picture sale. There were four oil paintings sold together. They went for a small sum, I think about a dollar apiece. When the buyer came to examine them and get the dust off, they were found to be signed pictures by an eminent French artist. A little later the set was sold for six hundred dollars. Then Roy began to look sharp at pictures, both for name and quality. He looked at them in earnest. A little later, in taking a walk, he saw a large German battle scene. It was full of figures, and well done. They asked five dollars for it. The frame was a good one, and that alone was worth more. He bought it. Within a week he was offered fifty for it, and sold it. A dealer bought it, and he sold it for a large advance. I state a fact. But such things do not often happen. But it does often happen that a man who is wide awake, and knows the uses and values of many things, can find a rich reward for his study. Once Baron Humboldt was travelling in Siberia. He saw

what was visible to his eyes alone. He called his attend-
ants. Said he, "There, in that mountain side, ought to
be found a most valuable plumbago mine. I see the
signs of it." They worked it, and found it. It is the
best plumbago mine in all the world, so far as I know,
the Alibert mine, that gives the richest supply for Faber's
pencils. It is a mine of wealth for Russia.

But Roy worked the hardest to find some value in his
own pictures. He gained upon it. What we have to
learn in this world is an appalling work. To begin, all
jammed up to a jelly, with only the breath of life in you,
among entire strangers, that never saw you before, only
about a foot long, and, small as you are, to be considered
the biggest joke of the season, when you don't know the
taste of your own mother's milk, if she has any, from
castor oil; with no sense or much feeling, and only the
least bit of a will of your own, which you inherit from
your mother, form a combination of circumstances
enough to take the gimp out of Mark Tapley. Roy
never thought of that, but he quietly kept on his work,
occupying a corner of Mr. Titcombe's studio.

The next June he exchanged Boston for the Bartlett
farm, until after haying. Mr. Titcombe took a sketching
tour of a week in Strafford County, with Roy. I have
some of the sketches that Mr. Titcombe made. Roy
painted pictures for his home. In that and later seasons
he sketched with Benjamin Champney at North Conway.
Roy loved the mountains as well as his father and
mother. Some of his excursions with them: — They
went to Portsmouth, the Isles of Shoals, York Beach, Old
Orchard Beach, Mount Agamenticus, Garrison Hill,
Grand Monadnock, White Mountains, and other places,

where, alone or with some good fellow of an artist, he made careful sketches in oil, water, or pencil.

He lived with the Warrens except the third winter, when they were in Europe. His pictures sold better, and he laid up money. He painted some the second winter with Mr. Champney. He joined the Art Club. He sold a picture to Mr. S. R. Knights, real estate auctioneer, and made a friend of him.

Not long after Mr. Knights called on him again. Said he, "Mr. Bartlett, I have a brick house to sell to-morrow. It is well mortgaged for half its value. The people wish the mortgage to remain, as they do not need the money. Now, Mr. Bartlett, there may be a chance for you to make something. If it sells for less than a thousand dollars over the mortgage, I wish you to buy it. If it brings more let it go. If it comes to you, you cannot fail to make from one to five thousand dollars on it. Do you wish to try? It is near Essex street and business is working that way. It is well let and the man wants a lease. I will warrant you to make a good advance."

Roy went with Mr. Knights and saw the estate. The next day, he bid a hundred dollars over the mortgage, and, although the auctioneer dwelt long for a better price, Roy was the purchaser. He had money enough by him, to pay. Within a week he was offered a thousand dollars for his bargain. Then they asked him what he would take. He did not say. He had several applications to rent it. The firm who occupied it, wanted it at a thousand dollars a year, if he would add two more stories with front battlement walls and a flat roof. He told them they could have it, rent free, for one year, by paying taxes only, if they would add the two stories satisfacto-

rily. They took it quickly and did well by it. At the
end of the year, Roy thought he owned six thousand
dollars in the estate. He told his father and mother
about it, and the Warrens also, but otherwise he kept his
own counsel. One day when it was quite rainy, Roy was
in the Athenæum. There was one gentleman there, looking over the pictures. So Roy took a chair to have a
good look at Allston's "Belshazzar's Feast." He took
plenty of time and studied it.

Said the gentleman, "What do you think of it?"
Roy looked up and saw a pleasant, middle-aged man.
Roy told him. They talked. Roy listened. They analyzed the pictures together. It was a pleasure to listen
to that man. He knew something. After half an hour
together, they paused before a small Fra Angelico. Roy
praised it. "Yes, it is good, but I have three better ones
by the same artist." Roy opened his eyes in astonishment.

"Can I see them?" asked Roy.

"Certainly, with pleasure."

"Where are they?"

"On Beacon street, nearly opposite the Athenæum."

"What is your name, please?"

"Gardner Brewer."

He did see Mr. Brewer's pictures and had a standing
invitation to see them again, when he pleased. He made
a splendid friend. This is written exactly as it occurred.
It was a joy to see those splendid Fra Angelicos, Verboeck-
hovens and all Mr. Brewer's beautiful pictures. There
were also many models of the finest of the ruins of Greece
and Rome. In the Brewer fountain, on the common,
Boston will long cherish the name of Gardner Brewer.

Roy thought to himself, what a splendid thing it is to be rich, to own works of art, to keep them in order, that people may see and enjoy them. What a blessing wealth is, for rich and poor alike.

But Roy soon met a different kind of a customer. He was walking out one day, and was attracted by a large number of unset stones, in a broker's window. It was a small place, but it contained several things of interest. Second-hand pictures, books, watches and jewelry. The proprietor Roy had seen before. There was a man about forty-five years of age, with thin gray hair, and the general air of a reformer, an animal too often met with. Although the proprietor replied not much, yet the man ventilated his opinions very freely.

He said, " Yes, sir. I assert that no man has a right to amass property. Property is robbery. All you get more than your equal share you rob from some one else. The time is coming, and soon too, when the poor will help themselves to all they want. Yes, sir, and yer capitalists' heads will fly like shelling peas." (Fact, word for word.) And turning to Roy he demanded, " What do you think of that, sir?"

Roy was not going to speak to or notice the anarchist. But he was appealed to, and it made him angry. His eyes snapped, his color rose, he clenched his fists and answered. " Think? Why, I think you are the biggest fool I ever saw in my life. You are crazy as Bedlam. Wealth is the poor man's blessing, more than the rich man's. If the wealth of the world was divided equally, some reckon that each would have a poor hut and a hundred dollars. There would be nothing bigger than a hut. Boston would be a collection of mud huts. There would

be no ships at sea, no railroads or any decent roads, no
decent houses; no literature, for it takes capital to pub-
lish a book; no art, for we should have to dig for subsist-
ence. Not a telegraph, or an electric or gas light. No
kerosene even, for it takes mighty capital to take it all
over the world and so wonderfully cheap. We should
all be a poor, helpless, hopeless, aimless, starving mass.
Oh, you gray-headed old fool, you know nothing at all.
Capital is the grain that Joseph saved in Egypt against
seven years of famine. Capital is your servant and help,
and mine and every one's. The clothes you have on, far
too good for you, would be out of your reach, for capital
makes them cheap. The watch you carry would never
be, but for capital. The flour from the West, the food
gathered from far and wide, the tea from China, the coffee from Java, would be impossible but for capital. Why!
we should not have a stage coach line or a baggage wagon,
and if our crops fail here, we might starve with plenty a
hundred miles away. But now Jay Gould is my servant
and he will carry me a short distance or a long one. All
rich men are a blessing and all capital is wealth, saved up
to help and bless mankind. Honor to the Astors. They
built much of New York. Honor to the Vanderbilts.
They built great steamships and railroads to carry food
for us all. Honor to Jay Gould. As soon as he touches
a railroad, it is at once a safer, better public servant to
carry a letter for me thousands of miles for two cents.
But the fool anarchist, that did not know enough to get a
dollar or to keep it, or to use one little talent wisely and
get a blessing out of that, had his talent taken from him,
and he was kicked into hell for his meanness. And it
served him right."

Roy ceased. He had freed his mind, and he had expected a fight. The anarchist had not uttered a yip. When Roy had done, the man said slowly, "I had not thought of it that way," and he went slowly out.

Said the broker, "I am much obliged to you, Mr. Bartlett. It is good missionary work. I hope that skunk will not come here again."

"Yet," said Roy, "I feel as though I had been doing a dirty act in talking with him. I shall have to go out on the common where the wind blows, and have the contamination taken away. Pshaw! Capitalists' heads fly like shelling peas? Still the wealth would remain, and capital represents all of God's blessing in life, and all that makes life desirable, endurable, or possible." Roy walked by the soldiers' monument on the common. He read the inscription upon it, written by President Eliot of Harvard University. If you wish to see a sample of as good English as ever was written, I recommend you to do the same. Gradually he forgot his resentment against the wretch, who could so ruffle such a quiet young gentleman and splendid good fellow. In 1888, the man with the one talent is acting like an awful fool, and I earnestly hope he will get hurt, until he learns better.

CHAPTER XVIII

WILL GLANCE HAS A DRUNK.

AFTER Roy had been in Boston a year, the neighbors noticed that Will Glance drank more hard liquors. Mary looked pale and anxious. Glance wanted to take loads of produce to Dover, and keep the money. Mr. Hoskins always paid him his twenty dollars a month, and he had no board to pay. One day Mr. Hoskins had been to market with potatoes. He had turned them in on account of groceries, and he had not much ready money with him. Glance had overdrawn his pay considerably, and must have had whiskey hidden in the barn somewhere, he smelt so strong of it, and was so ugly. Mary was afraid of him. Mr. and Mrs. Hoskins did not consider him safe. Sam Ellet had just come across the fields to ask the price of potatoes. Then they would know if it was best to dig them for the market. Glance came up to Mr. Hoskins, with an oath, and demanded money.

He was answered, "I do not owe you any. If I pay you any you will spend it for liquor, and I will not pay you any."

"Then," said Glance, crazy with anger and liquor, "I will kill you both." He pulled out a large Colt's revolver and fired at Mr. Hoskins's head. He missed. The ball whizzed by his head, and the flash singed

132

his hair. But in an instant Sam Ellet had him by the arm, and he and Mr. Hoskins tried to get the pistol away from the crazy wretch. Then, at once Sam clutched the barrel to keep himself and Mr. Hoskins safe, and as he gave it a twist, it was discharged straight into Will Glance's eye. He died instantly. The two women saw it from the house, and came running.

They both said, "Oh, father, I am glad it is not you! Oh, Sam, I am glad it is not you!"

"He shot himself," said Mr. Hoskins.

"Suicide," said Sam.

The women were told to go into the house, as it would be necessary to call the coroner. After they were gone Mr. Hoskins said, "Remember, Sam, we tried to get the pistol so he could not shoot himself, you know, Sam."

"I know," said Sam.

"Remember, Sam, he shot the first time at me, and then killed himself."

"Suicide," said Sam.

"Mind and tell it just right."

"Mr. Hoskins, I shall tell just as little as I can, and I shall say suicide, sure."

"Now, Sam, you stay here and watch the body. Say as little as possible to anybody. I will speak an earnest word to the women folks in the house. Then I will jump on a horse and go to Dover for a coroner. I will send Mary over to Mr. Bartlett's for help."

Mr. Hoskins had gone. Mr. Bartlett came, and soon after the coroner and a doctor.

"Now, Mr. Hoskins, just tell how this happened."

Mr. Hoskins began. "Mr. Glance was quite intoxicated and very cross.   Mr. Ellet here had just come over and was asking the price of potatoes, with regard to digging theirs, when Mr. Glance came up to us and demanded that I should pay him some money.   I had already overpaid him.   He had twenty dollars a month besides his living.   I did not think it safe to give him any more to buy whiskey with.   So I refused.   He at once swore he would kill Mr. Ellet and me.   He fired that large pistol at my head, and just missed me.   Then Sam and I tried to take it from him, but he turned the pistol to his own head and fired it."

It was a clear case of suicide.

The doctor said that the story was evidently true. The coroner picked up the pistol from the dead man's hand.   Two barrels discharged.   Correct.   "Now, Mr. Ellet, tell your story."

"It was just what Mr. Hoskins told," said Sam.   "It was just suicide.   And what he wanted to do it for, I don't see.   If he had not been drunk he would not have done it."

The coroner asked Mrs. Hoskins.   She was too much overcome; she could only groan, and utter "Suicide."

Mary said the same, "Just suicide; and why he did it I cannot tell, for we all used him as well as we knew how."

The coroner appeared to deliberate a moment.   Then he announced, that as there was nothing in doubt about it, all the evidence went to show that the deed was done with his own pistol, fired with his own hand; there was no need to summon a jury.   He should instruct the undertaker to report, that William Glance died by premeditated suicide.   It never was disputed.

The Hoskins family were too much affected to talk much about it. Sam Ellet knew enough to keep his mouth shut. He had good common-sense. Two days later Will Glance was buried in a small, new lot in Pine Hill Cemetery, in Dover. Mr. Hoskins told Sam, privately, that he would not bury his carcass in the Hoskins lot, as he wanted to rest quietly there himself, by and by. Will Glance's mother wept some for him, but she was the only one; and she wept more for what he might have been, than what he was. Will Glance was his own worst enemy. He did not live to see his son, born three months later; but it brought a ray of light to the Hoskins farm, where the shadows had been long and dark. Mr. Bartlett wrote his account to Roy. Sam wrote his. Sam's was peculiar, and Roy got an impression that Sam had adopted Talleyrand's theory, that language was a medium for concealing ideas. The Dover newspapers told the story as it was seen to be. So Roy got the different versions of it, and made his own conclusions. He knew when to let well enough alone. There was a feeling of relief wherever Will Glance was known. His mother seemed less anxious, went out more, and dressed better. Later it was ascertained that she had over three thousand dollars, that she had pretended was lost in settling her husband's estate; and she had been dressing poorly, and apparently living on her brother, to keep the knowledge of any property from her merciless, dissipated son. He had a plain white marble stone, with his name, age, and date. Almost as soon as the stone was set, some one had written the old rhyme, redolent of Tom Paine, but adapted to the occasion, —

" Poor Will Glance, here he lies,
Nobody laughs, nobody cries ;
Where he's gone, or how he fares,
Nobody knows, nobody cares.
One thing sart'in, that's a fack,
Nobody wants him to come back."

It was written with a heavy black-lead pencil, and nobody rubbed it out. Death is not so bad after all.

CHAPTER XIX.

ROY TAKES A STUDIO.

AGAIN it was the first of October, three years after we first met Roy Bartlett. In Lydia Maria Child's impossible, but very entertaining story of Hilda Silfverling, she writes, "So the years went by, and the earth rolled on, bearing with it the Alps, and the Andes, the bear, the wolf, and the maiden." So it has borne the choice spirits of my novel; and even later, for most of them are splendidly alive and smiling to-day. Roy painted a good picture, and had often been asked to give lessons. So he rented a good studio on Tremont Street. In movement there is hope; in stagnation there is none. He fitted it up simply, with a little that he bought, and some superfluous furniture that came from home. He hung his pictures, and they made a good show. His income from his real estate venture would support him, with reasonable economy. Then, if you had looked in the *Transcript*, you might have seen for two months the announcement, Mr. R. Bartlett will receive pupils in oil painting at his studio, Mather Building, Tremont Street. Pupils came at once, nearly all ladies. One of the old artists said he had quite a harem. Although he was a clean, handsome young man, with a love of a moustache, yet, strange to say, he did not fool or flirt with women, or try to keep them laughing. Every pupil that came must agree to

work their best, and try to improve. Some took one
lesson a week, some two or three. It was not long before
he had twenty pupils. Pupils came forenoons. The
afternoon he had for work or company. Company was
invited every afternoon. He sold more pictures. One
afternoon there came a knock at his door; a young lady
wished to see his pictures. She was welcomed. He
spoke of a few of them, without specially looking at her,
when, happening to catch a reflection of her in the cheval
glass, he was at once interested in his visitor. She was
two inches taller than the Medicean Venus, and many
times more interesting. She looked remarkably good,
and was remarkably good-looking. Her ears were perfect,
and the delicate purity of her neck contrasted with the
richness of her golden-brown hair. Her hands were
perfect, — Oh, rarest of beauties! — and there was no-
where about her a sign of slavery, mean thinking, or
coarse living. She asked the price of lessons. One
dollar each. She said she was living with her uncle, a
retired clergyman, who was steward of an estate, which
yielded him a living, and was likely to for some time to
come. The house they occupied was in Commonwealth
Avenue. She had painted some, and wished to improve
so that she could paint desirable pictures, and teach, if it
became necessary to make her own living. Roy said he
would help her all he could. It was a good thing for a
woman to have a means of support, for often resources
failed, then she was not left helpless. Her name was
Miss Graham. She said the establishment that her uncle
has the care of is a large one. There is a fine house, well
furnished. There are some servants, that are to be cared
for and retained. There is a carriage, and horses that

are to be used, and a pew in church that may be occupied. So, you see, since my uncle's voice failed, so he could not preach, he has had the care of this estate, and it may continue for some time longer. He gets a good living out of it, and has saved something. He has no children, and no heirs but me. I will send Fred, our servant, here this afternoon, with my painting materials. Fred is a light mulatto, as also is his wife. They are very faithful, trusty friends, as well as servants. The establishment pays them liberally. Fred's wife is Jenny. She is an excellent dressmaker, so that saves us something. I thought it best to tell you how I was situated. Here is the money for twelve lessons. I am to carry the receipt to my uncle.

Roy did not wish her to pay in advance, but she replied, that the money was already provided, and if paid, cannot be lost. Miss Graham selected a waterfall to copy, and the interview was over. As she gave her parting salutation, he had a good excuse for observing her critically. His pupils were gone and now he was alone in his studio. He took an easy chair and mused, and this was his thought. Another pupil and a good one. I am doing well. That young lady is sure pay. All young ladies are. She is safe, honest, careful, and intends to be efficient. Too bad that she is poor. I hated to take her money. She was well dressed but plain, still it was very pretty and very becoming. Pure honest eyes. I hope her uncle and aunt will save a dollar, so they will not have to depend upon her. If she gets short of money I may be called upon by myself, not her, to help her. Well, well. There are some white souls in the world, thank heaven. Pity she is an orphan. But let that go now, and perhaps good

help may come by her uncle. When Roy had finished
his musing, he arose and put the room to rights, ready
for the morning campaign. Then a walk, which ended
at the house of Warren, and brought the wild artist to
the supper table, and the pleasant society of three ladies.
The supper was what it always was, abundance. Roy
helped the ladies, to such as they preferred, while each
gave assistance.

Said Mrs. Warren, " I like to have the first course all
on the table at once, where it is only a small number like
ours. Of course it would not be practicable in a large
family or at a hotel, where there were waiters. But here
we need not be obliged to let a servant choose our food
for us. There is more liberty, and we can have our choice
of fat or lean, rare or well done, all the time. Here we
can have just what suits."

Said Roy, " You have one custom that I like very
much. Your dinner always has its first course of soup.
If one has no appetite, soup will almost create one.
Something warm, perhaps high seasoned, like broth with
a little red pepper in it, will arouse a sleepy stomach, and
prepare the way for a fine meal. Once a prime minister
of England had invited four noble lords to dine with him.
They came on time. The minister sent word that he was
detained by an audience with the king. They waited.
Other messengers came. He was still detained. More
than two mortal hours passed and the dinner waited.
Then the speed of his carriage was heard and the minister came in. I know how you feel, said he. He gave a
servant an order, while the dinner was served, and he
mixed the five hungry men, a dose of something hot and
strong, which was immediately followed by a mullaga-

tawny soup. Then came the roast and the famine was over. It was a splendid dinner. A man's best friend is his stomach. It supplies the motive power and is the boiler of the engine. A physician once said, a man ought not to be conscious that he had a stomach."

Said Miss Emily, "I think men enjoy the pleasures of food more than women."

"Yes," said Roy, "they have stronger appetites. When a woman wants labor done she expects a man to do it. He makes the roads, tills the land, builds and runs the railroads, builds the houses, and of course, needs a pile of fuel to sustain the wear and tear. So he eats."

"But," said Miss Sarah, "women work."

"Most certainly. The men sustain the world and the women sustain the men. For a general truth that is not far out of the way."

Said Mrs. Warren, "I am glad, Mr. Bartlett, that you do not take pleasure in saying spicy, paradoxical, and cutting things about women."

Said he, "Indeed I do not, and how could I after all the women I have ever known, and this almost without exception. If they knew my opinion of them, as compared with their nearest male friend, they would give me credit for a most generous opinion. Of course, we are all human. But where women have faults men have vices. Women are provoking where men are villainous. But all the women that I have known, have made it a joy to do them a service, at least, where it can be done easily. So if I find a nice young lady hanging upon a hook, it is always a pleasure to me to help her down."

The ladies laughed at the application of Roy's theory.

When the second course was served, Mrs. Warren asked, "Mr. Bartlett, can you cook?"

"Oh, yes, meats generally, and vegetables. I have made bread and some pastry, but not much. I think it well for a man to be able to help at home, in case of an emergency. In these days of uncertain servants, nobody knows what may happen." Said Roy, "Let me tell you something. Not long since I met one of my own teachers. She never would tell her age. But she would tell that her father died when she was fifteen years old, and a little later she told in what year her father died. Some rainy day I am going to get out my slate and pencil and figure up her age."

They laughed, and the ladies said they should have to look out for him. They adjourned to the parlor. It was Thursday evening and company came. Mr. Stacy and some lady teachers. They talked of subjects, not of persons. That is gossip. Educated people prefer subjects. It is abstract thought.

Said Mr. Stacy, "How is your art prospering, Mr. Bartlett?"

"Very well, thank you. I am selling some pictures and having a fair amount of pupils. Doing better than I expected."

Said Mrs. Warren, "Are there not desirable people among your artist friends and pupils, that you would like to invite here?"

"I have no doubt of it," he answered.

"Then please do. I have the room. My parlors are very large, and I can stand the wear of the carpets and furniture. Now, Mr. Bartlett, let us have a reception twice a month, on Thursday evenings. You invite only suitable people whom you know, and fill up the parlors. We can stop if we do not like it. Sarah can play, Mr. Bartlett and Mr. Stacy can read."

"I agree to it," said Roy. "But let us have no organization and no society with officers. Small societies consume all their time doing unimportant business. Call it simply the Art Coterie."

They all agreed, and the programme was left to Roy and the Misses Warren. The company made suggestions. They could have music, Shakespeare, literature, song or story, sociable or sermon, and those who do not like it, need not come again. It was agreed unanimously.

CHAPTER XX.

THE next morning Mr. Royal Bartlett descended from the sacred precincts of Beacon hill, feeling light, airy, and gay. He was conscious of a reasonable amount of greenbacks in his pocket, of plenty of the most agreeable work to do, and an abundance of the best companionship to enjoy. Father Taylor once said that he used to consider Boston hill a little nearer heaven than any other place. Here was Roy in Boston. He had not an enemy in the world. The only one he ever had, a child of the devil, who hated Roy without a cause, had just shot himself dead. It was out of Roy's mind. There were no outs about his life. Plenty of friends, and most true. No critics that he knew of. If any critic had sought to find a case against him, that case would not have had a leg to stand on. Make it too sweet? No, I do not. There are plenty of white souls that walk in the light of God and the love of man. I know plenty of them, and some of them are coming into this book later. Take a look at Roy as he takes his morning walk through the Public Garden and across the Common. If you do not like him, go down to the frog pond and drown yourself. Roy put the finishing touches on a picture, and hung it high, out of the reach of hands, where it might dry. Fred Annerly, the mulatto, Miss Graham's servant, came with her easel,

144

paint-box, and canvases. Fred was light for a mulatto, and Roy thought he might be more white than colored. He was very pleasant and gentlemanly. He and his wife had been born slaves, but they were free enough now. Soon Miss Graham arrived. She placed her easel in what Roy called fine light, and he said it might remain there, and she could work at other times when she was not taking her lesson, and no charge for it. A few directions were given as to what colors to use in the sky, how to lay it in, and to call for help when she wanted it. Miss Graham went to work. Other pupils came in. That forenoon he had seven at once, all he wanted to attend to. When it was near noon, Roy called their attention. He said, "Ladies, I have something to tell you that may interest you. There are a few of us that have met on alternate Thursday evenings, for social entertainment. No refreshments. No fancy dress and no expense. The lady of the house has kindly asked me to invite my pupils and friends. But they must be only suitable people. I should not dare to ask a man who was flavored with tobacco. First, I will begin with inviting all my pupils. Each can take one other as escort, if necessary. We have very large double parlors, really a fine large drawing-room, a magnificent piano, a music teacher in the house, and several talented readers and speakers who will come. But all will be informal. No ceremony; just simple and enjoyable. Now, ladies, will you come?"

They said "yes," every one.

"Please tell me who reads or recites. Who plays any instrument? Who sings?"

"One lady read when she was needed. Miss Graham played the piano, and had been known to sing."

"Have you played much?" asked Roy.

"Yes, considerably. I have had many piano lessons from Mr. Petersilea, and lessons in singing from Mr. Lyman Wheeler."

"Then I will risk you to sing," said Roy, "and it is fortunate that I asked you. If you will bring a piece of music, not too short or too long, a piece that you like yourself, and also a song, it will be a splendid contribution, and we will all consider it a good beginning."

Miss Graham said she would remain longer, and paint awhile in the afternoon. She did. When her day's work was finished, Roy was satisfied that she had laid in the picture so well, that he might have to scratch forward or the pupil would be equal to the teacher. At any rate, she could give lessons now, and would not be left helpless in case her uncle should die or lose his stewardship. That was a cause for thankfulness. Roy wanted a light lunch, but he first made a call. High up in his own studio building was an artist, Mr. Frank Wilkie, a man past thirty, a good painter, but a man who used strong stimulants. Roy knocked at the door. He heard a strong voice say, "come in." Mr. Wilkie was seated in an old-fashioned chair, and looking far from cheerful. "How are you, Frank?"

"All wrong. I should be well enough if I had any luck. I have not taken a dollar for a week and I am all run ashore. I should not tell every one, but I tell you, Roy."

"Well," said Roy, "I can help a little. I was just wanting a lesson from you and here is a dollar for it. I will go out to lunch and you must go with me. Then we will come back and I will take a canvas that I have and watch you while you paint, for an hour or two, you to tell me your colors and methods, and I to sponge all the art I can out of you, in a given time, and have the picture beside. Do you consent?"

"Yes," said Wilkie, "anything for a dinner, a dollar, and to oblige Benson."

Roy led the way down to the Quincy Market, where the eating-houses are, that keep the market-men so fat. Places there where they do not live by bread alone, but where they get the best the world affords, and oh, such meat, the biggest, fattest, richest, tenderest, juiciest cuts. And a man goes away plumb-full, although he was hollow away down to his heels. Roy had not lived in Boston for nothing, for when Sam Ellet had been in the city with Roy, they had fully celebrated the three great feasts of the Jews, namely : breakfast, dinner, and supper. So Roy led the way to a light, pleasant room, up one flight, near the market.

"Good morning, Mr. Blanchard. Can you give us two nice tenderloin steaks, well done?"

"I can just do it, Mr. Bartlett."

It came. Then two cups of coffee with potatoes, warm biscuit and butter, and condiments galore. It was a great, big, wide steak, tender and juicy, and thick as your foot. But that depends. It was enough for a man-o'-war's-man, or one of Jim Camel's amazons.

"There," said Roy, "that ought to stay your stomach, until you can get around to some hearty victuals."

That fancy seemed to chirk Wilkie up mightily, but it did not spoil his appetite. Each attacked his steak in less time than it takes to tell of it, and soon the relative condition was the same as when the lion and the lamb

lay down together: the lamb was inside the lion. "Have
a piece of pudding or pie?" asked Roy.

"Yes, if you please. About next week, I guess.
Couldn't do it much sooner. Oliver W. H. says, —

> "Three courses are as good as ten.
> If nature can subsist on three,
> Thank heaven for three, amen."

Jess so, as William Warren says. But my experience
tells me that one course has the breath of life in it, if it is
good enough, and there is enough of it. So I make no
mistake, nor degrade these two artist gentlemen, by
making them stub along on one. Then by special request,
Mr. Wilkie painted in Roy's studio all the afternoon,
Roy gave him another dollar and they were both suited.
Frank Wilkie was a generous, improvident fellow. It is
good to be generous at times, but there is much to be said
on the other side. The generous man helps people generously, and he often needs to be helped generously in
return. But the mean man, the man that is not half
generous enough, wins. He always pays his debts, you
can come down on his property if he does not do it. He
must do it. The generous man can't and don't pay. He
lives freely. When he has anything he goes through it.
He has nothing and you can get nothing. When he has
a streak of luck, he treats a squad of non-combatants, to
a champagne supper, and then, when he is clean busted,
he blows up his wife because the milk bill is so large.
The generous man wants you to sign a note with him or
be his bondsman for a large sum. He says you won't have
it to pay. You can catch a bear real easy, but you need
plenty of help to let go of him. The mean man signs

nothing, you can't get him to. The assessors hate him, and he, very properly, returns the compliment. The generous man pays a poll-tax, when he can put it off no longer without going to jail. His wife looks shabby and is worried about what will come next. The mean man's wife has good clothes, heavy warm shawls and wraps, and takes care of them. She has a house full of everything, so she does not worry, or care a continental what happens. The generous man's children ought to go to school more, but they can't. The mean man's children go enough, and they do not neglect their arithmetic, if they do their grammar. If the mean man's "darter" wants to take lessons in "ile paintin'" she can do it, and you ought to see the pictures. The generous man's wife, oh, so sweet and beautiful when she was married, grows lean and old before her time, she suffers and is neglected. She dies all too soon and is buried in coarse gravel. She has no gravestones. Her children are divided up among people that do not want them. The mean man and his wife both live to wear out several sets of store teeth. Their children marry well-to-do folks in the vicinity, and all do well. The mean man gets fat and his wife gets fleshy. He has the phthisic and she the asthma. Both live to be outrageously old, and die full of years and things. Silver handles on their coffins a foot long. Graves in yellow loam. They leave fifty dollars to foreign missions. Gravestones six inches thick, of splendid Italian marble, for the birds to roost on. I do not know what becomes of the generous man. I think he runs away with a medium, or something. He is always giving himself away. You may not believe all this, but I do, I almost think.

The next day Roy had the chagrin to know that Frank
Wilkie was shut in his studio, drunk. It cut him up to
know that so good an artist could be such a fool. Roy
made some calls in the studios, and, as he was always
free to welcome others, so they smiled back at him.
Honey catches flies; vinegar is not so popular. There
was hardly a room in his building where he was not
known. A man cannot paint ten hours a day, except it
be on a house or fence, which commonly does not strain
his intellect very much. So an artist refreshes himself by
a call, and returns with fresh eyes for color, and more go
in his imagination. Besides, it is refreshing to know
what a gaby another artist is making of himself, in his
frantic efforts to be original. Oh, there is a comfort, one
way or another, — either in the art in your own pictures,
or the want of it in another's.

Roy's pupils did well for him. They learned well.
Miss Graham worked several hours each day. Several
days in the week she helped Roy in caring for his pupils.
She brought him two pupils, that each paid him twelve
dollars in advance. If he wished to go out, she cared
for the studio, and taught the pupils. She was an acquisition. Her finished pictures increased in number. Fred
carried four home, which were disposed of. Roy congratulated her. Her pictures were good. Then came
the evening of the Art Coterie. It was a fine evening.
Roy had invited many of the artists, but not Frank
Wilkie, or any like him. The rooms were well filled and
comfortable. There was an intermission, and all were
asked to change their seats, so as to have no wall-flowers.
Some were standing.

When Roy called the company to order, he said: "The

lady of the house and her daughters have given me permission to invite pupils and friends to an informal social gathering. If the guests are pleased with this, there may be others. There will be no bills to pay, and it is only that we may be happier by entertaining and knowing each other. There is plenty of talent here, and I have arranged to call upon several. First, a musical selection by Miss Sarah Warren."

It was splendidly done. One part strong and grand, with all the power of the instrument; another light, airy, intricate, and sweet as the song of a bobolink. Henry F. Miller was there, and heard his piano played as he liked it, and Miss Sarah won a storm of applause. What an addition an accomplishment is to a human life.

Roy spoke again: "Ladies and gentlemen, in the old convivial times, when they met together, each one was expected to do what he could to entertain the company. He might tell a story, sing a song, or treat the company. I will tell you a story. It is of 'The artist that lived at Capri.' It is a story that Virgil Williams told me. He knew the artist, and was with him a long time in Italy."

There was an English squire, rich, aristocratic, and with sons and daughters. The youngest son was inclined to art. His father wanted him to go into the army, the navy, or the church. He wanted neither. He would not be a soldier, he hated a sea life, and he had no call to the church. So he learned to paint from Nature. He kept studying until he was a fine artist, and could sell his pictures. He travelled in Scotland and Wales. Then he went up the Rhine. He worked in Switzerland,

making sketches and getting photographs and stereoscopics. Lastly he travelled the Cornische road, sketching faithfully until he came to Rome and Naples. He
painted in both cities. He met his fate in a beautiful
Italian girl. He was a handsome fellow, and the usual
result followed. They were married. He sold many
pictures, and made money. Then he took his wife and
went to England. He arrived in the afternoon at his
father's house. He introduced his wife to his father and
mother. His wife was well dressed, virtuous, honorable,
and very handsome. He took supper with the family,
and stayed all night. He breakfasted with the family.
After breakfast his father asked him to go into the garden
with him. They went, but did not go far.

Said his father, " I do not want that woman here.   I
want you to take her away to-day.   If you go to Australia,
I will allow you one hundred pounds a year; or you may go
to India, and I will allow you one hundred pounds a year;
or you may go and live on one of the islands up the Mediterranean, and I will allow you a hundred pounds a year;
either of these three, and a hundred a year; or you may
go to the devil and have nothing.   But I want you to
leave here to-day, leave England soon, and take that
woman away from here at once.   Now which will
you do?"

He answered, " I will live on one of the islands in the
Mediterranean."   It was a savage piece of business; but
" it is English, you know."

He left his home that forenoon, went to London, Paris,
Geneva, Rome, Naples. He took his time about it.
After looking about him well, and consulting his wife, for
she was prudent as well as handsome, and she had no

notion of losing five hundred dollars a year when she could get it from the people who had used her so mean: he bought, for a small sum, a nice house on the island of Capri. He enlarged it, and made a villa of it, with gardens around it. It is in a high and beautiful place, with the most splendid views of Vesuvius, the coast, and the sea. Virgil Williams stayed at his home and painted with him. Everything is cheap at Capri, and he lived like a nabob. His wife was as handsome as ever, and much respected. Mr. Williams said the children of the blond Englishman and the brunette Italian were as beautiful as he ever saw. As he owned his own home, he could entertain the best of company, and sell his pictures before they were dry. He had boxes prepared, so he could enclose them before the paint was set. He had all the fine views of Vesuvius, Naples, Sorrento, and the coast. Every one who had any money at all, was glad to buy a souvenir of Capri and the artist. He also got orders from England.

> "And his bank account grew,
>   His good wife was true,
> His children were splendid, as ever you knew;
>   The climate was fine,
>   The scenery divine,
> His garden with sweetest of flowers did shine;
>   He lived happy and free,
>   And you never will see
> Such a joy as the artist that lived at Capri."

Roy made his best bow, and the general "stoop en tumble" of the whole thing pleased the company hugely. It was such a picture, so good a picture, and so many pictures. Alas! that we shall not see Virgil Williams, or hear his stories again here.

Roy announced a selection for the piano, by Miss Graham. It was a surprise and every way a success. It showed the finest taste and cultivation, and was well approved.

A gentleman told another story: — An artist was at work, when a knock announced visitors. Ladies came in. He showed them his pictures, and entertained his company. Above the line of paintings was a fine old engraving of the leaning tower of Pisa. One of the women looked at it critically. Ah, said she, Minot's light? Yes, marm, said the artist, as he turned away to hide his emotion. Another anecdote, also a fact, the author vouches for it. An artist was in a second-hand furniture store, looking at stray pictures. Among others was a colored chromo of the State Street massacre, with Crispus Attucks, just falling, shot, in the foreground. The owner said, buy that; it is cheap. It is true, too. The real thing. Real history. Corpus Christi was killed in State Street. This will be news to most folks. The artist was much affected by it.

The chairman called on Miss Graham for a song. After a short prelude she sang:

THE BIRD'S LOVE SONG.

"A bright bird of morning his love song was singing
To his mate, on their nest, in the leafy green spray;
And he poured forth his joy in such melody ringing,
That my soul answered back all his beautiful lay.
Oh, sing, happy birdie! Oh, beautiful birdie,
The echoes exultingly bear it along:
Oh, sing, happy birdie, Oh, beautiful birdie,
For love is the joy of your beautiful song.

"Then blest be your sweet home, and peaceful your slumbers,
Where love builds your nest in the leafy green tree ;
Let love be the joy that inspires your blest numbers,
And sing it, sweet birdie, Oh, sing it to me.
Oh, sing, happy birdie, Oh, beautiful birdie,
The echoes exultingly bear it along ;
Oh, sing, happy birdie, Oh, beautiful birdie,
For love is the joy of your beautiful song.

"Then love, pretty birdie, and tell your true story ;
And waft your sweet notes to the songsters above,
And mingle your songs with the angels in glory,
While heaven echoes back the sweet music of love.
Then sing, happy birdie, Oh, beautiful birdie,
The echoes exultingly bear it along ;
Oh, sing, happy birdie, Oh, beautiful birdie,
For love is the joy of your beautiful song."

Indeed, an English skylark could not have sung sweeter.
Miss Graham was rewarded as she should be.

After some select readings, Roy called for " Auld Lang
Syne."

Before it could be given, Mr. Cobb expressed his grati-
fication in a telling, witty speech, which took finely.

Roy said, "The notice of the Art Coterie will be posted
on my studio door. As there is a large delegation from
the Handel and Haydn society here, it follows that we
can sing. Miss Sarah Warren will please take the piano ;
Mr. Webb, the baton. Sing one double stanza, and repeat
if Mr. Webb orders it." They sang it gloriously. Miss
Warren put in a dainty interlude, and Webb led on.
When the full harmony of the glorious refrain, that
Jessie Brown heard at Lucknow, died away, there was
a clapping of a hundred pairs of hands, outside, in the
street. It was too much harmony to pass unnoticed.

The Art Coterie broke up, the young men and maidens paired off, and Mr. Bartlett was about to see if Miss Graham had company home, when Fred Annerly appeared at the door and asked for her. She came with another lady, older than herself. Roy was introduced to her. He saw their carriage near, and Fred Annerly acting as footman. He assisted them in, and the evening was done. The Warrens were well pleased, and so was every one. The next day, Roy had no end of congratulations. It was not long before he had more pupils. It never rains but it pours. Miss Graham received Roy's most hearty commendation. She seemed pleased. She was good help to him in teaching his pupils, and somehow she seemed to be a new white light in his life. But he did not suspect what it was.

CHAPTER XXI.

MARY GLANCE, whom I shall call by her maiden name, Mary Hoskins, lived quietly with her father and mother. The family were well, but kept mostly at home. Mr. Hoskins kept no help, so of course he could not do much farming. Mary's boy was near two years old. At first he was a thin, pale little fellow, and well he might be, for he was the child of fury and fear. But as he grew, and the disturbing prenatal influences lost their power in a mother's love, he grew stronger and handsomer. He was like his mother and her progenitors. Boys usually are. He clung to her mostly, going but little even to Mary's parents. His paternal grandmother came to see him and tried to pet him, but he did not take to dark complexions Little Walter was a good child and a comfort to his mother. Mr. and Mrs. Bartlett called often at the Hoskins farm, and when they were out, Sam Ellet managed to be at home, as major domo, and company for Canis Major and Grimalkin. But the Bartletts were in love with their home, and, as they had some company to come in occasionally, Sam had some time to make calls, and he used to neighbor with the Hoskins family. He pitied Mary for her sorrow, and the baby began to smile and play with Sam. About twice a week he was there, and the Hoskins family grew brighter under the sunshine of

Sam's visits. After supper and the chores were done, he remarked that he would take a walk over to neighbor Hoskins. When Sam came, the old folks chatted pleasantly a little while, but soon they went to bed. They always insisted that bed was the safest place, in spite of the ugly fact, that more people have died there, than anywhere else. Sam took the baby and frolicked with him. Mary sat and sewed or knit, or did nothing, but smile at the joy of baby and Sam. His visits became a necessity. Baby expected him. He laughed and made a break for Sam, as soon as he was inside the house. That which began in pity and sympathy, became a comfort and a healing. Although Sam was not conscious that he needed to be restored or sustained particularly, yet somehow the arrangement which had come spontaneously, was as much a blessing to him. If you paid no attention to other scripture, and remembered only that "pure religion and undefiled is, to, visit the widow and fatherless in their affliction, and keep yourself unspotted from the world," you would conclude that Sam Ellet was a very earnest Christian. There is a pile of joy in doing your duty, and, if you did but know it, it is very seldom that you have to go against the grain, at all. So Sam's happiness grew.

The path across the fields, that led from the Bartlett farm to the Hoskins farm, was well worn. They were good neighbors to each other. It was night again. After supper Sam said, I guess I will go over and have a sociable with the baby again. He was at home at once, they were so glad to see him. Mr. and Mrs. Hoskins were pleasant and glad to have him there. Mary had a gratified look as she resigned the boy to Sam. It was a pretty picture, that sitting-room, with the open fire-place, and the dancing light is very fine, if you do not need a steadier light, to read or work by.

" An' little fires shone all about the china on the dresser."

They told stories. They had some apples. Nice apples too. The old folks were simple unconscious folks. That is, maybe they were, and maybe they were still, quiet, long-headed people, content to let things go, if they went right, but to be counted on as a strong obstacle, if they went wrong.

" Short-handed, heavy-armed — a man that had been strong,
And might be dangerous still, if things went wrong."

At eight o'clock, Mr. Hoskins said, "Well, mother, I think I will disappear in a general way as Mark Twain's twin brother did."

Sam Ellet had read Sam Clemens's " Encounter with an Interviewer," and it pleased him to hear it applied so pat. Some New Hampshire farmers have a rich collection of dry jokes. A few minutes later, a little squeak or two told that farmer Hoskins had put himself in his little bed, in the corner bedroom.

Then mother Hoskins arose, went and bolted the back door, and said, " Now I guess I will go and see what has become of father."

It was a sweet bit of hypocrisy. There are some blessed little swindles in this world. Like the curl in a pig's tail, of no commercial value whatever, but, oh, so picturesque, and too sweet for anything. And when, after two little whacks, and a rustle or two, a squeak of the blessed old bedstead in the bedroom was faintly heard, then Sam looked with a sly smile at Mary, as if to

say: that is the most sensible thing they could possibly
do. Mary did not deny it. The baby was asleep. They
sat just easy distance apart, and in such a light as to see
each other to perfection. They talked of Roy and his
doings, of friends and neighbors, and Sam read some spicy
things he had cut from the papers. The hour was short
when the long clock in the corner, rang out nine, in its
silver chime. Sam said he must go. Don't hurry, said
Mary.

They walked to the front entry. The light was not so
strong as in the room, but they needed no hand-lamp.
They walked softly and slowly and Sam stopped in the
half-light, near the front door. He turned toward Mary,
and putting his hand on her rich dark brown hair, he
smoothed it down, as if in pity and sympathy for her
troubles, and he kissed her. She did not say him nay.
That one kiss put ideas in his mind. It was a kiss of
help and friendship. But his heart gave a jump and
demanded its rights for more. His heart ruled. He
put his left arm around her neck and with his right hand
under her chin, while she looked with great honest eyes
up into his face, and then he kissed her, for himself, and
for herself, and for love, and for luck, and for her father
and mother, and her distant relations, devotedly, raptur-
ously, gloriously. He kissed her for Christmas, Fourth
of July and Thanksgiving, and in a minute more he
would have kissed her for the world, the flesh, and the
De — claration of Independence, but she cried out, oh,
Sammy, don't, you hurt me. You don't want to bring
trouble to me, do you, Sammy. No, said Sam, I'd die
first. Then don't kiss me any more to-night. You have
been good to me, and the baby loves you. To-night,

was a saving clause, and Sam saw it. She opened the front door. Sam moved slowly out. Good-night, Sammy, come again. He could only say, good-night, Mary, I will come. It was all there was to say. He moved slowly through the front yard toward the road. The door slowly closed and Mary Hoskins went in, sat down in the big rocking-chair, and stretched her feet out to her full length, like one who stretches up after being long in one position; then with her lips pursed up she blew out her breath as forcibly as a boy, and said, softly, to herself, whew! what a siege. How Sammy did lose his head. Ha! ha! ha! she laughed — the demure little witch — Sam is a goner. He's gone. If I had made him eat a bushel of Turkish love powders, he could have had it no worse. Ha! ha! ha! That is a good one, and Sam is a daisy. Lucky I didn't lose my head though, she continued, in soliloquy, and then she added with a stern, set, severe face, and her fist doubled up as a woman always doubles it, with the thumb on the end of the four fingers, instead of in front of the middle finger, as a man does, and she shook her fist at some imaginary being in the air, and said sternly, and I won't lose my head, Sammy. I won't lose my head, Sammy. I have been a fool once, and that is enough. If I ever do marry again, it will be to some good, pure, true, clean, smart man, and it may be to you, Mr. Samuel Ellet, and she smiled very sweetly, as she spoke to the imaginary Sam. And she meant it. She was good enough for Sam Ellet or anybody else. She lay back in the rocking-chair, with her face wreathed in smiles, which played over her sweet face, in the flickering fire-light, like heat lightning. The clock struck again. She sprang up. My stars, it is eleven o'clock. Well, I don't care, Sam didn't stay until eleven o'clock, so people can't talk about me. But now I must go to bed. Wonder how Sammy is, I warrant he is not asleep. She hit it just right; a woman always does. Sometimes. Mary went to bed beside little Walter. But she had something in her mind, that kept her thoroughly wide awake, and she thought and smiled, and took long breaths occasionally, until the old clock chimed twelve, as sweetly, but not as sadly as it does at low twelve at the funeral of a master-Mason. Then she said to herself, now this won't do, I am going to sleep just as tight as I can. And she did. I find, when a woman says no, she means it, occasionally.

CHAPTER XXII.

THERE is an old and very witty problem, and it is this. "If an irresistible force comes in contact with an immovable body, what will the result be?" The question and answer are both full of wisdom, mixed with very refreshing lunacy. The wisdom is not so much in what you learn, as what you don't. The answer is just these four words: "the devil to pay." This describes the condition Sam Ellet was in, when Mary Hoskins said, good-night, Sammy, come again, so sweetly. He walked a few steps to the road, then he stopped, looked down a moment, sighed, like a cow that has just lain down, turned around, and looked at the house. It was not very dark or very light. There was a little of the old moon in the sky, and some light fleecy clouds. There was a light in the Hoskins window. He took two steps toward the house. He stopped again. He tried to find a reason for going back. · He could not find one; no, not one, or a sign of one. So he sighed again, looked east toward the Hoskins house, then west toward the Bartlett farm. The most of this deliberation was in the road. There were no teams passing, or he would surely have got run over. By a great effort he turned his back on Mary and went to the wall. He did not happen to hit the bars as usual, but he did not care. He could

163

straddle a wall, he could; and he did. He knocked
down some of the rocks and barked his shin. He was
over, anyway. He looked to see where he was, and
there was that big pair of bars within ten feet of him and
wide open. He laughed. It was very, very funny. I
don't care, said he, "The farthest way round is the nearest way home." This is a New Hampshire proverb. It
is awful good for folks who go wool-gathering. Sam
kept on a rod or two, and Mary Hoskins's face was so
plainly in his mind that he stopped to gaze at it. He
stopped for some time. He sighed, then shook himself
and went on. Again he stopped and looked back at the
light he had just left. He gazed hard at it and seemed
to see Mary Hoskins inside, sitting and thinking kindly,
safely, and prudently of him. He walked on. He
wanted to go to Mary, but his duty led him home to
Bartlett's. So, still keeping his mind's eye on Mary, he
unconsciously split the difference, and wandered off into
the field. He stopped once or twice, that he might gaze
the harder at Mary, in his mind. Then he slowly moved
onward by guess. It was a poor guess. He had not
gone far before he was over shoes in a mudhole. The
cold water gave his blood a start.

He took the back track in an instant, with "I declare,
here I am in the Hoskins mudhole. Well, well, I am
almost a fool. It is the only water within half a mile."
So he wiped his shoes on the grass, and then went
straight to the path which led to the getting-over place
in the corner. It was easy enough now; he could look
at Mary again. He did. He would just sit on the fence,
in the corner, and think big about Mary. Just as he got
into the dark corner, to step upon the fence, something

let out a blood-curdling yell, rushed by his legs with a great rattling of the bushes, and ran yelping away. He never knew what it was, but concluded it was some lost dog, and that he had not only disturbed his sleep, but had trod upon his tail. Sam was startled as much as the dog was. The course of his love did not run smooth a bit. So it must be true. Sam sat upon the fence, and gave his whole mind to Mary Hoskins. Probably she was running a battery at her end of the line. Then he descended from his roost, and dragging slowly his lengthening chain, he kept on to the Bartlett farm. He hugged Canis Major, and found some one to kiss him back. He stopped. Right there before him, he could see her with his eyes shut, was Mary Hoskins. The time passed on. Sam did not move far, and Canis Major wondered what had possessed Sam. Then he thought he would sit on the new board fence, and think sitting, taking it easy. He mounted it and began. He gazed in his mind at Mary, her eyes, her hair, and was conscious that he was sitting on a pain. It grew. Ah! Mary was very attractive. The fence was a mean seat, but he could stand it, I mean sit on it, to think of Mary Hoskins. Oh, good gracious! this fence; but Mary's sweet face, and her sweet invitation. Come again, of course I will. Oh, Great Scott, it is terrific! What in thunder am I sitting on? He jumped off and examined. It was a new, wany-edged board, as sharp as a knife. He had almost cut a gash a foot long. He rubbed the seat of war. He tried to straighten up, and by attending to himself exclusively, for a few minutes, he was able to see a light come into his mind. It was Mary Hoskins. Sam had outdone Mary. She was abed and asleep; but he had no more exposition of sleep than if he was having a tooth pulled. The small hours came on.

Sam took a big look at Mary, by faith, and went into the house. He took an allopathic dose of that element that killed so many in the great rain, and went up to bed. He straightened out and closed his eyes. A heavenly cloud came over him, and right in the centre of its celestial brightness was Mary Hoskins, looking ineffable sweetness at Sam Ellet. But, with a feather-bed under him, hot blood racing in his veins, and Mary Hoskins in his mind, he was soon hotter than a baked apple. He stood it as long as he could, then he rolled over to the cool side, to let it cool off. Then Mary came to the fore again, and in a few minutes he almost sizzled. He tried it cornerwise, but it began with hot spots in it, and ended by being hot all the way. He sat up awhile, and by shortening his interviews with Mary, he got asleep. Even then he went it all over again. First, he would walk out, worshipping Mary. Then he got in the Hoskins mudhole; then the old boy jumped out with a yelp, and ran off ki-yi-ing; then Mary beamed on him high up in the sky, much like the moon, much like Mary. She came nearer. The room, of course, grew lighter; she smiled; she looked Oh, so good! Oh, she was coming! Yes, she rushed into his arms, and was kissing him for all he was worth, an immense sum. He waked up. He was being kissed, but it was Canis Major. It was morning, and cow time. Sam had had a poor night. He got up; took a big drink of water; laved his red cheeks and hot hands; and went to milking.

Mr. Bartlett was already there. Sam sat down by Jerusha, and in an instant his mind was fired with Mary

Hoskins. Yes, dear Mary. Jerusha looked around to
see why he did not milk, if he was going to. Sam turned
away from Mary, and attended to Jerusha. Ting, ting,
ting ting, went the alternate streams of milk into the
pail, and soon Jerusha had yielded up her sweetness, like
a four-legged saint, as she was. Then he came to Dolly.
Dolly was a tall, proud young cow, that it was very hard
to convince that it was right for men to handle her. She
had been a queen in some previous state of existence.
She never allowed one to scratch her head. She had
learned that she must be milked, but she allowed no fool-
ing. This is a portrait: —Proud, airy, sleek, graceful,
lady-like, a bovine queen; she knew her rights, and was
one of the best of cows. Sam sat down by her side to
milk her, but sweet Mary Hoskins came into his mind,
and he sat still, and gazed at her. Dolly would not stand
it, and she up with her foot, and kicked him over. Sam
landed in the débris. He got sadly and slowly up, not
much hurt, but not so nice as he was. Poor Sam. He
was hard used.

Mr. Bartlett saw it all, for he knew what ailed Sam,
and being behind the cows, he laughed inside, as if he
would die. His old diaphragm jumped up and down, until he sweat. But he made no sound. He and his wife
had kept an eye on Sam all the time. Sam milked Dolly
and others, and the job was done. They went to breakfast. Mr. Bartlett helped Sam; but soon Sam's head
went forward, as if he was taking a big look at something. He was. It was Mary Hoskins. He ate something, but not much. He saw signs and wonders; had
visions without number; and right in the middle of every
one of them was Mary Hoskins. He forgot his pie.

Now, what condition can a Yankee be in, who can forget his pie ? He walked out. He stopped, and looked down. There was no flavor in anything but Mary Hoskins.

Those two old coots, Mr. and Mrs. Bartlett, watched him slyly, and were just ready to die with laughter. They knew how he felt, for they had had the same complaint. Sam worked a little between the visions. Nothing was right. His food did not interest him. His clothes did not fit him. Nothing ever would again but Mary Hoskins. Just before milking time, Sam straightened up, smote his right leg and said firmly, I'll do it, by thunder. He had been with Sam Weller. He got new strength from his decision, did his chores creditably, and ate a little supper. Then he shaved, put on his pretties, and went forth to meet the shadowy future, without fear and with a manly heart. The baby was glad to see him. Mary was handsomer than ever.

The old folks put themselves away in ordinary, very early. It was queer how much rest they did need.

Sam kept his vow. He began : " I have come over here to-night, to ask you to marry me. Will you, Mary ? "

" How about the baby, Sammy ? "

" I want him too."

" Do you truly, Sammy ? "

" Yes, I do. I will do my best for both of you as long as I live."

" Then I will, Sammy. But I'll ask father." She opened the bedroom door a little. " Father, are you awake ? "

" Yes."

" Father, Sammy wants to marry me."

"Well, why don't he?"

Sam smiled. So did Mary.

"Are you willing, father?"

"Yes, I am. Sam Ellet is good enough for you or any-body else."

Sam blossomed. He was happy.

"Are you willing, mother?"

"Yes, dear, and God bless you both."

Sam's happiness had come, and the old folks were not long behind it, for they got up, dressed themselves, and came out to talk it over.

Sam said he would try to hire a place or get Mr. Bartlett to suggest some way they could make a beginning, but Mr. Hoskins cut him short. "Why, Sam. Come and live with us. This farm needs you. I will give you your living and half or more of all we sell off. We can keep more stock and raise three times as much crops. Come at once, Sammy."

"I will if Mary is willing."

"You may," said Mary.

It was decided that the wedding should be on the second Sunday evening, at five o'clock. Sam was as quiet as a lamb. He told them that he should make the old farm shine. He did.

CHAPTER XXIII.

THE next morning Sam had a hard job to do. He had nearly finished his breakfast, and had scarcely known what he was eating, the subject in his mind had so occupied him. Then he told it. He began : " Uncle and Aunt Bartlett, I am sorry to say I must leave you. And it breaks me all up. You have been so kind and good to me. But I have been getting over head and ears in love with Mary Hoskins. It seemed the only thing to do. I have asked her to marry me, and she will. The old folks want me to live with them. They will give us a living and half that is sold from the farm. It is a good chance. There is no chance for any quarrel, for Mary is an only child. We are to be married a week from next Sunday evening, at five o'clock."

" Sam," said Mr. Bartlett, " you have done well. I knew what was coming. Mother and I have been laughing about it for a week. We are glad of your luck. It is a good job, well done. Mary will make you a good wife. She is about your age. Mr. and Mrs. Hoskins will both help you."

Said Mrs. Bartlett, " Yes, Sam. We rejoice with you. You don't need to say good-by, we shall see you so often. If you get hungry, Sammy, come over and get some of my cookies. Father," she continued, " what are we going to do for Sam ? "

"Oh, something nice, I guess. Suppose we give him Lady Fly."

Lady Fly was a beautiful half Jersey cow, kind and gentle, that loved to be petted, and was one of Sam's favorites. Mr. Bartlett said he was awful sorry to have Sam go, but the sorrow was all turned to joy, it was such a blessing to Sam. And again, the Hoskins farm joined the Bartlett farm, and Sam would be only over the fence, away.

A day later, Roy received this letter, —

DEAR ROY, — You will be surprised at the news I shall tell you. I am engaged to Mary Hoskins, and am going to be married a week from Sunday evening, at five o'clock. If you can come and see your friend off, I shall be glad to do as much for you. We shall live with Mr. and Mrs. Hoskins, and he wants me to make the farm shine, which I can easily do. It is a good home and a good situation. You know that I can save my money. I know it is young to be married at twenty-one, but it came to me so forcibly, that I thought it best. I shall be at the usual train on Saturday to see who is there.

Ever your friend,

SAMUEL ELLET.

Roy was not as much surprised as Sam thought, for he had heard from his mother. Roy remembered how Sam had saved him from Will Glance, and he went out and bought him a black walnut chamber set and also had a good-sized oil painting framed for him, for a wedding present. When he went home to the Warrens' that night, he told them the story of Sam's good fortune and the story of Will Glance, which interested them much. Before Roy went, the Misses Warren gave him a package, in trust for Sam, containing a quantity of silver spoons. Mr. Bartlett paid Sam all his wages, and on the Saturday before the day, Mr. Bartlett and his wife told Sam to stay in the kitchen and keep house, until they returned. This caused him some apprehension, as the diplomatic relations were becoming somewhat strained already. When, a little later, they came from the barn leading Lady Fly, with brass balls on her horns and the end of each horn decorated with a bow of white ribbon, then Sam's heart gave a big jump and danced Hi, Betty Martin, until the tears came in his eyes. They led Lady Fly over to the Hoskins farm, a good home for her and her descendants.

Saturday night brought Roy, sure enough, and Sam had already got his presents, which had been much admired at the Hoskins farm. When Roy greeted Sam with a cheery word and a hearty grasp, there was a toad in Sam's throat, that almost strangled him. He soon got his wind, and said he should have to get married often to get Roy home. That night Mary did not see Sam. The Bartletts had him. And every one had the same feeling, that, to take a poor, little, frail, half-nourished boy, too young to help himself, and no help but the God of the widow and the fatherless, and educate that boy fairly, make him healthy and strong, and grow a great, big, clean, white soul in him, loving and beloved, giving and hoping for nothing again, and have him turn out as well as Sam Ellet, was indeed a triumph for them all. Some people glorify everything they touch. They had their supper. Somehow they could not talk much, although they had a quiet evening together. The fact is, the whole family were feeling very mellow; and when, a little later, Mr. Bartlett read a psalm of thanksgiving, and prayed for them all by name, it seemed as if help must come of it.

The Hoskins family had a late breakfast, and a three o'clock dinner on Sunday. Mr. Hoskins had provided a huge wedding cake, so they could nibble that for supper. The Orthodox minister and his wife from Dover came up. The Bartletts were there, Mr. Hoskins's brother from Barrington, and some relatives, Elisha McDuffie and his wife, and Jean and his lady. There were no tears and no fears. All were glad of it. Mary and Sam were a handsome, well-mated couple as you often see. An hour later the guests departed, and Mr. and Mrs. Hoskins took little Walter and went to Barrington for a three-days visit, leaving Mr. and Mrs. Samuel Ellet to keep house as best they could, and investigate one of the problems that Solomon pretended he could never understand.

The whole thing had been a perfect success. It went up like a sky-rocket, like Dr. Marigold's entertainment.

The next day, Mr. Guy Bartlett brought home another boy, to see if he could stock him up with body and soul, victuals and drink, education and principles.

CHAPTER XXIV.

Roy was considered a rising artist. He kept his word, was especially faithful to his pupils, and he did not ruck or provoke his brother or sister artists with useless caustic` criticism. He was of the opinion that people learn more by the praise of beauty, than the condemnation of the want of it. And so am I. Roy had declined to take money from Miss Graham for lessons, she was so much help to him. This she would not consent to. Her uncle was allowed all he needed for family expenses, and her lessons were a part of it. They finally settled it by Miss Graham's proposition to take the studio with him, and pay half the rent. It was forty dollars a month; twenty for each. She was to get all the lessons she needed from him, and help teach his pupils for the practice it gave her. Inasmuch as the money came from a great estate, Roy consented, and Miss Graham had a studio of her own. The studio was not open evenings at all, Miss Graham never having been there, and Roy being so well situated for companionship, and with such easy chairs, papers, magazines, and Mrs. Warren's library, that he kept much at home. Roy was saving his money as much as possible to clear his real estate. He hoped to do it in a little over a year. He still had a good sum in the Dover Savings Bank, which he had never drawn upon. It was a favorite story with him about the Englishman

who wished to hire a coachman.   The Englishman advertised for a man suitable to drive his coach.   Three men
came.   He asked the first one how near he could drive
to a precipice, and do it safely.   He thought he could
drive within a foot.   He asked the second.   He thought
he could drive within six inches.   He asked the third,
a canny Scot, who answered, if I ever drive your coach,
I shall keep as far from a precipice as I can.   And the
Scot became the coachman.   It will do for a story.   But
all wisdom is not contained in one statement, scripture,
sermon, song, or sentiment any more than all beauty is
contained in one scene or picture.

The night for the meeting of the Art Coterie had
come.   The Warrens had often called at Roy's studio,
and of course had made the pleasant acquaintance of
Miss Graham.   They seemed to take to each other at
once.   When the Art Coterie was discussed, they seemed
to have a confidential understanding with Miss Graham,
which Roy felt was more than he ever possessed.

The studio door bore the name " R. Bartlett, Landscape Artist."   Underneath it, in smaller letters, " Miss
Graham."   For two days past the door had borne this
additional legend : " The Art Coterie will meet on Thursday evening, at the usual hour and place.   Per order."

If there is anything that has exerted a permanent
influence upon the human race, an influence that has
not yet entirely died out, it is curiosity.   You ought to
have seen the people stop and read that notice.   The
expression of their faces was, Wal, neow, wot in thunder
is that?   I do not say that any one in Boston ever said
such a thing, but I do say that all but the initiated went
off with an interrogation point in their minds, higher

than Bunker Hill monument. The eventful evening
came. When Miss Graham came Roy did not know.
Miss Emily said she was upstairs with Miss Sarah, and
was all right. The great double parlors and hall and all
available rooms were plum-full.

Roy took a prominent position, and began: "Ladies
and gentlemen, the Art Coterie has grown so fast that I
hardly recognized it. Remember, it is entirely informal,
and its entertainments are unique and entirely original.
I am happy to tell you that I have some one here with
me, but not in this room, where he can hear me, or he
would be too modest to allow me to say what I shall say.
The ladies have inveigled him away for a moment, so
that I can tell you about my friend, Doctor Alvah C.
Smith, whom I consider about the pleasantest, most
entertaining, and accomplished man and the best company that I ever knew. Of course he comes here to
entertain us only after much solicitation, for he is as
modest as he is accomplished. He is a regularly educated
physician, but he chose to teach. He has taught in the
grammar schools of Cambridgeport, for more than twenty-
five years. He is a fine scholar. He is teacher of the
guitar. He plays the organ and piano. He plays and
teaches the fife, flute, and piccolo. He can drum exqui-
sitely. He can make the old violin talk, and tell more of
the old hornpipes and queer old music than you ever
heard. He knows more

> " Quips and cranks and wanton wiles,
>   Nods and becks and wreathed smiles,"

than the whole of us, more jokes, problems, stories, and
songs than anybody. Don't any one dare to criticise it,

but give your whole mind to it, as Mark Twain did
to the interviewer. Banish dull care, lay right back and
smile when the time comes."

This was the keynote to enjoyment.

The Misses Warren escorted the doctor to the chair,
and Miss Emily said: "My friends, I now have the
pleasure of introducing my old and valued friend, Doctor
Smith, who has consented to entertain us this evening."

They cheered him so heartily that he saw some one had
been talking. He rose, bowed, and said: "If you are
disappointed in your entertainment, you can blame Mr.
Bartlett. He is a New Hampshire man, like myself. He
did it. Does any one happen to have a guitar in his
vest pocket?"

It came, having been tuned and put in order behind
the scenes. Without prelude he began to sing with the
guitar, "Happy are we to-night, boys," and a sweet interlude. Then the old-fashioned song, sung in old-fashioned
style, "Betsy Baker." They laughed. He played a military march. It was grand. How they listened. In an
instant the guitar changed to a wild fantasia on the flute,
which was slyly handed him by Miss Sarah Warren. It
was a beauty, and before they knew it, he was giving
them the interlude on the piccolo. He finished the interlude away up in the clouds somewhere. Then he sat
back and rested, smiling pleasantly, while the audience
made long continued and hearty acknowledgments.

The doctor said, "Excuse me, my friends, I'm dry."
He said it dryly. "I must have a glass of cider." He
held out an imaginary bottle in his right hand, and an
imaginary tumbler in his left. Then he made an imaginary pull on the cork, which came out with a loud pop.

He made believe spill some, and the imaginary cider gurgled loudly into the tumbler. He held it up, canted his head on one side, and looked at it smiling. Then, with wide open eyes, and the greatest gusto, with much noise about it, he took the imaginary long drink. He leaned back. He breathed out a huge, long breath, with Ah! h! h! and a strong blow, then saying, in a big voice, "That's good cider; give me another." It was done so hugely and ponderously, that they screamed with laughter. It was just fun. He called for the drum. It was brought. It had been previously and slyly put in order in the back cellar. It was loaded for bear. It was a fine drum, such as is used by a military drum-corps.

Miss Emily said, "Now, doctor, please wake us up with the drum; we shall all go to sleep."

He took the drumsticks. "Want to be waked up, eh?" He began a double-trouble fantasia on the drum, enough to split your ears. Then he changed, and if you never heard a first-class drummer drum, you can have no idea of the grace, rhythm, and expression of flim, flam, and flammadiddle, that he put into that blessed drum. All at once he stopped, as if scared, exclaiming, "Hark! the soldiers are coming." In an instant he whistled, making it sound afar off, but coming nearer, and louder, making it sound like fife and drum approaching, playing "The girl I left behind me." It was a fine illusion. The sound grew, until it was present, even passing the house, and feet were tramping the time, in simulated march. Then Roy clapped his hands to cheer the soldiers, while the Misses Warren waved their handkerchiefs to them, and the audience took the cue like fire. The doctor whistled and drummed furiously, and the tramp, the cheers, and Roy's command, "Shoulder arms!" liked to killed them. It was realistic beyond all reality. Then Roy and the Misses Warren, just as the uproar lulled a bit, waved their hands for hush; the soldiers passed on, the distance increased, the tramp grew fainter, the "Girl I left behind me" went farther off, the drum came down to a far-off sound, and all the imaginary pageant faded away.

The doctor called again. "Hark!" holding up his hand in command, when they were almost painfully still, he said in a low voice, and with a solemn face, my friends, a funeral is coming. It is a Lancer. Then the imaginary fife whistled Pleyel's Hymn, and the muffled drum came nearer, nearer, nearer. It was passing the house. Oh, the solemn muffled drum. They held their breaths and it had passed on, going farther, farther, farther away, until it died out in the distance. Two or three of the ladies really shed a few tears, like Job Trotter's latest effort, real water. Then, in an instant, when they were discovered, and laughed at, they laughed as hearty as anybody. "Oh, man, thou pendulum between a smile and a tear."

The doctor rested, and Miss Sarah Warren played a selection upon the piano. I need not say what her reception was. The violin came to the doctor. He gave selections from an opera, then changing to the old hornpipes and dances of fifty or a hundred years ago, he played ever so many pieces, better than you ever heard them. Said he, now I will make the baby cry. He did it. It was a dolorous howl but ridiculously natural. When the big baby had cried enough, the doctor told him to go to sleep; the imaginary baby said, "I can't help it," on the fiddle. Dr. Smith allowed the audience to call for old airs, and he knew them almost all. He played that old fiddle — the author owns it now — with a scamper of variations from the bridge to the nut. Roy called for an old song. It was perhaps never written before, and no one knows how old it is. The song is remembered entire by one who loves the doctor. It is given here, not from any literary merit, but as a specimen of the olden time, and as it was prettily and wittily sung by Dr. Smith. It is called,

"CASTLE OVER LYNN."

THE YOUNG MAN SINGS.

" Young man, are you going to Lynn,
    Castle over Lynn, castle lonely?
Give my love to the maid therein.
    Keedle oh, keedle oh, tally oh, tally oh,
    Castle over Lynn, castle lonely.

" Tell her to buy one yard of cloth,
    Castle over Lynn, castle lonely.
And tell her to make me a shirt thereof,
    Keedle oh, keedle oh, tally oh, tally oh,
    Castle over Lynn, castle lonely.

" Tell her to sew it up without any seam,
    Castle over Lynn, castle lonely,
And never to take one stitch therein,
    Keedle oh, keedle oh, tally oh. tally oh,
    Castle over Lynn, castle lonely.

" Tell her to wash it out in a dry well,   ·
    Castle over Lynn, castle lonely,
Where water never sprung and rain never fell,
    Keedle oh, keedle oh, tally oh, tally oh,
    Castle over Lynn, castle lonely.

"Tell her to hang it out on a dry thorn,
  Castle over Lynn, castle lonely,
That never bore a leaf since Adam was born, -
    Keedle oh, keedle oh, tally oh, tally oh,
    Castle over Lynn, castle lonely.

"Tell her when she will the shirt provide,
  Castle over Lynn, castle lonely,
To bring it up to me and she shall be my bride,
    Keedle oh, keedle oh, tally oh, tally oh,
    Castle over Lynn, castle lonely."

THEN THE MAID SINGS.

"Young man, are you going to Cape Ann,
  Castle over Lynn, castle lonely?
Then give my love to that same young man,
    Keedle oh, keedle oh, tally oh, tally oh,
    Castle over Lynn, castle lonely.

"Tell him to buy an acre of land,
  Castle over Lynn, castle lonely,
Between the salt water and the sea sand,
    Keedle oh, keedle oh, tally oh, tally oh,
    Castle over Lynn, castle lonely.

"Tell him to plough it with a hog's horn,
  Castle over Lynn, castle lonely,
And sow it all down with one peppercorn,
    Keedle oh, keedle oh, tally oh, tally oh,
    Castle over Lynn, castle lonely.

"Tell him to reap it with one penknife,
  Castle over Lynn, castle lonely,
And cart it all in with two little mice,
    Keedle oh, keedle oh, tally oh, tally oh,
    Castle over Lynn, castle lonely.

"Tell him to thrash it out with a goose-quill,
  Castle over Lynn, castle lonely,
And winnow it up into one egg-shell,

Keedle oh, keedle oh, tally oh, tally oh,
Castle over Lynn, castle lonely.

" Tell him when he has done his work,
Castle over Lynn, castle lonely,
To bring it up to me, and he shall have his shirt
Keedle oh, keedle oh, tally oh, tally oh,
Castle over Lynn, castle lonely."

The oddity of the old song pleased them. The doctor
got it when he was a boy. Miss Emily handed him the
fife while Miss Sarah had the drum at her side in real
military fashion, ready to mark time. The doctor said,
Soldiers, our company is full and we are ordered to the
war. Massachusetts expects every man to do his duty.
Forward! March! It was Yankee Doodle, played as
few have ever heard it, with the step kept by the doctor,
the Misses Warren, and Roy. Miss Sarah had practised
slyly on the drum and surprised them all. The audience
caught on, and they all marched triumphantly off to the
war, almost. Then the doctor practised a few capers and
quaint old tunes, coming back to " The girl I left behind
me." He next sang a song, accompanying himself on
his " bay window," his capacious vest. It was witty in
word, funny in conceit, and jolly, musical, and rhythmi-
cal all through. The " rocket cheer " was called for.
Roy said some knew it, and all would after one trial.
Nobody ever forgets it. There was a low clapping of
hands. The doctor made a racket, cried out, look out!
and began a terrible hissing of the rocket going up. It
grew fainter away up in the sky, for the doctor was a fine
ventriloquist. Then it burst in the air and at the sight
of imaginary stars they breathed out Oo! Oo! Oo! Then
the second far-off explosion came, with imaginary scr-

pents in the air, and all Boston Common breathed out Ah, h, h, h. Then clapping again. They all knew it now. They tried it again and again, and it was done. The responses came in a voice of thunder. Nor was it confined to the house, for the crowd outside prolonged the cheering vociferously. Then the drum rolled again smartly, and Forward! March! in a field-officer style and the whole audience tramped the time through Yankee Doodle.

Said the doctor, " Mrs. Warren, what do you keep that dog shut up, barking all the evening, for?"

They had not heard it before, but now they did. There it was in a room not far off. Bow, bow, bow. He barked louder. It was another of the doctor's illusions. He called, Rats! and a rat squeaked. The women shrieked and jumped, showing signs of standing on chairs, holding their dress about their feet. Soon they laughed. Sold again.

Said the doctor, " The last selection which these friends have called for is, 'Old King Coyne.'" Now this piece is full of acting. When he spoke of a thing he acted it. It was a real play on an imaginary fiddle or a real beat of an imaginary drum, on his "bay window." He imitated every motion. So this was a busy piece to sing. When the women yowl out in the last stanza, it scares them dreadfully, and they all hurry through most comically. Words can hardly reproduce it. Here is the text: —

"OLD KING COYNE.

"Old King Coyne he called for his wine,
  And he called for his fiddlers three;
  And every fiddler could fiddle well,
  For a very fine fiddle had he.

'Twas a Yankee doodle tweedle, said the fiddler.
O ne'er was a maid in old Scotland
Could play such tunes as these.

" Old King Coyne he called for his wine,
And he called for his drummers three;
And every drummer could drum well,
For a very fine drum had he.
'Twas a rubadub dub, said the drummer,
And a Yankee doodle tweedle, said the fiddler.
O ne'er was a maid in old Scotland
Could play such tunes as these.

" Old King Coyne he called for his wine,
And he called for his fifers three;
And every fifer could fife well,
For a very fine fife had he.
'Twas a rootle tootle tootle, said the fifers,
And a rubadub dub, said the drummer,
And a Yankee doodle tweedle, said the fiddler.
O ne'er was a maid in old Scotland
Could play such tunes as these.

" Old King Coyne he called for his wine,
And he called for his harpers three;
And every harper could harp well,
For a very fine harp had he.
'Twas a plim plim plim, said the harper,
And a rootle tootle tootle, said the fifer,
And a rubadub dub, said the drummer,
And a Yankee doodle tweedle, said the fiddler.
O ne'er was a maid in old Scotland
Could play such tunes as these.

" Old King Coyne he called for his wine,
And he called for his barbers three;
And every barber could shave well,
For a very fine razor had he.
'Twas a hold away your snout, said the barber,
And a plim plim plim, said the harper,

And a rootle tootle tootle, said the fifer,
And a rubadub dub, said the drummer,
And a Yankee doodle tweedle, said the fiddler.
O ne'er was a maid in old Scotland
Could play such tunes as these.

" Old King Coyne he called for his wine,
  And he called for his farmers three ;
  And every farmer could team well,
  For a very fine team had he.
  'Twas Iiish ! Haw buck, ye divil, said the farmer,
  And a hold away your snout, said the barber,
  And a plim plim plim, said the harper,
  And a rootle tootle tootle, said the fifer,
  And a rubadub dub, said the drummer,
  And a Yankee doodle tweedle, said the fiddler.
  O ne'er was a maid in old Scotland
  Could play such tunes as these.

" Old King Coyne he called for his wine,
  And he called for his ministers three ;
  And every minister could pray well,
  For a very fine prayer had he.
  'Twas a Lord 'a' massy on us, said the ministers,
  And Iiish ! Haw buck, ye divil, said the farmer,
  And a hold away your snout, said the barber,
  And a plim plim plim, said the harper,
  And a rootle tootle tootle, said the fifer,
  And a rubadub dub, said the drummer,
  And a Yankee doodle tweedle, said the fiddler.
  O ne'er was a maid in old Scotland
  Could play such tunes as these.

" Old King Coyne he called for his wine,
  And he called for his sailors three ;
  And every sailor could swear well,
  For a very fine oath had he.
  'Twas, O blame your eyes, said the sailor,
  O Lord 'a' massy on us, said the ministers,

And Ilish! Haw buck, ye divil, said the farmer,
And a hold away your snout, said the barber,
And a plim plim plim, said the harper,
And a rootle tootle tootle, said the fifer,
And a rubadub dub, said the drummer,
And a Yankee doodle tweedle, said the fiddler.
O ne'er was a maid in old Scotland
Could play such tunes as these.

"Old King Coyne he called for his wine,
And he called for his women three ;
And every woman could scold well,
For a very fine clack had she.
'Twas Yaah! yaah! yaah! said the women (this scares
them all),
O blame your eyes, said the sailors,
O Lord 'a' massy on us, said the ministers,
O Ilish! Haw buck, ye divil, said the farmer,
And a hold away your snout, said the barber,
And a plim plim plim, said the harper,
And a rootle tootle tootle, said the fifers,
And a rubadub dub, said the drummer,
And a Yankee doodle tweedle, said the fiddler.
O ne'er was a maid in old Scotland
Could play such tunes as these."

The clack of the women had scared them ridiculously. His imitations were very funny. There was one old fellow there that no one ever had known to laugh. But he let out a Haw! Haw! Haw! that caught like an epidemic. The Coterie had heard the oddest, queerest entertainment in life. I cannot begin to do it justice, on paper. Many who read this, will begin and read with a smile, which will cloud up to tears, and they will end at Dr. Smith's grave, in the cemetery at Reading, Mass. It is a break to put it in here.

The doctor said at the close, "I thank you, friends. I

have never had an audience who were more in sympathy with me. A little fun is good. The rocket cheer, the way you do it, is grand.   If anybody says that artists are not sympathetic and appreciative, I shall go for them." He bowed. Roy called for a vote of thanks. It was given with a will. Now, Miss Sarah Warren, please take the piano, and we will sing —

> " Over the mountain wave,
>   See where they come ! "

Copies were furnished: the simple song was grandly sung. There were many fine singers present, some from several choirs, well known in Boston, and as the last notes died away, there came to each a feeling, O how much comfort there is in common accomplishments, when so magnificently done.   Theodore Parker once said, " You strike flint and steel together, and you get fire. You strike two pieces of ice together, and you get nothing but cold splinters."

CHAPTER XXV.

Roy sat in his studio and thought over the situation. He thought whether he ought to be satisfied with his progress as an artist, or not. He had not really gained a large sum in three years or more, beside all his previous study in art. Still, by taking his real estate venture into the account, with some other sources of advantage, he had done well. He had about a thousand dollars in the Dover Savings Bank and had not drawn a dollar. He felt that to be an anchor of safety, if he should break a leg, or get a snowslide that smashed him down, or get an acute sickness, or get sued, or see a sure chance to make a pile at a small risk, when he might need a few hundred dollars in a hurry. Oh, he was cautious, Roy was. Tom, Dick and Harry did not know that he had means. So he was not teased to death, to cast it into the bottomless pit, by lending it to irresponsible persons. His parents knew all about it, and all his affairs. Miss Graham knew some, and Roy knew her to be prudent and safe. His pupils were many and good pay. Yes, he was satisfied with what he had done and he wanted to do more.

Miss Graham painted well. Not quite as well as he, but too well to have any need of paying him for lessons. She was gaining all the time. So was he. Hardly a week passed that one of them did not take one or two

188

lessons from some fine artist in Boston. They learned what colors were safe, what were changeable, what would fade, and what were solid and permanent. There is a great deal of treacherous color for sale. Sometimes it was a lesson from Mr. S. L. Gerry, or Mr. Benjamin Champney, or Mr. A. T. Bricher, or Mr. J. M. Stone, or Mr. J. W. A. Scott, or Mr. J. J. Enneking, or Mr. C. F. Pierce in cattle or sheep, or Mr. E. L. Custer in portrait. As they always paid cash, and did as they would be done by, in criticism, they were welcome everywhere. I know of no place where the golden rule is so much needed as in art criticism. It was good medicine for Roy that Miss Graham was there. Although he was awake, yet he had to keep his eyes open tight, or like many a boy in a spelling class, he would have had the chagrin of seeing a little woman walk right in ahead of him. He had no idea of that, so he kept gaining, often producing a picture that was a surprise to himself and to her.

I said he was sitting, thinking. When a wide-awake Yankee sits squarely down and makes a business of thinking, something ought to come of it. He spoke. "Miss Graham," said he, "I have quite a lot of pictures on hand. They gain on me. What luck ought I to have, if I sell my pictures at auction?"

Miss Graham thought a moment and replied, "You ought to have good success. But I cannot advise you, whether you will or not. I will help you all I can. It may amount to something, or not."

Roy said he would look it up, and he thought he would have the sale, and risk it.

He reported the process to Miss Graham, step by step. He laid out fifty pictures, from six by eight inches in size, to one pair thirty by fifty. McLondon's commission was eleven per cent. Roy would have to frame them all and the pictures would have to be sold with the frames. Roy would have the bill for the advertising and catalogue to pay. McLondon wrote the advertisements, and for several days, they were in half a dozen papers. The pictures were hung and on exhibition four days. The sale was to be on Thursday, at two o'clock. The number that examined the collection was good. Some of Roy's pupils were in to look, and they reported that the criticism was kindly.

The pictures seemed to be well liked, and several people were there who seemed to be looking to buy. Some of them had taken the names and numbers on cards and slips. It looked rather favorable. More than this, some one had caused to be inserted in the *Transcript*, a notice containing one very mild criticism, and considerable honest, judicious praise of this artist's work, and of this sale especially. Roy wondered who had paid for it. It must have been paid for. He asked the Warrens, and they said squarely they did not know. He asked Miss Graham but she said she could not help him any. He thought it might be Gardner Brewer or S. R. Knights, but he did not find out that it was. He reckoned that if he could only realize ten dollars each on fifty pictures, that would be five hundred dollars and he ought to do that above all expenses. Why! There were two that ought to bring a hundred each with the frame, easily. There were twenty that might bring fifty each. It looked sure every way. He expected but little and it might be a bonanza. Roy had cleaned and varnished every picture that needed it, and Miss Graham had helped splendidly. She was one

of those faithful souls that follow out the wisdom of
Charles Dickens's speech, which he made at a visit to a
school, at his last visit to the United States. "Boys, do
all the good you can, and make no fuss about it." It is
Bible boiled down to a diamond solid. Roy's pictures
were well framed. He had about a dozen on hand in the
studio. The remainder he had made to order. They
were all good gold frames, though some of them were not
very heavy. He got them of a frame-maker, and at a
satisfactory rate. The day of sale came. McLondon
sold furniture in a part of the large auction rooms, until
two o'clock, the hour of the picture sale. Still he kept
on selling furniture. There was quite a crowd present.
At ten minutes past two some one asked the auctioneer,
"When do you sell the pictures?" Very soon, he said.
Here is a small lot of furniture to be closed out, and then
come the pictures. He kept on selling furniture. Roy
was conscious of being defrauded. Twenty minutes
passed. Some began to leave. The public is an animal
that won't bear being fooled with. Whoever tries it
is apt to find out their mistake. Still selling furniture at
half past two. Strangers shot angry glances at McLondon. At a quarter of three he desisted and announced:
"And now, ladies and gentlemen, we sell the pictures."
Half the audience were gone. Others felt that it would
be spiting the auctioneer not to bid at all, and they did
not bid. The pictures went low, often less than the price
of the frames. Roy was present at the sale. There was
to be no limit on anything whatever. Miss Graham was
there also. She was pale and without a smile. As soon
as she saw the pictures begin to sell below the price of
the frames, she began to bid. She knew the value of

every frame. If a frame was not a new one she allowed
it to go for less. Roy took his punishment like a man.
There were not over fifty people present, and three or
four of these were Irish second-hand furniture dealers,
who only bought at half the price of the frames. The
sale went on. Miss Graham had bought eight pictures.
The second-hand dealers looked hard at her. Thirty pictures had been sold. Said McLondon to Miss Graham,
" Lady, are you bidding in pictures for Mr. Bartlett ? "
" No, sir, indeed I am not. I am buying these pictures
to sell again. I can easily get five times what I pay for
them. The money is all ready to pay for them, sir, as
soon as the sale is done."

The sale went on at about the price of the frames.
Miss Graham bought in all, twenty pictures. The frames
were all new, the most tasty patterns, and in most cases
the pictures were Roy's most careful studies. The two
that were thirty by fifty inches, came to Miss Graham, at
twelve and fourteen dollars each. Her bill was two hundred dollars. It was less than the cost of the frames.
Bad as the sale was, she had saved him a hundred dollars. She went not to the studio again that day. Just
at night, a furniture team from the West bay came to
McLondon's auction room, called for Miss Graham's bill,
paid the two hundred dollars, and took the pictures.
The frames had been hard used. One of the smaller
pictures had a long scratch across it. One had a corner
dented into it, that made a dimple enough to spoil it,
and one of the thirty by fifty sizes had a slit in it six
inches long. The whole thing was enough to make
angels weep, and Satan tear his hair. The pictures all
went, and well they might at the price.

Roy called at the counting-room. Melowney, McLondon's clerk, told him to call next Thursday morning, and he would get his money. It took about a week to make up the account. At any rate, it is good to give a victim a week to let his expectations evaporate, and bring him into a more receptive condition, and glad to get anything whatever. Reader, I am writing a realistic novel. The fact is, that this is just as it happened, and is real, with no "istic" or novel about it. I have seen it worse than I have written it. I know just what I am talking about. I know just as true, kind, honest auctioneers, as good men as are in the world, and most useful. And I have met some that the devil would blush to own as an acquaintance. I have known an artist take many thousand dollars for a two-days sale of pictures, fifty pictures each day. I have known a fair artist have far worse usage than Roy Bartlett, both in the management and the result.

The next day Roy was in his studio on time. He was, if anything, a little better dressed, a little handsomer, quite as smiling, and, what he did not often do except on coterie night or festive occasions, he had a bouquet on his coat, carnation pinks. He was a daisy. He might have been a lady-killer, but the fact that he presides in this book, is assurance that he was not.

Miss Graham came at nine. She was just her own pleasant, smiling, sweet self, or perhaps a shaving more so. I can say no better than that. It is the superlative degree before they develop wings. They were glad to see each other again. The time since yesterday seemed long. They were glad it was over. Now for work.

Said Roy, "Miss Graham, I wish to go out to make a

call. I shall be gone only a few minutes. If pupils come in, please to look out for them until I return."

He went out. He called upon a young lawyer in School Street, a Mr. Edric Lyman, whom he had known in Dover. Roy stated the facts concerning the sale, and all about it. He asked if he had any remedy. The lawyer thought a moment, and answered. You had better not consider whether you need a remedy, or not, until you get a settlement with McLondon. Don't sign a receipt in full of all demands. But I do not think McLondon will offer you one. He will offer you a statement of the result, with a balance due you which you can sign a receipt for. When you get your money, call again.

Roy went to work. Pupils were well cared for, and good results came from that forenoon's work. Miss Graham had a little lunch with her, and took it quietly in her corner. Roy went out to lunch.

While he was gone, a man came in and asked permission to see the pictures. Miss Graham said Mr. Bartlett had none done. She had a few. She showed them. One was a good landscape. He asked the price. She had done her best on it. She would sell it for twenty dollars. He handed her a new twenty-dollar bill, took the picture, would not have it done up, and went away.

Another knock on the door. Miss Graham answered it. A man inquired for Mr. Bartlett, the man that paints picters. He was gone out, but would be in again soon. Be you his wife? Miss Graham's face fairly blazed, she blushed so. But she answered with dignity, No, sir. He is no relation of mine whatever. I am his pupil. I beg your pardon, marm, I meant no offence.

Just then Mr. Bartlett came in and saw the man, and Miss Graham went to her easel.

He said, " I bought one of them picters of yourn. My wife used to paint some before we were married, an' she wants a mate to the one I bought. It is twenty by thirty. I'm a teamster. I dunno nothin' about picters, but I like 'em well enough, and I can afford one or two for such a woman as mine. Will you paint a mate to it, same size, some subject suitable for a mate to it ? "

" Yes," said Roy.

" When'll ye have it done ? "

" In two weeks."

" All right. Same price as the other, of course ? "

Said Roy, " What was that ? "

" Ten dollars."

" Not by considerable. The frame cost fifteen."

" Wal, that's queer," said the teamster. " Pooty queer for a man to have two prices for his pictures."

Said Roy, " Those pictures were put in that auction room with the expectation that they would realize from four to eight times as much as they brought. It was your luck to get one. But I do not believe that you will ever, in your life, get a picture of mine, which I can easily sell for thirty dollars, and a frame which I paid fifteen for, — forty-five dollars in all, — for ten dollars. I will give you twenty dollars for your picture and frame."

The man reflected a moment, then said, " Wal, it is so, come to look at it, ain't it ? Then you must have lost some money yesterday."

" I did," said Roy.

" Wal, it is too bad. I'm sorry. What would ye charge for a good mate to the one I had ? "

Said Roy, "I can get the frame made for you at cost, fifteen dollars, as it is not a very heavy one. I will paint you the picture for thirty more, and give you a good mate for yours. Don't do it if you do not want to, or if you cannot afford it."

Said the man, "Wal, now, I shall jest do it. Here's my card. Please have the picter and frame ready in two weeks from to-day. An' say, you must need money. I vow, here's yer forty-five dollars. Now give me a good one." Then, turning to Miss Graham, he said, "Lady, I hope you won't notice my rough ways. I don't mean to be rough to any of God's creaturs, leastways to a woman."

"You are very kind," said Miss Graham.

He was gone.

"Thank God for a man!" said Roy.

"Amen!" said Miss Graham, smiling.

The teamster got his picture, and it suited him and his wife. It was not the last that he bought for himself, or sold for Roy either. "Luck for both of us," said Miss Graham.

"What?" he asked.

Then she showed her twenty-dollar bill, and told of the sale she had made. It was Roy's turn to be pleased.

"Now," said Roy, "it is my turn to talk to you. You saved me money on my sale, or give-away, as McLondon managed it. You paid two hundred dollars in cash, for pictures and frames. I will take them all of you, and pay you the cash, if you will allow me to. You must have borrowed the money to pay for them, and it must make you cruelly short. Shall I send for them?"

She answered: "You need not worry at all about

my being short of money, for I have something from my uncle every month. I have sold pictures for good prices, and I had the money to pay for all I bought. You can take any one, any time you can sell it, and return just what it cost me, and no more. But had you not better select the best subjects, paint slowly and carefully some new pictures, and let the old ones go by? I am willing to keep them. I want some of them to hang in the house. My uncle will charge them to the estate, and I shall be paid for them at a profit."

Roy concluded to let them remain. He also concluded that Miss Graham had the best of common-sense, was a good manager, and would always do the best that could be done.

He got his account of the sale from McLondon. It was thus : —

50 pictures sold on account of R. Bartlett. .		500.20
Advertising, per bills	49.90	
Commission, 11 per cent.	55.02	
200 fancy linen catalogues	65.28	
	170.20	170.20
Cash paid R. Bartlett		330.00

Roy signed a receipt to that statement, took his check and a copy of the statement to Edric Lyman's office, in School Street. The lawyer looked hard at it, but did not keep Roy waiting, to show his own importance, the intricacy of the case, or the general ponderosity of the law. He took a little time to consider it, and went into it, like a sharp, wide-awake New Hampshire Yankee, as he was.

He spoke : "Mr. Bartlett, you have been used badly.

Swindled outrageously. Still an auction sale of pictures is a chance for an accident. But your sale was put off three quarters of an hour, until your audience, that you had paid heavily for, had largely gone, and the remainder nettled, and made cross, so they would not buy. You ought to have substantial damages, but you cannot get them. I have had an experience with McLondon before. He is slippery. You cannot hold him. He has no real estate. His wife has. She has a bank account. You cannot even tell him your opinion of him. It is a right-eous opinion. He would sue you. He might collect. You have real estate. I read the deed in the registry. You can collect nothing in my opinion. I will give you Peter Parley's prescription for the gout, ' Grin and bear it.' I am sorry I cannot be of real comfort and redress to you, for I know you have been swindled. Hereafter take care and look out who you deal with."

Roy took out his pocket-book. "How much is to pay, sir?"

"Nothing whatever. You have paid too much, now. When you want advice call in. If it is legal advice that saves or collects money or value for you, I will make a moderate charge for it. Otherwise make me a social call, ask me any questions on law or anything else and I shall be glad to answer free. That is the way I do busi-ness, and make friends and money. If you see any one wronged or robbed of their just rights, send them to me, and I will make the best fight I can for them, whether I get paid or not."

Roy thanked him, and said he would do it. He did, faithfully. He went back and told the story to Miss Graham.

She said, "It seems to me you have met another whole-souled man."

"Yes," said Roy, "he is. Thank God for an honest lawyer."

Miss Graham took his name and address for possible future use.

Roy had his figures now. His frames for his fifty pictures, including a fair valuation on some not quite new, made the amount just six hundred dollars. He received from McLondon just three hundred and thirty. So he had sunk just two hundred and seventy dollars in cash and given away fifty pictures for nothing. He was at least a thousand dollars out. Miss Graham asked if he had money to provide for it. She had disposed of some of those she had bought and he could have a hundred dollars as well as not. She should not use it. He said no. He was greatly obliged, but could get along, and by industry should soon get over his loss, while the experience was worth money to him. He never should forget it.

The next morning two new pupils came, both ladies. They paid for twelve lessons in advance. Miss Graham chanced to know them. She knew them to be suitable people, and they at once received their invitation to the Art Coterie. It was partly what they came for. There were eight pupils at work in the studio beside Miss Graham and Roy. There was a knock on the door. Roy opened it. A well dressed man of medium height was there. He had on a nice silk hat, plenty of jewelry, and the general air of a man of substance. He spoke loudly. "I want to see Bartlett, that sold the calamity pictures at McLondon's."

Roy answered, "I am Mr. Bartlett."

"Well, sir, I bought a picture there for an oil painting. It was on your catalogue as an oil painting, number fifteen. It is no oil painting at all, sir, only a cheap chromo. I consider you a fraud, a swindler, and a scoundrel." He raised his voice high and loud so that all Roy's pupils heard him, and many others in the building. Roy was angry. He was strongly tempted to smash his face, and he could have done it, and not much harm come of it, but the Bartlett brains prevailed, and he did not. "Where is your picture, sir?" "At my house. It is a chromo. My wife says it is, and she has painted some. She knows it."

Says Roy, "Now please give me your address. I will send a messenger to your house and if you have suffered any wrong or loss by me, I will make it good."

The man gave his name and habitation.

"Where is your place of business, sir? If it is nearer than your home on Columbus Avenue, I can send you word there."

He reflected a moment, and then gave Roy his place of business. It was a firm well situated and doing well. Roy stepped inside the studio again. He said to the ladies present: "Ladies, there is not the slightest ground for this outrage. Miss Graham will remember number fifteen on my catalogue. He bought it for less than the price of the frame. Of course no artist in Boston or elsewhere ever sells a chromo for an oil painting. Miss Graham, will you please write in ink, the date, the hour of the day, the names of the pupils present, with their addresses, and keep it as your property. I may need it."

Then Roy went out, and called on Lawyer Lyman

again. He was in. Roy told his story and the lawyer laughed heartily. He said, "If folks did not make fools of themselves, what would we poor lawyers do!" Roy could not come to laugh at it yet. He was too much provoked.

"Seriously, Mr. Bartlett, I do not think you can collect much, if anything from him, for calling you names, unless you can prove that you have sustained real loss therefrom. Now if you can prove that your pupils left you, or other real loss came to you, then you can force him to pay. But I guess I can get you some satisfaction if I do not get you much money. Mr. Bartlett, where do you get your artist's materials?"

"At F. C. Hastings & Co.'s sometimes, and sometimes at C. J. Edmands's."

Lawyer Lyman took the man's address and would report to Roy. He got one of the clerks from the artist's materials store to go with him at once to the man's house, in Columbus Avenue. The wife was at home. The picture was shown. It was taken from the frame. The clerk looked at it and smiled. Said he, "This is a Winsor and Newton canvas. I covered it myself. The picture is signed by Roy Bartlett. It is a beautiful dainty signature. It is not a chromo. It is a fine oil painting, worth about twenty-five dollars or more. The frame must have cost eight or ten."

The lawyer held the picture up to the light, saying, "See, lady, see the brush marks. See the linen canvas. See the store mark on the stretcher, are you satisfied?"

"Yes, I am. But it looked so smooth and shiny, I thought it was too good to be an oil painting. I am sorry, I declare."

"Yes," said Lawyer Lyman, "it is very bad. I will give fifteen dollars for what he bought for six. It is a view in Dover, New Hampshire. I know the place. And your husband went to that large building, and before many witnesses, and in the presence of several ladies who live in and about Commonwealth Avenue, he in a very loud voice denounced the artist as a fraud, a swindler, and a scoundrel. I have long known this artist as a gentleman, the soul of honor, incapable of a wrong act. Now here is my card. I am Mr. Bartlett's lawyer. If your husband comes to my office before ten o'clock to-morrow morning, he can settle. Mr. Bartlett does not propose to submit to such an outrage. If he does not come I am ordered to bring a suit at once, and the whole outrage will be in the newspapers. There are twenty or more witnesses. That is all. He cannot afford to let such awful blunders as that go before a jury."

The woman was pale and trembling. She had been the cause of it. The lawyer went back to his office. He asked the clerk to remain on the corner, in a store, a few minutes, and see if a woman left the house. He got back to Lyman's office almost as soon as he did, and reported that the woman went out. In a little over an hour the man came in to the lawyer's office, looking rather sober. He began, "You were at my house about that chromo, er, oil painting I mean."

"Yes, sir, I was. Take a seat, sir. That chromo is a fine, carefully studied oil painting, a view in Dover, near Mr. Bartlett's homestead. The Bartletts are a high-toned, wealthy family, with a great deal of pride, and a good record to back it up. They are descended from Josiah

Bartlett, the first governor of New Hampshire. I took the clerk up to the house, to identify the canvas it was painted on. Mr. Bartlett did not want you swindled, and does not propose to bear the name of a rascal or scoundrel. How that story would look in the papers. How it would sound, that you bought a fine oil painting and did not know it from a chromo. Living in Columbus Avenue too. Ha, ha, ha! you would be the laughing-stock of Boston. It would be remembered against your children. Of course, you cannot approve your action now, and you cannot afford to let it get out."

The man was pale, his hands trembled, his lips were gripped together and he could hardly articulate. He managed to ask, "What will settle it and keep it from getting out?"

"Will you settle?" asked the lawyer.

"Yes, if I can. My wife wants me to."

Said the lawyer, "Now I don't think Mr. Bartlett wants to take your money for nothing. He is not that kind. You are well situated in life, paying several thousand dollars tax and living in your own house in Columbus Avenue. Am I right?" He bowed, and visions of big money, going out from him to the lawyer, floated before his mind's eye. "Now," said the lawyer, "I think I can manage this thing easily for you, and honorably for Mr. Bartlett. There need be no suit. I should not be surprised if you were an honorable, upright man. Only you made a bad mistake. But you come honorably to me, at once, and offer reparation. These pupils and witnesses can be told that it all came by a mistake, that you have apologized, and got acquainted with Mr. Bartlett, that you have fallen in love with his pictures and have given him an order for two nice ones, and no suit and no damages to pay."

"Can you manage it?" asked the man.

"I will try it, and I rather think so," said the lawyer. "If you say so I will make this proposition. You write an apology, directed to Mr. Bartlett, saying it all came through a mistake. Don't for heaven's sake explain the mistake, or people will never get done laughing at you. Then say, please find enclosed two hundred dollars, for which please paint me a pair of landscapes, of such size as you can afford to, without frames, for the money. Pay the money to me, and I will give you a receipt for the money, for him. Also pay me ten dollars for my trouble. Mr. Bartlett will get the two hundred solid. If he does not consent, I will at once return the two hundred to you, but keep the ten."

"I will do it," said he, "and you let me know at once. Say, you must let me know at once, right off, now. I will wait. I can't go home until it is settled. My poor wife won't sleep a wink to-night, and of course that means me too."

That lawyer wanted to roar. He could hardly hold in. But he did. They always do. He said it was too bad for such nice folks to make such a mistake. Then Edric Lyman wrote the apology, and the order for the pictures. The man signed it and gave the lawyer two new one-hundred-dollar bills and a ten.

"Now," said the lawyer, "you wait here, and I'll see if I can find a night's sleep for you and your wife." He stated the case. Roy laughed. His anger was gone. He did not wish to keep the happy couple awake. "How much of the two hundred comes to you, Mr. Lyman?"

"Not a cent. I got ten dollars from our worthy friend. Do you settle?"

"Yes," said Roy.

"Then," said Lawyer Lyman, "I consider you are just two good orders in. I have got ten dollars to pay me for holding in, when I wanted to laugh. I also consider that you can afford to paint me quite a picture as a present."

"So do I," said Roy, "and I'll do it." He did.

The lawyer returned and the man's trouble was over. He was grateful. He was invited to call again, socially, or on business. The lawyer told him that he wished that all would settle their legal wrongs as honorably and promptly as he had. When the man left, he felt a something like a warm spot in his heart, as if he had parted with a dear friend, and that friend was Edric Lyman the lawyer. But it is not every lawyer that can do that. This man's wife had made a bad mistake. She had done what a woman often does, verdict first, evidence later. She had denounced a good picture too quick, and sent a good but impressible man off, loaded for bear. He had made a fool of himself, and paid the bill like a little man. The lawyer had made his share. Oh, I guess it was well enough, and as near God's justice as we shall ever get among men, whose ways are so unequal. Roy asked Miss Graham if she considered he had been hard on the man. She said no, at once. Easy enough, perhaps too easy.

CHAPTER XXVI.

Roy walked out upon the Common with Miss Graham, to the soldiers' monument. They were pleased and amused at the way the money had come in since the sale. I suppose there is no name to call it by, except a sale. When they reached the monument, Roy turned toward his home on Beacon Hill. He was inclined to laugh at the way the two law cases had turned out. The three ladies at home were much amused at some of Roy's experiences which he told them, leaving out the names. These suppers were very pleasant. Mrs. Warren was about fifty, and she refused to grow old. So she was as full of fun as a girl, and with a great deal more sense in it. There is a saying that a man is as young as he feels, and a woman as old as she looks, but like all sweeping assertions, it binds nothing, and leaves us all to look as young as we can, and feel as young as we may.

Said Roy, "It is astonishing how some people love Boston."

"How can they help it?" asked Miss Emily.

"How would it do to let the Art Coterie glorify Boston, at our next meeting?"

The ladies approved of it. They were all born in Boston.

Roy said "he was not, but he liked Boston very much.

206

He had met so many pleasant things, and so many true, splendid people, that it seemed to him there could be no city in the world more justly loved than Boston."

So it was ordered that the next Art Coterie should be Boston night. Miss Graham approved. When the artists and pupils were told, the idea seemed to take immensely. Whatever joy many people find in other cities, they keep their love for Boston.

Roy's studio door bore the usual Art Coterie notice, for three days. During those three days, his pupils were thicker than Indians. They averaged ten a day. He had to laugh, but it kept him and Miss Graham busy. The Thursday evening came. The rooms were full and everything was lovely. The iron namesake of the bird that saved Rome was suspended high. Obscure joke. When the company was seated, Mrs. Warren was observed sitting in a good corner beside a fine-looking gentleman about her own age, and they were having a most sociable time. Her daughters looked triumphant at each other.

Roy called the meeting to order. He said, "My friends, I welcome you here again, in the name of Lady Warren and her daughters. Our coterie has all the latitude that it needs, and any subject that the powers select is in order. To-night we have the most interesting subject in the whole world, 'Glorious Boston.' It is usual to divide a sermon into several heads. That rule will never apply to Boston, which is incapable of being divided. It can be added to, without limit. So we must consider it all at once. I heard a man who was coming to make a speech in Boston, say that he tried all the way to lay out some remarks to make, when he got here. He was utterly unable to do it, and come to get here, he found the reason. The city itself never was laid out. Now a man that could say that, ought to be laid out himself. There is a proverb in New Hampshire, that you die a fool if you do not see Boston. Who says she is not loyal? I do not intend to speak of the history of the past. The schoolboys know that. I do not need to tell of the present. We can all see it. But I should like to tell you of the future, and of the forces that will in all probability operate forever upon Boston. So the theme of to-night will take the form of Prophecy, Story, Poem, Song, and Congratulation. I did intend to speak of it myself, but I have had the rare good fortune to bring to you the sound of more than mortal voice, and to secure the opinion of one who, many years ago, loved and lived in Boston. For years and years he has been an inhabitant of the land of immortals ; yet knowing, loving, and watching over Boston. He is old and wise now, and makes no more mistakes. He has kindly consented to give us a

" *Sure Prophecy of Boston.*

"I now have the pleasure of presenting to you, an older inhabitant than you ever saw. Mr. Peter Rugg, who once lived at the North end of Boston."

He did look old. His face was fair; his hair was white like his long beard, white as snow. He was dressed in the style of Georgius Secundus. He looked about two centuries old. He was a noble, commanding figure, or man, or spirit, or whatever he was. He received instant attention, and when the room was almost painfully still, he began in a voice at first tremulous, which at once became magnetic, firm, rich, and strong.

My children, I come to you from that home which seems so far, and is yet so near. I take the old form which I lived in, and cherished. But a spirit does not grow old and worn out. O, no, my friends, we are up to the times. We know what is done, and can see much more that may, can, ought, and will be done. Else how can we keep you in all your ways, lest you dash your foot against a stone? I always loved Boston. She is an eternal city. No city on earth has more to make it permanent, than Boston. Few, very few, have near as much. She is a mighty gateway, in the highway of nations around the world.

Beginning at Eastport, there is no especial natural site until you reach Portland. That can easily be burned by war vessels from the sea. The same is true of Portsmouth. Boston is much safer and better defended, naturally. There is no more until you reach New York. Boston is by nature a strong city. No city in all the world has so many advantages, by nature, as Boston has for her children. Unlike our Southern cities it is not built on alluvial soil. Its foundation is hard and solid. Its rivers are permanent, and do not change their banks. The islands in the harbor are rocky and immovable. Our harbor is a good and safe one. The entrance to it is narrow, and well defended. Boston is situated in the toe-calk of a mighty horseshoe, for eternal luck. It is about a hundred miles around on the South Shore to Cape Cod. It is a hundred miles around on the North shore, and more if you count it. Oh, the handsomest rocky islands, green fields, pretty bays, sandy beaches, lighthouses, cities, towns, villages, hotels, summer houses, sparkling waters, tides enough to keep

them sweet, bright ocean, staving billows, vessels of all
kinds, oh, more beauty than any city can show this side
the New Jerusalem. The site of Boston will not wash
away. Her hills will always stand sentinels around her.
Her beautiful West bay is a water park fairer than
Venice ever knew. All the bright cities around her rise
up and call her blessed. What drives in summer.
What sleighing in winter. None can be better. No
stagnant waters like Marseilles and Mediterranean ports.
No earthquakes like San Francisco and Charleston. No
malaria. No cholera. No yellow fever. No fleas. No
chigos. No dykes like Holland. No little sewer of a
river like the Thames or Seine. No inland city like
Paris or Milan. No winter like St. Petersburg. No
heats like India. No tigers. No serpents. No white
ants to eat your house down. No centipedes or taran-
tulas. No volcanoes to shake your house down or burn
it. No London fog. No Bergen rain. No Texel wind.
No Denver dust. No Dakota blizzard. No Texas·
grasshoppers. No Egyptian ophthalmia. No overflow-
ing of the Nile. No washing away of the Mississippi.
No, my children. None of these.

When God made the ocean he said: " Thus far shalt
thou come, and no farther. Hither shall thy proud
waves be stayed." Internal water courses are very in-
constant, and depend upon the rainfall. Boston is
largely beyond all evil influences, a permament city, a
beautiful queen city. The ocean comes to its feet, bringing tribute from all the world. It has a healthy fertile
state, country, and great nation of near seventy millions,
the smartest, freest, most progressive nation on earth,
behind it, and Europe, Asia, and Africa before it. Oh, it

is a mighty gateway, for all the world to pass through. And they will pass through it. Mankind are increasing in the world. The sails, the rides, the drives around Boston, are a continual surprise, from the Fells to Franklin Park. Even the ocean is a beauty, and from afar can be seen the beautiful city that we love, with the sunlight reflected from her golden crown. Now here, my children, is the prophecy. Other cities shall decline and die like the cities of old. Boston shall live and grow grandly, gloriously. She shall have few misfortunes, few calamities. She shall be wise and prudent. She shall be loving and giving as now. She shall be Christian, hoping and trusting, an honor to God, and a blessing to all mankind. She shall grow beautifully, continually. And, my children, this shall continue, until the angel shall stand, with one foot upon the sea, and the other upon the land, and shall swear by him who liveth forever, that time shall be no more. So shall it be done to glorious old Boston. My children, farewell.

He disappeared behind a curtain. He spoke solemnly and impressively, as if he believed all he had said, growing more so, unto the end. It was listened to with almost breathless attention. Whoever he was, he had held them spell-bound to the close. They seemed to regret, when he had finished his words, so earnest and loyal, and they seemed most of all to sorrow, that they should see his face no more. This is Peter Rugg's last visit to Boston. Then Roy called for short stories about Boston.

A gentleman said: Not long since, two of us from Boston were in Philadelphia. We wished to see Benjamin West's large picture of "Christ healing the sick."

It was in the insane asylum, at West Philadelphia. We
went there. The matron admitted us and showed us
the establishment as well as the picture, most politely.
We expressed our thanks for her kindness. She asked,
" Are you English people ? " I answered by asking if we
were different from Philadelphians. " Yes, sir, you are."
" In what ? "   " In your language and pronunciation."
" Is it as good as Philadelphians' ? "   " Yes, sir, better,
much better. In fact I think it is the best I ever heard."
" Thank you, lady. We are from Boston."   " Ah, that
accounts for it," said she, and she added, " I was raised
in Philadelphia."

Another arose   He said, there is a lady artist here,
who makes fine crayon portraits, and fine as they are,
they are no finer than her loyalty to Boston. Here is a
favorite story of hers. There is a man, who married a
Boston woman. She died. He was inconsolable, as well
he might be. He sought a medium and called her up.
He asked her how she was and if she was glad to be
there. She answered that she was getting along mid-
dling well. Said he, are you not in heaven? Oh, yes, I
am in heaven. Well, are you not perfectly happy? Oh,
I get along very well, but it is not Boston, was the
answer. Miss White's story brought down the house.

A young artist arose, and said he liked Boston as well
as any one, but he lately heard of a sad thing that had
happened. He asked if he might tell it.

Roy said it was a pity to cast a gloom over so happy an
audience, but as he had excited their curiosity perhaps he
had better tell it.

Said he, It is a case where a gentleman artist caused a
young lady artist to suffer capital punishment. He had

been acquainted with her a long time. He had waited upon her, and showed her very pleasant attention. She was gratified. He invited her to his studio, a fine upper room in his dwelling. I have been in it, and it is a beauty. Unsuspiciously he conducted her upstairs. She admired the room, the light, the pictures, and the artist. Of course she did not tell him this last. It was time to go. She leaned against the dressing-case, apparently to arrange her bonnet, but in reality she secreted a fine, valuable oil painting, of a flock of geese, painted on a mahogany panel. She hid it under her cloak. I am sorry to say it of a Boston woman, but she did. She did it illegally, feloniously, surreptitiously, and with more or less malice aforethought. They descended the stairs, talking pleasantly, until they came to the large vestibule. They were alone. Suddenly she took the picture from under her cloak, and, handing it to him, she said: There, do, dear, take it. It is so good I could not help wanting it. He was aroused in a moment. Said he, in a stern voice, Oh this is dreadful! You shall suffer capital punishment for this. He caught her and held her fast. There was a little scream, a slight concussion, and all was over. They are going to be married next week. He sat down.

That young chap had done it. As Mr. Toots says: "It is not so much what he says, as the way he says it, that gives me an agreeable feeling of warmth, all up my back." Other stories were told.

Roy spoke, My friends, I wish there was a Boston Opera. I do not mean an opera in Boston, for that we have often, I mean an opera which shall contain Boston scenes, ideas, songs, stories, sayings, jokes, and fun. It would be all the better with Boston celebrities. Put in

"March to Boston" sure, and Yankee tunes. Have a procession, military, brass band, and the airiest drum-major in the city. Drum and fife. Have models, paste-board if you want to, borne aloft, of State House, Bunker Hill Monument, Soldiers' Monument, Old South, New South, Trinity, Faneuil Hall, City Hall, Equitable Build-ing, giant pot of beans, brown bread, big crackers, State House codfish, — that the aristocracy be not neglected, — Member from Cranberry Centre, and Hannah Partridge. Alarms of fire. Fourth of July. O hold me while I faint away. If made good, it would run a thousand and one nights. The audience approved.

Another gentleman arose, and said he would tell them a vigorous story of

" The Boston Centaur."

He was a Boston man, well situated, from one of the oldest families. He traced his ancestry away back into the dark ages. He was a graduate of Harvard, six feet high, a fine athlete, a man of fine taste in literature and art, and a man of bravery and honor. He liked to ride horseback. He knew he was handsome, and as he rode he was a picture to gaze upon. His mount was usually a bay stallion. Why should he not show his shape, and get the life that comes from horseback riding? Theodore Parker said the outside of a horse is good for the inside of a man. So one day this centaur was riding up Wash-ington Street, near the *Transcript* office. He passed a truck team whose driver had a long whip. It was an unlucky piece of devilment, that prompted the teamster to hit the stallion a cut with his whip. He sprang forward, almost throwing his rider, who saw the blow and later found the welt on the horse. He reined him in, by might and strength, and, turning around, he rode back and demanded of that teamster, in the best of English, "What did you strike my horse for?" "I didn't strike yer hoss." "You did strike my horse." "You lie!" and he added a huge double oath, that reflected upon the horseman's mother. The centaur rode on a little, turned into Avon Street, dismounted, asked a gentleman near, "Sir, will you hold my horse a few minutes, as a favor of the most valuable kind? It is a case of life and death." "I will, sir," was the answer. The centaur went out, and saw the teamster coming. He jumped upon the rear of that team, ran lightly up over the load, and, drawing a light, tough cowhide, he cowhided that teamster until he roared for mercy.

You ought to have seen the Art Coterie then. The house shook. Everybody was frantic with applause. The man had brought them all solid, and most impressively up to the climax, and carried the Coterie by storm.

Then he said, "This horseman was the manliest of men. Now I have almost told you his middle name."

The evening was getting along. Roy arose, and read the poem of

THE DISCONTENTED BOSTONIAN.

"There was a man in Boston, a native Boston boy,
Rich, airy, handsome, bright, well read, with plenty to enjoy,
And he grew discontented, chose to travel off apace
To see if he could find somewhere a nicer, sweeter place;
Says he: If I don't like it, I'm not obliged to stay.
He bought a strong and splendid trunk, and journeyed on his
    way.

" He went straight to Chicago, and vastly pleased was he,
At supper time the waiter brought a cockroach in his tea ;
The drummers huddled 'round him, to sell him each did try,
They did not understand a man that did not want to buy.
Says he : This place is much too smart, I do not care to stay,
And so he packed his trunk for luck and journeyed on his way.

" He journeyed to Dakota, where the emigration goes.
A blizzard caught him on the fly, and froze his ears and nose ;
The snow came down Spitzbergen drifts on all the prairies
    wide,
But he had splendid Boston grit, or else he would have died.
Then when the road was opened an hour he did not stay ;
As he had not unpacked his trunk, he journeyed on his way.

" Ah, Denver is the place you want, the speculators cry,
The ridgepole of the continent. O how is this for high ;
The wind came up and blew great guns, O how the dust did fly.
Says he : I'm in a hurry, friends, and not prepared to buy ;
Just wait a bit till I come back, for now I cannot stay.
He quickly checked his trunk again, and journeyed on his way.

" He went to Sacramento. Ah, this handsome place will do,
He took a drink of water and it waxed him through and
    through,
Says he : For active physic this water here is prime ;
Physic is good, but 'tis not well to take it all the time.
I like your pretty city, but I guess I will not stay.
Counting the scratches on his trunk, he journeyed on his way.

" He went to San Francisco, where the sun shines not in rain,
And nature shows her force as strong when she sends down
    the rain.
He tried to think he liked it, but its power made him frown ;
The fog came on and choked him up, an earthquake shook him
    down.
Says he : My friends, I've got to go, I have not time to stay.
When baggage smashers smote his trunk, he journeyed on his
    way.

" Down to Los Angeles he went, a country hard to beat,
Where fleas adore a Boston man, so nice and fresh and sweet;
They picnicked on him all the time, at every step he made,
Abed and up, in coat and boots, and breeches I'm afraid.
So to secure what might be left, he could no longer stay,
And so he scratched, and packed his trunk, and journeyed on
    his way.

" He laid off at San Diego. What heat was all around,
His blood did almost sizzle, he almost melted down.
Says he: Some folks may like this, tastes differ so, you see,
I know a city farther east that's good enough for me.
He bought another ticket, glad any price to pay,
To take him and his well worn trunk, to journey on his way.

" He stopped again in Texas, to see what fate would bring,
'Twas drought, or floods, or grasshoppers, or some infernal
    thing,
Texas vicissitudes are large, in such a monster state,
A quart of something that you like, a bushel that you hate.
As he was not obliged to come, he was not bound to stay,
That blessed trunk he took once more, and journeyed on his
    way.

" He went to New Orleans, among the Pelicans to stay,
Drank Mississippi water and the mischief was to pay.
They said: You soon get used to it, 'tis quite a job to try;
When you are well acclimated, you're safe without you die.
Fever and ague shook him loose, he could no longer stay;
Weary, he took his battered trunk and journeyed on his way.

" Over to Florida he went. Pine trees and sandy ground,
Where alligators, oranges, and rattle-snakes abound;
Mosquitoes are gallinippers there, their quality is prime,
They bit him quick, they bit him hard, they bit him all the
    time.
And when an ague chill set in, the mischief was to pay,
And begging them to spare that trunk, he journeyed on his
    way.

"Northward he took his weary way, in search of rest and ease,
Where Charleston's shadows hide away beneath palmetto trees;
He saw Fort Sumter's battered wall and sadly shook his head,
But not to mourn secession's doom or sigh for slavery dead;
When a great earthquake shook him loose. For more than
    double pay
He saved that trunk on board the cars, and journeyed on his
    way.

"He stayed again at Washington, our capital to see;
He found the distances so grand, a weary man was he.
Folks asked: What office do *you* want? What office want? he
    cried,
I want no office. Then they laughed. For sure they thought
    he lied.
Says he: 'Tis very lonesome here, I will no longer stay;
He took his poor, hard-looking trunk, and journeyed on his
    way.

"He went to Philadelphia, great city of our land,
They did not speak our language quite, though he could under-
    stand.
He tried to smile and like it, but ended with a sigh:
Great city of the checkerboard, I fear I'm going to die;
I'm stuck full of right angles, although I tried to stay.
He cobbled up his poor smashed trunk, and journeyed on his
    way.

"He went to New York city. Ah, this is grand, says he,
This Brooklyn bridge, this Central Park, Statue of Liberty.
He saw it all in such a whirl he had not time to think;
He kept it up by day and night, he could not sleep a wink.
Says he: Yes, this is awful, I'd almost like to stay.
He tied a clothes line round his trunk and journeyed on his
    way.

"When Boston's golden dome arose, his heart was tried and
    true,
Says he: My luck is found at last, O glory Hallelu.

I've wandered far away from home, returning, fancy free.
Hail, Boston, queen of heart and home, just good enough for
    me,
Hail, luck and love; Hail, food and drink; Hail, joy with which
    to stay.
No more fool's paradise for me, or journey on my way.

"And now he lives in Boston, so happy all the while;
He walks upon the common with a beatific smile;
He looks in the batrachian lake, and in it sees his face,
No more a tired wanderer, bereft of joy and grace.
With no more worlds to conquer, no higher joy to know.
If he could start for heaven to-day, I doubt if he would go."

There appeared to be no one asleep during the reading
of this.

Another story was told. Said he, There is always
something new to be seen in Boston: the exhibitions, the
meetings, the art stores, the galleries, the studios, O something all the time. I remember once, when calling upon
some of my artist friends, I was in the studio building.

I was talking in a corridor, when a friend came by and
said, "Call on me next, and I will show you a wonderful
sight, a sight that you will never see again." Very soon
I went. Near his studio door he had a fine telescope
set, and he invited me to see the transit of Venus. It
was a thrilling sight. To see that little base-ball looking
planet, passing clear as noonday across the face of the
sun, and showing the awful distances of the sky, better
than I ever saw it before, was a thing to happen only
once in a lifetime, and for which I shall always be grateful to the man who is at once engraver, artist, portrait-
painter, and generous good fellow — Mr. D. T. Kendrick.

Said Roy, "Now it is near time to close. Let us sing
the Boston Song."

It was distributed on slips. Miss Sarah Warren took the piano, and a dozen vocalists, who were not strangers to the public, gathered around her. I give the words of the solo and chorus.

THE BOSTON SONG.

" There is a handsome city, reflected in the sea,
   Upon a noble river, that pours its waters free ;
   Her regal beauties rising around her golden dome,
   And Boston proudly sits a queen with royal welcome home.
CHORUS — O roll away, roll away, Atlantic waves are rolling
            Up to the city of the golden dome,
            O roll away, roll away, ages onward rolling,
            Proud old Boston gives us welcome home.

" The sun lights up her harbor, sweet islands down the bay ;
   No fairer scene he shines upon in all his longest day,
   And east and west, o'er hill and wave, new beauty doth
       enfold,
   To glorify his setting in a sea of molten gold.— CHORUS.

" And history stands ready her brightest page to fill,
   The story of the Pilgrims, the fight of Bunker Hill,
   And deeds of daring sailors, and patriots tried and true,
   And soldiers, O we bless them all, our boys that wore the
       blue. — CHORUS.

" With learning, wit, and culture, with science and with art,
   With all good works of mercy old Boston does her part.
   When sorrow or misfortune falls, in near or distant lands,
   Her blessing flies with winged feet and open heart and
       hands.— CHORUS.

" Then hail, eternal city, sure founded on a rock,
   Thy granite harbors, forts, and walls, thy granite Pilgrim
       stock,
   Thou queen of peace and plenty, what harm can thee befall ?
   Refreshment of the nations, as they travel round the ball.
       — CHORUS.

"Now join we to salute her, and let the cannon roar,
We cheer, praise her, love her as our fathers did before.
For justice, right, and honor we keep our flag unfurled,
A beauty and a beacon to the nations round the world.
—CHORUS."

They made the most of the rattling song and chorus, and the crowd outside shared in the effect.

Roy again called attention. He said, "Now, in conclusion, we will listen to our hostess, by whose kindness our coterie is possible."

Mrs. Warren arose. She was richly dressed, and Roy did not know before that she was so handsome. When the noble lords and ladies of England await the coming of their queen, an equerry makes the announcement. The queen is coming; ladies bare their shoulders in the presence of royalty. Mrs. Warren had worn a mantle, very handsome, but now, as she arose, it fell upon her chair and showed full dress, suitable for the queen's drawing-room; a bouquet of appropriate flowers at her side, her hair crinkled a little, and yet showing her fine forehead, and a cluster of white light diamonds upon her bosom, that saw the light only on the most festive occasions. That dear old witch had fairly taken them all. The daughters looked at each other in triumph.

When the welcome was lulled, she said, "We are pleased to see you all so happy. The Art Coterie pays us well, as an investment. But I have a story to tell you. When I was a little girl, going to school here in Boston, there was a little boy in the same classes with me. He was about my size, and we went through the schools together. Sometimes one was higher in the class, sometimes the other. We have always known and respected

each other, and have always called each other by our
given name. So we have never grown old, and we are
still boy and girl together. He took a Franklin medal,
and wears it to-night. He has had many honors, and
deserved them all. He has done much for Boston, and
will do all he can. And you do not know with what
pleasure I introduce my schoolmate to you to-night, as the
mayor of Boston."

Mrs. Warren had designed to make a sensation, and
she had just done it. She was a long-headed woman. It
was an ovation and a reception. The mayor did not
make much of a speech. He was so broken up, he said,
he could not. He had enjoyed one of the happiest evenings of his life. Yet somehow it had pulled upon his
heart. He had tried to do all the good he could to
Boston and everybody, and if there was any good in him,
it was because he had known such loyal and true hearts,
such white souls as Mrs. Parna Warren and her daughters.
White handkerchiefs were moistened, and the Boston
night was in memory, a thing of beauty, and a joy forever.

CHAPTER XXVII.

A FRIEND IN NEED.

Roy attended to his pupils, and painted pictures besides. He made them just as good as he could. He was doing better than he expected. About once a month he went home to his parents, and a fine change it was to him, the two or three days he had with them. The home bond was strong. Miss Graham was in the studio four of five days in each week, sometimes only forenoons, and then, again, she was there until four or later. Roy took a walk every morning when the weather was fine, on the way to the studio. One morning he was walking briskly past the head of Hanover Street. Something jumped against him, and upon him, and, although a young Irishman pulled upon the chain, and shouted, O come off! still he did not give up jumping upon or towards Roy. He looked again. It was Canis Major! There he was, muzzled, and being dragged off by a young Irishman. In an instant he sprang, caught the chain, and held on.

"Leggo my dog! Leggo my dog!"

"You lie. It is not your dog. It is my dog," said Roy.

The man gave Roy a kick on the shin, and Roy returned the compliment by a big blow on the nose, that blooded his face. For a wonder, a policeman came along just in time to see the kick and the blow. He took the man by the collar. Right is usually with the best dressed man. Poverty and crime roost together. The policeman had not formulated that, but he usually acted on it. Both held to the chain and the dog.

"What is it?" asked the policeman of the Irishman.

"This divil warnts to stale me dog."

"How long have you had the dog?"

"'Bout foore months."

"Where did you get him?"

"Bort him."

"What did you pay?"

"Twenty-foive dollars."

·He turned to Roy. "Is the dog yours?"

"Yes."

"Can you prove it?"

"Yes."

"How long have you had him?"

"Five years. Since he was a pup."

"Who bought him?"

"My father. But the bill was made out to me; so he is my dog."

Then, turning to the man, he asked, "What is your name?"

"Maginnis."

The policeman laughed. He took Roy's card, and told him to take the dog, and have him at the police court at nine o'clock the next day. "Maginnis, you be there, and prove that the dog is yours, and you can take him."

Just then a friend came along, and went with Roy to the studio. If ever there was a loving, thankful heart, it was Canis Major. Roy sent out for Lawyer Lyman. He came. He knew the dog. He asked, "What evidence have you that the dog is yours? Any photographs?"

"O yes, several good ones, and stereoscopic pictures of the home. Canis Major comes into them all. They all have the date, and the photographer's name at Dover. Also I have painted him in oil, with the date each time."

"I guess you will do."

Said Roy, "I wish you would call at the Quincy House and telegraph to my father, that I have Canis Major, and for him to come to my studio in the first train to-morrow morning. He will come."

"What value do you put on the dog?"

"Oh, no money value. He is not for sale at any price. I would as soon think of selling my guardian angel."

The dog was next cared for. Roy petted him and loved him to his heart's content. Canis Major paid his respects to a pound of beefsteak and a drink. Miss Graham was presented to him, and he took to her at once. Roy sent word to Mrs. Warren about it, and said he should not be at home at night, but would sleep on the sofa in the studio, to be company for Canis Major. And would they send down his supper, and a few bits for his poor friend? I leave you to judge whether they did or not. No, I'll tell you. After supper, which was like the play of Hamlet with Hamlet left out, Mrs. Warren and her daughters came down to see Canis Major, and fell in love with him. It was a picnic for him every way. He had not been long from home, and was not much changed. He was a large brown and white Newfoundland. He was well petted. Roy could not be prevailed upon to take him out. The next day Mr. Bartlett surprised Canis Major, and had his welcome. They all went to the police

court, but the enemy did not put in an appearance. It
was too dangerous. Mr. Bartlett took the dog home by
the noon train for Dover. Roy saw them safely into the
baggage car, and Mr. Bartlett, with the chain on the dog,
seated comfortably with Canis Major's head in his lap.
He did not see the malicious, ugly eyes that watched him
from behind a bunch of feather dusters, the father of the
Irish American that had given his name as Maginnis.
But they were there, and watched the whole proceedings.

Roy went into Lawyer Lyman's office. "O give me
two dollars, unless you think it is too much."

"Not a bit."

Said the lawyer, "I did not quite think they would
appear, but sometimes such people will, and swear you
right out of court."

"How is that?"

"O courts go by the mass and quality of evidence.
If a rascal can bring evidence enough he can win his
case in spite of all the righteousness in the world. Law
is one thing, justice is sometimes another. Not long since
I had the facts in a horse case. There was a horse-dealer
who got his living by buying horses, fixing them up a
little, and selling them at a profit. Inasmuch as a horse
adds the price of his board every day to his cost, he soon
eats his own head off, without you use him. This man
was sharp, and with no more conscience than a man-
eating tiger. A young man rode a horse into his yard.
He had a light bridle, but no saddle. It was a young,
pretty, medium-sized horse. The man said he had been
selling sewing-machines. He had sold out. He had sold
his wagon and harness. The firm had appointed him to
take charge of the wareroom in Boston, and he wanted

an offer for the horse. The horse-dealer had his own ideas of buying a horse on a stranger's word, and said so. He did not want to buy the horse any way, and it was not safe for him to be out selling a horse that way. If he wanted twenty dollars for him he could leave him.

"Horse-dealer took a bill of the horse dated a year ago, the sum stated in it being a hundred dollars. Man signed it, took his money and vanished. The horse was kept in a tight stall, out of sight of visitors. He was driven out at night and proved from his speed to be worth from two to three hundred dollars. Not long after, a man was talking horse with him, and looking over his eight or nine horses. Said he lived a few miles away, in the next town, and wanted to buy. After a little criticism on the horses he saw, horse-dealer showed the horse in the close stall. The man recognized him at once, as his own horse, which had been stolen from his pasture, the night before the horse-dealer bought him. The owner of the horse made no sign of what he had discovered, but went to a country lawyer, an oldish man, and rather slow. He brought suit for the horse. The owner, the plaintiff, was in court himself, his wife, and his two sons. Four people all swore point-blank, that they had raised the horse, and the old mare, the horse's mother, was outside, hitched to the fence. They might go and see her. Nobody went.

"Then the defendent came. He had a dozen witnesses. They all swore that horse-dealer had owned that horse over a year. Horse-dealer showed his bill of the horse. He did not doubt that the horse was like the farmer's. It was a common kind of horse; but there was his bill, and he had bought the horse low, only a hundred dollars,

over a year ago. He had doctored him up some, and
now he was all right, and worth double. He could not
afford to pay for plaintiff's mistakes. So horse-dealer
euchred the man out of his own horse, and stuck him
with a large bill of costs. This story is a fact, every
word. I heard the story from the lawyers, and later,
horse-dealer told it to me himself, laughing heartily."

Roy went back to his studio again, reflecting on the
glorious uncertainty of the law. So the winter days
came and went, with pupils to teach, pictures to paint,
some of which sold at art stores, and some to Roy's
customers. Roy invited the man who had called him
bad names, and given him an order, under pressure, to
come with his wife and see how they liked his pictures.
He did come. The man had a painful look, as if he was
under restraint. Soon he began : "Mr. Bartlett, can you
ever forget how I treated you?"

"Yes, sir," answered Roy, "I can, and I do. And I
ask you to forget it, and never refer to it again, either of
you. Now please, not another word, ever, for each will
find the other better than he thought. Look at these
pictures."

Roy placed them in a good light. They were delighted. They praised everything. Soon Roy had them
at ease and they had a nice call. Roy asked if they had
heard of the Art Coterie. Yes, they had. Lawyer
Lyman had called upon him, and had told him that Mr.
Bartlett wanted him to see his pictures. Then Mr.
Lyman told him about the Art Coterie. Roy said he
should be glad to have them come, and that was what
pleased them most. The man fell in love with a nice
panel picture of Champney's fall and paid him thirty

dollars for it. The happy couple departed, smiling clear around their faces. Roy sat down and for a while was content to do nothing but smile, and feel tickled at the way the squall had cleared up.

One day Roy and Miss Graham were quietly at work in the studio. There was a crying and scratching at the door, then a terrible cry.

Miss Graham said, "O go, there is some one in distress."

Roy opened the door, and, with a suffering cry, in came Canis Major. Roy could hardly believe his own eyes. The dog came up, licked Roy's hand, and then his hinder parts swung around, and he fell upon the floor. He had a collar on, and had evidently broken his chain, as a piece of it hung to his neck. He was lean and exhausted. He had many bruises and sores, and his neck, under the collar, was raw and bleeding.

"O, my poor friend, my poor friend!" said Roy.

"Let us do something at once," said Miss Graham. "He is evidently starving."

Roy folded up an afghan, and covering it with papers, because the dog was bleeding, he cut the collar from his neck with many a kind word, which Canis Major acknowledged with a little wag of his tail, and soon the sufferer was lying more at his ease. Roy went out and got a pound of beefsteak. Canis Major was too far gone to touch it.

"Get him some milk and warm it," said Miss Graham.

Roy got a quart can of milk, and soon had some in a tin pail warming on the radiator. Then Canis Major got up on his fore paws and lapped a little of it. Later he took more, and the quantity was increased, and before night he took little pieces of beefsteak. But after he came, there was no more work done that day by Roy or Miss Graham.

Roy sent for Mr. Lyman. He came.

He said : "Of all persistent dog-stealers, these are the worst that I have met. This dog has some value, and would sell for anywhere from twenty-five to a hundred dollars or more."

Said Roy: "I believe in government and law. I also believe in punishing the man that stole this dog and abused him so. If the rascal is smart enough to cheat justice, I believe I am justified in punishing him myself."

"That is what I think," said the lawyer.

"Can you help me to do it?" asked Roy.

"Yes. I think so, but it will be at some expense."

"Go ahead then, and call on me for any sum from ten to fifty dollars."

"I will do it," said he; "and if I do not hit him somewhere, I will ask nothing for myself. Give me ten to begin with."

Roy gave it to him. He said, when he had anything to report he would call. Miss Graham bore a message to the Warrens, and they all came, bringing Roy and Canis Major no end of comforts, even to a custard for Canis Major. The dog knew them, and came to see each one and to kiss the hand that caressed him. Then he staggered back to his afghan and lay down. It was truly a visit of condolence. Roy stayed in the studio all night, and Canis Major slept beside the sofa on which Roy lay.

Somebody says: "The more I know of men, the more I respect dogs." Roy wrote home and said he had Canis Major, but he would not be well enough to go home for a week. Edric Lyman sauntered from his office in School Street, through Court Square and along Court Street with a problem in his mind of how to find the man who stole the dog. There were not many who would do it, as far away as Dover. He was a professional criminal, and either English or Irish. He looked at the hats in Taylor's hat store, on the corner of Hanover Street. Ah, there was the policeman that helped Roy before. The lawyer greeted him kindly. Soon he asked if he ever found out who Maginnis was, that had Roy's dog.

"Yis, sor, I have, an' he's a bad lot. There are two of them, father and son. They pretend to sell a few baskets of coal and kindlin's, an' they will stale anything, from a dog to a meetin'-house. The old man is not very old, and pretends to sell feather dusters. But it is only a chance to go around and find where to steal. They are the worst enemies the police have."

Then the lawyer told the officer the rest of the dog story and asked him to call at the studio, and see the dog. He did later, and had sympathy for him. The next day he asked the officer if he was situated so that he could get any one who was down on these people, to go and punish the younger one. They both had the same name, Shan Rines.

"Will ye kape it to yerself?"

"Yes, Mr. Officer. Neither of us will ever know anything about it."

"Correct," said the officer. "I know several who hate them like the devil. I can help you."

Said the lawyer, "Here is the proposition that I do not make, and you do not hear. You get somebody that is able to do it, to go and give him a pounding that he won't

get over in a long time.   Don't kill him, but hurt him bad.
If we can't have justice without a vigilance committee,
let us have it with.   Here is a five-dollar bill for the man
that does it.   When it is done let me know, and I will
give you another for yourself."

I am sorry to say this was against the law, but I told
you this story was in the actual, and it is history.   A
little later, but within a week, Shan Rines had a caller,
just at dusk.   He was a stout man with his neck done up
in a brown handkerchief.   His eyes were visible.   They
walked out into the shed.

"Wot's the matter with yer?" asked Shan.

"Neralgy.   Got it bad."   He asked, "Is the old man
round?"

"No."   The stranger leaned on his thick stick.   He
was lame.

"See that cat," said he.

Shan Rines turned to look at the cat and he got a clip
that straightened him.   Both hands were stamped on.
The thick muscles that he sat on, were clubbed into jelly.
One knee pan was split.   Both ears twisted, his nose
spoiled, teeth knocked out.   He was clubbed, kicked, and
bruised all over, and all of it was done before he knew it.
For a month he was the sickest chicken that ever was.   As
soon as the job was done, the neckwear came off, the
avenger called at the door of the house, and Mrs. Rines
came to the door.   Says he, "Wot's ever got Shan?   He's
out in the shed fainted away."

"I guess he's been a-fightin'."

"Shall I go for a doctor?"

The woman let out a yell and Shan had help.   They
reported it to the police and the police grinned.   The

neighbors were very sorry, but laughed inside. And everybody that loves justice at all, was glad of it. Later, both of them went behind the bars for burglary. The *Herald* had an item. The policeman got his five dollars. Lawyer Lyman called on Roy and showed the *Herald* item. He had no report to make, except that justice had been done, a little irregularly perhaps, but still nothing more than what was foreordained, from the foundation of the world, and an orthodox man ought not to kick at that. Roy saw the joke, and was amused at the application of the doctrine.

" How much ? "

"Oh, give me two more, and never tell the story."

It was done.

Said Roy, " I once thought I never should need a lawyer in my life. I never was going to sue anybody, or have anybody sue me. But I find it is not for me to say whether I shall have a lawsuit or not. All the world has the answering of that question."

" Right, sir," said Edric Lyman. " And among all the old proverbs, sayings, and chunks of wisdom that have come down to us, there is one which says : — ' Keep my purse from the lawyer, my body from the doctor, and my soul from the devil.' Generally, if a man kept the first two of these impossibilities, he would surely find the third. No, sir, we cannot live without law and lawyers. Now let me give you a better sentiment. Keep on the best of terms with a good lawyer, doctor, and pastor : with your wife, children, and conscience."

Roy laughed, " How if a man has not got any wife ? "

" Oh, you will mend of that later."

" I hope so," said Roy.

Said Lawyer Lyman, " If you want legal advice on that
or any other subject, you know where my office is," and
he went out.

Canis Major slept in the studio the first night, with
Roy. The second he went to Mrs. Warren's and was in
Roy's chamber. He behaved perfectly and made friends
like his master. The next day there were pupils and he
wanted to be at Roy's side all the time. It was too much.
It took the attention of pupils, and proved, as it always
does, that a studio is a poor place for a dog. Roy loved
Canis Major dearly, and I grieve to say it, Canis Major
loved him, and depended upon him so, and stuck to him
so closely, that, splendid as it was, it was a burden. So
on the next Saturday afternoon, Roy rode in the baggage
car, with Canis Major. Ned Foss, Mr. Bartlett's new
boy, was there with a team, and the home was happy
once more with Roy and Canis Major. Then Mr. Bartlett had accommodations for the dog to sleep in the shed,
under lock and key, and he went to Boston no more.
Roy called upon Sam and had a royal welcome. They
were all happy. Roy found his father and mother sitting
up for him, when he got home, it being a little later than
their usual bed-time ; the hymn was read, the psalm of
thanksgiving also, and then the master of the house gave
thanks to God for all his mercies, especially for the return
of his dear son and his faithful dog.

CHAPTER XXVIII.

IN THE STUDIO.

Before nine one morning Miss Graham and Roy came to the studio. Roy said he did not feel much like work and she said the same. He said, " Miss Graham, you have your name on the door with no initial. Yet once or twice, you have had a letter come directed to Miss Mary Graham, else I should not have known your first name. Mary is a beautiful name, that everybody loves in earth and heaven. May I call you by your first name?" He asked it very pleasantly.

She looked as though it was a doubtful matter for a moment, then she answered. " Let me first give you the reasons to base an answer on, and you may answer. If you alone were to have the privilege, I should say yes, at once. But if you do, others will. The artists, the pupils, and the errand boy will also. You remember that smart girl, Miss Lockwood. She is bright, pretty, pert, and smart. But she is not to blame. You remember, once when you gave her some instruction, she looked up in your face and said, 'Er which?' It almost spoilt the gravity of the class. She is evidently the only girl in a family of rough boys. She knows no better. Now if you and others do, the next time I meet her in the street, she will greet me with, Hello, Mary. And I should not like it. I believe in humility and I am not what is called

235

'stuck up.' When her majesty's mother died, she wept; and among other reasons for sorrow, it was that she had lost the last friend who had the right to call her by her given name. Some people do not care either way. I do. My people have been people of dignity and substance. It is a sacred right, seldom acquired and not transferable. If no one could use it but you, Mr. Bartlett, it might do. But even then I had rather address you as Mr. Bartlett than by any other name. I should honor you more. Now what is the answer?"

Said he, "The answer is that 'she who must be obeyed' shall be obeyed. And hereafter let no man deride a woman's reason, for you, Miss Graham, have given me the best of reasons. If any cheap people dared to use your first name, I should resent it. Now, Miss Graham, let us go out and see the pictures in the galleries."

They called at B. S. Moulton's in Hanover street, and at J. Eastman Chase's. They came back to the studio and found Roy's father and mother waiting for them. It was their first visit together. Miss Graham was introduced, and they were glad to know her. She said she did not feel like work and would go home. Mrs. Bartlett objected. She wanted to know Miss Graham, that she had heard so much about.

"Have you heard much about me?"

"Yes, dear, a great deal. And always that you are helping Roy, and doing a great deal of good to everybody."

"Thank you."

"Now, Roy," said his mother, "we are going home in the five o'clock train. Let us stay right here and visit you all the time. And, Miss Graham, stay too. By and

by Roy may go out and get some crackers and cheese,
or some little thing, to keep us from getting faint. Then
we can have a good long visit here all day. Ned will
meet us at half-past seven to-night, when the train comes
into Dover."

It was so ordered, and Miss Graham agreed to take
lunch in the studio with them.

Said Roy, "Now I leave you for a few minutes to
speak for our lunch. You can get acquainted with Miss
Graham." Roy went down to North Market street again.
"Good morning, Mr. Blanchard, I have company to-day,
and they will be at my room. I want something good
enough for my father and mother to eat. Can you take
a tray or box and send me up four tenderloin steaks, as
good as market-men ever get?"

"Yes, sir, I can. They are all ready to put upon the
gridiron."

"Good enough," said Roy. "You know where my
room is?"

"I do. You know I was there to see your pictures."

"Here is a card for the messenger. And here is the
order. Four tenderloin steaks, well done, good mashed
potato, two slices each of graham bread, celery, a quart
can of coffee, sweet, and milk. I have plates, knives,
forks, cups, saucers, salt and pepper."

"All right, Mr. Bartlett, it shall be done and up there
a little before twelve o'clock."

Roy went back and his visit began. He had an account of Canis Major, and of how content he was to stay
in the shed, in a good warm bed of his own, away from
danger. Miss Graham was seated beside Mrs. Bartlett
and they seemed to like each other well. Roy told them

of the Warrens, and all of his doings in art and the Art Coterie.

Said Roy, "You did not eat much breakfast this morning?"

"No, we had not time or appetite, we were so full of coming here. If we get a little lunch we shall do well enough until we get home and then we shall feast again."

"Well," said Roy, "I guess Boston will honor my father and mother enough to give them a good dinner. Let us set the table. I have dishes enough for a lunch, so I can have one here, when I choose to send out for it, or get it myself."

The lunch came on time and they were just surprised. Blanchard's steaks were as good as the queen could get. The coffee was perfection, and there was all they could manage, in one course. Miss Graham thought it was the best she ever had, although her uncle had orders to live on the best he could buy. That Bohemian lunch was a change and a surprise, something unique and to be remembered, as long as they lived. They invited Miss Graham to visit them in the spring, and Roy said he should ask her to make it the week that Whitsunday came in, so as to see New Hampshire when the apple trees are in full bloom.

When the time was up, the parents were escorted to the station, and the artists had found a day of vacation and a change. The next day there were pupils. It was a busy forenoon. If there is anything on earth that is entitled to respect, it is a palette of color. Without art, the poor tortured color becomes mud. With art, it has possibilities of all beauty. Some people have not much more idea of beauty than a horse. I was travelling among the White Mountains once, and stopped at a house to get a drink from their well in the yard. The view was of the very finest. I looked at it long and lovingly. A girl of fourteen came near. I said, "You have a splendid view of the mountains here."

"Yes," she said, "view enough for them that like it."

"Don't you like the mountains?"

"No, I don't; I hate 'em."

And from the way her eyes snapped, I knew that she meant it.

Said I, "Have you ever been on the mountains?"

"Yes, I have, an' it is the meanest, most misable place in the whole world. I wish I could never see another mountain as long as I live. I hate 'em."

Just then a four-years-old boy came along. He was a bright, pretty, well dressed boy, perhaps the girl's little brother. Said I, "Have you been on the mountains?"

He looked at me, and answered, "Do you think I am a fool?"

I have recorded it word for word. My companion was much amused by it. It was Mr. Lucas Baker, artist, late of the Massachusetts Normal Art School, now teaching in New York. I never was so completely shut up in my life. It was funny enough to last a fortnight. These were no poor people. But they had a knowledge of the mountains, as rocky, barren deserts, with possibilities of bears and wild beasts, and a place whence people returned tired and exhausted, and often wounded and bleeding. What to eat has often to be learned, what to admire more so. So these by no means foolish people had their own idea of the mountains. So people have their ideas of art.

Roy's pupils were getting a start in the right direction. After they were gone, the afternoon was more at leisure. Two artists called. They were neighbors, and were welcome. They looked over the pictures, gave him reasonable praise, and Miss Graham also, and did not score them down with caustic criticism. It is a good way, to enjoy a thing for what it is, and not sting the author to death for what it is not.

A gentleman and lady called. They were admitted, and at once Roy gave his artist friends an illustrated book to keep them busy, while he attended to the visitors. They were a good-looking pair, evidently well situated, and not very long married. The man spoke but little. There was that in his manner which seemed to say, Now I am the escort, and you have nobody to please but my wife. You take me in my own business, and I know my rights, and want them. He introduced them, saying: " We are Mr. and Mrs. Quince. Mrs. Quince wishes to take lessons in painting."

The lady opened. " Yes, Mr. Bartlett, I have long heard of you and your success in teaching, and I have seen your pictures at the Art Club and in the galleries. The elegance of the foliage, the buttery richness of foreground, the mysterious art of the perspective, and the general chiaroscuro, compel one to remain and enjoy the subtle beauty of your landscapes, until one almost forgets it is art, and not Nature in her happiest mood. O Mr. Bartlett, what a delight it must be to paint as you do."

Mr. Bartlett bowed ; her husband looked resigned.

" When can I come for a lesson ? "

" With the class, Tuesdays, Thursdays, and Saturdays,

at one dollar each lesson. Single lessons, on other days, one dollar and a half."

She answered, "I think I can come better on Tuesdays and Thursdays than other days. I will send my servant with easel and color box before next Tuesday." She looked at the pictures, and talked most elaborately. At last she swam to the door. Then, with a smile which was the consummation of all graciousness, an obeisance which was the combined result of all our highest refinements, and a nod from her husband, and Mr. and Mrs. Quince were gone. This is a portrait.

Roy came in after seeing them going downstairs. There was an amused smile upon Miss Graham's face, and a broad grin upon each man. Roy took a fan and sat down, saying, "I ain't well. Suthin's come over me."

He fanned a little, and they all laughed heartily.

Said George, " O we poor artists have a tough time. I often get an avalanche of the richest and most ornamental language slung at me, until I am stuck full of it; and it is a positive relief when some low-down comes in and says something unparliamentary. It is an awful responsibility that a poor artist has, to be obliged to skirmish round in art for his bread and butter, and to be in mortal fear of an attack of the dictionary."

Said Roy: "When will people learn the beauty of simplicity; that beauty when unadorned is adorned the most. When will they learn that the simplest language is the best. That

"'You see a woman simply drest,
You see that woman at her best.'

Of course, a dress may be ever so rich, and still have the element of simplicity in it. Even a glass of water is better in a large, plain tumbler than in a little, fussed-up one."

"Yes," said Frank. "I like a plain, unfigured tumbler best; but I do not choose a cheap, five-cent one. I want a good one. The fact is, that almost all truth is only part truth, and not of universal application. Nature is plain to severity, and she is ornamental and intricate beyond all expression. She has a plain sky, and soon she changes it to a mackerel sky that no one can paint. She has a plain moonlight, and changes that, and hangs out all the stars in the sky. She has a plain field of grass, and the next one is starred with daisies that no man can number. She has a calm sea, and in an hour it is beating its waves upon the shore, in the despair of art. And so I like plain things that I like, and I like a reasonable amount of filigree and ornament."

Said George: "That seems to give you all the latitude you want."

"Jess so, as William Warren says, and I like plenty of sea room. I do not mean to admire any artist's picture because it is the fashion to do so. Of course, no one can get to be the fashion in a great city, without being a good artist. But there are, many times, pictures that pass for more than they are worth."

"Whose, for instance?" asked Miss Graham.

"Corot's."

"I think so," said she.

"Still there is art in them," said Frank. "I attended a sale of a popular artist. His pictures brought from fifty, to several thousand dollars each. I since saw a large picture of his that was appraised at twenty thousand dollars, put up at auction and offered to be sold, if any one would start it at ten thousand dollars. No one offered to start it at ten thousand but after waiting a moment for an offer, a man offered to start it at six thousand. The offer was not taken and the picture withdrawn. Well, at this sale, there was one picture, about twelve by eighteen inches in size, entitled on the catalogue, 'Donkey Approaching a River.' I think it sold for a hundred dollars. It was a poor specimen of this artist's work. After the sale a messenger came for it. He had the bill receipted. They looked among the pictures and at last found it. They got it up in a good light. I was there and saw it. They laughed over it. Said the messenger: 'Are you sure this is a donkey approaching a river?' 'Oh, yes, this is it.' Then be kind enough to tell me which is the donkey, and which the river. They pretended to debate which was which. At last one man said he had found out how it was. Said he, pointing to the road, that led to the river: 'This is the river, and the donkey is the man that paid a hundred dollars for the picture.' This seemed to strike the crowd very cheerfully. But this artist, whom I have not named, did often get some very wonderful effects in his work."

Said Roy: "Now we have talked art, let us have a story. Mr. George, please tell us the story of the happiest day you have had, this last summer."

George looked up with a queer smile. Said he, "You've just hit it. It is a leading question. But you are such a good fellow, I am going to tell you the story of

" *The Artist's Happiest Day!* "

I was busy most of the summer in Boston. I only got away a little, and, as I had good orders, I made big money by filling them. There was a young lady whom I have known for some time, and, as she was not going away much, I proposed. Oh, you did, said Frank. Yes, I proposed that as we were two poor " onfortnits " that did not go to Saratoga or Newport, I thought we might go to Nantasket for a day. She agreed. I told her I would be commissary and provide. Only she had better bring a light waterproof, in case of weather. I could take them in my pocket or satchel. I asked her for them, when I met her, but she had them safe and ready for use when wanted. I like to help a woman, and I also like to have a woman have the will to help herself. Then she is able to do it, if obliged to. We went down in an early boat, the *Rose Standish.* I had a hand-bag slung at my side, and not at all in the way. Oh, the morning was bright, and just the right temperature. The lady was interested and agreeable. We intended to have a happy time, and there was not a jar or bit of friction, all day. We walked slowly up the beach toward Boston Light. We took our time and sat and rested when we wanted to. I had two or three books, and I read selections. She asked for my books and read me selections that I did not know of. There is no end to the possibilities of a Boston girl.

Miss Graham said: "Thank you, sir," which pleased them all.

I took some pencil sketches, and ourselves in them as figures, walking down the beach. We walked slowly down the beach to the cliff at the southern end. It was noon. We went upon the high ground where we could see the whole length of the beach, and south by Minot's Light and beyond. We had the whole Atlantic before us. It was a smooth, pleasant, grassy spot, where we sat down. I have it well marked. I said I was hungry, and asked her if she could get along on crackers and cheese. Oh, yes, well enough. I opened my commissary department, and took out a small paper bag with six crackers and a piece of cheese. I spread it out on a large napkin, and the napkin on a paper. I asked her if she could live on that until we got home. Oh, yes indeed, besides I have two apples in my pocket, and she laid them out on the napkin. Well, said I, I am not so easily suited as you are. I am going to have something decent for dinner. Then I took out a quarter box of Philippe and Canaud sardines, a lemon, two boiled eggs, two good slices of cold corned beef, two of bread and butter, two chunks of pound cake, a piece easily divided of wedding cake, a pint of cracked English walnuts, a pint of Japan tea sweetened, and some candy, two china plates and two silver cups. By Jove, you ought to have heard her laugh. We both had Nantasket appetites, and that is something phenomenal. We took our time about it, and I think we were through a little before two. That dinner had disappeared like dew before the sun. The air was just perfect, and the ocean as calm as in Landseer's picture of peace. We waited, we reclined on the grass, we rested. We voted it the perfection of all days, a summer vacation in itself. A thought which had long been in my mind, was present all day. I said : Then the day is a satisfactory one to you, Annie ? Yes, it is.

I am glad to hear you say so, Annie, I am always happy when I am with you. Are you? she asked. Yes, I am. I am glad of it, said she. Then said I, why should we not be one, and be together always? It has long been in my mind to ask you, and now I must. Will you, Annie? I will do my best for you always. There was no one in sight. I spread the umbrella and kissed her tears away. The promise is not yet fulfilled, but will be soon. The afternoon had sped away, and we took the six o'clock boat for home. As we sailed toward Boston, we saw our city, dressed in the golden glory of the setting sun. Apart from the day, and what we had promised, it was the most golden sea that we sailed in, and the effect of the luminous air over Boston, and a sky with small, but most brilliant clouds floating over all, fitly closed the pleasantest day of my last summer, as well as the happiest, most blessed day of my life. Mister George received the congratulations of the three listeners, and thanks for his most interesting story.

Said Roy, "O it is the old, sweet story, as old as Eden, and as new as the last love that has come to bless mankind. It is the Grand Old Passion that makes the world go round. So may it come to all of us."

CHAPTER XXIX.

HAIL TO THE CHIEF.

FOR three days Roy's studio door had borne a notice, saying: The Art Coterie will entertain itself on Thursday evening, at the usual time and place, perhaps, to see a vision of the man whom our country most delights to honor. People looked and wondered. Good artists had the tableau in charge. Miss Graham could keep a secret. The evening was pleasant, and the company was the size of the house. Miss Graham gave a selection upon the piano, and it was worthy of the applause it received. Then Roy called upon the veracious author of this book, to edify the company. Mr. Wiggin came forward with his heart and a lozenge in his mouth, but both went down, a moment later, and have not been heard of since. He began: Members of the Art Coterie, your chairman has introduced me in just the right way. I always get laughed at, every time I try it. This time I have all the latitude I wish. I cannot treat so large a company. You would not wish me to sing a song. I do not know how to make an entertaining speech, good enough for you, and therefore I must do that which most people like, tell stories. They will be true ones. How common it is to hear people called crank or fool. It has sometimes been my privilege to be so honored. It was written long ago, that he that increaseth knowledge, increaseth sorrow. It

247

is a half truth at best. The more a man knows of literature, the more he can enjoy of the stores of rich thought
of others. The more he knows of what is good in art,
the more beauty he can see in Art and Nature too. This
is a double blessing. Nature is like the sun, and Art is
like the moon, which reflects her light. We give thanks
for both. It has been my business to make some Art
goods, and I like to know as much of the use, construction, and value of what I see, as I can. If I go to an
auction sale, I look about me, and sometimes I find a
thing of use or beauty that is desirable. Once, however,
I attended a sale, and acted very ridiculously, without
being conscious of it at all. It was a large sale at
Leonard's, of portraits and other pictures, partly the remains of Ransom's estate. He had long made portraits
in Boston, and had left some unfinished pictures. Some
were portraits of old women, homely enough to stop a
clock. Nobody would bid. I went up and scratched on
one side of the pictures. If the result was satisfactory, I
bid twenty-five cents. It was struck off to me. The
next, the same, and so on for ten pictures. Then I shook
my head, instead of nodding assent. Well, how much?
asked Joseph Leonard. Ten cents. It was mine. The
crowd laughed. It was a very funny auction. I did not
want the pictures at all, but I could use them at the price
I was paying for them. The sale went on. Mr. Leonard
started them at twenty-five cents each, and a nod from
me accepted them. A few I took at ten cents. Every
time a picture came to me, they were merry over it.
There were some awful old virgins among them. When
the sale was done, I had about seventy pictures, and I
said to Mr. Leonard : I will send an expressman for them

this afternoon, so please have them together. If there are any which others have bid off, that are not called for, put them in with mine, at the price I bid, and, I added, I don't see what anybody but me wants of such pictures. The crowd laughed uproariously. All right, said Mr. Joseph Leonard. I went out and got my lunch. It was a pleasant day, and I was as quiet in my mind as a pan of milk.

Perhaps I had better say, right here, that I have no crazy blood in me. I can trace my ancestry back through good people, as far as any one I know. So I am not a luniac. I know you never heard that word before. Perhaps I had better explain and qualify a little. My mother-in-law had a cousin who was rather flighty. But I never could see that it affected my sanity. Here you can smile. So I persist in feeling perfectly sane at the bottom. Bunchy and full of the old boy, of course, but still more or less sane.

Here a friend of Mr. Wiggin, who had been on jolly excursions with him, let out a Haw, Haw, Haw, which became epidemic in the audience.

Mr. Wiggin resumed: Then I went along toward home. I called in at the artist's materials store of Mr. F. C. Hastings & Co. At the desk sat Mr. George Hastings. Said he, "Have you been to Leonard's auction this morning?" "I have." "What do you suppose I heard of you just now, Mr. Wiggin?" "I do not know; something pleasant, I presume." "Shall I tell you?" asked Mr. Hastings. "Certainly, I should be pleased to know." "Well, sir," said he, "there was a man in here just now, and he had come from Leonard's auction. He said he had seen the biggest fool that he had ever seen in his life.

A man perfectly crazy. And his name was Wiggin. He
stood beside the auctioneer, and bought a large lot of horrible old portraits and pictures, that nobody would bid
on. Everything that no one would start at any price, he
would take for twenty-five cents, except that once in a
while, he would only bid ten cents. O he was an awful
fool, clean crazy." I laughed, I had to. Said I, " Well,
Mr. Hastings, what did you tell him?" "I told him I
knew a Mr. Wiggin who makes goods for us, and he was
a long way from being crazy. In fact I told him that Mr.
Wiggin knew what he was buying." "I think you are
right, Mr. Hastings. Those old portraits were on extra
frames that I had made for a dollar apiece, and under
each worthless portrait was an extra heavy, clean canvas,
making them worth two dollars each, beside the
portrait. And some of the portraits are good. If I cannot get a dime out of that hour at Leonard's, then I mistake. But I was the only man in the room that knew the
value that was covered up under those portraits." "I
knew it was all right," said Mr. George Hastings, " and I
told him so." It is a good thing for a man to know his
own value. It is written, "What shall a man give in exchange for his soul?" Now, if it is wise to know one's
own value, it is wise to increase one's own value. This
the artist does, as he improves in his work. Let him be
very sure of what he can do, and not overestimate himself.

There were three brothers in Philadelphia, artists and
good fellows all. One was a photographer, and O the
beautiful, picturesque stereoscopic views he has made,
some of which I have copies of. One of the brothers
went to England. He made fine oil studies of the old

castles, ruins, and whatever was best material for him. I
visited him in his studio in Philadelphia, after his return
from Europe. Here is the story that he told.

The American Artist in London.

One day I went to the National Gallery in London. I
took my time about it, and looked over all the pictures.
I saw some being copied. I asked the janitor if it was
allowed to copy any pictures. Yes, sir. You can copy
hany picture 'ere. I told him I would like to copy "Turner's Shipwreck." I got the size of the canvas, and told
him I would send canvas and easel in the morning, as soon
as the gallery was open, and I would make it right with
him if he would care for them. This he agreed to do.
Then he went back to some men he had been talking
with, and I heard him say, 'Ere's a Hamerican wot's a-
goin' to copy "Turner's Shipwreck." Isn't it 'igh? They
all laughed. The next morning my easel and canvas
were on time, and I was ready soon after the gallery was
open. It was a good day. The janitor was having many
callers, and he told them all. They laughed and had no
end of fun of it. The presumption of these Hamericans
was 'orrible. I took a large palette and put on a pile of
color. I took my coat off. I got two or three measures
and then put a large patch of color right into the middle
of the canvas. They were immensely amused. There
were from six to twenty persons watching me all the
time. Soon there was a large piece of canvas covered.
Then I laid on my color to stay, and the picture began to
grow. As fast as I put the color on, it was "Turner's
Shipwreck." It was like it, and it was just as good.
They laughed no more. They tiptoed around me. They

looked through their hands. They did not cease to watch me. I did not see them at all, but I observed them all. I worked the best I knew, and I was satisfied with what I was doing. I knew their eyes were on me for criticism, and I gave them no chance. The janitor asked if I needed anything. No, I was all right. I must cover my canvas to-day. It ought not to be over a day's work to copy such a picture as that. He looked dismayed and I wanted to laugh, but I kept busy. One man asked if the picture was for sale. No, I did not wish to sell it. So I kept on. A little later, a fine-looking gentleman came up and praised my copy. In a few minutes more, he gave me an invitation to dine with him. I declined. When the light began to fail in the afternoon, my copy was done, and I had five invitations to dinner. The artist farther continued. Now all I have said is only on my assertion. But here on this wall is another copy of "Turner's Shipwreck," just a quarter of the size of the original. You can judge by this, whether my full-size copy was good for anything or not.

I gave my verdict, at once, that it was a wonderful, splendid copy. And I hereby add that the artist, Mr. Thomas Moran, is a splendid artist and good fellow, and the hour that I passed in his studio was most entertaining. His pictures are often in chromo. I have his photograph coming in with the Philadelphia Art Club. If there is anything I do admire, it is to see a man that knows something. I had a visit of several days in Philadelphia, and a good time in them all. I almost always do have a good time, for I keep them on hand, ready made, like an enterprising hardware firm that I once knew. They circumvented frozen ground by keeping post-holes, ready dug, for sale.

The Story of the Nun and the Artist.

The scene changes to a studio in Ohio. The artist was at work, one day, when a knock came on his door. He admitted a short, stout, clean-shaven man, who had on a Roman collar, and was a Roman Catholic priest. He looked at the pictures and talked of art. He asked the artist if he ever repaired pictures. Yes, often. He had studied with a figure painter and often had figure pieces to repair and varnish. The priest engaged the artist to go to an institution, a home of Sisters of Charity, and look at a large picture of the "Annunciation" in the reception room. He went there, examined the picture, and reported that it could be made as good as new, but it would take four or five visits to finish it, as the browns had cracked so badly in the bottom of the picture. The price was satisfactory. The picture was taken from the frame and the artist began his work. Two or three nuns came and looked at him as he painted. He was a fine looking and appearing young man, and a good artist. The lady superior was engaged with company, and after the other nuns had gone out, one remained to look at him. She was about twenty-four years old, tall and handsome. He spoke to her. Do you like pictures? Speak low, she said, the walls have ears. Yes, I do, very much. They conversed in a low tone. He looked at her, and what he saw in her face prompted him to ask, Are you happy here and glad to stay? She shook her head sadly. Do you wish to get away? I do. I was prevailed upon to come, and I have been sorry ever since. He said, I expect to come here again next Thursday. Try to come in and see me paint, and I will talk with you again about it. I shall be glad to serve you, for you have impressed me very much. Thank you, sir, she said. Yes, very much, he added. More than any woman I ever saw. Ladies and gentlemen, I am telling this story exactly as the artist himself told it to me. She went out of the room. He removed the loose crackly browns of the corner which were peeled up all ready to rattle off. Then he laid it in strong of umber, burnt sienna and ochre, leaving out the asphaltum which had made it crack. He left the picture one good stage towards stability. The lady superior came in. She asked if any one had been in the room. Yes, madam. Two or three people had looked in or passed through the room. There, said he, I will try to come again next Thursday, and advance it another stage. He picked up his color box and retired, leaving two people to think much of his next visit.

They say love laughs at locksmiths, and will go where it is sent in spite of bolts and bars. Certain it is, the nun had a picture in her mind, and it was not the " Annunciation," which she cared nothing about, but it was the honest young artist who had told her that rare and inspiring story, that she had impressed him more than any one, of all the daughters of Eve. And he painted and mused, and he sighed, and he painted.

The next Thursday brought him to the home of the Sisters of Charity. The lady superior met him and he was soon at his work. As it was reception day, she was soon busy with other visitors, who were entertained in the sitting-room or chapel, library or embroidery room. An hour elapsed and the artist's work was well advanced for the day. He feared he should not see the face he was so much interested in, when the door softly opened, and she was at his side. He shook her hand warmly. She said she was afraid she should not get a chance to slip in and see him. The artist was glad to welcome her, and he told her she was in his thoughts all the time, since he had seen her, a week before. She said she was glad of it. If she failed to see him the next Thursday, it would be because she was too closely watched, and could not come. She would see him if she could possibly. He hoped so. Now, said she, I must go. He looked at her as only a lover can, and they kissed each other. It was a sure thing after that. She was gone. He left his work well advanced, so as to be ready for the higher lights after drying a week. He went away, but he left his heart behind him. There was another in that great building, in the same condition. For two people it was a long, uninteresting week. Nothing had any flavor to it. Neither one had anything they wanted, or wanted what they had. Mr. Mantalini said, "My life is one demd horrid grind." I suppose it is not too much to say, that all who love beauty are susceptible people. It follows that all susceptible people are likely to fall in love. When they do fall in love, the Grand Old Passion possesses them to the exclusion of everything else. It is an awful condition to be in, and yet, I suppose those are the most truly unfortunate who have never loved at all. It is a nebulous kind of a paradox. Even Solomon, himself, a man of large experience, pretended he could never understand it. A woman may possibly be excused for not loving, because she, like Hannah Partridge, never had the chance. But a man, that is like an egg, so full of himself that he has no room for any one else, is entitled to the full benefit of my opinion. An old bachelor always reminds me of a mule, whom Sunset Cox has so happily described as "an animal without pride of ancestry, or hope of posterity." The nun and the artist were not that kind of people. They were willing to follow the example of the old gardener and his wife, whom we are all obliged to acknowledge as our ancestors.

The week went by on leaden wings, but at last it went, and Thursday came. The artist was ready to work upon the picture. There was a glass window on the back side of the room. It was transom-like, high up, and always closed. He spread out his colors and worked upon the picture. Visitors came and the lady superior was away with them. After a little time, the door softly opened, and his nun came in, softly closing the door after her. In an instant she was in his arms, and was getting such a kiss as — but there was a knock on the glass window, in the back part of the room. She turned pale, and almost fell to the floor, as the door opened, and the lady superior, with a scowl upon her face, took her by the arm, and led her from the room.

The superior soon returned, with pen, ink, and paper, saying, you need not touch the picture again. Make out your bill and receipt it. He did so without a word. She paid the money, opened the door for him, and in a moment it was locked behind him. He consulted a lawyer. The lawyer could see no daylight. He went to a sheriff, but he had no authority to enter the abode of peaceful people. He went to the governor and stated the case. The governor wished him well, but could see no chance whatever to help him. The artist had money but had no claim on any one to demand help. He did not even know the nun's name. What became of the woman he did not know. I could not comfort him, and I do not extenuate the crime of those who forbid marriage, in the face of the New Testament, which approves it.

I have told you the story just as the artist told it to me. I believe it fully. I think a bad promise is better broken than kept. I think that the son who said he would go to work in his father's vineyard, and went not, was a bad lot; I think the second one, who repented and went, did better. I think that Catherine Von Bora, who broke her vows as a nun, to marry Martin Luther, did right. The wrong was in the foolish, wicked vow of celibacy. It is as wicked and hurtful as to stick one arm up straight until it hardens there, as the fools do in India.

Thus far I have told three stories. Now let us have a more playful one. It is a story of

Apollo in Boston.

There is — now, to-day — in Boston, a young artist, quite a talented one, who is, like many others of his class, a daisy. Six feet high, fine form, handsome hands, clear complexion, dark hair, a moustache that is Cupid's bow in shape, red lips, splendid dark eyes, an Apollo in his own right, and strongly threatened with beauty all over. If he was the Marquis of Westminster's son, what a swath he would cut. If anything can surpass the way he plays the piano it is the way he plays the banjo. And he might be a lady-killer just as easy as rolling off a log. But he is not, and, on the contrary, he is the pink of propriety, and as safe as your grandmother. If I was the most modest, blushing young lady in the world I would not hesitate to be alone with him, he is so safe. I would risk the casualties. He has such an air, and a twist about him, and he can entertain friends, particularly ladies, just elegantly. O I tell you he is one of the gayest, airiest, of all the mortal gods that inspire our modern Olympus. Of course I mean Boston. Any one ought to know that. So I call on him, make him come and sup with me, make him talk, and put him through his paces, as Artemus his "amoosin' kangaroo." Somebody says, Every rich family in New York keeps a tame clergyman. I have a number of tame artists, and most refreshing people they are. Well, one morning this Apollo, junior, which is not far from his real name anyway, had arisen from his beautiful couch, — no levity, please, it is actual fact, — he had taken his bath, had dressed himself, as he always did, to look as if he had just come out of the upper drawer. Here I must digress again, and say, that Boston has a large percentage of this class, who are in striking contrast to some people who always look as if they had slept in the ash barrel. Apollo, junior, came sweetly down to breakfast. Sweet is no name for it. Everything about him was as sweet as a wrinkle in a fat baby's neck. Breakfast, I said. Now if any part of your life has been unfortunate, I beg you not to associate any coarse "grub" with this breakfast. No fried liver smothered in onions about this. Not much. Apollo junior would not touch it. No. He took some very nice, delicious biscuits, such as are evolved by the Boston cooking schools, a little delicate meat, one or two bulbs of the Solanum tuberosum, and a cup or two of male-berry coffee, such as Cleopatra refreshed Marc Antony with. Apollo junior would no more have touched female berry coffee than he would have put Prussian blue in a picture. He believed in the eternal fitness of things, and so do I.

So he had his breakfast, and was walking down Tremont Street, in that state of body and mind that the truly elegant Boston man loves to be. The smile upon his face was like the sunshine upon the sweet waters of the Batrachian Lake upon the Common. It was a cool morning. A tramp met him. The tramp was poor, ragged, dirty, pitiful, cold, shivering, and hungry. He was the antipodes of Apollo junior, in all things. He was very, very cold, you see. He had slept, or tried to, in a cattle car, with a slat bottom. Apollo was moved to pity, like old Grimes, and the tramp was moved to beg. O give me ten cents to buy something to eat, I am dreadful cold and hungry. Said Apollo: My friend, I will give you some money upon one condition; if you will solemnly promise me that you will give ten cents for a good stiff drink of whiskey, I will give you twenty five cents. If ever I saw a man that needed warming you do. Will you promise? Ye-e-e-s, I will, truly, said the tramp, shivering. He got the money, and took a bee-line for a saloon. The recording angel stood and chewed his pen for some time before he knew which side of the book to enter it. Finally he laughed. I'll do it, says he; and he wrote Apollo junior, credit, by cash paid the kingdom of heaven, twenty-five cents. A gift of pity and love. He called the wretch "my friend." If some folks I know of had known it, they would have been madder than wet hens. My stories are done. •

Roy Bartlett announced, that it was hoped there would be a visit of a spirit of might and power, that they might see, once in their lives, one whom we all delight to honor.

There was a dark curtain across the rear end of the parlors.

Said Roy, "It is usual, when we wish to get an audience into harmony and sympathy, to sing. This brings us to be all of one mind, and is supposed to make it easy for the spirit to appear. Now please sing that grand piece, Keller's American Hymn. All please join who have the gift of song. Miss Sarah Warren, please take the piano."

It was done. Of all noble songs, I like that hymn, and then they sung it with the spirit and the understanding also. The windows were open, and when it was done, they heard the applause from a large company outside. It was just fun for Mrs. Warren and her daughters. The applause came floating in like a sixth sense, or as the smell of gunpowder did, when the great peace jubilee in Boston sang the national hymns, with anvil and cannon accompaniment. Oh, that mighty tide of song. God bless P. S. Gilmore for that.

Then Roy said, "Now Miss Emily Warren will read a poem by John Pierpont, and sung once, on the twenty-second of February, in the Old South Church. It is Pierpont's 'Washington.'" In perfect stillness, with the lights turning a little lower, she read the poem beginning,

"To Thee, beneath whose eye
Each circling century
Obedient rolls."

When she came to the stanza,

"There like an angel form,
Sent down to still the storm,
Stood Washington.

Clouds broke and rolled away,
Foes fled in pale dismay,
Wreathed were his brows with bay,
When war was done,"

then, the piano being muffled, by laying a large, lady's
cloud, or hood, upon the strings (a trick which if done
rightly is a revelation), and a snare drum, also muffled,
and deftly played by Miss Sarah Warren, and the instruments were ready. The lights were very low.

Said Roy, "The Continental army is coming. Washington has taken command at Cambridge."

Yes, he is coming. There was a rustle of feet and afar
off was heard the piano and drum and the tramp of the
time-keeping soldiers coming nearer, nearer, nearer. It
was a fine illusion. It came near. Halt was ordered,
and the music ceased. The front door opened and rus-
tling and tramping seemed as if important visitors had
come. Earnest words were spoken. Has he come?
Yes, it is he. He has come. They are here. Oh, it is
a sight for a lifetime. Shall we see him? Perhaps, I
hope so. The room was perfectly dark and still. Then a
strong, solemn voice recited this adjuration,

"Hail, chieftain from the home above,
Come from the land of light and love;
Come to us from thine own blest place,
Let us once more behold thy face,
Thou, who didst lead our armies on
Till liberty and peace were won.
Chosen of God and heaven-sent,
Our leader, patriot, president.
Once more receive the homage due
A mighty nation pays to you.

Receive the praise so gladly given,
Welcome to God, and saints in heaven.
Come thou from home that saints inherit,
Come bless our sight, inspiring spirit,
We love thee, wait to meet thee here,
Great Washington, appear! appear!"

The piano struck softly a few bars of "My country, 'tis of thee." The drum rolled and the centre of the curtain was shot with light. The light at first was white. In a minute it was changed to blue, in another it was roseate. Then the curtain parted in the middle and showed two large, rich, silk, American flags, parted, and in a beautiful alcove sat General Washington himself. The parlors were dark, the alcove was light. It was a sight for a lifetime. The illusion was so good they did not think to criticise. Whispers were heard. One woman really asked: Is it Washington? What is it? Is he alive? No, it is wax. No, it is not. I saw him wink. And so, hungry eyes looked at that tableau. Whoever it was, played his part well, and looked our idea of Washington to perfection, like Gilbert Stuart's picture. He sat still. O what dignity and conscious power. The arch of evergreen, above all, the flags, the alcove lighted from invisible lamps. The drapery and lace curtain in the rear, the exquisite hothouse flowers. O, these ladies and artists had not studied art for nothing, and they did not lack for a dollar, if they needed it. Mrs. Warren blossomed. She was a girl again.

Said Roy, "Now we will have, 'Hail to the chief.' After which this illusion will change, and pass away, forever. If this is not Washington himself, you will never get a better likeness until you see him. Look at the fine ruddy color which Gilbert Stuart has twiddled into the cheeks of his portrait, and the hair and expression I have often admired in this gentleman. And they are more like Washington than any one I ever met."

Then, with bull's-eye lamps enough to see the score, with Miss Graham at the piano and Miss Sarah Warren with little taps and rolls of the drum, they sang that glorious song of The Wizard of the North, —

> " Hail to the chief who in triumph advances,
> Honored and blest be the evergreen pine,
> Long may the tree in his banner that glances,
> Flourish, the shelter and grace of our line."

O it is so good I can hardly refrain from putting it all in. And those magnificent sopranos, with an abundant support of choir singers and instruments, made such a triumphant song, as I never heard surpassed. They sang the whole four stanzas, repeating only the last line of each. Then the gas was turned on and the gentleman arose.

Roy spoke, " Friends, the vision has passed. I now have the pleasure of introducing to you a gentleman who looks like Washington, and is like him in noble and kindly character. He has been long and well known in Cambridge, both in business and the city government. He is the founder of the New Hampshire Club of Cambridge, and its first president. He is as popular and as worthy in his sphere, as Washington was in his. At any rate, a great many people love him, and so do I, and I gladly present to you Mr. Francis L. Chapman of Cambridge."

To say he had a greeting, is useless. He was known to several, and he had as much welcome, for his own sake, as for the great commander. Many were presented by name, and would persist in calling him General Washington.

It is a matter of history, how clean the streets of Jerusalem were once, when every man did his best to keep it clean before his own house. It is a matter of astonishment, how much enthusiasm there is in a society, where they all let themselves out to help all they can, and to enjoy it, whether or no. Churches, make a note of this; this the Art Coterie did. They did their best to make it good. They all owned it, and owed it allegiance. They smacked their lips, and made it taste good without criticism. If they had gone to a theatre or church festival, and paid a long price for admission, I am afraid their noses would have gone up into the air, like so many art critics'.

Roy said, "It is getting late. Let us sing 'Auld Lang Syne.'"

A gentleman jumped up and said, "I was at a late meeting of the New Hampshire Club in Cambridge, and the company would not let Mr. Chapman off, until he sang an old song, that used to give the firemen a chance to come in on the chorus. Mr. Chapman is a member of the old fire department, before the days of steam fire engines, and there is so much love and good-will among the ex-members, that they make him sing the old song as they used to, and all the boys come in on a roaring chorus. I move that we request Mr. Chapman to sing 'Lowlands Low.'"

Roy put it to vote, and the answer was a unanimous "Aye." They all laughed.

Mr. Chapman said he had sometimes been elected to

office, but never went in by a handsomer majority. He was no musician, and did not claim to sing; but the boys wanted a jolly chorus, and the old sea-song helped them to sing the chorus. The New Hampshire Club had ordered it, and he would give it to the Art Coterie if they would only come in strong on the chorus. The song is as old as the ocean, more or less, and here it is:

THE LOWLANDS.

"O I have a ship in the North countree,
And she goes by the name of the Bold Galatee;
But I fear she will be taken by some Turkish gallee,
As she sails along the lowlands.
  Chorus — Lowlands low,
        As she sails along the lowlands low.

"Then up steps the boy, and to his master said,
What will you give to me if I'll go and destroy?
O I will give you gold, and I will give you store,
And you shall have my daughter dear, when you return on
  shore, —
If you'll sink her in the lowlands.
  Chorus — Lowlands low,
        If you'll sink her in the lowlands low.

"Then this boy he bent his best and away swam he;
Swam till he came to the Turkish gallee.
This boy he bent his best and away swam he;
Swam till he came to the Turkish gallee,
As she sailed along the lowlands.
  Chorus — Lowlands low,
        As she sailed along the lowlands low.

"Now this boy he had an auger that bored two holes at once,
Now this boy he had an auger that bored two holes at once;
While some were playing cards and some were playing dice,

He let the water in and dazzled all their eyes;   ·
And he sank them in the lowlands.
    CHORUS — Lowlands low,
           And he sank them in the lowlands low.

" Then this boy he bent his best and away, away swam he;
Swam till he came to his own ship's side,
Dear master, pick me up, for I'm drifting with the tide,
And I'm sinking in the lowlands.
    CHORUS — Lowlands low,
           And I'm sinking in the lowlands low.

" I will not pick you up, his master he replied,
I will kill you, I will shoot you, I will send you down the tide,
And I'll sink you in the lowlands.
    CHORUS — Lowlands low,
           And I'll sink you in the lowlands low.

" Then this boy swam around all on the larboard side,
Then this boy swam around all on the larboard side;
Dear shipmates, pick me up, for I'm drifting with the tide,
For I'm sinking in the lowlands.
    CHORUS — Lowlands low,
           For I'm sinking in the lowlands low.

" Then the shipmates picked him up all on the larboard side;
They laid him on the deck, where he soon revived;
And then they called the captain unto the larboard side,
And they chucked him overboard, with a fair wind and tide,
And they sank him in the lowlands.
    CHORUS — Lowlands low,
           And they sank him in the lowlands low.

" Now this boy he won gold and silver bright,
Now this boy he won gold and silver bright,
Now this boy he won gold and silver bright,
Likewise his master's daughter, to be his heart's delight,
As he sailed along the lowlands.
    CHORUS — Lowlands low,
           As he sailed along the lowlands low.

" Come weigh up your anchor all to the bow,
Through this wide ocean we have to plough,
Through this wide ocean we have to plough,
Till we get her off the lowlands.
    CHORUS — Lowlands low,
        Till we get her off the lowlands low."

To say the Art Coterie sang, was no name for it. Those splendid sopranos outdid themselves. When the chorus struck the " Lowlands low," it was immense.

The basses sung in a voice like a fog-horn. Nobody said it was or was not classical music, but some of them said Beacon Hill never heard the like, or anything they relished so well. Ask any one of the company to-day, and they will laugh. The crowd outside joined in, and it is even said that away down the harbor, the sculpins came to the surface to listen, and even the sea-serpent put in an appearance, off Apple Island. This I cannot vouch for, as I wish to be entirely circumstantial and avoid even the appearance of exaggeration. But I do know Mr. Frank Chapman sang the old sea-song, and we enjoyed it hugely, even though it is flavored with tragedy, even as the rhyme of the Nancy Bell. However, none laid it to heart, and we all went home happy, even as happy as a pair of twins.

CHAPTER XXX.

THE next day Roy was at the studio, bright and early. Miss Graham was there not long after. There was plenty of fun among those who sang at the Coterie. Everybody was as pleasant as a basket of chips. A New Hampshire proverb. Miss Graham brought Roy a note. It read : —

MR. ROYAL BARTLETT, Dear Sir, — You are kindly invited to dine with us this evening at six o'clock. Truly yours, —
WILSON GRAHAM.

It was from Miss Graham's uncle. Mr. and Mrs Graham had often been in the studio, where they had met Mrs. Warren and her daughters. They were all agreeable people, and had been often in the studio and at the Coterie.

Roy said : "Miss Graham, I am glad to receive your uncle's kind invitation, which I shall have to answer."

"You are welcome, sir," said she, " and you need not send an answer, but just go across the Common with me, when we are through work. I told my uncle, I thought you would come, and they will take it for granted."

" Ah," said Roy, " your uncle has good fortune. It is real luck for a disabled clergyman, to have an estate all furnished, to care for, with an income and a good living."

"Yes," she said, "I am glad uncle is so well provided for. But the estate he cares for, constantly increases under his management, so he really earns a great deal more than he costs the estate, by his judicious investments. He has taken the earnings and bought land in New York, that he has built business blocks upon, so that the owner can see the estate grow largely every year. He has never lost the estate a dollar, and he has gained it many thousands."

"Ah, yes," said Roy: "honesty and stability of character are a double blessing. They help everybody. I am thankful that, since his voice became weak, he has such a chance to show the sterling gold of his character. A faithful Christian minister deserves that the world shall use him well. Some people never see any one situated as he is, without feeling envious, and wishing all the blessing was theirs; but I never feel that way. I never expect more than a competence, and I am fully prepared to be happy and thankful with that. I have a good time all the time, now, and I hope he will long enjoy the trust that is laid upon him. Of course, that means you too, Miss Graham."

"Thank you, sir," she answered.

There came a knock at the door. Roy admitted the visitors. It was the man who had called Roy a bad name. His wife came too. They had their pictures hung up and liked them ever so much. He was one of those men who when they have done a wrong, and have seen it, can never do too much to repair it. So he told Roy that he had an offer for his house, of far more than it cost him, with all the furniture, and also the pictures. He said he was on his way down town to close the bargain and should want some more pictures. Would Mr. Bartlett take a commission for some more?

"Certainly."

"Then as soon as the trade was made sure, he would call and give his order. He thought it was all right now as a thousand dollars had been paid, and the papers drawn; but if Mr. Bartlett would allow his wife to remain there, he would slip into Mr. Lyman's office and complete the trade."

He did. He was gone about half an hour, and came back with the whole amount deposited in the bank.

"It was sure, surer than certain," he said, and, he added, "as I do not own a house, or pictures in it, and also, as the pictures helped very much to sell the house, here is a check for five hundred dollars. Mr. Bartlett, you please take that check, and paint me what pictures you can afford to for it. If you can give me one thirty by fifty and others smaller, say four or five in all, all right. And do what you can afford to, without the frames. As fast as you get them done send them where the last were framed and let me know. And here is a check for one hundred; will Miss Graham paint me a pair of upright waterfalls for that?"

She would.

"Miss Graham, please choose some of the pretty waterfalls in the White Mountains."

It was so ordered, and the pay was sure; indeed, they had it already. Roy said he would do his best to please such a customer, and do it at once. "He never neglected a friend," he said, "and always tried faithfully to do as he would be done by. Would he and his wife look in, in a week, and see how the pictures were coming along?"

They would.

"And would they be at the next Art Coterie? Something nice was brewing. They would be notified."

The call was over, and these people had done a very graceful thing. They had proved, out and out, that they did not think Roy was a scoundrel, for the man had trusted him with five hundred dollars, with permission to pay it in such quantity and quality as he pleased. Truly Roy had not seen such faith, even in Israel. But he had found it in Boston. He went along, and sat down beside Miss Graham. They smiled at each other.

Said he, "Surely, goodness and mercy shall follow me all the days of my life, and I will dwell in the house of the Lord forever."

He said it solemnly and reverently, and he was thoroughly glad Miss Graham had a check for a hundred, and he wished it was for five instead. She deserved it. He was glad Miss Graham had some luck come to her through being in the studio with him, and he hoped more would come, for she had helped him; and if it had not been for her, his auction sale would have been a calamity indeed. Roy said he intended to keep that five hundred whole, so as to pay it on the mortgage of his real estate.

It would not be long before that would be clear.

Roy said he hoped Miss Graham would begin a savings-bank account, if she had not already done so. She thanked him, and said she had money laid away, so if she wanted a hundred dollars she could get it. She laughed. She said she was quite a capitalist, in her way. She did not waste any money.

They had a rush of pupils that day. Young men had lessons by themselves; but the busy day was when every

mother's son of them were women. I hope I have not
dropped a word wrong. It is written that Moses was a
proper child. I never was. I always relish some comical
irregularity. Henry Clay buttered his watermelon.
Sydney Smith was once drinking water, and he said, " O,
that this were a sin, just to give it a relish." The water
was lost, but the bright saying has tickled the fancy of
millions, even until now. There came a knock. It was
the postman. Here is the note.

MR. BARTLETT, Dear Sir, — I have sold the pair of pictures
I bought of you. If you have on hand, or will paint another,
same size, same price, or about that, of a pleasant subject, I
will take them.   Truly yours,
                                   B. S. MOULTON.

He passed the note for Miss Graham to read, and
added, " You furnish one of them, and have half the pay."
She thanked him.

It was a cheerful day. Fred Annerly, Miss Graham's
servant, called at the door. Roy sent word back by him
that the invitation to dinner was accepted. Miss Graham
said he need not write it, as they did not make ceremony
with him. In the afternoon he went to Mrs. Warren's
to tell her he should not be at home to supper. He was
going to dine out. Yes, I know there is a discrepancy,
but I like it. Then Roy went through those toilet mys-
teries which are past all understanding, and came down to
Mrs. Warren for inspection. He passed muster elegantly.
On his way back to the studio he mounted a buttonhole
bouquet, — moss rosebud and sweet-scented geranium leaf,
— and then, I do declare, he looked good enough to eat.
Miss Graham cast him a look that gave him quite a turn.

There are a few men, and more women, who remind me
of the little child's prayer: "O Lord, bless me, and give
me a new heart. Lord bless brothers and sisters, and
give them a new heart. Lord bless papa, and give him a
new heart. And Lord bless mamma, and you needn't
give her any new heart; she's all right now."

They took their way across the Common, over the
bridge in the Public Garden, that the critics suffered such
agony about, but, alas! it did not kill them, then past
the mighty bronze equestrian statue of Washington, and
to the home of Wilson Graham. Fred Annerly admitted
them. It was a splendid house. The centre of it was
the large and elegantly furnished reception room they
were in. Looking out of it, in front was the parlor.
Here were pictures worth looking at, in all the rooms.
Among the artists represented were Claude, Gains-
borough, Sir Thomas Lawrence, Verboeckhoven, Meisso-
nier, Turner, Bierstadt, Heade, Kensett, Bricher, B.
Champney, S. L. Gerry, Brackett, Hunt, Church, T. Moran, Virgil Williams; and Roy was surprised, as well as
pleased, to find two out of his own sale, that Miss Graham had bought. They were hung in a good light.

Mr. Graham and his wife had taken Roy in hand as
soon as he came in, which gave Miss Graham a chance to
slip upstairs, and even up toilet matters. A woman
will not let a man crow over her, if she can help it. It
was easy for Miss Graham to be good-looking, for she
always looked good; because she was good. Another
advantage she had, Jenny Annerly, Fred's wife, was a
fine dressmaker; and with her help in my lady's chamber
Miss Graham soon came down, looking O so sweet that
Roy's gizzard got another twist. It served him right.

He had not seen her in full bloom before.

Roy said, "Mr. and Mrs. Graham, and Miss Graham, I am very greatly obliged to you for hanging my pictures in such good company. I am afraid you have used me too well."

"I think not," said Mr. Graham. "Your pictures are good work. You have studied with Mr. Gerry some, and have caught a little of the charm in which he idealizes a picture. If you do not go to Europe and learn the broad crude way that some paint there, you have a fine future before you, in art. Are you doing as well as you ought to expect, Mr. Bartlett?"

"Yes, sir, better. Especially since the sale, which was bought experience."

"I am glad of it. Now let us go to the dining-room and see what they have for us. As our party is small, Mrs. Graham and I will lead the way, and the next couple forms of itself." When they were seated at the table, it was Mr. and Mrs. Graham as opposites and Roy and Miss Graham also. Mr. Graham gave thanks.

Roy said, "Ah, you arrange as Mrs. Warren does. She has a quartette, only in that case three are ladies."

"Yes," said Mrs. Graham. "Our family is small, only three of us. Although we often have company. Mr. Graham often meets some of his clerical friends, or college chums, and then we are social. But no one ever need be lonesome in Boston. It is so compact together, and is in such endless variety, that all can be amused, instructed, or interested. It was one of the glories of Jerusalem, when in her grandeur, that she was builded as a city that was compact together, but Jerusalem in her palmiest days never saw the time when she had a quarter part of the things to interest one that Boston has to-day."

"Well done, aunty," said Miss Graham. "That is the longest and best speech you ever made."

"I don't care," said she. "I am a Boston girl and I know whereof I speak."

The first course had been soup.

"Do you like turkey, Mr. Bartlett?" asked Mr. Graham.

"Indeed I do. I think it ought to be our national bird, instead of the eagle. An eagle is a tyrant and villain in his life and useless in his death. A turkey is a harmless good citizen in his life and a feast for good Christians in his death."

"Then," said Mr. Graham, "you will like this one, for it is a large and fine hen turkey as I ever saw."

Said Roy, "I never heard but one criticism on turkey in my life."

"What was that?"

"A man of large appetite once said: 'A turkey is the most uncomfortable bird in the world. It is rather too much for one, and not enough for two.'"

The dinner was a social one. Each tried to see how much he could do for the others, and Fred and Jenny waited upon them, as if they were trying to do all they could, also, to supply their wants. And they were spoken to in such a considerate pleasant way that it seemed like a realization of what was once spoken, "Hereafter I call you not servants, but friends."

Roy had seen it in his own home and he was glad to find it here. They had an abundant dinner, everything at its best, and took an hour for it. Then they went up

to the reception room, and up another flight of massive
mahogany stairs, to a very large front room, the drawing-
room. A low bookcase of heavy carved black walnut
was on the whole length of the west side of the room,
while upon it were bronzes, reproductions of famous
buildings, the Temple of the Sun at Baalbec, the temple at
Jerusalem, the Temple of the Sybil at Tivoli, the Parthe-
non, the Napoleon column, Michael Angelo's Moses, the
statue of the Nile, the statue of Ocean, the pilgrim statue
of Faith, and I don't know what. The cases were filled
with books of the best, and at their best. The pictures
were large and splendid. There was nothing there that
said, I am here for show, but all said, here is a good and
valuable thing, that you may appreciate and enjoy. It
was the richest and best furnished room that Roy had
ever been in. Of course Roy knew temples and palaces,
without and within, and he knew what was in Europe
and Asia, better than half that had been there. And why
not? He was familiar with the stereoscope, and had a
thousand views of his own. He had seen many thousands. He knew the palaces of Europe much better than
many who have been there. But here were so many
points of interest he was charmed at once.

"Now," said he, "before we sit down let us walk
around the room and see how many of the models and
bronzes I can name."

Mr. Graham was curious to know. He went slowly
around, giving the right name and history to every one,
except one, which he was not quite sure of. He thought
it must be the Alexander column at St. Petersburg, but
he was not sure of it as he had never seen a photograph
of it. It was a correct guess. Mr. Graham was pleased,

Very few can do it. Mr. and Mrs. Graham had been in Europe, but Miss Graham had not.

"And so you like stereoscopics?"

"Yes indeed, I do," said Roy.

"I am glad of it, Mr. Bartlett. Sometime we will have a quiet evening with the stereoscopics. This estate contains some fine pictures in glass and paper. We will have a chat to-night, but later we will travel in the stereoscope, and enjoy foreign parts without going out of Boston."

Said Roy, "With good company, this drawing-room is the perfection of comfort. There is beauty wherever you look, but no fashion or style that is trying to assert itself. No angular Eastlake style that is trying to be in fashion. Comfort and beauty in perfection, and suggestions of that which the world has praised and admired for ages."

Said Mr. Graham, "Do you enjoy life, Mr. Bartlett?"

"Yes, sir, I do. I am in perfect health, fairly situated, have no friend in any sorrow or trouble, and I have nothing to worry me. I remember the injunction, 'Rejoice, O young man, in the days of thy youth,' and I do not forget the remainder of the injunction. Of course I can never be situated as you are here, but I think I shall get as much blessing and cause for thankfulness in life, as almost any one you will see."

"What church do you attend, Mr. Bartlett?"

"The Orthodox. I like the old name. I go to Park St., except that I often go to hear Phillips Brooks, Doctor Bartol, and others, who give me a good quality and variety of instruction. What was your denomination, Mr. Graham, before you gave up your pastorate?"

Mr. Graham smiled, "O the old Puritan faith, the

New Testament in practice. There are some little variations in our evangelical churches, but they are near enough alike to work together and love each other if they will."

Said Roy, "Just see how nicely we four people are seated. What a nice picture it would make, looking either way."

Miss Graham said, "Yes, these social home scenes are always attractive."

Mr. Graham asked, "Have you studied medical books any, Mr. Bartlett?"

"Yes, sir, I read several hours each day, and I often choose a medical book. I should be a good nurse, and I could play doctor, in the absence of a better man."

"What is your favorite school?"

"I suppose the allopathic, but perhaps the modified allopathic, or the eclectic, perhaps."

"How about the homœopathic?"

"Well, Mr. Graham, I do not believe there is enough of it to amount to a distinct system. Of course I do not object, if any one chooses to use it. Many nice people will have no other. Oliver Wendell Holmes once brought down the house with this exhaustive statement, ' Homœopathy has long been encysted, and is carried as quietly on the body politic, as an old wen.' I heard him say it. I have no prejudices against it, but if anybody recommends homœopathic medicine to me, I always think what occurred to a friend of mine. I know the man well, and I know he told the truth. He had not been feeling well, and had some rheumatism. He consulted a homœopathic physician, a good man, whom I also know. He put up quite a large bottle of sugar pellets, which he was to take, four at a time, three times a day. The patient stayed at home, and was company for his grandson, a boy of about three years. He took out his pellets, and set the bottle down on the table. The medicine had little taste or smell. It melted in his mouth and was gone down the red lane. He mused a little and queried in his mind, if so little cause could have much effect. It seemed queer, so small an atom, on so large a man. All at once he remembered that he was watching the boy. It was poor vigilance. The boy had been suspiciously still, and lo, he had just eaten the last one of that lot of pellets. The old man was scared, but he did not run. The boy was all right. The old man did watch him now, for a change of color, or a sign of pain, or some sign of result. And the result was, there was no result. The boy played all the afternoon. Nothing came of it, except that the old man was much improved by laughing at the loss of his medicine. And since then, when I hear of the blessed little pellets, I think of the boy and the picnic he had of them. However, I think that homœopathic patients are not often hurt by too much medicine, which is more than I can say of some other practice. So it is certainly a negative good, and sometimes it may be a positive."

"You are not very belligerent, Mr. Bartlett."

"Why should I be? I should gain nothing by it, and be in a worse condition to learn wisdom, than if I was a strong partisan. So I fight no windmills."

"I wish more people thought so," said Mrs. Graham.

"Come, Mary," said Mr. Graham, "please to give us a song."

"What will it be, uncle?"

"O let it be my favorite, 'The Maid of Dundee,' and another that you like yourself."

The large Chickering piano gave them a beautiful prelude, and Mary Graham sang, O so sweetly. It was a ripple of sweetest melody. I have heard her sing it, and never heard a song that I liked better. Then she played a selection. It was followed by "Homeward Bound," as played by Prof. E. L. Gurney, of Cambridge, and it was full of wonderful variations. She ended the theme by singing the majestic hymn —

> "Out on the dark heaving ocean we glide.
> We're homeward bound, homeward bound."

It was an uplifting song, and when the last sweet notes died away, the clock chimed the hour of ten.

Roy said, "Mr. and Mrs. Graham, it is time to go. I am obliged to you for one of the pleasantest evenings of my life."

"I am glad of it," Mr. Graham answered. "We hope to have you here again soon."

Miss Graham honored the going guest, and he bade her good-night at the door. The night was cold. Roy cast his eyes up at the house, as he went toward Beacon Hill. "I declare, that is a beauty," said he to himself. "O it is past all belief, how beautiful is beauty, and cleanliness, and love, and song, and Christian living, and hoping, and aspiring. Mr. and Mrs. Graham are as fine people as I ever met. Why, I don't see but what they are as good as my father and mother, and that is good enough. And Miss Graham is a very talented and accomplished young lady. To play with such phrasing and expression, and to sing with such feeling. Well, well, well, and to paint so well too. It is rare to find one accomplishment that is really good enough to entertain you, but here is a woman with three. If she has human faults I have not seen them in an acquaintance of several months. Well, well, well. There are some white folks in this world, surely. And the Warrens, too, blessed people. Yes, yes. There is a heaven, and even here it is begun. And there is a hell, too, to put dog-stealers in, and they are already in it, and it is in them, or they would not steal Canis Major. Well, well, well, I am blest."

Now, reader, don't you think he was? I do.

CHAPTER XXXI.

THE days went pleasantly along with Roy Bartlett. As soon as the studio was open, one day, there came a knock on the door. It was Edric Lyman, Roy's lawyer, about Roy's age. It was a pleasant meeting.

"How is business, Mr. Lyman?"

"Very good. Mr. Bartlett, I had a queer thing happen yesterday. Have you time to hear it?"

"Certainly. I can paint any time and all the time. So if something happens to you, that I ought to hear, please tell me."

"Some days ago, one morning, as soon as I got into my office, there came a man whom I had known as a real estate agent. He looked all around, and, seeing I was apparently alone, he sat down. Want a case? said he.

"Yes, sir, lawyers always want cases."

"There is a mortgage," said he, producing it; "it bears the signature of Eli Bertram. It is his own signature, I saw him sign it. It is for ten thousand dollars. The property is worth about fifteen. So it is sate. I do not wish to foreclose it. It is recorded all right and no one can find any irregularity about it. I will discharge the mortgage for a little less than the face value, and I might reduce it to one-half rather than fight it. But I should not want to. Here is his address. See if he will settle and what he will pay. I will look in every morning. If

282

you have not heard anything, shake your head and I will
go out. If he has been in, beckon with your finger and
I will come."

"Yes, sir. Now please tell me, who does this mortgage
run to?"

"Me, Solomon Shavin."

"Well, Mr. Shavin, what objection will he bring to
paying this mortgage?"

"He will say he never made a mortgage, never signed
a mortgage, never got the money."

"What shall you say?"

"I shall show his real signature, his seal, and his acknowledgment of the deed, before a justice of the peace
who happens to be my clerk. There is also another witness. Oh, I have got him strong. He can't get away."

"Was the money paid to him by a bank check?"

"No. It will be proved that the money was paid,
a part in cash, and a part in settlement of an old claim
which I had against him."

"Did he acknowledge this claim?"

"Yes, er, no, he didn't really, you know, and there is
where he will stick. But I can prove that I paid him a
large sum of money, which I really did, you know, that
is, it was a large sum to look at, and my clerk will swear
it was a large roll of bills. But really, the bills were
mostly small ones."

"Now, Mr. Shavin, you have not told me the whole
story. How can a doctor cure a patient when there is
something the matter and the patient won't tell? He
can do nothing. Neither can I. You must tell me
everything, then I may be able to help you get your
money."

"All right, I guess I must. I'll begin away back. If you help me to collect this money, I will pay you ten per cent. of it, and it will make you rich. Will you do it?"

"Of course I will, if it is all right," I answered.

"Bet yer life it is all right. I've got it strong," said he. "Now listen. Many years ago, there was a vacant lot of land at the South End. There was a large mortgage put on it. I knew the land well, and played on it when I was a boy. The mortgagee was a friend of my father. This man was cast away at sea, and, as he had no heirs, it never was paid or discharged. My brother died a spell ago, and left me that mortgage, and the old note that never was paid. So you see it is very valuable."

"See here, Mr. Shavin, you made that mortgage, didn't you? you copied it out of the Suffolk registry, didn't you? word for word, on old paper of course?"

"Wal, if you must know, I did, an' you can bet it is on old paper, for both mortgage and note are on paper cut out of one of old Billy Gray's account books. You can't hoot me down on that. Not much."

"I see," said I, "you have it strong. Did you make the mortgage exact?"

"Yes, I did. Every word. And the note is in all the old-fashioned spelling. Oh, I have any amount of old papers to go to."

"How about the ink?"

"Wal now, I am all right there. I just made my ink out of an old resate of logwood, nutgalls, old nails and vinegar, and it is just yaller with age. So I have a big and solid claim to land that has big blocks on it now. I told Eli Bertram that I had a claim on his land, and my clerk heard me."

"What did he say?"

"He said he had heard of me before. He owns a part of the land. I went on his piece and did a little damage, for which he demanded a small sum. I told him to call and get his money. He came. I told him my pens were poor. I like a goose quill. I made a bill for twenty-five dollars due him, fixed it in a little frame I had, to make it lay flat, and he signed it, or thought he did. There was a crease just above his signature and when that bill was taken off, there was his signature to this mortgage due in three months, for ten thousand dollars. The consideration is twenty-five dollars in cash, and a release of my old mortgage on his real estate. My two clerks are witnesses. They get a dime when I win. Don't you think I have got him?"

I told him it looked so, decidedly.

"Well, well, well!" said Roy, "I shall give up."

"Don't give up yet," said the lawyer, "for the best is to come."

"Now you see," said Mr. Shavin, "my brother was a bachelor. I looked out that his will was all right for me, for he hadn't much, and I started this thing some time ago. I let him have money to carry him through, on condition that he assigned these papers to me, and willed everything to me. He did it easy enough. The note was assigned by the mortgagee to him, and now it is legally and honestly mine. The mortgage is sound, and the interest is very large. The best part of it is, Mrs. Parna Warren and her daughters own a part of the land, with big stores on it, and they are rich, and I can just make them settle."

Roy jumped when the Warrens were mentioned.

"Mr. Shavin continued," said the lawyer, "But Eli Bertram is old and failing, and can't live long. If you scare him a little, and tell him his memory is poor, he will settle. That will establish a precedent, and the others who own the mortgaged land will come down easy. The old mortgage and the note have been carried in my pocket, to make them look old. They have had tea stains on them, and iron rust. I have them in my safe, and they are just the honestest-lookin' old dockiments you ever did see. Now when will you write to Eli Bertram and start toward your ten per cent.? You can take the money yourself, and pay me mine. Then you will be safe and run no risk. I think they will all pay without a suit."

"Then that is your case, Mr. Shavin. If I understand you right, the old mortgage is a real one, in the registry. So it makes little difference whether your copy is real or not. The old note was assigned to your brother, or appears so, and was willed to you, and Eli Bertram's mortgage is based upon that. It is really three forgeries, when we are all alone by ourselves."

"Yes, but don't speak so loud," said Mr. Shavin.

"Well, Mr. Shavin, I don't want your case."

"Why not?"

"Because I don't want that kind of cases."

"Won't you if I pay you a bigger per cent.?"

"No, sir. If you would give me the whole business I would burn it. I don't get money that way."

Mr. Shavin looked as though he had met a setback.

"Wal, I'm sorry, an' mebby I sha'n't do it." He went away. I got up and opened the window, for the air seemed poisoned. I stepped to my closet, only four feet

away, where my typewriter and copyist girl happened to
be, and I said, "Miss Carter, did you get my signal?"

"I did."

"Did you hear that?"

"I did, every word."

"What do you think of it?"

"I am almost ashamed of mankind."

"Will you take pen and ink, and sit down and write,
day, hour, and minute, a correct statement, as you can
remember, of the whole interview. Did you see him
plainly?"

"I did, sir. And I know him well besides. He
brought in claims against my father's estate, that my
mother always said were false. But he got his money."

"Mr. Bartlett, yesterday I had a call from another
man, and who do you suppose it was? Well, sir, it was
old Eli Bertram."

"Was it?" said Roy. "Good, good enough."

"Yes, it was," said Edric Lyman. "I touched a spring
— but don't you tell of it — that called Miss Carter
where she could hear the interview. He began: 'Are you
Edric Lyman?' 'I am.' 'Mr. Lyman, I am the victim of
a damnable conspiracy.' 'I know it,' said I. You ought
to have seen his eyes open. 'You know it? How do
you know it?' 'If you are my client, Mr. Bertram, you
will find out later. But not now. I assure you, I know
it, and all about it.' 'Can you help me, Mr. Lyman? and
will you serve me honestly and faithfully if I pay you
well for it?' 'I will, sir, and to your satisfaction, both in
the work and the pay also, if I serve you at all.' That
pleased the old man. He had got a lawyer's letter, and
of course it was from a shyster of a lawyer. He had

read the rascally demand, and had gone to an honest friend for advice. Now, Mr. Bartlett, who, among all the sons of Adam, do you suppose it was that sent Eli Bertram to me, as an honest lawyer? Well, Mr. Bartlett, it was the man who called you bad names, settled it like a man, and then came back and gave you five hundred dollars for more pictures."

"I declare, I am surprised again," said Roy.

They both laughed heartily at the luck.

"The next thing to do, Mr. Bartlett, is to see Mrs. Warren and her daughters, and the other occupants of the mortgaged land, to find out whether they wish to be my clients or not. The case is mine now. I own it. I can crush the whole villany, and the man who did it; but I doubt if another man can. You keep your own counsel, Mr. Bartlett. Speak a good word for me to the Warrens, and I can save them many thousands of dollars. I know it is irregular, after you know a man's case, but I should be a scoundrel myself if I do not stop this villany. But I am taking too much of your time. I must call on Mrs. Parna Warren. I thought it would not do to keep any of this from you, as it came remotely by you. I also thought it would not do to visit the Warrens without letting you know it."

"Mr. Bartlett, I wish to ask you a leading question."

"Go on," said Roy.

"Mr. Bartlett, are you paying especial attention to Miss Sarah Warren?"

"No, Mr. Lyman, I am not, and I never did. But I regard her as a friend, and a very amiable and accomplished young lady."

"Thank you, sir. That gives some one else a chance."

"I wish you good luck," said Roy.

"Thank you again."

Mr. Lyman went to call on Mrs. Warren. Roy sent a note, saying it would be pleasant to him if Mr. Edric Lyman was invited to their six o'clock dinner. The case was stated to Mrs. Warren. She was surprised, but would consider it. It would be agreeable to Mr. Bartlett to have his friend dine with them, and Mrs. Warren joined in the invitation. The invitation was accepted, and Edric Lyman said in his heart, bless Roy Bartlett for that. He has done me a good turn at once. I do not need to say that the dinner was a good one. The Warrens always had something to eat. Miss Emily was good at conversation, and Sarah was vivacious and splendidly musical. Mr. Lyman had met them often on coterie nights, and they seemed like old acquaintances. You let people laugh together, and they will soon be acquainted. It was settled that Mr. Lyman should consult with Mrs. Warren's lawyer. Then they went to the drawing-room for music. During the evening, Edric found time to say to Miss Sarah Warren that he had been worshipping her at a distance for a long time, and might he call on her sometimes, and get better acquainted? Will you be real good and desirable? she asked, with a smile. Yes, I will, truly. I will always do my best to please you. She made just a little comical bow, and he whispered, O thank you; I will try to deserve it. Then there were two more young folks, each with a bright, beautiful, new idea in their minds, both willing to keep the new commandment. When Edric Lyman had gone, and Roy had ascended to what he funnily called his boudoir, Mrs. Warren was alone with her daughters. She had a spice

of mischief in her.   She said, "Did you have a nice
confab with Mr. Lyman, Sarah?"

"Yes, mother.   Your daughters can never come up to
what their mother used to be.   But they will do their
best."

"Yes, you seemed to be doing very well, Sarah.   That
was a most gracious bow you gave him.   I should not be
surprised if something came of it."

"All things are possible," said Miss Sarah.   "But our
mother has made such an elegant married woman, that
it is to be hoped that her daughters will follow the example of their illustrious predecessor."

Mrs. Warren had not made much by trying to poke
fun at Miss Sarah.

Sam Tamper was the lawyer that had taken the case
for Solomon Shavin.   Whether Shavin had told the
whole story as he had to Edric Lyman, I do not know.
But as I think he had not, this gives Sam Tamper the benefit of a large doubt.   He was known as a sharp lawyer,
who would take any case, right or wrong, but perhaps he
would not disbar himself by any suicidal villany like this.
Mrs. Warren got a letter and a demand for a settlement
from Sam Tamper.   She at once sent it to Edric Lyman.
He, in turn, called on Mrs. Warren's old lawyer, and
showed the letter.   The old lawyer was one of those old
settlers, that believe in themselves, faithful to his clients,
honest as lawyers go, slow, a man of property, family, and
position.   He would take no suggestions from a young
lawyer until he was obliged to.   He read the letter, and
said he did not believe any one was going to run away
with Mrs. Warren's estate.   He thought not.   He looked
up through his glasses, and beamed all his magnetic eyes
at Edric Lyman.

"That depends something upon me," said Edric Lyman.

The old man's back was up in a minute. He was often called to suppress young lawyers. If, like a butting goat, who was driven off with brick-bats and clubs, and got the worst of it, even though vanquished, he could argue still. Said he, "And do you think that you, a boy, although admitted to the bar, are the only man in God's world that can win a case?"

Edric Lyman laughed a mischievous little laugh. Said he, "Mr. Strong, if you and I were to fight two cases alike, with just the same evidence, you would undoubtedly win best, from your fine position at the bar, and with your large experience. But if we had two dangerous cases, and your enemy had all the evidence he wanted, right and wrong, and you had none, and, if I have my case with all the evidence I want, together with a full admission of all the perjury and forgery in it, before a good witness, then who would win?"

"Is that so?" asked Lawyer Strong.

"Yes, sir, that is just so. I have such evidence that Solomon Shavin will not dare to attack Mrs. Parna Warren or Eli Bertram, and, by the way, I have Eli Bertram's case now, and seven other occupants of this mortgaged land. They are all my clients now, and I think I can say, I am absolutely sure, that if Solomon Shavin does fight these cases I can win for all my clients, and send him to state prison for life. But I have no idea he will do anything, but surrender, when he finds he is surrounded. Now, Mr. Strong, Solomon has a strong case. He has the original mortgage and note, or what looks like it; all the witnesses he wants, and the whole business legally willed to him by his brother. The chain is very strong and apparently complete. If I had not the whole thing confessed, with a witness, I could not hope to win the case, and even now, it must be very well managed to win. Still, with what I know, I think I can add collateral evidence enough to win a vindication. So I need your help, Mr. Strong. There are parts of this case that I wish to manage in my own way. If you will see Sam Tamper, and get copies of the mortgage and note, and a copy of Eli Bertram's mortgage to Solomon Shavin, so that I do not appear in it at all, and not let any one know that I am in the case, I will work on it in another direction, to as good purpose. Don't let Sam Tamper or Solomon Shavin know that I am in the case at all, or it will spoil all."

Mr. Strong had been deferred to, kowtowed to, mollified, soft-sawdered, and more than all convinced. An old lawyer likes taffy as well as a girl, and they will take a bushel of it. So Lawyer Strong concluded to be gracious. If he had an idea that Edric Lyman was leading him, he would have kicked like a steer. But Edric Lyman was leading him.

Lawyer Strong called on Sam Tamper, and was taken to the office of Solomon Shavin, as Mrs. Warren's attorney. It was his right to see the mortgage and note. It was shown. It was old and looked honest.

"Have any of the others offered to settle?" asked Mr. Strong.

"Yes, sir. Eli Bertram did, but he is sick of it now. These old men change their minds as well as young ones."

Mr. Strong looked carefully through his glasses, at the

mortgage note, and Solomon Shavin looked at him. Mr. Strong spoke slowly, " I do not know what Mrs. Warren will say to this, if she has to lose a part of her estate. But a mortgage is a mortgage. What part of this land does her estate cover ? "

" About half of it," said Shavin.

" It will be quite a bill if she has to pay it."

Solomon Shavin nodded.

" It seems to be complete," says Mr. Strong. " I should like a photograph of the note to show Mrs. Warren. It will not cost me much, and I will think it over in my office. It will not do to surrender too quick. I will send my son with a photographer here. I wish you would quietly figure up what you will settle for, and send it to me by mail. Now make it low and save bother. Just state for what sum you will release your claim on Mrs. Warren's estate. It did not cost you anything, and you had better take a part than risk all. A good run is better than a bad fight. I shall have a job with Mrs. Warren and she may want to fight it any way. You never can tell just what a woman will do, or a man either, for that matter. Now make it low."

Mr. Strong was gone. He had done well. He was an old fox. Solomon Shavin smiled, rubbed his pockets, and almost felt the shekels pouring into them. The photograph was taken, both of the note and the mortgage. Shavin sent his terms, what he would release Mrs. Warren's estate for. It was lower than Edric Lyman had thought.

Mr. Lyman had a young friend who was studying law in another office. He went to him. He asked him if he did not wish to take some lessons in the manufacture of paper, and its age. He said, "I will give you the money. I wish you to go to some one familiar with old paper, who can tell about when and where it was made. Pay him a dollar for a lesson. Most any one will do it for that. Take several lessons and read up on it. You make a collection of old writing paper, with the date, as well as you can, and the maker's name. Get facts and record them. Get thirty or forty kinds. It will do you good. Then take your collection to Solomon Shavin, and give him a dollar or two, for a lesson or two. He has one of old Billy Gray's account books. Don't let him know you know it. Get a sight of it if you can. Then if you can borrow that old book, bring it to me. I wish to see it. Don't for the world let him or any one know that you are doing anything but studying up on paper. If you succeed in borrowing the book, or if you can buy a leaf out of it for a dollar or two, and get Solomon Shavin to write on it, that it is a leaf out of old Billy Gray's account book, that will do as well. Then I will give you ten dollars for the leaf out of the old account book. Now mind your eye, and don't scatter."

The young man was a sharp one, with fun in him. He looked up in a comical way, and said, "Do you see any chickens about me?ʻ Treat a poor boy 'spectable if he am brack."

"You will do," said Edric Lyman. "Now put it through as fast as you can. Here is a V, to start on."

Four days later, the student called with about fifty different kinds of old papers, mostly notes, deeds, and legal documents. Also a page out of old Billy Gray's account book, endorsed as such, by Solomon Shavin. It was wanted as a souvenir and a specimen. It cost a dollar. It was a nice bit of evidence. Edric Lyman allowed him to retain a quarter of the leaf, told him to record the getting of it, in his diary, and gave him ten dollars. Both were pleased. Then Lawyer Lyman called on Lawyer Strong. He told the old man what he had done. Furthermore, he had gone away back in the Suffolk registry of deeds, and had actually found the original mortgage, which had never been taken from the registry by the mortgagee.

Lawyer Strong laughed. Said he, "Do you always have such strong evidence in your cases?"

"I do not take any case that is against right and justice."

"That is a splendid sentiment, Mr. Lyman. You ought to have success in this life and the next."

"Thank you, Mr. Strong. I hope to have your approval always."

O an old goose will take a pile of stuffing.

"Then," said Lawyer Lyman, "I am all ready to sit down on Solomon Shavin. Suppose you invite him to call here at your office, at nine to-morrow morning, and bring the mortgage and note with him. You do the talking. He is already threatening Eli Bertram strongly. You state the case. You can show the leaf from old Billy Gray's account book. I shall tell him that I am paying attention to one of the Misses Warren, and don't propose to see her robbed if I can help it. Then I shall demand the note, the mortgage that he cooked up, and the discharge of Eli Bertram's mortgage, and Eli Bertram's note, which is also a forgery. Then you, Mr. Strong, ought to demand about five hundred dollars damages to you, for conspiracy. After I come in, I will have an

officer at your door, for contingencies, and a blank writ
on my desk. Then it is either settle or state prison."

It was done. Solomon Shavin was scared almost to
death. The finding of the old mortgage in the registry,
and the leaf out of old Billy Gray's account book, convinced him that his cause was lost. He paid Mr. Strong
five hundred dollars for damages, upon condition that the
false mortgage and note, and all evidences of his crime,
be burned in the grate, then and there. He signed a
discharge of Eli Bertram's mortgage, and gave up the
forged note, which was burned. Then the scoundrel departed. Edric Lyman asked Mr. Strong what part of
the money he would take.

"O give me a hundred, and keep the balance yourself." It was done.

Said Mr. Strong, "Mr. Lyman, I congratulate you on
the way you have managed this case. It is a credit to
you. You will stand high in our profession. You will
never want a good word from me."

Edric Lyman thanked him, and went out with four
hundred dollars in his pocket. He showed a splendid set
of teeth under his moustache, he smiled so sunnily
as he said to himself, "I captured that old egotist, hook
and line, bob and sinker. Cast thy taffy upon the
waters, and thou shalt receive it again, after many days."
He went into his office and sat at his desk. He touched
a spring with his foot, and Miss Carter came to him. He
said, "Miss Carter — Old Solomon Shavin went after
wool, and came back shorn. Please accept fifty dollars
extra pay, for the help you were to me in my office, and
for general faithfulness." She blossomed. Eli Bertram
set the price for Edric Lyman's faithfulness. It was lib-

eral. All the other occupants paid fairly. It was cheap, indeed, for them, for it saved thousands, and made a handsome sum for Edric Lyman.

Then he called on Mrs. Warren and announced that it was all settled forever. She asked for her bill. He would bring it the next time he dined there. It was a cheeky proposition, but Edric Lyman was a lawyer. Besides he was fast acquiring rights in Mrs. Warren's house. Who ever heard of a modest lawyer? If such a thing could be, he would never be heard of. I mean nothing invidious. Had not this man thwarted crime, protected the innocent, and saved many thousands of dollars, all for a very moderate sum? What profession can do as much?

"Then," said Mrs. Warren, "please dine with us this evening, and let us have it out."

They did dine together, and they had a good time. Before they left the table, Edric Lyman gave them a true and careful statement of old Shavin's villany, and of the big money he was offered to win the case. And, said he, "I think I could have won the case, and have got twenty per cent. or more for doing it. But I told my mother, I would never take a case that I could not ask God's blessing upon; and I will not, however profitable. I never had a case I was more rejoiced to win than this one. I have made a friend of Eli Bertram, and he says he will put me in his will. Never mind that. But let us be thankful that right is triumphant, and rascality punished a little. Now, Mrs. Warren, here is your bill." It read, —

"Mrs. Parna Warren, Miss Emily Warren, Miss Sarah Warren, undivided estate, to Edric Lyman, attorney at law, debtor, For legal services against the claims of Solomon Shavin.

Sum unstated, but very large. It is paid in full to this date, by the kind regards of the aforesaid Mrs. Warren and her daughters.

"EDRIC LYMAN, Attorney at law.

" Witness : JONATHAN STRONG, Attorney at law."

Edric gave her the bill. She was surprised indeed. She had expected to pay a large sum. She urged. No, never. Not a cent. Then she came around the table and kissed him.

" My turn next," said Roy. Sure enough it was. The ladies laughed heartily.

Said Edric, " I will wait a moment and see if any other lady is taken that way," and you ought to have heard them laugh.

The daughters arose and ran upstairs to the drawing-room, followed by the gentlemen, who were not in any state of dejection. It was a happy evening. Music and song, poem and story. It was ten o'clock before they knew it. Perhaps I ought to have said that Edric Lyman was a fine-looking fellow. Pleasant, kindly, and wide awake. First, one took Mrs. Warren's bill, and analyzed it, then another. It was very interesting. Roy Bartlett was glad that it had come to them by their acquaintance with him. It was time to go.

Said Edric Lyman, " Miss Sarah, if you will escort me to the door I will go home. Good night, dears," he said, and bowed.

Miss Sarah opened the door for him, they passed through and he closed it. They were in the hall. His hat was in his hand, he whispered a word in her ear, there was a slight explosion, and, " good night, dear," and Edric Lyman went home as gay as a lark. He was not much

of a stranger in Mrs. Warren's house after that. He took
to Sarah Warren as naturally as chickens do to corn, or
robins do to cherries. He went out with all the Warrens,
to concerts, and society. He did not neglect Mrs. Warren or Miss Emily.

One evening, a little later, at the table, Mrs. Warren
said, "I think we had better have the Grahams here to
dine with us. They are three, we are four; that makes
seven of us. Just a nice little party for an evening.
What do you say?" They said yes, only Miss Sarah
quietly remarked, that it would be an improvement to
make it eight.

Mrs. Warren exclaimed, "I beg your pardon, Miss
Warren. The all-important legal eighth one shall be invited. And you please write all the invitations yourself."

"All right, mother. It shall be done."

It was done. It was as near a perfect evening as it
could be. Still, if we must criticise it, then whatever
criticism we might make, would arise from the fact, that
there were only three men to five women. I say no more.

The winter was going along finely with them all. It
had got to be the twelfth of February, and about nine
o'clock on that morning, Edric Lyman might have been
seen coming out of his office in School street, and taking
a bee line for the office of Jonathan Strong. He was in.
He greeted Mr. Lyman warmly.

Mr. Lyman said he had a case on hand, that involved
the future of two people certainly, and maybe even the
lives of others, and he wished to have a certain document
so strong, that it would be perfectly and legally sufficient.
So he wished to submit it to the learned counsel before
him.

Talk about flattering a woman. You ought to hear a lot of old lawyers soft-soap one another. It is, "my learned brother," "the eminent counsel," "the honorable counsel," "my scholarly opponent," "the great legal light," and so forth. But it might be more foolish. They do not wear wigs and gowns, as they do in England. Let us be thankful for that. After they were closeted together, Edric Lyman handed the learned counsel a nice, large, formidable-looking envelope.

Mr. Strong blew his nose sonorously and adjusted his glasses. Then he slowly and ponderously opened the envelope, which was unsealed. Edric Lyman stood with a sober face, watching him. In a moment the old man began to grin, the second line the grin grew broad, and shot from ear to ear. Then he would read a line and laugh, then another and hold on to his abdomen and remark, " Haw, haw, haw ! " and look up at Edric so irresistibly that he caught the infection of the learned counsel. Finally, in instalments, he took it all in, and poking Edric in the ribs, he said, " you dog, of all lawyers, you do beat the devil." This was superlative praise.

"Then you think it will do ? "

" Do ? It will be sure to win."

" Then witness it, please, and I am safe."

With alternate writing, and spasm of the diaphragm, in laughter, he got it down in a hand as large as the Irishman who wrote a letter to the deaf woman. There it was.

" I am obliged for your kindness," said Edric Lyman. " Call me when you want me, and receive the continued assurance of my most distinguished consideration." He crossed School Street again and was in his office alone.

When there his face relaxed into a smile, he snapped his eyes and said, "I made the old fellow grin once."

On the morning of Saint Valentine's day, a large, rich-looking envelope lay on Edric Lyman's desk, while beside it was a large sheet of legal paper done in splendid writing, and colored inks. Edric Lyman had been airing his penmanship. On the top were two doves, billing, in the most suggestive manner, while down the sides of the sheet ran wreaths of flowers. At the bottom was a cottage and vines in green ink, and a happy couple near the door. Underneath was "Home, Sweet Home." He looked it over for the last time and examined the formidable-looking seal, but did not seal it. "There," said he, " I guess that will do."

He touched the bell and it brought the office boy. The directions were given and obeyed, and this messenger started on his journey.

It was a — Lawyer's Valentine. Miss Sarah Warren was summoned to the door. It was Mr. Lyman's office young man. In a stern voice he asked, "Are you Miss Sarah Warren?" (He knew well enough she was, for he had carried her notes and bouquets.)

"I am, sir."

"Then," he said, solemnly, " it is my duty as an officer of the law to serve this writ upon you. Please sign this receipt." She was startled, but she did.

Here is what she saw on the great envelope.

WRIT OF HABEAS CORPUS FOR MISS SARAH
WARREN.

This was written inside.

COMMONWEALTH OF MATRIMONY, Suffolk, SS.

To Cupid, Esq., high constable of the Court of Hymen, Greeting: — We command you, that the body of Miss Sarah Warren of Boston by Mrs. Parna Warren and Miss Emily Warren imprisoned, and restrained of her liberty, as it is said, you take and have before a minister of the Court of Hymen, as soon after the receipt of this writ as she is willing to go, to show cause why she should not be married to our beloved Edric Lyman, and conform to the mandate of said Court of Hymen. And you will also summon the said Mrs. Parna Warren and all other kin concerned, to show cause why they should detain the said worthy and well beloved Sarah Warren, any longer. And have you there a license from the city clerk with your doings thereon.

Done at the Court of Hymen, on Saint Valentine's day, in the year 188-.   Hymen, Judge.

By EDRIC LYMAN, Attorney at law.

Witness, JONATHAN STRONG.

God save the Commonwealth of Matrimony.

If you want to describe Miss Sarah Warren's sensations as she read this screed, I can only say, "she thought she should have died." But she did not. It was too good to keep, Sarah's valentine was, so before long, her engagement was an open secret. Miss Sarah Warren is the only woman that I ever heard of who received an offer of marriage by a writ of Habeas Corpus. Plenty of people got copies of it, and it advertised the smart young lawyer, no end.

CHAPTER XXXII.

Roy Bartlett was prosperous. First-class people came to him and gave him an order for a costly picture, upon condition that they had an invitation to the Art Coterie. Tickets were issued and not transferable. His pupils were many. Edric Lyman gave him a check for fifty dollars, and Roy painted one for him. And, would you believe it, Eli Bertram did. · He was grateful. Roy did not neglect his home or his friends. Sam Ellet got a hearty letter as well as Jean McDuffie, and it came to pass that no interest was neglected. Miss Graham was in the studio four or five days in a week. She sold several pictures, or at least they disappeared, like Mark Twain's twin brother.

It was a rainy, blowy, slushy day. Miss Graham came to the studio in a carriage, and Fred Annerly opened the carriage door. She was dry and in first-class condition, as she ran up the steps to the studio.

"I did not think I should see you to-day," said Roy.

"Yes," she said: "Aunty wanted something in town, and I could send it back to her. So I could come as well as not, and I shall stay and work awhile."

No one came in. It was a still day. Roy asked if she had heard of Miss Sarah Warren's valentine. She had heard of it and seen it. It was an open secret. It was very refreshing, and very honorable.

"Miss Warren was wealthy, was she not?"

Roy said he supposed she was, but he had no idea that a money consideration alone would attract Edric Lyman. He was no fortune-hunter at all.

Said Roy: "If there is anything in the world that I despise, it is a man that hunts a woman for her fortune. I shall marry a poor girl. I should not have courage enough to ask a rich one. I had rather a woman would depend upon me for all, and then she could judge whether I loved her or not, by the way I treated her. I should try to bear the most of the burden and make it as easy for her, as I possibly could."

"Then a poor girl would stand a better chance with you than a rich one, Mr. Bartlett?"

"Yes, I think so," said Roy.

"That is rather hard on the poor rich girl, is it not?" asked Miss Graham.

"Oh, I guess no rich girl will ever care for me," said Roy, "and perhaps no poor one will either, although I hope so."

"Perhaps some one will, if you only will them to," she answered.

"Miss Graham, did you ever hear the story of the cork leg?"

"No, I never did. Please tell me."

"Very well," said Roy. "It is a still day. The rain beats hard against the window. Tremont Street is almost deserted, and we have had good luck in selling pictures; so we have quiet, and a reason for a little rest. Now please put down your palette and brushes, and I will tell you an old story, for too much work is not good for us. This story has, I think, been printed, but it was told me by a friend, and I liked it so well that I filed it away in memory, so as to tell it to some one that I was anxious to please."

"Thank you, sir," she said.

Roy smiled.

"Once upon a time there was a woman, and she was tall and fine-looking, well dressed, sensible, entertaining, and attractive. Not the most beautiful in the world, perhaps, but still a fine woman. It was not so much that she was so good-looking, but she looked good, and she was good, and she was an Irishwoman, in society, living in London. She had plenty of followers. They talked with her, and when they came to enquire about her, lo, she was poor. Her aunt gave her a living. Then this admirer came no more. A middle-aged man became acquainted with her, and said he was much interested in her, and would she tell him how she was situated in life? She frankly told him she was dependent on her aunt. If she had been differently situated, he would have been glad to have said more. Then came another. He did not care for her poverty, if she would live within his moderate income. She added also: there is another thing I must tell you, I have a cork leg. Then he would say no more. But at last there came an earnest, honest man, who admired and loved this beautiful woman, if she was poor and a cripple, although she did not show it, when she walked. He urged his suit. She told of poverty and the cork leg. He did not object. He would do his best to love and serve her, in spite of poverty and misfortune. Would she marry him? She would; and the day was fixed. They had a quiet wedding at her aunt's house. He had offered her money, but no, thanks to the liberality of her aunt, she had enough for the present. When the wedding was over, she said she was glad to tell him that things were better with her than they had appeared to be. She said she was poor yesterday, but her aunt had held a large amount of property, which she had conveyed to her to-day. She told her husband that she was glad and happy to be married for herself alone. She was glad to tell him she was rich, and out of all danger of fortune-hunters. And about the cork leg, she said, I shall have to tell you that I have two cork legs. I was born in Cork.

> And this splendid husband, so loyal and rare,
> Was glad that his wife was so perfect and fair;
> All the love and the wealth that to her he had given
> Came gloriously back, with the blessing of heaven;
> ·Ever so may they come from the powers above
> To the man who gives all for a true woman's love."

Roy waited a moment.

She said, " Thank you, sir." After a pause she asked, " Is marriage the highest ideal of life ? "

He answered : " To me it is, and the only one. Of course there may be reasonable excuses, but Tupper says, ' Marriage is a duty to most men.' I have no doubt about it. It is to nearly all, and women too. I never, for a moment, contemplated a single life. When I see my own father and mother, and your uncle and aunt, I am satisfied that such marriage is beyond all price. Does it not seem so to you, Miss Graham ? "

" Yes, Mr. Bartlett, where good people marry intelli-gently, for love, it ought always to be the highest joy."

Said Roy : " Sometime I wish you would take that volume of Tupper's Proverbial Philosophy that lies upon that old sideboard, beside the Milton, Montgomery,

Burns, Shakespeare, and the Bible. It has Hammatt Billings' autograph on the first leaf, and is out of Titcomb's library. Find the article on marriage. It is the best I know in the English language. I do not see how it can be better."

She said she would read it.

Roy said: "A little later, I hope to be better situated financially, so I can be sure of a moderate income if I get disabled. Then I shall consider it."

"I should think your father and mother were very pleasantly situated," she said.

"Yes, they are. They are content. They have enough, and as good as they wish. They prefer to work, to help each other, and they like to have a good, productive farm. They help many, and harm none. I do not see how they can do better. I cannot see why my parents do not live free from wrong-doing. They try to. My father does not care at all for liquors, and he never used tobacco. Of course, plenty of good people do use it, but I think they would admit, that they would be whiter and cleaner without it. I never use it, and I am glad I was prevented from using it."

"What prevented you, please?"

Roy stopped, and appeared to muse and think. She waited. He turned, and looked steadily at her. "I have never told it," said he; "but if you will keep it for yourself alone, I will tell you. When I came to Boston, about four years ago, it was Monday. On the Saturday before, we were picking apples in the orchard. There was no one in the house but mother. I had not been gone out long when I thought I would go in for a pitcher of water. When I came to the door, I heard my mother's low, but most earnest voice in prayer. And this was the burden of her prayer: 'O Lord, keep my boy from liquor and tobacco. Keep him clean and white, as he is now. O Lord, thou hast promised to answer prayer. I claim it now. I will never cease to claim it. O Lord Jesus, keep my boy pure and clean from liquor and tobacco.' Again and again she begged for me. She does not know I heard her. And I made up my mind, that it should be the joy of my life to answer my mother's prayer. I do not use liquors, I never touch tobacco, and I never will. It is not self-denial at all. It would be self-denial to use them. I would not be hired to defile my lips with tobacco. You have my secret."

"I thank you, Mr. Bartlett. I think you will find I can keep a secret, even if you had not asked it. It is refreshing what people there are in the world, when you know them."

"Thank you, Miss Graham. Few people ever know what it is to be loved as my parents love me. It is not to be spoken of to every one. It is too sacred. Let me show you something, Miss Graham. Here is this large row of books. The Bible my parents gave me is here. Let me show you what is written in it. Here it is:"

"TO ROY.

"My son, I wish you, while you live,
The highest good this life can give:
So read this book, for thus you may
Learn of the straight and narrow way.
And peace shall all your life attend,
With Christ, your Saviour and your friend.
"Your father, Guy Bartlett."

"My son, your mother's love and care,
  Your mother's hope, your mother's prayer
  Are all, that Christ shall be your joy;
  That he shall own and bless my boy —
  For present peace, for future bliss,
  My son, there is no way but this.
            "Your mother, MARIAN ROYAL BARTLETT."

"We join to wish you, while you live,
  The highest joy this life can give;
  And when its joys and griefs are past,
  We all may meet in heaven at last —
  No more of sorrow, care, or fear: —
  So may it be, God bless you, dear.
          "GUY BARTLETT.
        "MARIAN ROYAL BARTLETT."

Miss Graham read it with strong feeling, for it was like her own parents, and she was an orphan. A tear fell down and moistened the page. She said, "O I am so sorry to blot the page."

"Never mind," said he. "It is all the more sacred to me. There are many people who would think lightly of such an expression as is here written. For their opinion I do not care. When the Master asked Simon, son of Jonas, 'Lovest thou me?' he wanted Simon to both say he loved him, and to show that he loved him. And so do I. The love that never finds expression, is worse than the deaf and dumb alphabet of signs. Canis Major tells me he loves me in every wag of his tail. If I had a dog that never told his love to me, by a loving look or a wagging tail, I should appoint his successor. I like this beautiful stanza —

  "'Love is the golden chain that binds
      The happy souls above.
    He is an heir of heaven who finds
      His bosom glow with love.'

"Now I do not mean that love should be limited to a man and a woman, or to relatives only. I like the way Edric Lyman treats me; and Sam Ellet, and Jean McDuflie, and the man and his wife who called me bad names, and Jonathan Strong; and your uncle and aunt, and Fred Annerly and his wife also, if they are tinted Americans. He seems to be a kind, sensible gentleman."

"You never said a truer word," said Miss Graham. "He is a part of the estate, and his wife also."

Said Roy, "It is duty, pleasure, philosophy, common sense, and religion all in one, to put as much love and good will into our lives, as we can. For surely life is a tragedy. It begins with a cry of pain, and ends with a dying groan. But O, what growth, what love, what hope, amusement, cultivation, beauty, art, literature, music, song, what fun even, lie between the coming and the going. Some one addressed a new-born soul thus: 'O little one that comest into this life, while all around you smile, so live that thou mayest go up into the higher, holier life, while all around you weep.' These are great thoughts, and they tend upward. So every time I think of what my parents wrote in my Bible, I rejoice, and my heart is full of love and loyalty to them."

"I am glad," said Miss Graham.

There was a knock at the door. It was the janitor.

"Mr. Bartlett, have you any influence with Frank Wilkie? He is two months behind on his rent, and I must make him move. He is drunk all the time."

"I do not know, Mr. Janitor, whether I have or not. I will go and try. Please make no move until I see what I can do."

"All right, Mr. Bartlett. I will look in to-morrow."

Roy took a long breath and said, "Now I will go and see what can be done for Frank Wilkie."

Roy went up to the top of the building, and knocked on Frank Wilkie's door. No answer. He heard just the least noise within, and was just sure he was there.

Then he spoke and called, "Mr. Wilkie, Mr. Wilkie, a friend wishes to see you. It is Mr. Bartlett."

There was a stir, and he came to the door, which he slowly unfastened.

"I want to see you," said Roy, "you need help."

"Come in," said he.

Said Roy, "The janitor asked me if I had any influence with you. He said you owe two months' rent, and he is responsible to the owner."

Wilkie sat down and covered his face with his hands. His room was a lair. Behind a screen was an old lounge, which was his bed. He did not take off his clothes at night. There were no pictures of any account in the room. It was dusty, forsaken, and mean, and the man was the meanest thing in it. There was a choking odor of stale tobacco smoke, which, with an unclean man, who was saturated with beer and whiskey, right in the middle of it, made it a sight over which angels might weep. It is lucky that a woman never does such a trick. Ten men do it, where one woman does. Yes and more. Ten times more, I guess. Right in the midst of it sat Frank Wilkie. He sat down as soon as Roy came in. He did not reply for some time. He was dirty, suffering, wretched, ashamed, and partly drunk.

Roy said again, "Mr. Wilkie, you need help. I will pay one month's rent for you, if you will let drink alone, and go to work. If you do not, your things will be put into the street to-morrow. I will help you. Will you try?"

Wilkie trembled and said, "Yes, I will try again, I promise it."

"Then," said Roy, "I will open the window and door a little, so I can breathe, and I will send out and get you some coffee and biscuits, and will you sweep up and arrange your room?"

"Yes, I will. I would go to the river and jump in to drown myself, but I can swim like a duck, drunk or sober, so that is no use."

When Roy came back he brought a can of hot and strong coffee, from the Oriental tea store, and a loaf of graham bread and a piece of butter.

"There," said he, "that is good for you to sober off with. Now what colors do you lack?"

Roy looked in his color box, and it was lean indeed. He went downstairs to his own room, and got canvases, and a dozen tubes of paint.

"Now, Mr. Wilkie, go to work. It will steady you as much as anything. Paint this waterfall and make it good enough for me to keep." He promised he would, only he wanted a bit of fresh air. "I want to go out. As soon as I brush myself up, and walk around the Common, I will return and work for you, all day."

"Very well," said Roy. "I will look in again by and by, and I will get your supper."

Wilkie locked the door and they went downstairs together. Roy met another artist at his door, a sharp, witty one, who is always saying something brilliant. Wilkie kept on with a downcast look, but his wretchedness was apparent.

Says the artist, "I do like to see a man enjoy himself."
Roy had to smile at such an absurdity. Wilkie soon
returned and went to work faithfully. Roy paid a
month's rent, only ten dollars, and bought pictures of
him, which he did not want, to get his money back.
Frank Wilkie got upon his feet again. He might have
made from one to three thousand a year, if he had been
the man that Royal Bartlett was. It is more in the man
than it is in the business, usually.

Miss Graham tendered a five-dollar bill to help pay
Frank Wilkie's rent, but Roy declined it. He said, "a
woman's money comes harder than a man's, and he should
feel happier to know that she was saving hers, so that
she might be well provided for, in case of misfortune."

She laughed a merry laugh, and said, "she hoped she
should not be so disabled that her music or her art would
not give her a living."

CHAPTER XXXIII.

THE GREAT ENGLISHMAN.

Roy Bartlett's studio door had for three days past borne this notice, —

ART COTERIE, THURSDAY EVE AT 8.
SHAKESPEARE AND ENGLISH NIGHT.

The company was a rich one. The curtain concealed the rear end of the great double parlors, and was an interrogation point of great suggestiveness.

Roy Bartlett announced, " Ladies and gentlemen : We vary our programme to suit ourselves. The first thing this evening is a new song to an old tune. It is a rattling college song. ' Vive la Compagnie.' Only one stanza is to be sung by one person, and only that person, and one other, knows the one stanza which he is going to sing. We hope you will all sing big on the responses, and jump on when the chorus comes around. Miss Sarah Warren will preside at the drum and Miss Graham at the piano."

She played it through with variations and queer little capers. The lines were sung solo, and the refrain and chorus by all. But the way that drum came in, marking the time, right on the dot, and with a judicious roll on the chorus, was very exhilarating. There were no critics there, so I leave you to judge whether it was fun or not. Here is the song, —

Sung by Miss Emily Warren.

O welcome, dear friends, with the sunshine you bring.
Vive la compagnie.
We welcome you here to be happy and sing,
Vive la compagnie.
CHORUS—Vive la, vive la, vive l'amour,
Vive la, vive la, vive l'amour,
Vive l'amour, vive l'amour,
Vive la compagnie.

Sung by Miss Graham.

This life is a blessing so pleasant and long,
Vive la compagnie.
With love and good company, music and song,
Vive la compagnie.
CHORUS — Vive la, etc.

Sung by Roy Bartlett.

When a splendid young lawyer has fallen in love,
Vive la compagnie,
It is time to give thanks to the powers above,
Vive la compagnie.
CHORUS — Vive la, etc.

Sung by Edric Lyman.

When a rising young artist is well known to fame,
Vive la compagnie,
It is just about time he was doing the same,
Vive la compagnie.
CHORUS — Vive la, etc.

Sung by Mr. Stacy.

Hurrah for sweet Cupid, and may he live long,
Vive la compagnie,
Hurrah for old Hymen, so wise and so strong,
Vive la compagnie.
CHORUS — Vive la, etc.

Sung by one of the members.

May the blessing of heaven crown every glad year,
    Vive la compagnie,
For our hostess so kind, who has gathered us here,
    Vive la compagnie.
CHORUS — Vive la, etc.

By the young man who told the capital-punishment story.

Now a blessing, a cheer, and good luck to you all,
    Vive la compagnie,
So says every one of us, so say we all,
    Vive la compagnie.
CHORUS — Vive la, etc.

There was a spice of mischief in the song, but they knew how to take a joke, and it went well. It was a roaring chorus. Then Roy announced that they would listen to Mr. Edric Lyman. He spoke almost without notes. Yet a few heads of subjects, numbered, and well arranged, he held in his hand, and taking his story easily, and hardly making a set speech, or argument of it, he began, —

"Ladies and gentlemen, if you were asked to give the first name in English literature, for all the past, you would all, undoubtedly, unite upon Shakespeare. And the questions, Who was he? what did he do? and what is it worth? are questions of interest to all thinking men and women. Lately, these questions also involve the same questions concerning Sir Francis Bacon. I have no theory to prove as barrister, but I have a verdict as juryman. I have read Shakespeare well, have been in clubs for his study, have heard readings and recitations many, have heard and seen his plays on the stage, and have read about fifty volumes of his critics. What I have to present to you is not intended as an argument, to compel you to my way of thinking, but as a slight summary of the result of all I ever heard or read of Shakespeare. You can think what you please of it. More than three hundred years ago he was born. More than two hundred and fifty he died. He was thoroughly English, of the great middle class, that own property and do business. He and his ancestors were all Roman Catholics. Now, and here, let me say, that of all the critical books upon Shakespeare, not one stands so high in my estimation as 'Shakespeare, from an American point of view,' by George Wilkes. To be a Protestant, in that age, meant that a man protested against the customs of the old faith, because he found the new faith a higher and purer one. Consequently Puritans were moral and religious men, while easy-going Catholics might be moral or not. Charlecote Hall was a noble manorial residence, then and now. I have a picture of it. It was the residence of Sir Thomas Lucy, knight, and member of parliament. It was a spirited thing to do, to steal a deer of Sir Thomas, and a dangerous, as well. There was an added flavor in the fact that Sir Thomas was a Puritan, a Protestant. I have heard old fellows tell of their exploits in stealing watermelons, but I never thought any more of them for it. Indeed, I think decidedly more of the man that never was a thief. Still it must be remembered that these were easy-going times. Sir Thomas had it all his own way, being a magistrate, and young Shakespeare was fined and whipped. It also must be remembered that Lucy's game, his deer, in his park, were as much his cattle as his cows. It is a big crime in England to-day to steal a deer. No wonder William got himself into trouble. The name Lowsie Lucy was a spite. But you cannot prove anything against Lucy as an honest, good man.

"It did not hurt Shakespeare's conscience, for he never had much. He was a good-sized, auburn-haired man, gentle and pleasant in his ways, when he left his wife and three children, and relieved Sir Thomas Lucy's jurisdiction of a poacher by going to London. Perhaps Shakespeare's family needed the meat to eat. He liked the stage, and took to the theatre. The Puritan element and the theatre element were a long way farther apart then than to-day. Now the stage is purer and better, and the Puritan is not so particular. If he wrote the plays and poems that common-sense gives him credit for, he knew the flavor of sin, and liked it. If he wrote a few verses, even the lampoon of Lowsie Lucy, before he was twenty, then later and often he wrote more and better. It is a natural sequence, as many artists and others know. Who is it that says, —

> "' 'Tis true, what every poet knows,
>   Dull souls shall always think in prose;
>   But whose rapt soul hath numbers given
>   Shall sing them both in earth and heaven'?

"It is said that he taught school. School-teachers are usually sharp. They see so much dulness, that they hate it, and put themselves far from it. This helps Shakespeare again. He wrote the sonnets, 'Venus and Adonis,' and the 'Rape of Lucrece.' These would take a higher order of talent than any of his plays. The poet outranks the prose writer, as the sculptor outranks the brick and stone layer. The prose of the ancients is lost. The poetry lives. That Shakespeare wrote these poems is undisputed. It is a higher order of talent to write good poems that shall live, than good plays, that may or may not live. What countless cartloads of plays have been written, and are gone forever. But Shakespeare wrote history in plays, and they live. He is compiled and illustrated more than all. There are plenty of as good plays as ever he wrote. The old English comedies, 'School for Scandal,' 'London Assurance,' and the like. That he had a large vocabulary, and the gift of expression in the highest degree, no one disputes. He said things elegantly and refreshingly. He was a master stagewright too. He pleased his sovereign and the nobility. He made friends, and he made money. Best of all, he knew the value of money, and how to keep it; and how to keep himself respectable. A man or woman that cannot keep a secret, or a dollar, is despicable indeed. The man with the one talent, that could not navigate that to advantage, had it taken from him, and he was thrust out. So will it ever be.

"How easy it would have been for Shakespeare, in those drinking days, to have fooled away every penny as fast as he got it, and have effectually prevented any accumulation. Many theatrical people do. He was in a place of supreme temptation, and he saved his money, supported his family, bought real estate, and got rich. He ennobled the stage. He ennobled himself. Bad as his themes were, the theatre began to be a better entertainment. Do you ask me what I object to in Shakespeare? He was in and of his age. There was a spirit of protest against the ancient looseness of speech and life, among the Protestants. It wrought slowly upon the stage. What immoral people some of his characters are. If drawn from life, they were no less unpresentable. He wrote to please, never to instruct. He wrote without any moral purpose whatever. He almost always bowed down to priests, friars, and nuns, and he spoke of Romish ordinances with deep respect. He made a martext of every Protestant in his play. He treated a Jew as they have always been treated in the Ghetto at Rome. In his 'Merchant of Venice,' his Jew, Shylock, is really the best man in the play. He makes his self-styled gentlemen to spit upon him, to cheat and swindle him without stint, and to ruin him. No wonder a Jew hates such Christians. Anybody would. No wonder he wants a pound of their flesh. I should, and more. The Jews are the great nation of the olden time. They have always been an educated people, loyal and true to their history, their faith in God, and their Hebrew nation; and if Jesus Christ is my Lord, my hope, and my Redeemer, he will be glad to have me honor his ancient nation, and think justly and kindly of his people. And I do. What abuse did ever Shakespeare condemn?

"Dickens was always fighting some ancient wrong. Now it was the chancery court, now imprisonment for debt, now the law's delay, now the tyrannical schools, now the rapacity of lawyers, now the shiftlessness of inefficiency, now self-righteousness and pomposity, and all the time he did amuse, he did instruct, and he did point the road to a better way. When her Majesty, a woman who is a legal, rightful ruler, and is, by the grace of God, loyally anchored in the hearts and pockets of all true Britons, when she sent for him to read, before her, at Windsor Castle, he declined to go as a reader, where he would not be admitted as a gentleman. He showed his right as a free Englishman. But I am sorry he did it. Even sovereigns are entitled to some consideration. Especially so in the United States, where no man can tell how soon he will be called to be sovereign himself. But Shakespeare was always, in every play, ready to do foolish homage to a king and to insult the hedge-born, common people, of which he was one. It is painful. But Shakespeare was an agreeable man, handsome, with winning ways, a fine poet, a master of expression, a first-class stage manager and playwright, a well read, well educated man. Many men are well educated without a college diploma. All this in one is very, very rare. There are in literature about three hundred allusions to him, by contemporary writers. All of them speak of him with honor, with scarce an exception. They speak of him as 'The sweet swan of Avon,' 'Gentle Shakespeare,' and other endearing names.

"About thirty years he lived in London, sometimes coming home to Stratford-on-Avon, a journey of about ninety miles. It is a pity that the great fire in London and other fires have burnt up all his plays, so that not a line survives. Only five poor signatures are left. Thank Heaven, his tomb remains, although if the rascally cremationists had lived then, we might not have had even that. For two hundred and forty years after he died, wealthy and honored, his right to his own work was undisputed.

"Then Miss Delia Bacon wrote a book to prove that all Shakespeare's Roman Catholic flavored plays were written by Francis Bacon, a Protestant, a man through whose influence, largely, it was that Queen Elizabeth cut off the

Roman Catholic head of poor Mary Stuart. Emerson gave Miss Bacon a letter of introduction to Carlyle. He wrote back, 'Oh, Emerson, your woman is mad.' An exhaustive statement. She died in an asylum. But says some one, Lord Palmerston is said to have thought that Bacon wrote Shakespeare's plays for him. Think what you like. I do not believe it. Pope spoke of Bacon as 'the wisest, brightest, meanest of mankind.' He was just about such a Protestant in theory, as Shakespeare was a Catholic in practice.

"Shakespeare wrote 'Romeo and Juliet,' also 'Troilus and Cressida,' 'Merry Wives of Windsor,' and others. These were lushy love stories. That was just like Shakespeare. He was married and had three children at twenty. It was his characteristic through life. Francis Bacon, Lord Verulam, was married at forty-six and had no children. Any 'Romeo and Juliet' about that? Bacon took a dose of nitre, a strong diuretic, every morning for the last thirty years of his life, and was dosing himself continually otherwise. Any 'Merry Wives of Windsor' about that? Not much. It never lay in his body or soul, to write the virile plays that Shakespeare wrote.

"Printer's ink did not flow as easy then as now, yet Francis Bacon's works were much in print. His income allowed it. He is described as of medium height, of a pleasing, open, and venerable appearance. With all his philosophy, he had plenty of superstitions, and very foolish ones. He was subject to certain epileptic or fainting fits, at certain times of the moon.

"Epileptics are not very fertile. Shakespeare was blond, winning, true, and, with all he has written, not egotistical. Bacon was a sublime egotist, and cold-blooded as a snake. Please notice the high-sounding titles of his works. The first was 'The Greatest Birth of Time.' Could anything be more grandiloquent! And yet that book, written by a man with abundant means, who married a rich wife, a London alderman's daughter, — that book is lost, and there is not a copy in all the world. You can draw an inference. His next work is 'The Grand Instauration of the Sciences.' Here let me ask, is there any person present that can repeat a few lines from Bacon's works? No one answered. What! not a bit of Bacon in all this company? And yet, some pretend that he wrote Shakespeare. What infernal folly."

Then they laughed.

"Notice how Bacon begins his 'Great Instauration.' 'Francis of Verulam thought thus, and such is the method which he determined within himself, and which he thought it concerned the living and posterity to know.'

"Posterity is full of Will Shakespeare, but it does not distress itself about Frank Bacon. The Earl of Essex was Bacon's friend and helper, until Bacon became Lord Chancellor of England. Bacon repaid his noble benefactor, by bringing him to public execution. I respect Shakespeare, I do not respect Bacon. Bacon wrote one or two plays, to be acted before Queen Elizabeth. But they were so full of adulation and soft-sawder that they are as dead as the Pharaohs. Bacon's books do not contain one bright saying, which is quoted and ascribed to him. But Shakespeare has done more to improve the English language than any man that ever lived. What expressions, what 'elegies, and quoted odes, and jewels, five words long, that on the stretched forefinger of all time sparkle forever.' Truly he is not 'of an age, but for all time.' Bacon's wife survived him twenty years. She had no children. Like Hannah Partridge, which dear old Mrs. Vincent acted, she never had the chance.

"I cannot stop to quote Bacon. He is as dry as dust. His philosophy is mental, often obscure, oftener fanciful, frequently only partially true, and often false altogether. His style of mind is as much like Shakespeare as Thomas Dick is like Lord Byron. Bacon's writings are as much like Shakespeare's as Dr. Watts's hymns are like Roderick Random. Nobody but a fool would 'try to make them read alike. The very fact that Bacon's high-sounding title, 'The Greatest Birth of Time,' written and published by a rich man, who was soon after Lord High Chancellor of England, and in a land, the richest. of all the earth, in colleges and libraries, a land that has robbed all other lands, by purchase and loot, of books and manuscripts, — a land of scholars and ideas, — a land of the British Museum, and private collections, — a land where its kings were often scholars, like the mighty King Alfred, — a land conservative and preservative of all good thought, — a land where original manuscripts can seldom be bought, and where first editions sell for enormous prices, — a land full of Shakespeare societies, — a land barren of Bacon societies, — a land loving, reading, quoting, studying, spouting Shakespeare, — this land, even England, cannot show one copy of a live lord's first work, and in one sense alone does not care to save its Bacon.

"Shakespeare died an old man at fifty-two. I can tell fortunes pretty well. Show me an August sweeting, and I can tell you that it will be dead and gone in October.

Show me a russet, firm and hard, ripe in the last of October, and I can tell, of positive knowledge, that with care it ought to keep till May. Show me a young man who grows slow, and does not get his beard until he is long past twenty-one, and I know that he ought to live to be eighty or more. Early ripe, early rotten. Show me a Shakespeare, omnivorous enough in the good things of this life, to be the husband of a woman eight years older, and with three children at twenty, — a man out of a family that nearly all die young, and I can show you a man that will have sucked his orange dry at fifty-two, — will have retired from business, will have paralysis enough to spoil his autograph, and will be ready to take his quietus in a rich dinner.

"I have seen Rufus Choate's writing, and I could hardly read it. I have heard him plead, and people came from far to hear him. Shakespeare's tomb and bust tell the story of what Stratford knew about him. Bacon died and had no monument for years. His rich wife raised none. But after many years, a man who had been his servant, and had profited by the money that Bacon had lavishly spent, he, out of gratitude and pity, raised a small monument to author, philosopher, lawyer, courtier, judge, lord, viscount, and High Chancellor of England. He was buried where he died, away from father, mother, kindred. He was not loved or lamented. Shakespeare was, and to-day there is no shrine on earth more precious. Of his own time, Bacon is neglected, and Elizabeth despised. Elizabeth ordered Shakespeare to show Falstaff in love, and he wrote the 'Merry Wives of Windsor.' Rare Ben Jonson knew Shakespeare well, and he wrote: —

" ' My Shakespeare, rise : I will not lodge thee by
Chaucer or Spenser, or bid Beaumont lie
A little farther, to make thee a roome ;
Thou art a moniment without a toombe, —
And art alive still, while thy books doth live.
Sweet Swan of Avon, what a sight it were
To see thee in our waters yet appear,
And make those flights upon the banks of Thames,
That did so take Eliza and our James.'

" Again he said, 'I loved the man, and do honor his
memory on this side idolatry, as much as any. He was
indeed honest, and of an open and free nature — had an
excellent fancy, brave notions, and gentle expressions,
wherein he flowed with that facility, that sometimes it
was necessary he should be stopped.' Ah, indeed, rare
Ben Jonson was a true, loving friend ! He also says, 'I
remember the players have often mentioned, as an honor
to Shakespeare, that in his writing, whatsoever he penned,
he never blotted a line.' Certainly, he could do it
easily, and he did it. Many of Bacon's platitudes remind
me of a certain windy orator, who said, 'I have considered that small towns and sparsely populated do not contain as many inhabitants as larger towns more densely
populated.' With this exception, that any one ought to
grin at this. But I never found a chance to smile once
at all the prolonged dreary dulness of Bacon. Twenty-
four years after Shakespeare died, Cote's edition of
Shakespeare was published, and this poem by Leonard
Digges is prefixed : —

" ' Poets are born, not made ; when I would prove
The truth, the glad remembrance I must love
Of never-dying Shakespeare, who alone
Is argument enough to make that one.

First, that he was a poet none would doubt
That heard the applause of what he sees, set out,
Imprinted:
Next Nature only helped him for look, thorow
This whole book, thou shalt find he doth not borrow
One phrase from Greeks, or Latines imitate,
Nor once from vulgar languages translate.
Nor, plagair-like, from others gleane,
Nor begs he from each witty friend a scene
To piece his acts with. All that he doth write
Is pure his owne: plot, language, exquisite.'

"Of all the asinine foolishness that the nineteenth century has envolved, none is more stupid than the Bacon-
Shakespeare controversy. You all know the poet's
epitaph. Let me supplement it, in closing, with a stanza
of my own:—

"Good friends, for Jesus' sake be true,
Give Shakespeare honor, richly due;
And cursed be he where liars dwell,
Who says he wrote not, long and well."

The address was done and the attention had been perfect.

Roy Bartlett said, "We have with us a delegation
from a loyal British society. And they can sing.
They will sing a new song. Their soloist happens to
have the same name as Queen Elizabeth's music teacher,
Mr. John Bull; and we can all join in the chorus, in a
word of praise to our Mother land." John Bull was a
beauty.

He was a large florid Englishman, with ruffles at his
wrists, and a bosom full of them. Then with Miss Graham lightly marking time on the piano, and Miss Sarah

Warren with dots on the drum, on the solo, but full
sounds and "tutti" on the chorus. Then John Bull
sang, —

"WHERE THE BOW BELLS RING."

An English song of home.

"Come join in a song of our mother land,
A song of old England so mighty and grand.
The land that we love, and the song that we sing,
Is the happy land where the Bow bells ring.
CHORUS — Where the bow bells ring, where the bow bells ring,
        Old England is fair as the flowers of spring.
        Ring on, sweet bells, your music tells
        Of the happy land where the bow bells ring.

"The British bells ringing glad and gay,
And we seem to hear them so far away,
And home comes back in the songs we sing,
The happy land where the Bow bells ring. — CHORUS.

"As the bird flies home when his wing is free,
Our mother land, we come back to thee,
In the tales we tell, and the songs we sing,
Of the happy land where the Bow bells ring. — CHORUS.

"Old England's flag is flowing free,
Britannia sails on every sea,
All round the world true Britons sing
Of the happy land where the Bow bells ring.—CHORUS.

"God save the queen and England's power,
God save Old England in danger's hour,
God save true Britons, wherever found,
While the world swings on in its mighty round. —
CHORUS."

The parlors were warm and the windows were open.
The applause outside was big and strong. The chorus
woke the echoes on Beacon Hill. The lights slowly de-

clined in the parlors. The piano gave a few chords,
which grew fainter as the lights went down, then, slowly
sinking, they went out and it was dark. Then a woman's
voice called firm and strong, —

> " O Shakespeare; come to us to-night,
> Come from thy home of power and might,
> Whose work the years have borne along,
> Replete with beauty, joy, and song.
> Spirit of power, inspire this place,
> And let us now behold thy face."

There was a clap of the best stage thunder, and with
bass notes on the piano, Miss Sarah's drum rolling, stamp-
ing feet of the initiated, a bass drum and a big gong
in the cellar and you would have thought the heavens and
earth were coming together.

But there, before the curtain, stood an English warrior
in armor on one side, and Queen Elizabeth in all her
jewels, ruffs and stomachers, on the other, with crown
and sceptre galore; while between them and behind the
curtain, in strong light, and in contrast to the darkness
of the rooms, sat Shakespeare. The same high forehead,
light complexion, pleasant face, Vandyke collar, bouquet
on table, library background. They were indeed surprised, and they greeted the first Englishman of all time,
with round after round of applause. Even the British
flag, the cross of Saint George above it all, was not forgotten. They looked with hungry eyes, and well they
might, for never did I see but this one man who was an
ideal Shakespeare. I have heard many speak of it.

When they had looked long, Roy said, " Friends, I am
glad you are pleased. This gentleman is a worthy rep-

resentative of the great poet. He is a literary and Shakespearian scholar, long known in the city of Cambridge, in the old Franklin Library Association, and the Irving Literary Association, and now well known in the city hall of Cambridge, most kindly and pleasantly, as Mr. John McDuffie. I am obliged to him for his assistance and for our pleasant illusion. Now we can afford to sing 'God save the Queen,' one stanza, to close our pleasant evening."

It was done, and the way that British delegation sang was an inspiration indeed. The Art Coterie took their enthusiasm with them and they always had it. Mr. McDuffie was very pleasantly greeted after the company broke up and the Warrens had abundance of approval of their receptions.

CHAPTER XXXIV.

THE ARTISTS OF BOSTON.

THE Mr. Stacy who had been a visitor at the Warren home, with his wife, was at all the Art Coterie entertainments. His brother also came, and was very pleasant company. He was a teacher in one of the best private schools in Boston. It was said, what a splendid match he would make for Miss Emily Warren, and it was not long before they began to be of the same opinion. They were very quiet about it, but still they allowed the idea to dawn upon them, and to interest them.

It was getting toward spring. Roy had made an exchange with a tailor, and sold him several pictures, which gave him all the clothing he needed. Eli Bertram had sent in a man with an order for pictures, and had paid it in cash. Roy had shown how grateful he was, and was giving him love and warm welcome in return. Some of the most loving, grateful people I have ever known, have been aged people. Sometimes they are hungry for love. Roy never forgot a friend.

He and Miss Graham called on the other artists, in studio hours. They went to the galleries, the Art Club, and the Art Museum. It was a change and a recreation, to study the work of others. He dined with Miss Graham's uncle and aunt, and a fine time they had with the stereoscopics. There are some fine collections in Boston.

They are the best pictures ever made, and they ought to take a revival. Our government ought to have views of every fort and fortification, every ship and public building, of its own. There ought to be a stereoscopic department Nothing shows, educates, and delineates so much. I know one man who has thousands of glass pictures, and another who has ten thousand views of all kinds. Roy enjoyed the society of Mr. and Mrs. Graham. They had travelled and seen much. Miss Graham did the honors, picking out the views she liked best, and Mr. Graham would tell some story or make some comment on some of his pictures. Long as the evening was, it was gone before they knew it.

Then Roy went home, musing as he went. He took it slowly, but undoubtedly he was doing a little quiet thinking. He paid no especial attention to the way home, but when he was on the top of Beacon hill, he paused, and said to himself, " Yes: I will think of it, but I will not hurry it."

Not long after this there was a dinner party at Mrs. Warren's. Although I have no especial warrant to do so, I will couple the names together, as they did in their minds: Mr. and Mrs. Alfred Stacy, Mr. Edward Stacy and Miss Emily Warren, Mr. Royal Bartlett and Miss Mary Graham, Mr. Edric Lyman and Miss Sarah Warren. These eight people did Mrs. Parna Warren entertain. To say that they had a fine time, would not be strong enough. Birds of a feather flock together. Here were four as good honorable men as you can find, and all they have to do, is to eat and drink, and entertain four as honorable and interesting young women, as ever were seen since Jacob kissed Rachel and lifted up his voice and wept. Jacob was Rachel's uncle. Jacob must have had it bad. These young people got through the evening without a tear. But they often laughed heartily at Edric Lyman's stories or Edward Stacy's. Lawyers and school teachers are frequently awful sharp.

Miss Graham's carriage came with Fred Annerly. Roy asked permission to walk home with her. He got it and sent the carriage home empty. He walked the long path with her, across the Common, and saw her safely in her own home. It was a pleasant walk, but without anything especial to report to you, who read this.

With industry, good management, a good number of pupils, and attractive ways, Roy was doing well. He enjoyed life thoroughly and thankfully. He would not be morbid, and he did keep sweet as a rose. Much depends upon the will. So the days went along until one Wednesday morning, when the janitor called again. He said: "Mr. Bartlett, do the artists want to try to rescue Mr. Wilkie from himself? He is down again, financially and morally. He is almost in delirium tremens."

"I will call on him," said Roy.

He did call and knock at the door. After a long wait, Roy heard shuffling feet coming to the door, and Frank Wilkie was a sight to behold. I need not describe a man saturated with whiskey and tobacco. But he had consciousness enough to be ashamed. He looked it. He began to stammer an excuse, but Roy stopped him.

"Mr. Wilkie, you do not need to say a word. Let me talk to you."

There was a light knock at the door. Roy admitted Miss Graham, and Frank Wilkie was ashamed indeed. He blushed.

She said, "I pitied you, Mr. Wilkie, and I want to help you and save you."

Said Roy, "Why will you go to hell this way?"

"There is no hell," he answered.

"There is," said Roy, "and you are in it and it is in · you. You are full of it. You are almost out of your mind with the poison of alcohol. When you say a man is intoxicated, you are simply saying he is poisoned. Toxicon is the technical name for poison. You are poisoned, almost crazy. Your clothing is poisoned to rags. Your money is all gone and poisoned out of you. Your self-respect is all gone. Your good name and clear conscience are all gone, and you are poisoned, body and soul. You are in hell if ever a man was. You are suffering. Sorry and ashamed. No drunkard hath eternal life. No drunkard shall inherit the kingdom of heaven. Frank Wilkie, I know you had a good mother. How must she feel to look down upon you now? Here Miss Graham and I have come to help you and rescue you. As soon as the janitor told us we came."

Frank Wilkie was weeping and shivering in agony.

"Oh, do give it up forever," said Miss Graham, and she wept and pleaded with him.

"There is no hope," he sobbed.

"Yes, there is," said Miss Graham. "I know there is hope, for you are loving and giving to all but yourself. I saw you lay a silver dollar down before a poor woman who was washing up the stairs. And I know you almost supported a poor girl, who got sick last winter. You gave her money to go to her friends in the country. Oh, give it up," said she, and she begged and wept alternately.

Roy kept silent while Miss Graham pleaded with him.

"What shall I do?" Frank Wilkie asked.

"Sign a solemn agreement never to use alcohol or tobacco again," said Miss Graham.

. "Good men use tobacco," said Wilkie.

"Yes, Mr. Wilkie," said she, "but the best and cleanest men do not. You will never be clean and safe until you give them both up forever. Tobacco is a vice, and you have had enough. Oh, be a clean white man."

She wept as she pleaded with him.

"Then, I will sign it," said he. "I was in despair. I thought I had no friend on earth, but I find I have two faithful ones. Miss Graham, I never will disgrace my name again. I never will grieve my sainted mother again, or bring tears to your eyes. Hereafter I use neither, again, as long as I live. Mr. Bartlett, please write an obligation, as strong as you can make it. Miss Graham shall prevail and beauty shall conquer the beast."

Said Roy, "Miss Graham, will you remain here until I return with the covenant?"

She would. Roy went down to his own studio and soon returned with the following, handsomely written on large note paper.

"This certifies that I, Francis Wilkie, do hereby and herein solemnly swear, upon my sacred honor, by all I hope for in this life, or the life to come, by the memory of my sainted mother, that I will Never again use intoxicating liquors of any kind, or tobacco. So help me God, and keep me steadfast."

With tearful eyes and trembling hands he signed it.

Roy added, "In our presence" and handed the pen to Miss Graham and then it bore the names of Mary Graham and Royal Bartlett as witnesses.

"Shall I keep it and bring you a copy?"

"Yes," said Frank Wilkie.

Miss Graham would insist upon leaving a ten-dollar note with Roy for Frank Wilkie.

"Now," said Roy, "I will get you some strong coffee and a lunch. If you can ventilate and right up this studio to make it look as if a temperance man lived here, it will be in order."

Roy soon returned with a can of coffee and a good lunch. Miss Graham returned to their studio, but she was tired. The strain of anxiety concerning Frank Wilkie was so great that she needed rest. She did not work, and went home early. While Frank Wilkie was having his lunch, which he needed to sober him off, Roy went up to his wardrobe at Mrs. Warren's, and got a second-best suit, which was just right for Frank Wilkie. This he gave him, and soon had the satisfaction of seeing him look like a man again. It touched him all the more. He was completely subdued. Then Roy led him out to the Turkish baths in Beacon Street and put him in charge of Mr. Haggerty, with instructions as to what he had been, what he had agreed to be, and to make a three-hour job of it, to keep watch of him, and to let him sleep if he would. He took his bath splendidly and was as quiet as a lamb. He rested while Roy got his own lunch and put in three hours good work.

After Roy closed the studio, he went to the Turkish bath rooms and got Frank Wilkie. They went down to Marston's, on Brattle Street, and got a tenderloin steak, with a cup of strong tea. It went well. He had been cleaned, rested, fed, employed, and when a man is thoroughly busy, the devil has little hold on him. Then Roy took him to his own room, and, with illustrated books and many other things to interest him, he left him, and descended to his own supper. I am afraid I use some words interchangeably, but I do not forget the traditions of my ancestors, and I cannot forget the customs of fine people of the present day.

Roy explained to Mrs. Warren enough of the situation, but not recounting all the objectionable points, for it is not always best to horrify a woman. If every woman knew what manner of man was near her, she would shrink much oftener than she does now.

Roy shared his bed with Frank, and they both rested well. Frank was still pale and unsteady, and Roy located him in his own studio, with colors and canvas, to work. He did not leave him long alone. They both applied themselves to work during the day, and Roy paid ten dollars for rent for Frank Wilkie. He brought back the receipt, giving it to him, and got a look of thanks and grateful acknowledgment.

It was the evening of the Art Coterie. Frank Wilkie did not wish to be visible at the meeting. The notice on Roy's, door announced that the entertainment would be "Sketches of Boston Artists." There was a screen near the desk in Mrs. Warren's parlors, that effectually cut off a corner, but left room for a chair behind it. In this chair sat Frank Wilkie, to hear all, but to be invisible. No one outside the family knew he was there, or suspected it. One of the older artists, that had long been in Boston, was introduced, and took the stand to speak. He said : —

Ladies and gentlemen, — Art is long. Its ways are various, and the many ways that artists have of holding

the mirror up to Nature give us infinite varieties of
interpretation. There need be no antagonism, because
we have not the same likes, or because we have not the
same facility of expression. Now I have before me a
peculiar task, and if you can help me by giving me permission to speak what you may not assent to, and let it
pass for what it is worth, to enjoy all you can, and to
refuse to be fretted by what you do not agree to,
then my work is easy, and all is pleasant. I have my
likes and dislikes as much as any, but I do not under-
value an artist that paints a cheap picture. The ancient
statement, that all men are created free and equal, is to
be taken with great allowance. All men are indeed created free, within certain very narrow limits, but they get
into trouble if they exceed them. In a few rights they
may be equal: but for the most part they are utterly and
eternally unequal, and I think they are more so in their
perceptions of art than in anything else. In some it is
utterly wanting, a minus quantity forever; while others
are pilgrims of beauty and children of light until they
are translated.

The numbers by which I denote these artists do not
indicate any quality, but are given as they occur to me.
No. 1. My friend, whom I shall call number one, was
born in 1817, in New Ipswich, N. H. I have known
him many years. I suppose he must be a sinner, if all
men are; but why he should submit to such an insinu-
ation, I never could see. I never found anything to base
such a statement upon. I think he paints as large a percentage of pictures that I like as any man living. It is
always a beauty. His colors are always pure and clean.
His summer home and studio are at North Conway.

The views of the mountains, the valley, and the world of wonder near home, give him beautiful subjects. I have one view, near his home, and Thomas Starr King watched him while he painted it. I have another, in the Cathedral Woods, with his own son, Kensett, in the picture. His lilies and roses, his kalmias and apple-blossoms, his corn and "punkins," his woods and waterfalls, are beauty pictures. He has had many pupils. Not long ago I heard a young artist say, "I have just been up in this artist's studio, and he has quite a harem of women, all painting in oil; and I'll be hanged if there was not one pupil sixty-five years old. Ha! ha! ha!"

He laughed heartily. After he was gone out, I told the others that the pupil in question was seventy years old, and could paint a much better picture than this critic could. Then they all laughed. I always enjoy a call at his studio. He is a kindly critic, and carries no tomahawk or scalping-knife. So the merciful find mercy. His name is in the later encyclopedias, and it is very pleasant to know that his winter studio is in Boston. For the sake of Boston and North Conway I might wish him to live forever, but it would not be fair to keep him out of heaven so long. So, inasmuch as I do not know what specific good to wish for Benjamin Champney, I shall leave it for the Almighty Power that gives, to select the gift.

> "May he have all, in one true wish exprest,
> Whate'er God gives to those that he loves best."

No. 2 is an Englishman, "For he himself has said it, and 'tis greatly to his credit, that he is an Englishman." He has crossed the Atlantic many times. He has gone back many times, to care for his sisters in England.

He is one of the kindest and best of men. While he attends, the Art Club will be sure of a total-absti- nence, anti-tobacco man. The woods are not full of such men. Everybody speaks of him in the kindest manner. His studio is a hive of pictures, many flowers, landscapes and souvenirs of old England. He plays the flute finely. It is very entertaining to hear him tell of his little adventures he has met in his travels across the ferry, and in England. Not long since I called at his door, and, without meaning it, I gave a Masonic knock. It was answered in kind, and in a moment more, I knew what I did not know before, that Henry Day had given me the welcome of a Master-mason. As Rip says, May he live long, and prosper.

No. 3 was born in Raymond, N. H. Forty years ago he was for a while a salesman in a dry goods store. But all the time he was studiously learning to draw and paint. Soon he began to paint all the time. He has had a great many pupils. He has had an art school in Bos- ton for many years, teaching several branches of art. He loved pictures, and illustrated books, beyond any one I ever saw. Some said he was a miser in art. If it is a fault to love art and beauty so much, it leans to virtue's side. Better love beauty than something worse. Later, when his strength failed, he sold off about four thousand dollars worth of books at auction. He must have had many thousand dollars worth of books, engravings, and works of art. Illustrations by Turner, Stanfield, Pyne, Calame, Harding, Bartlett, etc., and O how many port- folios of engravings and prints. I think he knew more of art in all its branches, than any man I ever knew. His pictures sold for moderate prices, but he was very prolific in them. I have been on summer tours with him several times, and it was very enjoyable. But one day in February, 1888, a few pupils and friends gathered at his studio, at the corner of Essex and Washington streets, and listened to his burial service by Rev. Dr. Bartol, and later, William H. Titcombe was borne to the graves of his family, and laid beside his father and mother, in Raymond, N. H. Age 63. He had no vices. He loved poetry, beauty, and art without limit. He was ready to impart what he knew. He had taking, pleasant ways. He was full of fun, and the best of company. He was Bohemian enough to make the best of life. And to him I take a cup of kindness yet for "Auld Lang Syne."

No. 4 is a lady artist. She has a home in Middleboro and Boston. She just believes in Boston, which is assurance of the highest taste. She paints in oil, and has many orders for crayon portraits. She does fine crayon work. Not long since, she paid a visit to Southern California. That was a good thing, but it was a better thing to come back to Boston, where she is known and appreciated. The name on her studio door is Miss Sarah D. White.

No. 5 is a man who paints many pictures at moderate prices, and gives as much art for the money, as any man I know. He has been in Europe, and travelled much in America. He is honest and true, easy and kind. He is so good to me that he will not chide me, even for this portrait. He is a Second Advent Christian, and don't care who knows it. He is teetotal and anti-tobacco. He is smart and industrious. It is pleasant to meet him here, and it would add largely to the promise of the sweet by and by, to know that I should have for a near neighbor, Mr. E. W. Parkhurst. Perhaps we might go sketching together.

No. 6 was a queer compound. He was small in size. Sometimes he would dress fairly well, and soon he would be shabby. He was embalmed in tobacco, and he often heightened the flavor with whiskey. But he could paint in very attractive color. He would take a palette knife and dab on bright color; then wobble it into a sunset effect that would charm you. His pictures would always have some past-finding-out effect, that would take with you. But his affairs were always at a crisis. He got locked up for his thirst. His pockets held nothing. He is gone. He was a scattering genius, with several vices. Alas for No. 6! What a pity he was.

No. 7 restores pictures, and does it admirably. What beautiful things I have seen in his studio. In all the picture work that I have met, I have found no restorations that have pleased me more than his. Fine specimens that are far too good to lose, come back with the same feeling and the life renewed. Some that seem cracked and darkened to death, come to life at his bidding. I always see something new in his room. He does the best work, and pleasant as that is, the artist himself gives the work an added charm. Mr. Harold Fletcher does not need to ask my blessing. He has it all the time.

No. 8 paints flowers, and does it splendidly. His studio has been in the studio building for years. He has had many pupils. I have a picture of his, magnolia buds and blossom. He manages to give the charm of Nature and art in his pictures, in a way to make them very interesting. I give Mr. George W. Seavey my kindest regards both for the man and his work.

No. 9 paints portraits. For good, faithful, durable work they are splendid. I have two of them. One is my son Bert, at three years old, with light curly hair. I have had people say they had rather have that picture, than any in the house. It is perfectly satisfactory. I have also my own portrait by him. ·It is satisfactorily and confoundedly like me. What a gallery his portraits would make. Several of his are in Mechanics Hall in Worcester. He has painted Lincoln, Garrison, Gov. Andrew, Col. Ward, Sumner, Webster, Phillips, John B. Moore, M. P. Wilder, Gough, Parker, Parker Pillsbury, S. G. Foster, and ever so many more. For the best of work, done by the best of men, I recommend both the man and his work, with lifelong regards for Mr. E. T. Billings.

No. 10 is a Boston boy. He was born in 1813, in Atkinson Street, now Congress street. He has been in Europe, and has painted long and well in Boston. He has had many pupils. Some artists take a subject, and paint nature in cold hard facts, grimly true. This artist will take the same subject, and, while being faithful to the scene, he will idealize it, and make it mysterious and attractive, so that you will wonder at the secret of his art. I like the pictures and the artist. His work is in the best houses, and wherever it is, there is a subtle something about it, that is the quality, that is almost the despair of art. What pleasant calls I have had at his studio. The percentage of his pictures that I should be glad to own and see every day, is large. They are vastly superior to many of the French pictures that sell for so large a price. Here is a poem of his which I appropriate. It is a view from his own house.

THE WILD ARTIST IN BOSTON.

THE REVOLVING LIGHT.

By S. L. Gerry.

'Tis dark. My children sleep.
'Tis dark. Yet day begins to creep.
'Tis dawn. Yon harbor lights have shone all night,
　　Till day's first peep.

Now bright it burns, now fainter turns,
　　Now dark as Egypt's night;
Now brighter gleams, now stronger beams,
　　Now full-orbed light.

My eyes still seek the distant streak
　　Where day the ocean meets,
Paler the light revolves as night
　　The morning greets.

Yet still it burns, and lights by turns
　　At danger's treacherous edge,
Where breakers dash, and sullen lash,
　　O'er sunken ledge.

Yon little star that pales afar
　　Hath faithful vigils kept,
At danger's post, guarding the coast,
　　While men have slept.

Its work is done. Behold the sun,
　　And now its little ray,
Mingling its gleams with God's own beams,
　　Is merged in glorious day.

And so, for all he is, and all he has done, I vote that Samuel L. Gerry is an honor to himself, to art, and to Boston.

No. 11 is composed of two ones, side by side. Consequently they are twins, C. and D. They were born in Malden, in the same room that Adoniram Judson was. I do not know them apart and cannot consider them apart. They are very talented men. One paints pictures, the other is a sculptor. One or both designed the soldiers' monument in Cambridge. They are musical, witty, literary, artistic, and if you need daylight on any thing that is nebulous to you, it is safe to consult them. Is it a lecture on music, literature, art, sculpture, Shakespeare? Well, it is a blessed thing to know something. I give kind regards to the brothers Cyrus and Darius Cobb.

No. 12 is a widow with an invalid depending upon her. She had a little money to begin on, and a love for art, but no genius. It was uphill work. She took a few lessons, and painted some almost hopeless pictures. Her courage was good and she did improve. So by main strength and will power, she would learn to paint. Now she paints a fair picture, has many pupils, at a low rate, and compels art to be her servant. Art shows good taste by surrendering to such a pleasant, true-hearted lady. We cannot all be grenadiers in art.

No. 13 and his wife came eight years ago from East Prussia. They lived in Washington at first. They are just married lovers, and it is refreshing to visit them at their home. They have quite a picture gallery and studio beside. Scenes in or near Washington, Boston, and in Germany. Their pets are many. Canaries, rabbits, doves, Angora cats and several monkeys. Dandie, their black monkey with a white face, gives me the kindest greeting. These people are fine artists, and I give my kind regards to Mr. Albert and Mrs. Ottilie Borris.

No. 14 is a young man who loves art. Usually it is a blessing, but with him it is a pity. Because if he hated it, he would let it alone. But now he has a studio, and paints pictures. Some are of barn-door size. O the roses, the landscapes and the figures. Of course there is no valid and sufficient reason for profanity; but if there was his pictures would be that reason. They are as far from being works of art as dock mud is from being wedding cake. Any artist would almost be justified in breaking out in wild, wicked, elaborate denunciations of such work. He painted a little child kneeling at prayer. Going by his door I saw it and I never wanted a tomahawk so badly in my life. A teamster saw it, and went off gritting his teeth. The little girl's bare foot was too big for a man's arctic. A descendant of the laughing philosopher got a glimpse of it and went off, holding on to his abdomen. And yet, that artist might have been a success driving a tip cart. Usually it is better to paint a poor picture than none, but there is a limit. He will not see this, and I will not tell his name.

No. 15 was born in Boston and lives in Malden. I had a chance to see him and his pictures within a week and I never saw a finer moonlight than he showed me. I do admire all his work. This picture was the bay of Naples by moonlight. Vesuvius of course. About the year 1837, when he was in Italy, he lived awhile at Albano. Mr. S. L. Gerry went there and was with him for some time. They went sketching together. With a hope of doing him some good, Mr. Gerry one day asked him, Why do you not give some thought of the life to come, and look forward and upward sometimes? It will make a better and a happier man of you. He answered, I do not trouble myself about the future, for the present is all I can attend to. Nevertheless he remembered Mr. Gerry's kind words. A little while before, some friend had given

Mr. Gerry a small Bible as a keepsake. He lost it. He thought the custom-house folks got it. But no, it was left with Mr. George L. Brown at Albano, and he thought it was left for him to read as a bit of missionary good work from his friend Gerry. Later, when Mr. Brown was sick from brain fever, he read Mr. Gerry's Bible as he recovered. He learned to love it and believe in it, and Mr. Brown tells, that the story and faith of Christ has brightened his life, and made a better man of him. He lived many years in Rome. He had good success in selling his pictures. I think he was born in the same year as Mr. Gerry. Both Boston boys. What bright splendid pictures Mr. Brown does paint. There is a might and power in the expression that he finds, in a palette of color. I return his parting word to me, his hearty "God bless you."

No. 16 has long been a portrait painter in Boston. His work ranks high, and goes into the best places. I do like the art he gets in his pictures. For a long time they will be in Boston as memorials of people of character, and souvenirs of remembrance of the artist, Mr. J. Harvey Young.

No. 17 is a lady who has painted in oil, has had her pictures reproduced in chromo. Her oil studies are always pleasant. She makes New England scenes attractive. Of late she gives the most of her time to crayon portraits. I see them well spoken of in the papers, and know that she is doing excellent work. Her pupils and friends will testify for Miss A. M. Gregory as a faithful and successful artist.

No. 18 is an artist, and self-appointed art critic. I have heard unconcise people say, a picture of his was

"good." They must have given the priest something to
pay for lying. Once in a while he praises a picture that
he did not paint, but usually he flays them alive. I never
knew him to sell a picture for cash. Still, with his art
and his rich relations, he manages to stub along somehow.
As I do not wish to fight, I omit the name.

No. 19 is a very odd number. I had him in my employ
when he was fourteen years old. He was a lean, cadaver-
ous, poor little boy. The freckles on his face were more
than sporadic, they were multitudinous and confluent.
The warts on his hands were more than social, they were
gregarious. Some were on foot and some were on wart-
back. He never had eaten an orange. I went out and
got him one, and before I knew it he had eaten the peel
also. He could not tell the time of day, as he had never
been where clocks were. He was mild, shy, and afraid.
I told him a funny story, and he smiled. I told him
another, and a funnier one, and he roared. I was bound
to start him. Then we were acquainted. I asked him
questions, pumped him in fact. He said he had made a
sketch in ink of his grandfather's turning-lathe. He
showed it. There was merit in it. He told me how he
had longed for paints, to paint pictures. I bought him a
kit of Winsor and Newton's water-colors, a good one.
He sat up late, and I was surprised at the good work he
had done. Soon his warts were all gone, and the freckles
largely gone after them. Since then he has been a
designer for calico. I have souvenirs that I keep, that
came out of his waste basket. One is a little marine
water-color. Another is a picture of thistle blossoms
with bees on them. Those bees and flies, drawn with pen,
are fine. I held the picture near my ear, and heard a

buzzing. Perhaps it was the bees in the picture. I have it framed, where I can see it every day. He can draw or paint fruit or berries admirably. He has designed and drawn for some of the best agricultural papers in New. York. He has made new headings for several. He can take an intricate oil painting and copy it good enough to puzzle the man that painted it. He will take a pen and draw blackberries better than any man I ever saw. He has no vices that I ever heard of. He is no financier. He has more genius than any artist I ever met. His bank account is so small that he can put it " all in his eye," and wink real easy. He was always true, kind, and grateful to me, and I earnestly hope that God's blessing will come to lighten his life, and shine brighter unto the perfect day.

No. 20 lives in Cambridgeport. On a corner, behind a high hedge, among trees and vines, is his home and studio. His pictures are mostly landscape, with some marines, flowers, and still-life. His trees are beauties. His country roads and waterfalls please me much. He is past seventy, and his pictures never were better. He had a son, Charlie, an artist, who died at North Conway. He was clever, in both senses of the word, and a real good fellow. Whoever has a picture of No. 20 gets an honest one, of an artist who is anxious to leave behind him work true to nature, and a credit to the artist, Mr. John W. A. Scott.

No. 21 has lived and painted in Boston, but now lives in Malden. Fine portraits, pleasant landscapes, and O such grapes, peaches, cherries, and other fruit. I give kind regards to the artist, Mr. H. R. Burdick.

No. 22 was a pleasant gentleman and a fine portrait

painter. He would paint the picture of an ordinary, uninteresting person, and, while making it a good likeness,
would idealize it, and make it a grand picture. It was
high art. I have three of his portraits. His wife and he
were called away in middle life. They were a fine couple.
I gladly give this word of kindly appreciation to the
memory of Mr. and Mrs. Edward L. Custer.

No. 23 is an absorbent. He will get all he can out of
this world, and give just as little as he can for it. He
can paint a fine portrait or a bright landscape. If he can
get into your debt he will stay there. The idea of loving
and giving, hoping for nothing again, never entered his
mind. The more I see of the man, the more I admire —
everybody else. He will never learn the truth of that
scripture, " There is, that scattereth and yet increaseth,
and there is that withholdeth more than is meet, and it
tendeth to poverty."

No. 24 is a lady artist, and all her surroundings are
as pretty as pinks. She lives in Cambridgeport, among
the pleasant, sunny houses not far from Brookline bridge,
and the views of Boston and Charles River from her
home and studio are fine. She paints many pictures that
I like, especially flowers, and many pupils come to her.
The situation, the city, the skies, and the river must be
full of pleasant suggestions for the artist, Mrs. J. A.
Wiggin.

No. 25 is a Boston boy. It is a splendid beginning.
He has been long and well known here. He paints landscape, marine, game, and fish. O ever so many things.
He is always good to me, and I fully believe he is to
everybody. Every summer he goes sketching far and
wide. Now in Maine, then in New Hampshire, and

again in Vermont, or in New York, among the Adirondacks. He has had some funny experiences. Once he was out sketching in a book. A curious countryman hailed him with, Hullo there! Practisin' singin'? No, I am sketching. Wal, I thought it looked like a singing book. Again he was under his sun-umbrella, sketching in oil. Hullo, are you shadin' a sick critter there? Not much. Wal, I see yer had yer umbrella spread, an' I didn't know but you was shadin' a sick critter. Wot ye doin'? I am painting a picture. Sell 'em? Git yer livin' out of 'em? Yes, I do. Wal, now, I wouldn't give ten cents for a barn full on 'em. It was very funny from the artist's point of view; but a countryman need not be a brute. Another time he was in New Hampshire. A farmer came out laughing. Ho, ho, ho, my wife thought you was a tramp, that had been stealin' our apples; but come to find out, you are the painter feller that boards down to Fogg's. Again he was making a sketch. A farmer came out and enquired. Cipherin'? Another time one enquired of another who it was. Is he crazy? He walks along a short distance, then stops; looks around, stops again; acts real funny. Curiosity was relieved when they found it was a still-hunt for beauty. On the seashore he was walking along with his sketch-box. A lot of boys came running after him. "Be you the man that vaccinates boys?" Again he walked out with his box. "Be you a pedlar?" No, sir, I am not. Wal, sir, it ain't nothin' to object to. John Jacob Astor was a pedlar. An artist sketching is a great wonder to an enquiring mind. It is a good thing to find a large, handsome pickerel, then take him to your studio, paint his picture, and then eat him for dinner. I should like to see all the

pictures that this industrious prolific painter has painted.
Now it is a derby hat with a rat-terrier in it. Then it
is a straw hat with a Malta kitten. in it. Now a fish, a
Florida red snapper, in the gayest of color. Now shad or
· salmon, perch or smelts. Landscapes in color, or black
and white, like a steel engraving. Then mountain, woodland, lake, and river in color. If any shall succeed in
being a better artist, they will find it hard to be a kinder,
better fellow than Mr. Samuel W. Griggs.

No. 26 is a marine painter. He gets as much of the
spirit of the sea in his pictures, as any one I can name.
A faithful student, and very popular. I like his pictures
thoroughly. Once he painted a large picture in six
hours, and sold it for six hundred dollars. I need not
say it was a fine picture, but it was a risky thing to do.
A house with one coat of paint on it is not a well painted
house. No more is a picture. It will soon grow to look
thin. He wins fame and fortune, and he deserves it
well.

No. 27 paints portraits, landscapes, and interiors. He
is doing excellent work. Lately I saw an interior, a parlor scene, with a lady sitting, reading. It was an elaborate picture, and a study of mysterious color. Several
portraits, some of them children, were being done.
There is power and promise in the work of Mr. J.
Wagner.

No. 28 was born near the Grand Monadnock, in south-
ern New Hampshire. His summer home is in Peterboro.
He paints cattle, sheep, and landscape. In these sketches
I am giving my own loves and opinions only, and not an
art criticism at all. Neither am I advertising an artist.
There is nothing mercenary about it. I have known this

man since he began, and I never knew aught about him
that was not the kindest and best. All the force of his
life has been to be the best artist that he could possibly
be. He paints cattle and sheep splendidly. If I wanted
a picture of New England cattle or sheep, I had rather
have one of his, than any artist that I ever saw or heard
of, not even excepting Rosa Bonheur, or Eugene Verboeckhoven. His sheep and cattle are a triumph of art.
He gets large prices and might increase on them. His
pictures get the best places in the exhibitions, and go
into the best houses. To the man and the artist I give
my kind regards, to Mr. Charles F. Pierce.

No. 29 is a fine lady artist. She paints airily, ideally,
admirably. Can I criticise her? Yes, I can; but I
won't. She has two always apparent ruling motives.
One is to paint the best possible picture, and the other is
to get the largest number of shekels for it. I envy her
her art, and give it the continued assurance of my most
distinguished consideration.

No. 30 paints marine pictures. If he could arise, as an
artist, to the level he has attained as a kind good fellow,
he would get the highest bounce he ever got in his life.
Still he gets about twelve or fifteen hundred a year, out
of it. We cannot all be Raphaels. It is better to be a
saint and an artist of moderate merit, than to be a
supreme artist and a Satan. I cannot paint a picture all
in white and cadmium. I cannot declare all artists Claudes
and Murillos. This gives me some fine shadows between
the high lights.

No. 31 is a poor artist. Poor every way. He was
born out of a poor family, and I think it would have been
a fortune to him if he had never been born at all. He

pays a poor rent for a poor studio, when he pays it at all.
He paints a poor picture, when he paints at all, with poor
paints, on a poor canvas; and it sells for a poor price
when it sells at all; and the buyer, when there is one, is
a poor judge of pictures, and makes a poor trade. This
poor artist lives in a poor way, dresses poor, and has a
poor look ahead. He sometimes wonders why this world
is such a poor place for him; and perhaps, I cannot say
for sure, he makes a poor effort to improve things. But
it is such a poor effort, of course it has a poor result. I
am sorry to hang such a poor portrait among such rich
color, but we are not all brigadier-generals. Some must
be high privates.

No. 32 is a young lady, pretty as pinks, and sweet
enough to cut up for a salad. She lives out of town,
coming in to take a lesson once or twice a week. She
paints a real good picture, so good that you would marvel
at it. She is engaged to a fine young man, and I should
like to kill him. I know I ought not to, for he must be
nice, or she would not tolerate him. I cannot really
blame him for wishing to forsake father and mother to
become one flesh. But it cuts me up all the same. They
will please receive the old beaver's blessing.

No. 33 was born in Ohio, in 1841. His home and home
studio are in Hyde Park, Mass. He has been in Europe,
in all about seven years, studying with the best masters.
He paints wonderful pictures. When the Mechanics'
Association and Boston Art Club buy a man's pictures,
it is a sign that he has a standing in art. His autumn
landscapes and twilight skies are very fine. He has
plenty of pupils and paints some portraits. One of his
pictures is in my sitting-room, where I see it every day.

My wife has voted unanimously, that she shall keep it there. That suits me. He has fine success in art, and I never heard even an art critic dare to criticise him as a man. If the prayers of the righteous prevail, Mr. John J. Enneking will live long and be happy. It is a pleasure to see what a power he is in art.

No. 34 paints cattle, sheep, and landscape. He has had very successful sales, has been in Europe and California. He has a fine standing among Boston artists. His late exhibition was interesting and popular. It takes merit to attain a position in art like Mr. J. Foxcroft Cole. Next to the poet, the artist lives in the work he leaves behind him. The gift of expression, always made valuable by development, is one great gift, whether in construction, invention, enunciation, or delineation. But words do not express the thought. They fit ideas as sabots do feet. They are wooden and clumsy. The thought is beautiful, flexible, and graceful. Happy is the man who can give it expression. Happy is the artist who can show the beauty pictures in his mind. Of course I cannot know many of the artists of a great city. But what I have known of them has, in general, been very pleasant. Indeed I think, as a class, they are the most enjoyable people alive. One more picture and I am done. Ladies and gentlemen, I have not spoken to win your applause, neither have I set down aught in malice. Every word I have spoken has been carefully written, well considered, and is true. A mean person, low, drunken, dirty, or selfish, will be that although he may try to do the noblest work. O the pleasant people I have met as artists. I give them kindest regards. If one utterly lacks self-control, woe is for him, unless he assert himself. A runaway horse is poor property, but alas, for a runaway soul. Once in a while we do see one.

No. 35 was one of the best marine painters I ever saw, perhaps quite the best. O his mighty ships, his ocean waves. He was a true genius, good size, florid, handsome, able to sell his pictures readily and for good prices. I have seen a picture of his marked two thousand dollars. He might have been immensely rich, and have gone into the most honored society. I can go where his pictures occupy splendid places. They are magnificent. But he wasted his talent and his young life. He died of a complication of everything that he could blame himself or a woman for. The artists subscribed money, some of them, with great self-denial, and buried him. More, they bore his coffin to a little chapel, and a dreadful office it was, and one they will not soon forget. I am sorry to bring such a picture before you, but I had a motive, and I must be true. And I have a little more to say, and perhaps I do an unpardonable thing, but I do it with a kind loving heart.

There is an artist now in Boston, that is going down to a drunkard's grave. He is a good artist and a generous man. He only lacks the saving grace of self-control. I never was intimate with him, and so I have no influence over him. I hope some of you have. His condition is well known to many. I should not be surprised to hear of his death at any time. I saw him yesterday, almost on the rocks. I earnestly entreat of any of you, that have any influence, to use it at once, to do the noblest deed of your lives, to rescue poor Frank Wilkie.

The address was done and the suspense was painful. What was it to the man behind the screen?

Roy Bartlett took the stand and for a moment was unable to control himself. He began: "My friends, I am glad for the kind words that our brother has spoken. With such as he, art and heart are near together. And I am glad to tell him, and you all, of something that will rejoice your hearts. What our brother has said, was true, yesterday morning. But now, Frank Wilkie is in the hands of devoted friends, and better still, has voluntarily signed a solemn obligation, by his sacred honor, by all he hopes for in earth or heaven, by the sacred memory of his mother, that he will never use intoxicating liquors or tobacco again, while he lives."

Roy Bartlett had made a sensation. Again and again there came a storm of applause, until weariness compelled them to cease.

Then the artist who had addressed them said, "I feel, to thank God. I should like to sing, ' Praise God, from whom all blessings flow.' "

It was done. Their thankfulness found expression. There were plenty of splendid singers present. They sang that glorious song of praise, and Frank Wilkie sat with bowed head and heard it all. The hour was late, but they felt thankful.

Handel's "Hallelujah Chorus" was called for. Miss Warren had some copies in books and they sang it with a will. Then the people in the street cheered, which pleased the coterie.

A gentleman arose and said, "I should like to hear this company sing, ' We won't go home till morning.' "

The idea took at once. Mr. Bartlett called Mr. Webb to take charge of it and sing the second stanza, "For we are all jolly good fellows," if ordered.

Mr. Webb asked Miss Graham to preside at the piano. Said he, "I once heard this man-song, sung by a wagon load of girls from a female seminary, and they sung it. *Dolce andante sostenuto.* I have not got over it yet. We will sing it to old 'Malbrook,' and please give it *staccato*, with force and precision. Sing big, and between the stanzas, Miss Graham, please give us a fancy interlude."

They arose as Miss Graham gave a line of the roistering old song. The director was wide awake. If you have ever heard it sung by a good smart chorus, as I did that night, you have heard a good thing, well done. Then came Miss Graham's interlude. I heard a graphic young man telling it the next day. He said: "I tell you she did everlastingly maul that piano." At the close of the interlude, her notes climbed by pleasant fugues to the top of the highest, and prettily trilling there, she came lightly and sweetly by the common chords, alternating with funny little capers, down to the tonic, and then she looked up for orders. She might have had all the applause she wanted, but it was not permitted. The order, Ready, sing, came short and sharp, and "For we are all jolly good fellows" was music and song, truth and poetry. The parlors were soon empty, and Frank Wilkie was conducted to Roy's chamber.

He said: "Mr. Bartlett, how pleasant it is to be loved and honored as you are."

"You can be," said Roy.

"I will try," said he.

CHAPTER XXXV.

The next morning, the first train bore Roy and Frank
Wilkie, with color and canvases, to Dover, New Hampshire, and Frank was left in charge of Mr. and Mrs.
Bartlett, with a full statement of the case. He was cared
for, guarded, made happy, and at home. He was cherished and prayed for, and it did not hurt him a bit. He
painted a good-size picture of the homestead, to begin
with, a daylight scene. When it was done he had been
so impressed with his surroundings, that he painted the
same scene, the Bartlett home, by moonlight. There was
the same light in the sitting-room windows, and in Roy's
chamber. There was the full moon above it all, and the
smoke from the large chimney came up in the form of an
angel, with shadowy arms, held out in blessing. The
bright moon was in a clear space, but just outside of that
were clouds suggesting cherubs' heads, like the angel
arch in Raphael's "Madonna di San Sisto." In one corner, on a rock, was printed, "The Angel of Peace."

Frank Wilkie worked like a beaver. He went to
church with Mr. and Mrs. Bartlett, and it did him good.
Mrs. Bartlett knit him stockings, and made him shirts,
and Mr. Bartlett bought him a new suit of clothes. He
learned to milk, and did so morning and night. When
the two pictures were finished and dry enough, Frank

gave them to Mr. and Mrs. Bartlett. He said he should
like to have them go to Boston for Roy to see. They
did go, and were shown, handsomely framed, at the next
Art Coterie.

Then Frank wrote a letter, thanking all his friends in
the Art Coterie, for their sympathy and kindness, and
Roy read it at the time he called attention to the pictures. It made the best of thankful feeling. Then it
was not long before he sold some pictures in Dover.
The dollars began to come in. As he had no vices, they
stayed in. He asked permission to prolong his stay.
He would help milk, would work some on the farm, and
if he could stay until next October, he would help do the
haying. He had never found a place that had so much
of peace and God's blessing. The author used to think
so himself, when he went there. Or he would pay cash
for his board and help some beside.

Mr. Bartlett refused his cash but said he could stay,
and help a little. So Frank Wilkie was changed from
what he was, and stayed all summer. He sent money to
Roy to pay his back rent, and the janitor stored his few
things at a low rate. Frank sent pictures to people in
Boston, who were glad to get them at the price. One
day Eli Bertram was in Roy's studio. He said he had
no relations living. Roy expressed his sympathy. He
went further. He said, "Mr. Bertram, you have been
good to me. Give me a chance to serve you sometime.
If you are ever sick, or in need of a friend, let me know
it, and I will come to your assistance. Don't hesitate to
send for me, day or night."

"I give you the same permission," said Miss Graham.

"God bless you both," said Eli Bertram. "I think,

however," said he, "that I have means enough for all I shall want, and the folks I board with are good to me. I board with a widow, who has an aged mother, and it is home for me, and help for both of them. But as I said, I will let you know if I need you."

Then Roy showed Mr. Bertram Frank Wilkie's pictures, and told him the whole story. The old man was pleased enough. Eli Bertram had the name of being a close-fisted man. Solomon Shavin would have testified to it. But he tried faithfully to do the most good he could. He had supported this widow, Mrs. Francis, whom he boarded with, and it had made a home for both her and her mother; and without it, they might have both gone to the almshouse. He loved those that loved him. He would have loved more, but they would not.

When Roy told him the story of Frank Wilkie, he was glad, and taking twenty-five dollars from his pocketbook, he said, "here, Mr. Bartlett, send this to him, and tell him to paint as good a picture of your homestead as he can afford to for that, and send it to me. And tell him to come and get boarded where I do, when he returns, and I will help him sell his pictures."

So Frank Wilkie had a splendid summer, made friends and money and grew in favor with God and man. He also made up his mind to go to board with Eli Bertram, when he came back in the fall, but it was not to be. Mr. Bertram's health declined visibly. He called on Jonathan Strong and made his will. No one else knew it, and although a copy was left with Mr. Strong, the original was left in his safe, in his boarding mistress's parlor. He told her of it later, and said he had left her something. Roy and Miss Graham came often to see

him, and Roy was with him when he passed away. And
Eli Bertram's will was a surprise. Not so much in what
he owned, as in what he did with it. He owned ten
brick houses in one block, worth over ten thousand dollars each, beside considerable other real and personal
property. He gave the houses to these five persons, for
their own use forever. Two to Roy Bartlett, two to
Miss Graham, two to Edric Lyman, two to Frank Wilkie
with a proviso, that he kept his obligation, otherwise it
went to his residuary legatee, and two to his pastor.
Roy and Edric Lyman were to be executors, and Roy
was residuary legatee. He also left the house and a
package of government bonds to Mrs. Francis, his housekeeper, the widow that he had boarded so long with.
She was worthy of it. They were all surprised every
way. There was no one to dispute the will.

Now Roy was well situated. He congratulated Miss
Graham and she thanked him. Frank Wilkie gave
thanks to Roy for it all. Well he might. There are
some sponges, that you may waste all human and divine
love upon, and they will never love you back again. Eli
Bertram was none of that, neither was Frank Wilkie, or
Edric Lyman, or Roy Bartlett, or Mary Graham. I do not
know which it was that loved first, but I do know that
the love was there, and one of them at least could say,
"he first loved me."

The next and last meeting of the Art Coterie was a
short one with more sketches of Boston artists and plenty
of music. Of course Boston artists were not half represented. Mrs. Warren received several pictures, as souvenirs of the artists. There was a genuine regret when
they sang "Auld Lang Syne," at the close of the

evening. Roy had hosts of friends, and a kind thought for all.

One day he had a letter from home which made him laugh. His mother had written what they were all doing, how Frank Wilkie had prospered, how industrious he was, and all the news. Then she wrote that Canis Major wanted to write a word, and as he had just come out of the meadow, she got a good impression of his big, muddy paw, which she dried, and added, "Come home, Roy," as the dog's invitation. Roy also got this letter, —

"DEAR FRIEND ROY, — I have heard from your father of your good fortune, and my wife and I are rejoiced indeed. My father owned a large house here in Dover, which did not pay very well. I have taken it, and fitted it up as a hotel and boarding house. We are doing well from the start. Father gives me the rent and supplies from the farm, and I give him a part of the money. We have splendid sings, and plenty of company. McDuffie's Hotel will welcome you at any time. When you are married, please come and pass your honeymoon with us. We have plenty of horses and carriages, and you shall have the best of everything, free. I am glad of what you have done in art, and in property. Now please let us see you in Dover, and we will have no end of a good time. My wife sends her love to you, and so do I.

"Ever your friend,
"JEAN McDUFFIE."

"He is a true heart," said Roy, as he folded up the letter. "He lost his self-will in the Isinglass River, and since then he has been grateful and loving."

Somehow Miss Graham did not seem elated over Eli Bertram's splendid gift, and Roy sat down to consider it. He was truly grateful to the old man. Was Miss Graham cold-hearted? Then he thought how ready she was to

give money to all who needed it, even more than Roy
thought best. Yes, indeed ; and how she pleaded with
tears to save Frank Wilkie. No, she was not cold-hearted,
sure. She was not. If she was not elated over wealth,
that was virtue and common sense. She was not ex-
travagant. She had not begun to tell what she would do
or buy. Her expenses were not increased. She dressed
well, but modestly. Nothing loud in color. He tried to
criticise her, and he began to feel ashamed of himself
inside for doing it. If any one had said a word against
Mary Graham, he would have resented it hotly. And
she, just quiet and faithful, helped his pupils, and walked
in Roy Bartlett's mind, the bright eclipse of any and all
other women. He mused. He looked with his mind's
eye, Horatio, at her, from every point of view, in every
relation of life, for time and eternity, and the little
modest woman unconsciously bore the test.

CHAPTER XXXVI.

SOLOMON IN ALL HIS GLORY.

The winter was gone, and it was May. Roy was well situated financially. He had a good bank account. With the brick store property, which came by the kindness of Mr. S. R. Knights, and the two brick houses that Eli Bertram left him, he was having an assured income of twenty-five hundred a year, beside what his art brought him, which was no small sum. He had not increased his style of living. His home with Mrs. Warren was good enough. It was the middle of May.

One morning Miss Graham came in and Roy asked "if it was not time to consider their trip to Dover, to see the apple trees in bloom."

She said, "she was ready, when the best time came."

"That is what I am looking for," said Roy. "The Whitsunday is about the twentieth of May. Suppose we go on Thursday, before the Whitsunday."

She said, "yes."

"Can you stay a week?"

"She could if it was suitable, and nothing happened at home."

So it was agreed. They took the morning train for Dover. The pupils had been notified and the studio door said: "Gone sketching for a week."

When the battle of Lexington was fought, on the nine-teenth of April, the peach and cherry trees were in full bloom, and it was so hot a day that some were overcome with the heat. A hundred years later, I went to Lexing-ton, and saw General Grant at the centennial. It was a cold raw day. Our party went out in the woods and made a fire to eat our lunch by. We saw several small snowdrifts, and although our party were all born Yankees, yet we were bluenoses, every one. Not a blossom or a sign of one. But the Whitsunday, a month later, is quite sure to show the apple-blossoms, that surpass Solomon in all his glory.

Mr. Bartlett met Roy and Mary at the station. He had killed the fatted calf, he said, and the prodigal would get some veal worth eating. Mother Bartlett was happy again now Roy had come home, and Miss Graham was made at home, and free from all restraint at once. Canis Major rejoiced with joy unspeakable to see Roy and Miss Graham, whom he remembered well. Frank Wilkie was there, and it was good to see how handsome he had grown. The great orchard was becoming a cloud of pink and white blossoms. In the afternoon the three artists walked out around the house and garden. Canis Major and Grimalkin went too; Frank Wilkie carried Grimalkin. A man that does not love cat or dog is a pig of a man any way. Roy showed Miss Graham where Will Glance had jumped out at him, and struck him with a club. The scar still showed. They were all as pleased and happy as Canis Major and Grimalkin, but Roy and Miss Graham were almost too quiet. Frank Wilkie noticed it, but did not remark. Mr. and Mrs. Bartlett were in the house. Mrs. Bartlett was fixing up something nice for tea, and he was all around, playful, paying attention to her, and courting his wife over again. "What is the matter with Roy?" he asked.

"Well, what is?" she asked.

"Why," said Mr. Bartlett, "he is as solemn as an owl. He has not smiled once since he came."

"Don't you know what ails him?" asked mother Bartlett, as she elevated the range of her specs, and looked her old husband-lover in the face.

"Liver complaint?" he asked.

"Liver cum-granny," she said. "Don't you know better than that? you old bunch of sweetness. It is a heart disease, and it will take a woman about the size of Miss Graham to cure it."

He laughed. He said he was getting a little mixed. He could not tell art from heart, at all. There seemed to be no boundary line between them at all. So Roy's father and mother kept up an awful thinking, and Roy was not a bit the wiser for it.

Take your excursion the first fair day, you can let it rain any time. So the next morning was sunny and pretty. They had an easy-riding top buggy, with rubber blanket and robe; then they were ready for casualties and showers. Roy and Miss Graham took sketching books, and were off at eight o'clock. They took the road through Barrington, over Waldron's Hill, by Jonathan Drew's and Gilman Hall's, past the old Judge Hale place, and by the old Doctor Woodbury farm, and so on to Bow Pond. They call it Bow Lake now. Roy told the names of the farms as he drove past, and they made an outline occasionally. It was a succession of exclamations. Oh! see this, or, Oh! see that, very often. I have often done the same journey, with an artist, but never with so interesting an artist as Roy had.

What a beauty New Hampshire is when the apple trees are in bloom. They kept to the east of Bow Pond, after passing the village, and when they came to a fine view of the lake, which is three miles long, they found a place to dine. The horse had his harness off, to cool off. Roy brought a pail of spring water instead of champagne. He took the supplies out of the carriage, and, with a tree piled with pink apple blossoms low down over their heads, they sat down to dine. Cold coffee, bread and butter, fatted calf, apple pie, doughnuts and cheese, with honey in the comb, do not amount to any great self-denial, and they began to be merry; that is — no, they didn't. They were as quiet and steady as two people frequently are in same condition. They ate their dinners, and were grateful to all who had contributed to them. The horse was rested, and entertained as well. These two people were satisfied to be together, for this visit of Miss Graham's might be the last forever. They were very pleasant to each other, but there was no fun, no laugh, from the rising of the sun to the going down thereof. It was a ride, it was beauty, it was apple blossoms, O handsome as paradise. It was nature, it was art; and if it was another thing, the Lord only knew it, or what it was. They did not. They returned by the green hill road, and they had found a long, quiet, happy day.

Sam Ellet and his wife came over in the evening. He was as full of fun as he could stick. His wife tried to suppress him a little, but he let out another joke, that made her snort right out with laughter. Then Roy laughed too, and Miss Graham also. But this was after sunset, mind you; so I have told you no lies. Sam was solemn enough the night he walked into the Hoskins mudhole. But he outlived it.

Saturday it rained. They all stayed at home, and Jean McDuffie and his wife came up. Roy was his mother's boy again.

On Sunday they all went to the brick Orthodox church, in two teams. It is a good way to spend Sunday. I have been there myself many times, in the days when Rev. Homer Barrows preached there. Miss Graham just enjoyed her visit, every minute. Such good, safe, clean, white people. They will labor for you. They will pray for you. Let them.

Monday morning they took to the road again. This time they went by Hicks's Hill, and straight to Lee Hill. O the apple blossoms. Many a tree was one mighty and splendid bouquet. O the glorious apple-trees! They went through Wadleys Falls village, and Roy told her stories of farms and people as they passed. Wilson's mills had formerly been Bartlett's mills. They kept on through New Market. They went slowly, for there was much to see. There was the bridge over the Lamprey River; on the eastern end, is where a plank was laid across, to save distance, and one Sunday evening Mary Rendall, while returning from meeting, fell off and was drowned, fifty years ago and more. On the hill, a few rods east of the bridge, is a huge rock, close beside the road, with a large dark stain on it, on the side of the rock toward New Market. Roy told her the Indian legend, how a young settler had come and built his house near, and they ordered him to leave, but he would not go. They shot him, and killed his wife and child on the top of the great rock, dashing the child in pieces where the great dark stain now is. The stain is still there, and every one sees it as he crosses the bridge from New Market to Durham. Beautiful trees. The river glimmers through them.

They had their dinner in a quiet place near the road. They had a twenty-mile ride, and so much beauty to see, that their eyes were tired with seeing. But they got home just in time for a cup of tea, and Mother Bartlett's cooking.

There were several people here, doing some tall thinking. Another day they took the carryall, and Mr. and Mrs. Bartlett went with Roy and Miss Graham, first to Garrison Hill, then to Great Falls, and Salmon Falls. The omnipresent apple-blossoms followed them all the way. Solomon did have some luxuries, but there were three things that he owned right up he could never understand, and here was Roy, a Boston artist, trying to find out the hardest one. No wonder it stuck him. Mr. Bartlett talked as they rode, and Roy and Miss Graham had the back seat all to themselves. It was a Quaker meeting.

They had two days more. Roy asked her, "Did you ever catch a trout?"

"No, I never did."

"Do you wish to?"

"Yes, I do."

"Then," said he, "we will go up to the old trout brook to-morrow, trouting. Perhaps we may get a string. The wind is south, and I guess it is a good time. Now, Miss Graham, I want to consult your wish. I will bait your hook, take the fish off, if you get any, and be your helper, so you need not soil your hands. But once you said you wished to help yourself where you can, and be independent. In that case you will have to take the worms, and bait your own hook, and take off your fish. Your hands will not smell nice; but soap and water soon cures all that, when you get home. Now, what will you do?"

She answered, "If you will please to show me how to bait the hook, and how to fish, I will get along alone, as long as I can."

He would show her. He did. He showed her how to walk softly, and not jar the ground, and scare the fish; not to let her shadow fall in the water; not to speak or make a noise, to fish cautiously and patiently, and not get her hook caught, but if she did, to break it and tie on another. He would be near. There were no snakes to hurt, no wild cattle, no danger. Beckon, if she needed help. His eye would be on her. It was a long lesson, and a good one.

Roy did not drop a line in the water, but showed her all the art. She had on light rubber-boots, and a gray dress. He took his sketch-book along, and she began to fish. She was noiseless and wary, and she caught them fast. At first Roy thought she would not fancy baiting the hook, but she did it, and as soon as they began to bite, that little witch took out the speckled beauties, many small, but some of good size, until Roy was hardly pleased to see her get along so well without him.

He made some outline sketches of her as she fished, with the winding brook beyond her. It was sport for her, and a heart-ache for him. Not once did she call him, but kept to her sport like an old fisher that supplies the White Mountain hotels. She lost one or two hooks, but she soon supplied their places, and she did not tie

them on with a granny knot either. ˙She had had a man's
instruction. It was a weaver's knot, and it held. Now
she let her line drop in the ripplings. Now she let it drop
in a dark, deep pool, like a grasshopper. She handled
that light pole like an old fisher. And while she fished
like Isaac Walton, she also unconsciously fished like Simon
Peter. She stepped as softly as a cat. No fish saw her,
until they had the good fortune to be caught by her.
When she had gone a long way, and ought to have been
getting tired, Roy came up and whispered that she had
done enough. He looked in her basket, and it was
another surprise. She had done splendidly, better than
he had supposed. They gave it up. Roy took her tackle
and fish, and they drove home.

It was a splendid ride. When his mother saw the
trout, and heard the story, she said it was the beatermost
thing she ever heard of. Roy cleaned the fish, and it was
a good mess, enough for all. He ate some of them, but
they rather stuck in his crop. I am not posing for elegance, but I must be graphic and forcible. This is a
man's statement. He was as solemn˙as two owls, or
Deacon Bedott, and he grew solemner. He had seen that
she could get a living out of a piano, out of singing, out
of painting, and he was almost afraid˙she could out of
fishing. One of the old English writers once said, " God
never made an independent man." But Roy was afraid
he had, by mistake, or otherwise, made an independent
woman.

The morning for their return came at last. Frank
Wilkie and Ned Foss had said their "good-by," and gone
ploughing. Miss Graham thanked them all for the
pleasantest visit of her life. Mr. Bartlett brought up

some sweet cider that did not appear before Frank Wilkie, and Miss Graham had a little of that.

Roy said he should be home in June for haying, but could not tell whether his next winter would be in Boston, or where. Miss Graham gave him a very earnest look at this, but made no remark. She went upstairs to complete her wraps, and they were not long waiting for her. Mother kissed her, and said, "God bless you, dear. Come again."

Miss Graham's eyes were tearful. Then four solemn people parted. Roy and Miss Graham to Dover station, and Boston, and away into the blue. Roy spoke but little. He cared for her splendidly. He called her attention to Hicks's Hill, and Madbury Station; to Durham, and New Market; to the glorious apple-blossoms everywhere.

At eleven, they took a hack, and went, with no other passengers, to Commonwealth Avenue. On the way she thanked him for all his kindness, but he said he was sorry he could not have done more to entertain her. Would she grant him a favor? He had something to say to her. Would she let Fred Annerly call at the studio at two o'clock? Then he would be sure the message would reach her. She would, and they parted at her door. Fred Annerly called. Roy shook him heartily by the hand, and Fred said, "Mr. Bartlett, please let me know if I can serve you in any way. I will do it if it is in my power."

Roy thanked him, and his commission was to bear this letter, and deliver it at once to Miss Graham, and to her hand alone. He would do it faithfully, and at once. Roy tried to make him take a five-dollar bill, but it was declined. No, he could not take anything from him; but he would serve him with all his heart. Then Roy knew his friend.

Roy's message went at true love's speed across the Common and Public Garden, to her hand, and in her chamber she read it.

"Miss Graham, I do not know as you are prepared to understand this, but I must write it. You have pleased me, impressed me, helped me, and have been growing to be the best part of my life, ever since I knew you. Now I can keep silent no longer, I must speak. Nothing seems of any value without you. Can you join your life with mine, and be my wife? Answer now, even if you have to ask time to consider. If I can be of any service to your uncle and aunt, I will gladly do so. I wanted to ask you all the past week, but did not wish to spoil your visit, or take you at a disadvantage. Please let your trusty messenger bring my answer.

"Ever yours,

"ROYAL BARTLETT."

In about an hour it came.

"DEAR ROY, — Do your parents know of this? and do they approve? Yours,

"MARY GRAHAM."

In less time, Fred waited outside the studio for the answer, and bore it to her.

"DEAR MARY, — Yes, they do. You remember my father gave you some sweet cider, and then you went upstairs to get ready. Mother looked up to me and said, 'Roy, that is the woman that I want for your wife.' It almost choked me. When I could speak, I told her I would get you if I could, and she said, 'Thank God.' She said, 'Father, I do not often taste cider, but you may give me some on that.' They poured out some in two tumblers, and she held it up and said, 'Roy, may you get the woman that you want,' and father said, 'Good luck to you, my son.' Yes: we will all love you forever. O tell me, Mary. I will wait in the studio.   ROY."

At five o'clock there was a knock on the door. Fred Annerly gave him a letter. Fred gave his hand fervently, but whether in pity or congratulation, Roy could not tell. Fred said that no answer was needed. Roy's heart sank within him. He entered the studio, closed the door, and was ready, as ever he would be, to meet joy or sorrow. His destiny was before him. He opened the letter and read.

"MY DEAR ROY, — You shall have your answer. Take your Bible, find the book of Ruth, and dear Ruth's answer shall be mine. It is the first chapter, and sixteenth and seventeenth verses. Rest to-night, and see my uncle to-morrow morning at nine, in the library.

"Yours forever,

"MARY GRAHAM."

With trembling hands he found the book of Ruth, and he read: "And Ruth said: Intreat me not to leave thee or to return from following after thee; for whither thou goest I will go, and where thou lodgest I will lodge; thy people shall be my people, and thy God my God. Where thou diest will I die, and there will I be buried; the Lord do so to me and more also, if aught but death part thee and me."

He covered his face with his hands, and murmured, "Thank God! thank God!" and he bowed his head upon his mother's Bible, and it was moistened with his tears.

CHAPTER XXXVII.

IF this novel, which is one of the truest books ever written, had been written by a woman, it would have bobbed off as short as a rabbit's tail, at the last chapter, but it is a male book. Whether Roy Bartlett or Mary Graham slept well that night, I do not actually know. But I do not think they did. There was a pile of thinking to do. Love is a mighty and disturbing force. I know it is, for I have had a touch of it myself. Here please smile. A joke. Better labelled.

Then next morning, Roy went across the Common, with a bit of bouquet on his coat, looking so handsome that people stared at him. I met him as he went through Park Street gate, and wondered what was up. I found out soon, and congratulated. At three minutes before nine, he went up the steps, and was about to ring the bell, when the door swung open of itself and he entered the vestibule. The door closed and Roy Bartlett stood in the presence of his queen. I know novelists have great privileges, but I was not allowed to be present. Some things are sacred. You can let out your imagination. If you think they stood at opposite sides of the vestibule, and criticised the weather, I hope you will never read another book of mine as long as you live. Mrs. Graham kept guard in the hall, inside. A sermon

has two heads and an application; good thing. Five
minutes later, this happy couple entered the hall, and,
without looking to, or for anything or anybody, they
passed through the door into the parlor, and she called
Roy's attention to the pictures. It was a good thing to
consider art for a moment, and let nature cool off. To
let the eyes dry and the cheeks subside from peonies to
blush roses. Not that they cared particularly for art,
just then. A few minutes later they came out and Roy
had a hearty greeting from Mrs. Wilson Graham. Then
Miss Graham escorted him into the library. Kindly welcomed by Mr. Wilson Graham.

Roy took the bull by the horns. He said: "I have
asked your niece to be my wife, and she has consented."

Mr. Graham smiled. "How soon would suit you,
Mr. Bartlett?"

"The sooner the better."

Mr. Graham laughed. "My niece is twenty-three at
the twentieth of June. The autumn is a good time to
marry, or next spring."

"Why not this spring, say, on her birthday?" asked
Roy.

Mr. Graham was amused. "Well, I do not blame you,"
said he. "Mother and I had been acquainted a long
time, but when we found we wanted each other, it did
not take us long to get ready. Ten days, I think."

Then Roy laughed. "That is a long time for us to
wait," said he. "About three weeks."

Mr. Graham said, "Well, Mr. Bartlett, I will make you
a proposition. This estate is not mine. But I hold it, and
am required to use it, as if it was mine. You young folks
can be united on the twentieth of June, upon condition,

that you come here and be my guests, for one year, without cost to you. You can be perfectly at home, you can use the carriage, and the servants will serve you."

" It is not accepted," said Roy. " I shall be glad to come, but I wish to pay."

" I was afraid I should find an objection," said Mr. Graham.

" Then let me pay a fair bill," said Roy, " and later, when you give up your stewardship, you come and live with us."

Said Mr. Graham, " Do you think my niece is a woman of good common sense? And am I also such a man ? "

" Most certainly."

" Then," said Mr. Graham, " when you understand it better, you will agree with us. After you have been married a month, if you think you must pay, I will take it. Until then, you may consider your wedding-day the twentieth of June, and keep your money."

" I will do it," said Roy, " for you, most generous of men."

Then Mr. Graham touched a bell, and aunty and Miss Graham came in. He at once told them that the wedding was fixed for the twentieth of June, Mary's birthday. She stole a glance at Roy's face which made his heart dance a fandango beyond anything they have in Mexico.

The drawing-room was visited, Mr. Graham did the honors. He led them along before a grand sofa, before they knew it, and, placing them, he stepped back, and, looking them over, he said, " there, my dears, is the place for you to be united, and you will make a very handsome couple."

Roy laughed and both blushed.

Said he, "Now, Miss Mary, you may show your young man around the house."

She did. All the chambers, her own boudoir, which was the large front chamber over the drawing-room, which, she shyly said, might be theirs, sometime, if he was good. They took their time about it. They went into each room. They sat and talked it over. They went upon the roof. They visited all the rooms again in succession. He found several of his own pictures, some of them hung in her own room. Before he knew it, it was lunch time. They were called below, where Roy had a rousing greeting, from Fred Annerly and Jennie, his wife. Nor were the cook, Mrs. Simpson, and her daughter Mollie forgotten. Roy had his lunch with them, and after a little time in the library, he wandered into the drawing-room, and around into quiet places, with Mary. Then he was escorted through the vestibule again and went across the Common, once more, to the studio. He wrote a letter home, thus, —

"DEAR FATHER AND MOTHER, — You are invited to my wedding on the twentieth of June, at Miss Graham's home, on Commonwealth Avenue,
"Your son,
"ROY."

He posted his letter. He tried to paint, but he could not get ahead any. He made calls. He called on Mr. Billings, Mr. Griggs, Mr. Shapleigh, and Mr. Seavey. He took a walk. He could not keep still. He killed the day. It was a peculiar day. Love is crazy business. He was warmly welcomed at Mrs. Warren's, and after dinner, he told them of his happiness. He got rather a

setback from Mrs. Warren, who said she had been ex-
pecting it for centuries.

Roy ate a little dinner, but could not settle down to
anything. He could not stay with the Warrens, nor in
his own room. So he walked out, and before he knew it,
he was gazing at a certain house, from the opposite side
of Commonwealth Avenue. He took a long earnest look.
It was a condition to be in. O the Grand Old Passion is
the strongest current a man ever meets. About a woman
I cannot say, as I never was a woman. If Pope had
said, the proper study of mankind is woman, he would
have just done it. Been and gone and done it.

Roy was irregular at his meals at Mrs. Warren's, but
Edric Lyman and Edward Stacy were there so much, that
Miss Sarah or Miss Emily Warren did not lose any sleep
on that account. If they did on any other account, they
might charge it to that particular account. The day
after his engagement, Roy called on his friend, Benjamin
Champney. Of course Mrs. Warren might have expected
something to come, but did any one else? He would go
slow. He began: " Mr. Champney, shall you be at home
at North Conway in August ? "

" Yes, probably."

" Then I may call on you, with my wife; I am engaged
to Miss Graham, and shall be married soon."

Mr. Champney replied, " I supposed you were engaged
long ago, and everybody considers it the most suitable
and elegant thing you could possibly do. I shall be glad
to see you at North Conway, at any time. Drop me a
line a few days before, and we will surely be there to
welcome you."

Alas for Roy's little secret. It had long been expected

on earth, and was written in heaven from the foundation of the world. If you cannot hurl in a little solid doctrine occasionally, what is the use to have any. Roy came to consider it, although, O so sacred, as something the public must know. So he made no bones about it. But that sweet June was a gusty kind of a time. You ought to have seen Miss Graham look at him. It gave him a sensation. Roy wrote to Jean McDuffie.

"DEAR JEAN, — My joy is coming. I shall be married on the twentieth of June. We shall take the five o'clock train from Boston and get to Dover at 7 :45. If you will meet us at the station, rain or shine, unless it is an awful dangerous storm, we will stay with you, perhaps a week. But I will pay, or I won't come. I will pay you fifty dollars for the week, and carriage hire, and other expenses extra. Will you be ready?   Yours,
                                    "ROY BARTLETT."

The answer came true and hearty, and Jean would be there to wait for him. At last, things seemed to be getting into line, and this planet did not seem to be quite so panicky as it was. If Roy was slightly irregular to his meals at Mrs. Warren's, he was regular enough at Mr. Wilson Graham's. He was there once a day at least, except that he went to Dover once, and stayed over Sunday.

He called on Sam Ellet, and gave him an invitation to his wedding. Yes, Sam and Mary would come. It was arranged that they would stay at Mr. Graham's two or three days, after the wedding. Roy's father and mother were to remain a week, also, and at the end of that time they were all to meet at the Bartlett farm.

This programme was fully carried out. Sam and Mary

had a three-days visit to Boston, and O the rides they had. One day a picnic on the summit of Milton Blue Hill; one day to the Middlesex Fells; one day at Nantasket. Then, after Sam and Mary had returned, Mr. and Mrs. Wilson Graham had Roy's father and mother alone to entertain. That was easy enough, for Boston contains enough variety to entertain a savage or a saint, from a prayer-meeting to a policy shop; from art to anarchy. So these older children had no end of larks, and did not worry about the rising generation.

But I am getting before my story. Roy arranged that Mrs. Francis, who was a young and comely widow, and needed a change after caring for Eli Bertram, should go to the Bartlett farm for a visit. So she went there with him. She was to keep house for Frank Wilkie and Ned Foss, while the old folks went to the wedding. She knew the story of Frank Wilkie. So she had her change of scene, and Frank had an awful nice time admiring the widow. Ned Foss was mightily interested in the developments. His moustache was getting a good start, and it was attracting much attention among the girls.

While the June roses were coming out, all the bright flowers were blooming in the kingdom of love. It was arranged that Edric Lyman should occupy as Roy's successor, in the Warren family, at which Mrs. Warren laughed, Miss Emily smiled, and I don't believe Miss Sarah ever shed any tears over it. It was the rarest and longest of all June days. The wedding party was a unit, in the love and best wishes that they brought. It was a new and holy love, not built on the ruin of broken hearts. Here are the guests who came, glad and smiling, to grace the wedding of Roy and Mary, —

Mr. and Mrs. Wilson Graham and relatives,
Mr. and Mrs. Guy Bartlett and relatives,
Mrs. Warren and the Mayor of Boston,
Mr. and Mrs. Alfred Stacy,
Mr. Edward Stacy and Miss Emily Warren,
Mr. Edric Lyman and Miss Sarah Warren,
Mr. and Mrs. Jonathan Strong,
Mr. and Mrs. Samuel Ellet,
Mr. and Mrs. S. R. Knights,
Mr. and Mrs. Fred Annerly,
Mrs. Simpson and Mollie,
The coachman and servants.

There was also another couple present, fine-looking people. Roy thought he had met the man somewhere. He was introduced to him as Mr. Arad Phillips, Mrs. Warren's and Mr. Graham's banker. That is, he was president of the bank where they deposited, and was their business adviser when called upon.

Miss Graham's pastor was called to perform the ceremony, assisted by Roy's pastor from Park Street, and the Orthodox minister from Dover, N. H. Brides are always lovely. It is beyond my power to describe the wedding. A healthy imagination is a blessed gift, and furnishes the best the market affords. So please to do justice to this, the most blissful of all occasions. Life has three great crises. The first is a little before our time. The last is decidedly subsequent to it. But with Roy Bartlett as groom and Mary Graham as bride, this, the sweetest of all the sacraments of this life, is entitled to everything in the superlative degree.

After the ceremony was over, and all had been presented, and had congratulated, there came a lull.

Like the man who courted a girl, got married, took his

wife home, and "went out and sot down on a rock," Mr.
Phillips remarked that it was a very solemn time. Then
they laughed. The servants retired to prepare lunch. It
was past noon. All were to remain.

Mr. Phillips asked, "Mr. Bartlett, do you remember
when you first saw me?"

Roy did not.

"Do you remember, when you first came to Boston,
that you said, in a studio, that you wished to find a boarding place like your own home?"

"I do," said Roy.

"I was there," said Mr. Phillips. "I reported to Mrs.
Warren that she had better send you a note, and she
did."

"Thank you, sir," said Roy.

"And I have kept my eye on you ever since. A little
later I told Mr. and Mrs. Graham of you, and suggested
that Miss Mary might study art with you. And she
did, and more too. I also told Eli Bertram of you."

Said Roy, "Why, Mr. Phillips, you have been my guardian angel."

"Hold on," said he, "I am not done yet. You know
that Mr. Wilson Graham is not the owner of the estate
of which this establishment is a part."

"I do," said Roy.

"Do you know who is?" he asked.

"I do not," said Roy.

"Then it gives me a great deal of pleasure to tell you.
Your wife, Mrs. Royal Bartlett, is the rightful owner.
She inherited it all from her father, except what it has
increased by the good management of her uncle. And her
first offering to you is this check, which I hold in my

hand, which commands the bank of which I am president to pay to your order fifty thousand dollars. It is on deposit at my bank, in your name. Here is the bank-book, your wife's wedding gift to you." Mr. Phillips presented it. "You know, Mr. Bartlett, that you were no fortune-hunter, and Miss Graham wanted no fortune-hunter. So we think we have managed it finely. Your wife's estate is not far from a million, and it may be more. And, Mr. Royal Bartlett, I congratulate you, for I think, apart from the money, you are just about the luckiest man in the whole world."

Roy turned all the colors of a dying dolphin, as this was all unfolded to him. At the close, he contrived to say, " he would try to bear up under it, but to have so much of happiness and God's blessing thrown upon him at once, was almost enough to kill him."

He thanked Mr. Phillips and them all. Many of the guests were surprised. A fine box of wedding-cake was labelled for each one present, only to be the forerunners of many more, sent out later. After the refreshments, Fred Annerly and the coachman were ready to take the happy couple to the station. Roy's father and mother, with Sam and Mary, remained to have their visit with Mr. and Mrs. Graham, at the home on Commonwealth Avenue.

CHAPTER XXXVIII.

It was a short ride, that seventy miles more or less, to Dover. If any element of happiness was lacking, they were too happy to miss it. In the dusk of the evening, they rode into the station. Jean McDuffie was there, and his face shone with joy. The carriage took them to McDuffie's Hotel, and it was a nice place. Mrs. McDuffie met them, and led them at once to their rooms. It was a surprise. The dressing-case was a bank of roses. On the table was a large satin cushion, and fastened upon it were blush prairie roses, forming the names Royal, Mary. Flowers everywhere. Two of Roy's pictures hung in the room. After they were settled, and the toilets arranged, Jean escorted them to the tea-table. Jean and his wife, and Roy and Mary. They were happy in each other. That is the way to be. "For no man liveth to himself." Of course selfishness can stay around a long time, but it does not live.

After tea, Jean showed them around the house, and they had much to tell. So the time flew away, and the Dover factory bell rang for nine o'clock. Jean said that there were some singers coming, and if Mr. and Mrs. Bartlett would sit in their room, with the light turned low, they could hear the music at its best. The house had a wide hall, and a fine piano was in it. Jean had invited Myra Pinkham, and a whole chorus, that he be-

longed to. He had told them he wanted them to sing,
for it was in honor of a man who had risked his own life,
and saved his, and that brought the music.

Jean and his wife were popular, and they did sing. It
got told around town, that there was to be a big sing at
Jean McDuffie's on the eve of the twentieth, and a large
chorus came, and plenty of outsiders. Ned Foss and
Frank Wilkie guessed whose concert it was, and they
left Canis Major to keep house, and took the widow, and
went down to listen outside. They kept their surmise to
themselves. So there was a piano, quite an orchestra,
and plenty of chorus. Roy and Mary sat in their bower
of roses, and heard the concert in their honor. The hall
was soon occupied, and by the people in all the rooms
below, there must have been a large delegation. Myra
Pinkham could just play the piano, and sing to perfection.

Roy said to Mary, that Jean was trying to outdo himself. Their door was wide open, but was guarded, and
Jean and his wife sat upon the stairs. Jean announced
that the concert would commence with —

THE SUMMER MORNING CAROL OF PRAISE.

· [SOLO AND CHORUS.]

"Morning comes and day is breaking,
Night is done and earth is waking,
All around the joy partaking
Wake a song of praise.
Birds are singing, flowers are springing,
Incense bringing, light adorning,
Gladness comes on wings of morning,
Full of love and praise.
CHORUS — Glory, beauty, power, and blessing,
Seemeth heaven the earth possessing,
We, the heavenly light possessing,

Gladly sing Thy praise.
Hallelujah, Hallelujah!
Gladly sing Thy praise, Amen,

"Lord, I thank thee for this being,
Living, hoping, loving, seeing,
Light shone in and darkness fleeing,
See the sunlight blaze.
So Thy love is shining ever,
So Thy mercy faileth never;
Blessed be Thy name forever,
All my hope and praise.
    CHORUS — Glory, etc.

"Lord, accept my invocation,
Low I bow in adoration.
Rise, my soul, in exaltation.
Thou, from whence I came:
Thou hast been my habitation,
Thou shalt be my expectation,
O my soul and all within me
Bless His holy name.
    CHORUS — Glory, etc."

It was finely sung. After a few minutes' rest, Jean announced —

THE NEW HAMPSHIRE SONG AND CHORUS.

"O beauty land, New Hampshire hills, fond memory comes to
    me,
And brings a song with music sweet, a loyal song to thee.
While youth and beauty, love and home come back again so
    fair
That all the past seems bright with flowers, so sweetly
    blooming there.
CHORUS — My dear New Hampshire home, where'er my feet
    may roam,
My loyal heart still claims a part in thee, New Hampshire
    home.

"O mighty mountains glowing light with morning's early
    beams,
O beauty hill-tops shining bright with evening's latest gleams,
O ever changing wonder-scenes wherever we may go,
With rivers, lakes, and sparkling streams, whose laughing
    waters flow.—CHORUS.

"O wonder-scenes of ice and snow, amid the winter gloom;
O handsomest of all the world, the apple-trees in bloom;
Sweet breezes playing in the grass, across the summer
    plain,
And Autumn loaded down with fruit, and piled with golden
    grain.—CHORUS.

"How blush the raspberries by the road, inviting as we pass,
How sweet the strawberries hid away so modest in the grass:
What blackberries shining dark as night, and ripe enough
    to fall,
And blueberry bushes hanging full of sweetness for us all.
    — CHORUS.

"God bless thee, O New Hampshire dear, my heart is true to
    thee.
God bless thy children everywhere, on every land and sea;
Firm as thy mighty mountains stand, pure as thy winter's
    snow,
God bless thee while thy sweet flowers bloom, and spark-
    ling waters flow.— CHORUS."

Myra Pinkham sang it beautifully. She is a New
Hampshire girl, and it was a home song to her. The
chorus was strong and the cheers outside the house, this
splendid June night, told how well the loyal song was appreciated. Truly Roy's honeymoon was a beauty. The
moon was at its full, and the days and nights were alike
glorious.

Then a lady sung a queer song, to a funny little minor
tune. It was the

"POOR OLD BACHELOR.

"There is a poor old bachelor we often see about,
Like half a pair of scissors that has lost the rivet out;
He is always hunting after something, always gone to pot,
And he never, never finds it when he can as well as not.
CHORUS — He's a poor old bachelor because he is afraid,
  When he might be so happy with a sweet old maid.

"His coat and vest need fixing, you can hardly call them dress,
And those continuations O you really can't express;
From the poor old fellow's hat, full of dust as it can be,
To the poorest darned old stockings that you ever yet did see,
  CHORUS. — He's a poor old bachelor.

"The boudoir of a bachelor is a wonderful old lair;
The blind, that cannot see it, can smell it in the air;
It has no angel's visits to keep it sweet and true,
For everything is crazy there, and everything askew.
  CHORUS — He's a poor old bachelor.

"On the coldest nights of winter he can lie abed and groan,
In solitude, to hate himself and shiver all alone;
Because he never hunted for a better way instead,
He ought to have some broken crackers, scattered in his bed.
  CHORUS — He's a poor old bachelor.

"The wise ones often tell us there is nothing made in vain,
The reason of a bachelor is not so very plain;
Perhaps to teach young people to remember love's young
  dream,
Or to occupy his bosom when you want to freeze ice cream.
  CHORUS — He's a poor old bachelor.

"So he lived his lifetime all alone, to grumble and to mope,
He often asked the value of a shilling's worth of rope;
As he had no wife or children, he did not want to stay,
There came an east wind from the west, and then he blew
  away.
  CHORUS — He's a poor old bachelor."

She sang it comically and it was jolly. Then Myra Pinkham sang "To charm the night away," a negro song, and the chorus did their part. A young man with a sweet voice sang "The sweet bells of heaven" with chorus. Then a lady sang "The birds' love song," warbling and trilling like a bird.

The Barrington song was called for and Myra sang it, and the whole house sang the chorus, —

" O shine the rising morning, O glow the setting sun,
The sweetest spot between them both is old Barrington."

Jean called for a Rochester lady to sing "The bald-headed man," and requested all to pile on to the chorus. It was very funny, and the lady made the most of it. But when the four parts sang big with piano and orchestra, —

" O the bald-headed man, deny it if you can,
The prince of all good fellows is the bald-headed man,"

it was a roaring chorus, and somehow they managed to accent it with a bass drum. The boys caught on, and the whole neighborhood sang. It was too good to forget, and the street urchins picked it up, and roared it, all the way from Garrison Hill to Sawyer's mills, all summer. When a countryman took out his bandanna, to wipe off the great desert, he was surprised to hear them sing, and thought the devil had got into the boys. He did not know it was a part of Roy's wedding chorus. I am afraid this is a digression.

Jean McDuffie said, "now we will have two songs more. One is, —

"THE GRAND OLD PASSION.

*A love song dedicated to all true lovers, old or young, married or
single, all round the world, by one of them.*

WORDS AND MUSIC BY J. B. WIGGIN.   SONG AND CHORUS.

"Young Love came down when old Time was young,
  And he made all the flowers of spring ;
He started the world in its tireless round,
  And he started the birds to sing.
CHORUS — Beautiful love, the glory of life,
         On angel's wings comes down ;
         Rejoice, rejoice, for the Grand Old Passion
         That makes the world go round.

" Young love he met a man and a maid,
  And he gave them the sweetest pain ;
He bound their hearts with a silken thread,
  And they never got loose again. — CHORUS.

" They lived together and loved each other,
  And young loves came at their call.
They worked together and helped each other,
  And love inspired them all. — CHORUS.

" The twain were one in their hearts' desires,
  As true to love as the sun ;
To love each other beyond the river,
  Whenever their work was done. — CHORUS.

" Their children grew to be men and maids,
  And in love's sweet meshes were found ;
They all rejoice in the Grand Old Passion,
  That makes the world go round. — CHORUS.

" Then open your heart to this beautiful joy,
  The sweetest that ever was found ;
The blessing of life is the Grand Old Passion,
  That makes the world go round. — CHORUS."

Myra Pinkham did her best with this song, and was well rewarded at the close. Jean stood in the hall, and announced, "Now we will have the last song. It is a waltz song, 'The Balmy Sleep,' a solo song, of loving care and protection. It is late. I have travellers and dear, valued friends in the house. This concert is in their honor. Especially this last piece."

Then, with prelude and interlude, a lady sang, —

"O come, balmy sleep, with thy wonderful healing,
  Like a fair summer eve, when the winds are at play;
O bear us from care, all its shadows concealing,
  As the thistledown floats on the light breeze away.
Then welcome light slumbers, to musical numbers,
  As they peacefully flow on a fair summer day,
With bright blossoms falling, and mating birds calling,
  And the music of bright waters flowing away.

"When sweet peace has found you, and slumber has bound you,
  And true hearts around you, in safety to keep,
With loving hearts blessing, and music caressing
  Like angels possessing, and wooing to sleep,
Then welcome light slumbers, to musical numbers,
  As they peacefully flow on a fair summer day,
With bright blossoms falling, and mating birds calling,
  And the music of bright waters flowing away.

"With the bright land before us, and the kind Father o'er us,
  And the angels in charge, his beloved to keep;
While true love around us, with sweet bonds has bound us,
  Then trustfully, blissfully, peacefully sleep.
Then welcome light slumbers, to musical numbers,
  As they peacefully flow on a fair summer's day;
With sweet blossoms falling, and mating birds calling,
  And the music of bright waters flowing away."

Some one called, "So say we all of us," and you could not stop them. It was sung to "America," and they all did their best, in the house and out, while the bass drum marked the time, so it could be heard all over Dover.

They cheered and shouted, " Good night, Jean," enough to wake up all Pine Hill.

Roy and Mary laughed some, and they felt that they were loved and honored indeed. Soon Jean was putting things to rights, and it was near eleven o'clock.

Roy came out, dropped the night-latch, and came down to talk to Jean. " Well, Jeanie, what is the programme for to-morrow ? Is it Agamenticus?"

" It is Agamenticus," he replied. " I have a nice, easy two-seated carriage, and span of horses. I have Linward Waldron and Sidney Wentworth both here, on their summer vacation. They are a little past twenty-one, about of an age, splendid fellows as ever grew, both Dover boys, out of our best New Hampshire stock. One will drive the team, and the other will guide you up Mount Agamenticus."

" Just the thing," said Roy. " Jean, you are a jewel."

" So my wife thinks," said he, laughing ; " and so does yours of you."

" I hope so," said Roy.

" Then," said Jean, "if the weather is suitable you can take an all-day trip, and sketch as you go. The commissary will be attended to, and you will be happy." And Jean sang, —

" Up in a balloon, boys, up in a balloon,
Kiting round the little stars, sailing round the moon,
Love will go beyond the clouds, love is kind and true,
Love will go beyond the stars, and navigate the blue ;
Up in a balloon, boys, up in a balloon,
Kiting round the little stars, sailing round the moon."

Roy laughed. He looked at his watch. " Good night ! " said Roy. " Time is up."

" Good night ! " said Jean, " and pleasant dreams."

CHAPTER XXXIX.

AGAMENTICUS, A PILGRIMAGE.

AT half-past six next morning Roy came down, like a son of the morning. Jean met him gayly, and showed him the little room set for breakfast for four. It was pretty as posies, and awaiting the arrival of Lady Bartlett, whom Roy soon ushered in to breakfast. They were four. It reminds me of a man who asked a blessing in this wise, "O Lord, bless me and my wife, my son John and his wife, us four and no more." I want to tell you all about this breakfast; everything. If I give you all the facts you have something to ornament. With your artistic knowledge and fertile imagination, you can get up a scene that is a credit to you and the book. I do not wish fiction too fictitious. It gets thin and uncertain. These people are real people. They are all alive to-day, and I love them and visit them. I have lived pleasant years in Dover. So Jean and his wife sat opposite, and Roy and Mary could do no less. There never was a kinder, more devoted quartette. I knew Roy from boyhood, and Mary soon after he did. I never knew an act of their lives that I regretted. If Job was a just man, and so good that some people think him an impossibility, an allegory, a poem, and a no-such-thing, why may not my friend, who is the hero of my book, be as much of a man every way as the nomadic old Jew? It is easier than rascality, and pays better every way. So love and gratitude prepared the breakfast, and joy and thankfulness ate it.

Soon after, they were called into the parlor, and were introduced to Lin Waldron, their guide, and Sid Wentworth, their driver. The time had gone to eight o'clock. The supplies were aboard. Mrs. Bartlett came down in a neat gray dress, and she and Roy took the back seat in the carriage. Jean gave them parting instructions. It is anywhere from twelve to twenty-five miles from Dover to Agamenticus, according to who tells the story.

"Now drive carefully," said Jean. "Take care. Don't miss the road. Get home by five."

It was a red-letter day. I have been over the road again and again, but not with a bride. The young men had received their instructions. Safe and honorable. No devilment in them. It was a splendid ride.

When Roy wanted to stop ten minutes or more, to sketch an outline, Lin Waldron did the same, for lo, he was a bit of an artist. Sid Wentworth told a story that was very funny, and now our two lovers could laugh heartily. A change had come o'er the spirit of their dream, or rather the dream had ended in a blessed awakening.

After the usual episodes of a glorious June ride, they came to the old homestead, deserted the last time I saw it, at the west end of Agamenticus. Sid took care of the horses, and remained with them, having his lunch by himself. This gave him a little time to geologize among the rocks. Lin Waldron, taking the basket, preceded Roy and Mary, each with an alpenstock. It was quite a climb, though not dangerous. It is called about six hun-

dred and eighty feet above the sea, yet it is so prominent,
it is seen from afar, and seems much higher. They were
not long reaching the summit, and O what a sight it was.
The day was cloudless. There was a good breeze upon
the mountain. Lin Waldron sought a sightly, sunny
place, in the shelter of a boulder, out of too fresh a breeze,
and began to prepare the feast. Mary was delighted.
There was the ocean, about eight miles away, a mirror of
light, with white dots of sails. Away to the west was
the line of York beach, and the rolling summer landscape.
Afar to the east, the ocean dissolved into the eternity of
space. To the northeast the farms and forests of the
Pine Tree State. They saw it hand in hand.

They turned to the north. Mary said, " Why, what a
peculiar cloud ! "

" It is peculiar," said Roy. He looked at her, and
watched the varying emotions of her face.

"O what a beautiful day," she said, "what a mighty
view of the ocean, and all the country ! And that wonderful, wonderful cloud. It is low down, yet it must be
high where it is, and it has angles and battlements, and O
it looks like a heavenly vision, O so white ! "

Roy smiled. He had been on Agamenticus before.
He looked in Mary's eyes and asked, "Mary, is that a
cloud ? "

She looked puzzled as she gazed at it, and answered,
hesitatingly, " Yes, Roy, it is a cloud, is it not ? A white
cloud."

Roy smiled, as he asked her, " Mary, what is that great
mass that occupies the whole of the northern part of
New Hampshire ? "

She looked earnestly to the north again. There was

the great white cloud. In a moment more she cried, "Why, it is the White Mountains!"

And as she gazed, the depth of her emotion dimmed her eyes with tears. There the great mystery shone, glowing in its dress of winter, soon to be changed to a warmer color. And so our lovers saw and worshipped.

I state an actual fact. I tell you I am writing a true book; I saw the same sights, on a beautiful day in June, and I gazed with wonder and astonishment at the mysterious cloud, and I saw it as such, several minutes before they revealed themselves to me. I shall never forget it. Two men, not artists at all, were with me, and they saw the mystery only as a cloud, until I declared it was the White Mountains. And my splendid Roy and Mary — for there are splendid men and women on earth, as well as in heaven — saw the mountains transfigured before them. Roy told me the story in the presence of his wife. It is well worth a pilgrimage to see. They were quiet. They looked love and joy to each other, and felt that they were near to each other, and to Nature's heart. Some splendid man has said that Nature often puts on her finest dress to receive an appreciative spectator. So did Mount Agamenticus to-day. And she entertained her visitors better than ever did the Mount of Olives. They heard a voice singing the old song, —

"When up the mountain climbing,
I sing this merry strain, la, la,"

and they listened. Lin Waldron could sing. When the song was done, he was near them. He lifted his hat, made a bow, and said, "Agamenticus will receive her guests at dinner." There was a cushion for Mary, and a

picnic surprise on the ground. The stuffed chicken was
a beauty. Roy cut it up. Lin had made a cup of tea.
They had cold coffee, and a bottle of milk, boiled eggs,
bread and butter, sardines and a lemon, cake and mince
pie. Candy, of course. Jean knew they would have
mountain appetites. And they began to be merry. Yes,
they did. And they kept it up. That dinner disappeared like dew before the sun. Roy said it was lucky
there was no more. Then Roy held up his hand and
said, "God bless Jean McDuffie." "And his wife,"
added Mary, "for I saw her put up the dinner."

Then Lin Waldron topped out with, "and as Tiny Tim
says, God bless us every one."

"I accept the amendment," said Roy.

So that dinner was a picture in memory, and a joy forever. They cleared away the wreck, and Lin packed it
up, much lighter than it was. They sat down, and Lin
recited "The Burial of Moses." I have had him do it at
my house. It is grand. And how appropriate for a
mountain top.

"Now," said Roy, "it is said that the old chief Agamenticus is buried upon this mountain top. Let us walk
around and see if we can find his tomb."

They did walk, but like Moses, "No one knows that
sepulchre, and no one saw it e'er."

They looked long and earnestly at the scene, and at the
mountains especially, long and lovingly.

Roy asked, "Mary, is your honeymoon good enough?"

"Yes, my husband, it is perfect. O God, thou hast
blessed me. I ask for no more."

"Mary, answer me one question. When did you first
begin to care for me, or to feel any interest in me?"

She answered, " Won't you be proud and uppish?"

"No," said Roy, smiling.

"Will you love me a little more?"

"I can't. I love you with my whole heart now."

She laughed. "Well, Mr. Bartlett, the first time I came to your studio, and saw you, I made up my mind if you were as good as you appeared to be, I would get you if I could. That was what I took lessons for. Now please don't take advantage of it."

Roy laughed heartily. He said "he was happier than he supposed he was, to be wanted and cared for so long."

They "cast a longing, lingering look behind." They left the old chief Agamenticus, "alone in his glory."

When a part way down, Lin let out a locomotive whistle, and Sid had the team ready, while Roy made an outline of the old farmhouse and trees. Lin and Sid strayed out of sight a few minutes.

Sid began: "Well, Lin, what do you think of it?"

"I think it is great," said he.

"So do I," said Sid; "it is the richest thing I ever struck."

"My sentiments," said Lin.

"How long have they been married?"

"Jean did not say. He said they were young married people, and we had better not discuss marriage, or anything about it. My opinion is they have not been married many days, and maybe not many hours. They have not got used to each other."

"Just so," said Sid. "Just see her look at him! I hope my wife will look that way at me."

"I guess she will," said Lin, "from what I hear. At any rate, you are man enough, and she is woman enough, and I hope my wife will," continued Lin.

"And I guess she will," laughed Sid Wentworth, "from what I hear."

Then they could both laugh.

"Say, Sid," said Lin, "I guess it is a case of love in all corners."

"I shouldn't be surprised," Sid answered.

They bade good-by to the lonely homestead. They saw the family burial ground, beside the road near the house. They had just about time to go home, and get there at five o'clock. They all voted that the day was a beauty, and Lin Waldron said it was as handsome as a bride. Sid laughed, and said that a bride was the nicest thing in the whole world; and Roy gave just a queer little look at Mary. She kept her face straight, and was serenely unconscious, but it took an effort. Jean received his company back again, safe and sound.

As they alighted at Mac's, Mrs. Bartlett thanked the young men, and said, 'If each of you have a lady in Dover, that you are interested in, if you will call here this evening, I will sing you a song."

This was a leading question, to be acted on.

"Will you come, Sid?"

"Yes, Lin, if you will. It is a giveaway," said Sid, "but I will try it."

Lin lifted his hat to Mrs. Bartlett, and said, "I thank you for your kind invitation, and I fully expect the lady will be glad to come. If she does not, I will come without her."

"So will I," said Sid Wentworth.

"Come from eight to nine," said Mrs. Bartlett, as she went up the steps.

They did come, with two of Dover's daughters, and

Roy and Mary were glad that these two splendid fellows were having a touch of this old, old complaint. Mary sang like a bird, and played the piano like a witch. Jean . McDuffie offered the young men money for their service, but they declined it. It was good enough without. They went on other excursions; to Garrison Hill, to Locke's Mills with Jean and his wife, to Stonehouse Pond, and the diamond rock in Barrington, and they had a picnic at them all.

On the afternoon of the twenty-seventh of June, Roy paid his bill of seventy-five dollars, which Jean begged him not to pay, but he would and did. He said, "Jean, if I am any good to you, pay me in love."

Later, Mrs. Bartlett sent Mrs. Jean McDuffie a check for a hundred dollars. Jean and his wife rode with them to the Bartlett farm, where they met Roy's father and mother, and Mary's uncle and aunt, just arrived. Ned Foss smiled all over. Canis Major almost turned himself wrong side out with joy. Ned was dressed all in his pretties, and had a bouquet on his coat. He had the parlor all decorated with flowers. Mr. and Mrs. Jean McDuffie were ushered in. There were four married couples. All had just arrived. Frank Wilkie and the widow had welcomed them, but all at once they had disappeared. Ned was radiant.

"Now," said he, "please to take seats for a moment, for I expect company."

What was coming? A touch of a bell was heard, and Ned stepped to the front stairs. There was a rustle of silk, and a sound of people descending. He came in as marshal, followed by Sam Ellet and Mary, who stood before the great sofa, and between them Mr. and Mrs.

Frank Wilkie. Frank had married the widow. Ned announced the fact. It was a surprise. It was all right. But it was so queer. Ned did the honors. He presented each, and they all said God's blessing was in it. Roy had written to Edric Lyman, and Frank Wilkie also had. So Edric was well posted. These four couples were here at the Bartlett farm, and as they had excursion enough, they all joined in the haying. After the Fourth of July was over Roy rode again a conqueror, to the rattle song of the mowing machine and help was so plenty that it went with a rush.

CHAPTER XL.

AFTER Roy and Mary had been gone four days, that evening Edric Lyman and Edward Stacy came home to dine at the Warren home. They sat down to the table. Edric did not eat. He sat back and said, "O dear, the world goes hard, and things don't suit me."

"What is it?" asked Mrs. Warren; "does not the dinner suit you?"

"O yes, the dinner is very nice, what there is of it, and it is abundant, such as it is, and it is altogether splendid, like the lady that presides over it, and that is not the trouble at all."

"Then what is the trouble?"

"Why! here those two infants, Roy and Mary, have been and gone and got married, and ended that dreadful single life, and I don't see why poor Sarah and I can't, or poor Edward and Emily." Mrs. Warren laughed. She said it did seem too bad somehow. She was willing. Sarah and Emily tried hard to keep from laughing. Edward sighed deeply, although he almost laughed too.

Said Edric, "I suppose that the happy pair will go to the Bartlett farm, on the twenty-seventh, and I move that we four people be married on the first day of July, and all four go to Mac's hotel for a week. We can go to

Agamenticus. We can run up to the Bartletts', we can have high jinks for a week, and come back to our splendid mother-in-law, and live happy ever after."

"Second the motion," said Edward. "All those in favor of this arrangement, please hold up their right hand."

Edric, Edward, and Mrs. Warren voted "yes."

Contrary-minded was called. Not a hand was raised. The ladies put their handkerchiefs to their eyes, although there was nothing to cry about. "It is voted unanimously," said Edric Lyman. And he snapped out, to Miss Sarah, "I guess you need not cry. I feel as badly about it as you do," and she snorted right out with laughter.

Edric Lyman had fun in him.

Said Mrs. Warren, "You have done a large amount of business, now eat your dinner. Your soup is cooling. Pepper it well, and it will do."

It was agreed that a public wedding was impolitic. They would have to leave out some, they were so well known. It would include so many of Edric's clients, and he mixed his friendship all in with his business, so his clients were his friends, and all the teachers, and the Art Coterie friends, and they were so well known in the West Church it was impossible. So they had a family wedding. Now, reader, look and see. The summons went to Dover, and was a cause for congratulation. Roy and Mary just rejoiced over it. The first of July came. The Warren parlors held a select company. Not selected for style, wealth, or any quality, but love and good-will. Here are the guests, after the wedding, at least:

406 THE WILD ARTIST IN BOSTON.

Mrs. Warren and his Honor the Mayor,
Mr. and Mrs. Jonathan Strong,
Mr. and Mrs. Arad Phillips,
Mr. and Mrs. Royal Bartlett,
Mr. and Mrs. Guy Bartlett,
Mr. and Mrs. Wilson Graham,
Mr. and Mrs. Samuel Ellet,
Mr. and Mrs. Fred Annerly,
Mr. and Mrs. Frank Wilkie,
Mr. and Mrs. Edric Lyman,
Mr. and Mrs. Edward Stacy,
Mr. and Mrs. Alfred Stacy,

and a few relatives and others. It went off like a sky rocket, like Dr. Marigold's supper. The mayor gave the brides away. I cannot describe it. All adjectives fail. Here was a room full of white souls. Most of them always had been white. Later, they had a Pullman car, and almost all the party went to Dover. Some to Mac's. Some to the Bartlett home, and some to Sam Ellet's. It was a happy time. They met at the Bartlett farm some evenings. Edric Lyman outdid himself. The wild artist in Boston had been a perfect ten-strike. Some people are. Some people glorify everything they touch. This good time was not very long ago, either. At the date of this book, they were every one alive, and in some families the number was even increased. So runs the world away. Let it run. It is the best thing it can do. Reader, I should be glad to know how you like my story. If you will write me, state any objection. I will do you a good turn if I can. Send your address. Direct to " J. B. Wiggin, 13 Pleasant place, Cambridgeport, Mass."

Mrs. Warren's daughters live with her. Her house and heart are big enough to contain her sons-in-law also.

They are rich and can take care of it. Mr. and Mrs. Guy Bartlett are just the same sweet honest souls as ever, and their house often shelters some splendid people. Sam Ellet makes the Hoskins farm shine, and Mary likes it. Mr. and Mrs. Wilson Graham live with Roy and Mary. Fred Annerly and Jennie are there, and they prove that God puts as white souls in bronze as he does in marble. Frank Wilkie promised to go to the Methodist church, with Mrs. Francis, and, now she is Mrs. Wilkie, he goes. He has joined them, and is one of the stewards of the church. He is a splendid man. Jean McDuffie and his wife are prosperous and happy. Mr. and Mrs. Jonathan Strong are all right, and he defers to his colleague, Edric Lyman. Mr. and Mrs. Wilson Graham are much, in summer, at the Bartlett farm, and Mr. and Mrs. Guy Bartlett are often, in winter, at the Bartlett home on Commonwealth Avenue. Selfishness enters not into their thoughts. And my splendid Roy and Mary are rich every way, and they use it, and they both enter into the spirit of Him who first loved us, and gave Himself for us; and thus they exemplify in themselves that grace of loving and giving which is the crowning beauty of a glorious life.